# A Soul Remembered

A Soul Saga

## Raquel Gabrielle

Dark Storm LLC

# Also by Raquel Gabrielle

**A Soul Saga Novel:**
A Hollow Soul
A Soul Forgotten
A Soul Remembered

**Standalone Novel:**
Legend of the Forest (2024)

*This is for the dreamers out there.*

# Chapter 1

"That's right, get nice and cozy with one another. We are going to have to get along as we make our way to the Dark Court. Don't forget to rely on each other's strengths and watch out for one another's weaknesses during our travels," Robert says. Riding on horseback through the rough terrain, coming across a large dark stain across the sky.

"I just don't understand why he has to be here." Natasha's eyes narrow at Zeek.

Robert holds up a finger to list off the reasons. "One, you have an arrangement that makes it almost impossible for him not to come along. Two, if he wasn't here, you would wish he would be. Three, he has a contract to cash in on at the Dark Court. Four..."

Moving her horse up to Robert, she shoves hers into his to make him stop counting. Robert's horse snaps at her as her horse dances away. "You can stop now. I get it, Zeek is needed."

I fiddle with the chain of the necklace that is partially hidden under my shirt. The three charms at its end lay safe and sound against my chest. Before leaving, I worked with Ms. Moshner, a talented jewel forger. She helped teach me how to forge the red ruby into a heart and create a hole in it to run the chain through. Of course, I couldn't tell her about the stone for fear of her realizing I stole it from her.

Instead, I learned from Ms. Moshner on the sliver of black onyx rectangle; I showed her how I temporarily wrapped twine around and hooked it to the chain. She explained it wouldn't hold. She helped me buff the stone into a new shape and create the hole to put a link through so I could hook it on to my necklace. After that project, I worked on some other for her getting the hang of it. In between those projects, I would sneak the ruby into the machine to create a heart pendant to attach to the necklace with the other trinkets.

One is a black stone from my mother, and Flit. I picked it up shortly after the flower. Another was a useless flower charm that has been with me since the beginning and used to connect Shade and me together. The last is a larger ruby that houses the soul of a siren now turned into a heart.

My fingers rub at the shapes, a heart, a flower, and the last in the shape of a rectangle. Looking ahead, the dark slash in the sky grows bigger as we move closer. "Are there no other people that go this way? Is there even a path?" I ask interrupting their fighting.

"No, there is no path to or through this place. Every time they tried; it would disappear as soon as it started. The workers would go missing or get lost," Robert throws over his shoulder. He moves away from Natasha, giving a scowl in her direction.

"Zeek and him have all these little nuggets of information," Natasha says sarcastically.

"You will be happy for that knowledge when we make our way through in one piece. Zeek!" He calls out. Zeek has gone up ahead to check things out.

He gestures by shaking his two fingers forward, which Robert nods to.

"He is checking to see the best entry point," he says before Natasha can make a comment.

"Those two have their own language. I swear if I didn't know better, there might be something going on there." She waggles her eyebrows.

"It wouldn't be so bad if any of us could understand what to do or not because of it," I chuckle.

Jazmin travels in the back with Natasha and I in the middle. Zeek usually covers the rear, but he tends to roam around, checking on things. He trusts Jazmin to watch our six when he couldn't.

"We have only just begun our journey and already I know I'm going to be irked with those two." Natasha grinds her teeth.

"At least we will all know each other better," I say, looking for the silver lining.

"When did you start looking at the positive side of life?" She gives an expression of disgust. "Don't be going and changing on me. I mean, sure, get rid of the woe is me and the naïve parts, but leave the rest." She gives an exasperated sigh.

"There are plenty of doubts going on in my head. Don't worry. Learning about our traveling group is just not one of them. I'm more concerned about this dark stretch and the monsters we may encounter there. I'm also anxious about the Dark Court and the secrets it may hold. It's just another place and set of people that will think of me as inexperienced."

"There she is." She gives a little wave. "You have been missed. I thought she got rid of you for good." Stretching her arm out, she pulls me into a side hug.

I scrunch my nose at her as I shake my head.

Tina, one of the fire elements I carry within me, shoots up off my arm and jumps on the top of the horse's head. She peers at the darkness that looms over us. "They are close!" She says excitedly. "Taz is close by!" She doesn't wait, just slides down the horse's nose and jumps over the dry, cracked earth that is turning to sand. Her little flame body jumps up and down as she races over the bare ground to Zeek and Robert. Her body is darker, almost black compared to the bright flame that surrounds her.

The horse I'm riding on skitters away and raises up. I grip on the horn of the saddle, my fingers turning white, not wanting to yank the reins too hard. My legs clench around the horse, my fingers clutch at the saddle to hold on as my heart races. Blood rushes to my ears as the horse races forward. My pack comes off the back of the horse, falling to the hard dirt packed ground.

Robert gives a piercing whistle. The horse turns toward the sound and slows to a trot, making its way to him.

"Tina slow down. You are spooking the horses," Robert says in a calm voice. Raising his hands to the horses so they would know he has everything handled.

"You said to let you know as we move through the Dark kingdom if we felt our sister's presence close. I'm telling you; she is close." Tina raises her arm and points her tiny light toward the darkness that swatches over the horizon. "In there."

"Are you sure?" Zeek's horse trots back to us as Jazmin and Natasha catch up. "I wanted us to stay on this side of the dark stretch until we have to make the trek across. To be as close as possible to make it the shortest path through this thing. If we enter now." He gives a shake of his head, frowning. "Crossing into a section I have never been in will not be easy. I have only traversed through a small part further down. I do not recommend this."

"That is saying something with all that you have dealt with in your lifetime and even you are warning against this place." Robert's face falls while his eyes scan the black scar.

"I'm sure they are in there." Jumping up, Tina stands on the pommel of the saddle in front of Robert. Her stance is firm with her hands in fists at her side, her flame fully lit. She looks as if she could take off at any moment. "I need to know that she is at least safe and not lost somewhere in there."

Zeek gets down, getting my pack. "You can't. The creatures would eat you alive in there. Your essence, your light, would be a beacon to them in there. Not even full daylight pierces those shadows. This place doesn't run like normal and consumes anything bright or that shows light."

"I could make it. I'm strong," she barks out. Making the leap from her perch to Zeek's shoulder, she stares at him.

He stares back and gives a low grunt. "This place isn't like anything you have ever seen. Even I do not know all that happens in here. I have never had to enter this place for very long. I can only go off of stories I have heard."

Jazmin comes to Tina's aid. "It is better if we have this Shade fellow in our company. It will make Alexia stronger and more put together."

Robert continues to gaze off into the distance, his face haggard. "We have to, Zeek. Both Tina and I have to know that Taz is okay. Since those three sisters came into our lives, I don't know... but they changed things for me and Margaret."

"Fine. But Tina, we need you and Trill out of sight. If you girls come back out again, you need to have your flame at the lowest setting almost fully out, or if we are covered, like in a tent." A tick in Zeek's jaw twitches.

Tina gives a nod. She slides off the horse and makes her way back over to Robert. Their voices are faint and low, comforting one another.

"Trill," I call out.

Trill raises her top half out of my arm as I hold it up in front of me. Her warmth heats it with her flame, but doesn't burn me.

"Yes?"

"We are going to be going into something called the Abyss. It is a very dark place and you and Tina will have to stay hidden while we remain in there. So make sure if or when you come out you are at your lowest setting or wait till we are in a covered area." I recite the same message to her, not taking any chances.

"I understand," she yawns as she sinks back down into my arm.

A while later, after stopping for a break and getting a plan together. We make our way towards the Abyss. I make sure Tina and Trill are both out of sight. Grabbing my pack that is half hung off the back of the horse, I pull it back through and tighten the straps to make sure it won't be going anywhere if the horse takes off.

I only brought the essentials, so I need everything and don't want it strewn across the desert. My mother's journal I kept back at the house, safely hidden under the dresser. There's barely enough room to get the book under there, so I don't really think anyone will find it. The necklace and clothes are the only things I had to my name, other than a few books here and there to help me learn about myself and powers.

As we ride, the vacuum gets larger until it is filling our vision. The darkness doesn't just appear; it is more subtle than that. Little tendrils of dark fog start to roll in as the light fades away. Little by little it gets hazy. The horses stop and turn as the light dims. It is difficult to see very far in front of us.

"We will have to walk the horses through this part. With us unsure in this place, the horses will become restless. We will be their guide," Robert states as he slides off.

Sliding down off the horse, the sand pulls at my boots with every step I take, making this worse. The sun we left had been high in the sky, yet barely any of it pierces this dark veil. We are all quiet for fear of this new place. The horses move, but their hooves stomp the sand as we guide them. The light barely stays with us as we move further into the shadows of this place.

As we continue to move forward, the light continues to dwindle as the dark takes on an opaque quality.

"What are we going to do if it becomes pitch black?" I whisper to the group that is fanned out beside me.

"That shouldn't happen. It is just after noon and we have plenty of daylight to travel by," Zeek whispers back.

Looking next to me, I see his hands disappear into the folds of his many pockets in search of something. "I can barely make you out, let alone anyone else." My eyes squint at our surroundings. "It looks like this place isn't governed by the same day and night schedule that the normal world sets."

One moment we can see at least a little bit and the next step we are in total darkness. A stick of gray light glows next to Zeek. He hands the glowing light stick to me; it turns green with black flecks. He then finds another in the many pockets of his dark cloak, giving it to Robert and the rest of the group down the line.

The green glow illuminates my immediate area so that I can see the others. After a few minutes, I twirl mine through the darkness, liking how the light leaves a faint line behind in the darkness.

"Why the different colors?" I ask. Noticing Jazmin's turning a bluish green, with purple hues blended throughout.

"It picks up on what kind of magic you use," Zeek explains. "You can also elongate the stick into a long staff. Just press down on the ends and it will spring out into a staff."

I press down on each end, watching it spring up in the sky. The light fizzles out but illuminates when I catch it, bringing it close to my body. I flick the long stick, spinning it around.

"What are you doing?" Natasha asks from my other side. She stops my staff with hers, which causes a low pop when they hit one another.

"Jamming out to the voices in my head," I retort back as I twirl around under the reins that I hold in my other hand. I bring up the green light, tracing it across the darkness. My boots fall heavy on the soft sand as I plod my way across, following the other's light. Zeek and Jazmin move up ahead as Robert falls behind, leaving us once again in the middle to do what we want.

Her light is a pretty blue. She also moves hers around. "That's kind of nice to look at." She trails it over my dying light when I get too far away.

We twirl around, making shapes with the light between the two of us, swirling green and blue together. Both of us humming to a tune of music that we make up. We erupt in giggles as we race around one another to make shapes and designs. Our lights come together, making a brighter and harsher light than just them on their own. We cross the tips of the sticks against the other by accident, making a harsh pop echo around us.

Freezing we, both stop what we are doing coming down off the high of our dance. "You did that on purpose," I hiss, ducking my head down as Zeek glares back at us.

"Me, you did that." She elbows me in the arm.

"Did not." My anger sparks as I push her back.

"You so did," she giggles as she raises her stick like a sword. "Put your weapon where your mouth is, traitor!"

"You may beat me in an actual battle, but a battle of color. That is where you will fall flat, just like your hair," I quip.

"Going after a woman's hair? Oooo, that will teach me. What's next? You going to diss my shoes?"

"I was going to kick lower, but last time I checked, you didn't have any balls, and weren't getting any either."

She flicks her stick in my face, wiggling threateningly.

"I told you that in confidence. I was teasing Zeek," she stresses his name, whispering. "Unfortunately, it backfired on me and is driving me crazy!" She says. Natasha continues to come at me, pushing me back out of hearing range of Zeek.

"I didn't say it loud enough for all to hear," I say back. Tripping backwards, my arms pinwheel to catch my balance, and the stick flings around with my movements. She bats at mine and they both come together, causing a louder boom and a flash of light which encircles our group. The light stays for a few moments long enough for us to see many dark creatures circling around us and waiting to pounce.

We all freeze in fear, no one making a move or saying a word in this moment as we take everything in.

There are bigger and darker creatures further away that we can barely make out. Heads poke up from the ground from under the sand. Spikes cover their colossal head; they look like something between a snake and an enormous cat as they dig their way out of the ground. A loud shrill comes from Zeek's direction as something he is holding goes off. He takes off and many of the monsters pull off of our group to follow him.

"What was that?" Jazmin asks in confusion.

My head whips around, trying to keep up with what is happening.

"A warning, come closer," Robert bellows.

"Fuck! We are surrounded," Natasha says. The light fades as the rest of us race closer together.

"How can that be? We weren't just a moment ago."

"Most of them came from deep underground. They were not registering our normal movement until you guys started dancing, making noise, and created a light show." Robert grabs the glowing lights from each of us, shrinking them back to palm size, hiding them away back in his cloak.

"How do you expect us to fight them if we can't see?" I ask.

"I think you have helped enough," Robert says. "Jazmin raise the dead. We are going to need as much help as possible here." He races away.

Zeek races in as Robert takes on the next wave of monsters fending and guiding them away from our group. "Bring the horses here at the center, stay on the outside of them. We will need them if we want to live through this. They are the only things that could out race some things in here," he says as he pulls this and that from his pockets but keeps a square device in his hand, watching the screen.

"Is that what made that shrill noise earlier?" I ask.

"I silenced it, but it tells us if there are enemies around and how close I noticed the other ones further back, but they never came too close for worry. These—" he shows the screen of the smaller dots that have clustered around us, blocking us from the other creatures. "—were all underground. We must have stumbled through their home, or this could be their nesting site. It would explain why there are so many here and why they are so pissed."

"Why haven't they attacked yet?" I ask.

"They are watching and waiting for the perfect time. Robert is distracting them, buying us time while Jazmin raises the dead. That's if there are enough bodies left for her to animate. There might only be bones left."

Natasha quickly changes as she takes in the situation and flies past us in her other form. Ice is already pouring from her. Her wicked wings are sharp and ready to shred others that get too close.

"Damn it, I needed her to help protect the horses," Zeek curses under his breath.

"Shouldn't she go help Jazmin, since she has more active power? Why aren't you out there with them and Robert back here? I know I'm not the best in a fight." I shrug okay with the fact, but apprehensive if I shouldn't have focused more on training when I came back from the past.

Growls and a huffing noise come from my right next to the back of the horses.

"Robert has his own kind of power that he can rely on. Being a Kitsune is more than just his spirit," Zeek barks. "You need to call on your animal."

"I can't," I say through gritted teeth. "It comes out all on its own when I'm scared or pissed."

He grabs at the front of my shirt, pulling me close. So close I can feel his hot breath on my face. "You better get to one of those quickly before they tear you up and make your bones a part of their desert canvas. Unlike you, all of us have other ways to get through this wasteland. You are slowing the group down and need to be better, do better." He tosses me away from him, his eyes take on a golden hue, getting brighter as he brings out a couple of sharp daggers. Twirling them in hand, he races to the back of the horses, scaring off what creatures thought about attacking earlier.

My eyes dance around the darkness, begging to find something that they could see. As I move closer to the horses, their outline comes into my vision. My fingers brush across the softness to calm my nerves. "What does he know?" I mutter to myself. My horse that I have been riding for the last couple of days nuzzles my face in comfort. "I need you to hang on to something for me." I take off the necklace with the trinkets and tuck it into the saddlebag. "Don't lose this. If I change, I can't risk looking these trinkets. Please." Patting the side of the horse's neck, I hope she understands my need. I feel the fur inside me bristle, claws rake the sides of my arms. Trying to call on the animal inside me, I move away from the horse slightly, not wanting to spook them anymore than they already were.

Yipping sounds scatter around, I hear ripping and tearing as the things attack. Since I couldn't see very far, I had to hope that the group was doing well and not laying lifeless and being devoured by these creatures.

I'm not a very good witch or shifter. I'm a human that has fallen into this messed up world. "Come on." I squeeze my eyes close not seeing the point to keep them open to just possibly see teeth coming at me. Pounding at my head, I try to call on my animal by harming myself.

Pulling my hair, I squeeze back between two of the horses they have all huddled together. Their hooves make small stomps as they worry together about the sounds going on. Someone trained them well to not break formation during dangerous times.

I could sense something crawling closer surrounding me. It just felt icky and wrong.

"You are not worth the trouble. You are not the savior, and you will never learn your powers and how to use them." Many voices whisper around me.

Shaking my head, my eyes spring open, hoping to not be surrounded. The horse skitters backwards as they feel something wrong coming toward them, just as I do. "No, I can do this." I shake my head, trying to call my animal eyes and claws. "Badger eyes would be helpful; I would at least be able to see what is about to attack me and then hopefully defend myself."

A ghostly chill runs down my spine as whispers tickle my ears. "Just wait. Someone strong will come and save you?" The voices laugh in a high-pitched squeal taunting me.

"No!" My ire shoots straight up as I push forward away from the horses. "I will not sit around and wait to be saved. I'm tired of waiting for shit to happen! It is about time I learn how to do this on my own."

A low growl emits from right in front of me.

Fear skates through me as my eyes begin to turn and things begin to lighten and crystalize as they become clearer.

This enormous cat with spikes down its head and back crouches low to the ground. There is no fur, only scales like that of a snake. It hisses at me and large teeth drip liquid as it stays low, getting ready to pounce.

*Is that thing more snake or cat?*

Another creeps up the side, dancing behind me, pawing at the ground. The first one creeps closer but stops when my eyes zero back in on it. A strong yank on my ponytail pulls me all the way back. I go down, gripping my hair. The snake cat is behind me now and has a lock on my hair, pulling me over the ground. Kicking my feet, I try to keep the one in front of me at bay.

"Let go of me!" I scream out as it tugs at my hair, my fear becoming too much for me to process. My wild eyes search the dark depths, hoping to land on a friend but only finding enemy after enemy. These two are the only ones close enough to see. I hear another monster, but it makes a clicking sound and dashes off to my right.

"These are sand burrowers. As long as you stay away from their claws and teeth, you should be good. Don't let them get in your head. They will try to unhinge you," Zeek yells out.

"They are blind, so stay quiet. Zeek and I are going to try to call them away," Robert adds in being extra boisterous. Stomping his feet and being as noisy as possible to bring them his way.

The one still has ahold of my hair and kept drags me over the ground. The sand pulls at my pants, slipping and scratching my skin. I hold my screams in, even though my whole being wants to scream at the top of my lungs. The one at my feet keeps pouncing from where my shoes connect with the ground and makes noise, but the other one pulls me further away, making it miss each time. Fighting over me to see which one would devour me first.

Tears run down my face, trying not to sob too loudly. The terror and helplessness I feel is enough to throw me over the edge. My legs shorten as my body contorts to the change. My hair falls away from me, bringing the creature both closer but then further away as it feels like it has gotten a prize. Rolling through the sand, I come up in my little fur body with all claws and teeth. The one creature leaves, finding better prey with the other two, which only leaves one more. My eyes lock on and grow sharp as they grow accustomed to the dark, liking how the darkness hides me fully.

Squeaking and hissing in frustration, I slash with my claws at the blind creature, still trying to sense where I went. It hisses back at me in answer, launching for the scruff of my neck. Powerful jaws encompass my throat crunching down, my claws swipe at its face and neck but can't find purchase on the slippery scales. Small whines bubble up out of my throat, along with a screech of terror. A blue glow zeroes in on us as ice daggers, both small and large, drop around us, pelting both the creature and I. The larger chunks hit the creature, causing them to ease up. The pressure on my throat eases. One long, sharp looking ice spear shoots through the creature, cutting through its side, causing it to yelp in pain. I lunge for it, tackling it to the ground, slashing at the wound in its side, cutting it fully open so its innards spill out. This one would not be getting back up, I make sure of that.

Blood coats my fur and claws. I could not enjoy my winning spoils because right behind the one I just took down; another takes its place. This one has a wide mouth with sharp teeth and is making the same clicking noise I heard before. I hunker down close to the sand, crawling close to the ground, not wanting to make myself a bigger target. I scuttle away and retreat into a pack that is left on the ground, near where our team had been confronted originally. My heart beats in rapid fire as I settle in letting the others fight. Staying silent, I hear the battle all around me. Grunts and yells of pain, along with hisses and chattering from the creatures.

I lick at my paws, cleaning the blood from them along with checking my neck. Moving it too much causes me to whimper. Teeth definitely sliced into me there and would take time to heal. After many minutes pass, the battle still rages on. My animal tires and I still worry that more are out to get me. I worry my friends are out there hurt or possibly even dying. My stomach turns, but I'm unsure if I can make myself move to help. As things quiet down, my eyes begin to droop and solve that issue for me. My animal needs the rest to heal, and I don't want to listen to what is happening out there anymore.

Many hours later, I hear the group coming together and talking in hushed tones.

"Where did she go?" Robert asks.

"I saw she had changed into her badger form. I helped her out when she was getting attacked," Natasha huffs.

My badger animal is cozy, curled in the bag. The warmth of fur calls me back to sleep. Lifting my head up, I can see them, but the sand has blown around us, causing a small hill hiding us effectively. There grating voices interrupt my dozing.

"Do you think she will come back?" Robert looks to Zeek. "Do you have a read on her?"

"No." He shakes his head and goes back to studying the device.

Peeking my nose out, my eyes continue to track them as they walk further away. Natasha holds a glowing ice light that keeps it dim enough not to call attention but bright enough to see by.

"Would she go after Shade on her own? Or would she have run out of this place?" Zeek asks Natasha.

"She might. She was very adamant about finding Shade." Natasha gives a shrug; her wings flutter to keep her afloat.

"That girl needs to make him give her back what is hers. She needs the witch powers and her badger powers to bring the masses together," Jazmin pipes in.

Shaking my neck slightly, I lower my head back on my paws, settling down. The twinge in my neck lets me know I have not rested long enough.

"What if he doesn't come with us? What are we going to do? Make him? Have you given thought to that Jazmin?" Robert asks. "Do we have a backup plan?"

"Why would he not come with us?" Jazmin asks.

"He left for a reason. And he hasn't come around at all during that time. What makes you think he wants to? Now that we have come looking for him," Robert says. "What's stopping him from attacking us for not leaving him alone?"

"It doesn't matter how we do it as long as we do. Get him and her to the Dark Court and we can take care of the mishap with him taking her powers." Jazmin grimaces.

A dark black skull floats in. "Spells and spells make a witch. She will be whole once fixed." Trix spins around, singing. His red eyes shine extra bright in the darkness. "None know what she will be, savior or terror, or maybe all three." He cackles.

"What will that do to one that has no soul?" Robert asks.

Jazmin gives a shrug. "What does it matter?"

"I think Alexia will have a problem with that." Natasha throws some ice balls that she makes at Trix. He dodges them as she lobs them in his direction. "You only show up after all the fighting? What use are you?"

*I would never do that to him. He is a person regardless if he has a soul or not! He protected me when no one else would and I will do the same. I don't know why he is doing what he is doing and maybe I don't need to. I just need to trust in him.* These thoughts spin through my mind. I shuffle restlessly as I hear them try to make plans I'm not on board with.

"Shouldn't we wait to talk this over with her?" Natasha tries again.

Jazmin waves her off. "We know what is best for her."

"Perhaps Natasha is right," Robert agrees. "No matter how much that kills me to say."

Zeek just grunts in answer, focused on something else altogether.

My paws scratch over the bottom of the bag in happiness. My claws sink into something and get caught there. Pulling my claw up to my face, I see some beef jerky that is stashed in this pack. Nibbling at the beef, I grunt and hum in a soothing way. Happy grunts escape me as I flump back into the pack, safe, and sound and proud of the people I have people around me who respect my thoughts. Or at least willing to wait to decide for now.

"What was that?" Zeek calls out.

The pack moves and I freeze in answer, snuggling deep down into the pack, making sure they could not see my face.

Natasha says over Zeek's shoulder. "Did she fall asleep in there? While we were doing all the fighting." She gives a bout of laughter. "Good for her!"

"At least we found her and don't have to worry about where she went and what she is doing." Zeek breathes out a sigh of relief.

# Chapter 2

"Let's go people, let's not waste daylight." Robert states as he claps his hands together.

"We are not all morning people like you," Natasha grumbles. Her hair is messy and there are bags under her eyes. She doesn't appear to be having fun this morning.

"I thought you sleep in four-hour intervals; this should be easy for you," Robert says.

"On a normal day, there are four hours twice a day at specific points that I sleep. This is throwing everything off. I'm not always ready for rest when we must stop and when it is time to move, it feels like I'm in the middle of needing to be asleep. I will be glad once we are through this place."

"Traveling like this is taking a toll on all of us. We have been in this place for a couple of days now. It's to be expected," I say in answer, trying to keep the peace we are all a little riled up.

"Robert and Zeek are used to this lifestyle. They aren't like the rest of us." Natasha's lip raises as she gives a snide look.

"Careful, your inner bitch is showing," I whisper.

She rolls her eyes and goes back to the tent that Jazmin, her, and I all share. As she stomps, dust clusters up from her boots.

"Do you think you should do that after last time?" Jazmin comments, her one purple eye glowing. "Not you, I need you to scour the sands for other dead," she mutters to something I can't see.

Natasha's steps soften, but she ignores Jazmin and continues with what she has to say. "We have been on the road for what, four days now? We are not them. I'm not used to these harsher conditions." She gives a huff and throws the tent flap to the side. Jazmin and I both look at each other for a moment before I jog forward to grab it and walk through, letting it fall behind me.

The sand beneath my feet is cool in the early morning. "There isn't much light to travel by, so I can understand why we have to take advantage when the light is present." I try to reason with her.

"After our first night in this place, we quickly learned that it did more harm when moving during the full dark times. We didn't even see the snake like creatures, but they sure felt us as you two danced around and made a show of yourselves. They had us surrounded, their nests deep underground, where they could hear and feel our vibrations making us easy targets," Jazmin says as she enters the tent.

"Whose side are you really on? Just be miserable like the rest of us," Natasha says.

"She is just crankier since she can't get any alone time with her death dealer," Jazmin coos.

Jazmin, who is usually dolled up in an extravagant dress, has switched to a dark purple full suit that covers her entire body with billowy pants and the top is tight across her chest. It looks like she could easily move and traverse this place.

"Are we close to the Dark Court?" I ask as I stuff some of my things into a bag and change into my riding clothes for the day. I make sure I'm facing away when changing my shirt to make sure the necklace is safely tucked underneath, and not viewable by others. Heat emits from the ruby heart at a low thrum. It is nice since the desert remains cool and dry with the lack of light or sun to warm it.

"We are southwest of where the court currently resides," she states as she rolls up her blankets in a tight burrito so she can easily pack it.

I struggle with doing the same. Kicking at my blankets, I kneel to start the arduous project of rolling them away. "What do you mean currently resides?"

"The Dark Court moves around at its own whim. Keeping enemies at bay by pure chaos alone," Jazmin cackles.

Natasha shakes her head. "Don't listen to the crazy lady. Where ever Flit goes, the Dark Court follows. When he came into power, he never stays in one place long. He said life would grow boring if he stayed in one place too long or something like that. So, his court is one that moves around to where the wind takes him."

"Will it still be in the same place? It will take us longer to get there since we now have this new lead on Shade to deal with?" I ask.

"Since the Dark Court is throwing a huge celebration soon, yes, it will. Flit usually commandeers one of his people's places for such an event as this. I believe there is a castle in this town," Jazmin states, looking away from us.

"Do you think Shade knows we are after him? Maybe that is why he is in here, so we can't follow him very well?" I say.

"I wouldn't put it past him." Natasha throws her bags that are already packed out of the tent flap.

"Did you even sleep? You were up before any of us."

"No." She gives a grimace. "This whole place is throwing me off. Hopefully, this light session isn't too long since I feel like it is getting close to the time I usually sleep."

"I know we have not had a lot of time together to talk," lowering my voice. "You know just us two without others around."

Natasha stops what she is doing, her eyes zero in on Jazmin. Jazmin continues to stare off at the corner of the tent, ignoring us. "With these people, there is no such thing as personal space. If Shade is doing this to throw you off his trail, he needs to stop it."

"That reminds me, Zeek will need to know the direction we need to head in. Trill are you up?" My hands are sore and as I massage them, deep grooves and cracks emerge. They ache as I handle rolling the blankets.

"Yes, Alexia." She pulls up off my hand and twirls on the sand. Heat comes up off her as she burns brightly.

I hiss at the pain that tears through my hands. "Man, my hands are not used to this kind of wear and tear."

"This place sucks the life from all that it can." Jazmin comes out of her trance. "Here, try some of this." She tosses a container to me as she finishes up with her bedroll.

"Did I hurt you?" Trill asks. She stops twirling, rushing back to me. She gives me a look of concern as she tries to grow her flame higher in order to see my palm.

"No, of course not." My fingers pry open the jar. I lower my nose to take a whiff of the contents. My eyes tear up and I quickly move it away from my face. "That is strong."

"Good, it should be. Let's you know it will do the job," she says.

Nodding, I apply a generous helping on my palms as my eyes track to the closed tent flap and then back. "Let's hurry before Robert or Zeek come in here and yell at us for wasting more time." The light under the flap is a dull gray and is barely able to be called light. "Trill is Shade nearby? Or, I mean, is Taz close by? If so, what direction do we need to head in?"

Her voice comes out quiet as she shuts her eyes to concentrate. "They are still moving to the south at a steady rate. They are closer, but that is all I can sense."

"We can't tell if he knows we are following him or if Taz is helping him?"

"I wouldn't see why she would help him and keep him ahead of us. She knows we travel with you, so she wouldn't want us hurt even if she is working with him." Trill's voice comes out stronger as she fights for her sister.

"I know you have said this before. I just hope we don't find your sister abandoned somewhere alone."

Trill's flame grows even brighter, her heat reaching the top of the tent. "He better not!"

I glance up in surprise and try to push her and the light back down, not physically, but by crowding in on her. "No, no, I know and we will deal with it if it comes to that, but I was just speaking about some fears or worries I have spinning in my head. I'm sure we won't." Motioning to Natasha with my head to go out of the tent and stop Zeek or Robert to let one of them know.

Natasha grumbles under her breath as she lifts the flap. A tendril of smoke escapes. Trill lowers her flame back down.

"I'm anxious and us not getting any closer makes me worry even more." She lowers back down to her normal small size. Trill launches up on my shoulder, coming closer to my ear. "It has taken all of me to keep Tina in line and not have her race across the desert to find Taz. They are a lot closer than Taz and I were, but they are both my responsibility."

"You are the same age as your sisters. You have no more responsibility than any of your other sisters do!" Giving her a harsh frown, I shake my shoulder, wanting her to see reason.

"I'm the eldest and had to help Mother with the other two. That means I have more responsibility than them and they both know it. I have always taken care of this family and made sure we stayed together and safe." She stomps her tiny foot on my shoulder. A sizzle of her flame can be felt through the layers I wear.

Robert sticks his head in to the tent. "In five minutes, this tent is coming down, whether you all are in it or not." The flap falls down to the sand as he exits, already being done with our communication.

"He's not lying either." Jazmin throws the rest of the stuff in a bag and tosses it to the ground at the front of the tent. "The second day you guys were cleaning up at the stream, I wasn't moving fast enough and he closed down the tent that I was still in. He tried to roll me up and throw me over the horse to carry."

"I remember we came back, and you had called up some dead things to aid you. You both looked like you wanted to kill each other," I say.

"He just doesn't like necromancers since I control the body, stealing some of the spirit or essence left in the carcass after the soul leaves. He is a spirit animal and worries I will steal his body if he leaves it unattended."

"I can understand that if you threatened to do just that. Why do you antagonize him?"

"I might have threatened someone a time or two. It's really hard to recall, as it's a lot of fun." She smiles and makes her way to the front, sliding past me. "I will hold off the brute until you're done."

I nod and hurry at getting my things together, putting the jar in my pack. My hands would thank me later. I bring my cheek against Trill, who is still on my shoulder. "Do you think we will come across them today? Are we that close?"

She concentrates and takes a moment to think through things or search for her sister. "We are close. They are on the move right now. Depending on what we find throughout our travels, we may catch up to them. Shade has magic to help him through this. Though we have a death dealer, we are just surviving and hindering him through this process."

"For one so young, you are very knowledgeable."

"I need to be in order to help my sisters and I make the best decisions and gain strength as we continue to grow. One day we will be strong enough to be big like Mother, maybe even take on human form. I hope to visit her world, but she warned us to be strong before entering that world. With what happened to her. She did not want that happening to her own children." She crouches and leans down on her hip, resting on my shoulder as I finish packing up my bag. Trying to move slow and fluid, I grab it and make sure not to jar her. I make my way, pulling the weighted bag beside me as it slides over the sand.

There were some books that Natasha and Margret made me take with to do some reading on the road in order to learn more about my animal and magic. They were so sure I would get my magic back or that Shade would eventually give it back. Magic was more of a pain than help. Spells just don't act right around me. It might be better that I don't have any powers to rely on. After that last spell almost killing me, I think I can do without magic.

Regardless, we need to get going and catch up with Shade. I need to be there for him like he was there for me in the past. I just hope it's a better reunion than the last time I saw him.

"Make sure your flame is the lowest it can go." Waiting until Trill dims her light, I move forward. "Ready," I say as I make my way through the flap. Robert is pacing by the horses, getting them ready for our ride. Zeek and Natasha were nowhere in sight. Jazmin is just ahead, bringing her bags to Robert. My muscles scream out in pain, but I lift the bag and walk slowly to where we are leaving them. I rush back to the tent to disassemble it since I'm the last one out. Waiting for Robert to take care of it would just be asking for trouble, since he's in a mood this morning.

"He doesn't do well away from Margret," Jazmin whispers as I race around the tent.

Digging through the sand, I pull up the spikes that are holding it in place. Making sure to not make too much noise for fear of attracting something to us again. Jazmin watches me closely but doesn't come to help me.

Soon the tent is down, and I set to work on packing it away. My legs cry in pain as I gasp at the quick movements I'm making to put this tent away. Making my way, I put the pack near the other traveling gear. Every part of my body is sore and there isn't enough of a break to get used to things or let my body fully rest. Natasha said there were other ways to get through here, but none that we have access to at the moment.

Soon we are all back and packed up and on the road. "Hang back with me," I whisper to Natasha before she can get on the horse and to the front of the line. She likes to be towards the front these last couple of times because she feels she could be the best line of defense since she has ice magic. It also is to stay far away from Zeek, since he brought up the back of the line most of the time.

Natasha gives a whining noise but nods, regardless.

After shooting death glares at Zeek, he eases back far enough for me to feel comfortable talking with Natasha. She gives a small silent laugh, but I can see her shoulders shake each time I glare at him.

"What did you need to talk about that is so important and couldn't wait till tonight or another time?" She shoots a curious look but makes sure her head stays forward so Zeek cannot read our lips or body language.

"We haven't had time alone since I came back and we need to discuss what is happening."

"What do you mean?"

"Don't play dumb with me. I overheard your deal that you made. Tell me everything." I nudge my horse into hers, making her horse neigh and dance away.

She gives a glare but slides it into a sly smile. "It sure has been interesting for me. I torment him a lot, though he knows how to give it just as good as he receives. You know this all already though." She scrunches her face in anger.

"So, working on it or what?"

"Definitely working on it, I guess. He isn't making it easy to just have fun. He can be a stick in the mud." She pulls up a hood, looking to the side so he cannot tell. She chews on her lip. "Part of me is terrified. The part that is terrified knows he isn't caving in because he is playing for keeps. Another part, though a tiny part that I keep hidden and will deny all night long, enjoys it and thinks maybe, just maybe, there is a reason so many people want this."

"It's good you need that in your life." I give a quaint smile. My eyes slide to the side, checking he is far enough back for my liking. His head is low and bent forward as if he is reading something.

Our horses are close, so I reach out a hand and place it on her shoulder. "I think he will challenge you in ways that you need. I don't think he will ever in ways that harm or hurt you."

She leans into the touch and then pulls away. "I know, and that worries me. I have a feeling I'm going to mess this up more than he ever would or I will chicken out and run like I always do."

"Even if you do, I don't think you will get very far."

"Yea, it is a good thing he is a death dealer, otherwise he may never make it." We travel in silence for a while. "What about you? We are growing closer to the Dark Court. Do you think you will run in to Blaise? Are you nervous?"

"It's a possibility. I'm not sure how to feel about everything. He is complicated to be with and after everything I have been through, I want something easy."

"But the sex is hot, is it not?" She gives a frown.

"Yes, but a relationship needs more than that to continue off of."

"That's what people say," Natasha says. Looking back, she stares at Zeek. He has not raised his head throughout our whole time of talking, but at that moment he raises it to stare back at Natasha.

I feel very in the middle as his hot, molten eyes capture Natasha's. Clearing my throat. "He had not looked until just this moment. Is he not supposed to be keeping an eye out for enemies?"

Her gaze keeps to his, but after a moment, they slide away. He slumps back down, his gaze falling back to where he was looking previously with his head down.

"He sees all, even if he doesn't look like he does. It is easier to trick your enemies in to making a mistake of their own."

Under the cloak, I clutch at the ruby and press it against my chest, feeling it warm up. I haven't told her of the siren and didn't think I could not without giving more details. Part of me craved to talk to her about it so I could get some advice. A lyrical tune echoes inside my head, as if calling to me. I let the trinkets fall from my hand. Right now isn't a good time for that or him, perhaps tonight would be better. A wave of heat pours into me from the necklace as if he heard my words and liked what was to come.

"It's just sometimes Blaise is fantastic, and then there are other times where he is almost cruel, mean, or detached and doesn't want me closer. I crave close contact even if he doesn't. When it is good, it is so very good, but then comes the pitfall of not so good. It just feels like a continuous ride. Are soul mates not allowed other partners? I mean, obviously they can, since Robert and Margret are an item, but is that just an exception to the rule or what?"

She bursts out in hushed laughter. "No, not at all, and if he is telling you shit like that, then he isn't for you, even if there is a tether."

"No, just my curiosity." Shaking my head vigorously so she knows he isn't trying to cage me into something I don't want.

"Good, we can't have that. Soul mates have a choice before the union. It makes you crave one another but that can be ignored if needed, I have heard it isn't pleasant but choice is there. Also, being with just them, that is bull you can be with another and so can they. It just means nothing. Back in the day, soul mates used to be a lot stricter, but with all the problems that caused, they just let it run its course now. Some groups, of course, keep to the old ways, but others have evolved from it and others have forgotten it all together."

"So ultimately it is our choice and nothing really happens to either of us if we choose not to go through with it."

"Not nothing. You may feel empty or as if you are missing a part of yourself. There may be other adjustments that might have to be made." Seeing the hint of fear on my face, she backpedals. "Nothing may happen. It depends on how far the bond has been allowed to grow before a decision is made to not complete."

I bite at my lip, unsure how much further to go. I shrug my shoulders and just let go of a pent-up breath I'm holding. If I couldn't tell her, then who could I trust to tell?

"There is another that is easier to be around and is more open," I say in a low hushed voice.

"What?" She gives a screech. Looking around quickly, she ducks her head and whispers back vehemently. "Another? Who? You little vixen." She gives a thumbs up and beams at me as if proud.

"No one you know he is being held with Blaise. He is a siren." I shrug. "He is just different and makes thing easier. He has his own set of problems, yet talks through them with me and explains things instead of shutting down."

"When did you meet him? You like danger, don't you?"

"I guess I have a type." Giving a chuckle. "I haven't really met him in person yet."

Confusion passes over her face. Her eyes are pinch as her lips purse with worry. She grabs the reins of my horse to slow us both down even more. "What do you mean you haven't met him physically yet?"

I squint ahead at Jazmin and Robert, who are getting further away. Zeek has stopped all together and is waiting for us to continue. "I'd rather not say."

"We need to get you dealing in reality first. This will be much easier to deal with then. Girl, are you sure that heat cycle didn't just go to your head? Since you did that spell in the middle of that cycle, it could have messed with things."

"I'm glad it hasn't been physical except the one time with Blaise I don't think I could handle that right now. I can barely handle what I'm doing. How do I do this? I don't want to screw any of this up. They are all adults. I should just be able to talk to them about this. Right?" My eyes flit between Robert and Zeek, worried one of them would interrupt.

"I don't think men can ever be adult. It's funny that you think so, especially if there are feelings involved." She nudges her horse forward, making mine trail behind, keeping us close together. "I'm intrigued how you would make a go of that, though."

"We kind of talked about things and I promised Blaise I would come to him first if I needed something," I say worrying my lip.

"And?"

Ringing my hands together. "Well, I didn't need something, per se. I just wanted to talk mostly, and the siren was there. He is easier to talk to than wondering where Blaise and I are headed at least."

"This siren doesn't have you under his spell, does he, with his voice?" She taps her fingers against her throat.

"At first maybe, and he admitted to that, but no, he hasn't used it unless he is teasing." I smile to myself.

Natasha gives a humph noise, stuck in thought.

"Or I beg for it," I blurt.

A huge smile appears on her face as her eyes light up. "Perhaps you are learning more than you think, just not in the way some of us want you to." Natasha nudges my arm. "Perhaps we are not incentivizing you the correct way."

I think back to what Domini and I were doing when he gave me his word his voice would only be used for teasing. My cheeks heat up in thought as an echo of his voice sings through my mind. I roll my eyes and remember to be problematic for him the next time we meet. He wants to tease me while there is nothing, I can do about it. Two could play that game.

"Whatcha thinking about?" She gives a knowing smile. "I know exactly what you're thinking about by that face." She gives a wicked expression.

"You already know it." I glance away.

"Soooo a siren," she gives a musical hum. "What makes him better or different from Blaise?"

"Do you want to share more with you and Zeek? I will not be the only one sharing on this subject." My eyes cut to hers, holding them, raising my chin.

"Mostly we sit in silence. I know so hot," Natasha complains. "Though he has gotten me to open up about a few things. I have persuaded him in only the best ways." She gives a wolfish grin. "Which he has declined so far, but he likes to watch, I can tell. I think I have a creeper on my hands." She lowers her head and leans closer to me. "But like a cute creeper, you know?"

"Can a creeper be cute?"

"Shhhh. Not so loud." She shoves my head down, looking back to make sure Zeek hasn't lifted his head. Peeking to the side, she turns her head to mine right before he looks up at her. "It's not creepy, more in a hot way. He enjoys watching me, if you catch my drift." Her eyes widen to entail what she means.

"So, you haven't done it yet."

"Not for lack of trying on my part." We both continue to talk in low tones as the horses walk faster to make up the distance. "At the next place we stop at something is going to happen. I need to find a party and just see what happens when I go for someone else."

Trill raises up on my other shoulder. "Alexia, you are becoming very warm at an alarming rate. But I hear what is causing all the excitement now," she gives a giggle.

"Shit is one of the fire sisters out." Natasha rubs the back of her neck the hood falling down. "Margret is going to have my head for this. She is always yelling at me to be careful of my words around the young ones. Shit. Fuck. Damn it, see, I can't stop." She places a hand over her mouth, forcing her to stop.

"I can go up near Robert. He might not like to hear what you guys are discussing, though." She gives a tiny twirl and looks away shyly.

"Fine, you can stay, but if Margret hears about this, I'm coming for you and only you." Natasha glares at the tiny flame and shoots a tiny ice ball at the dancing flame, missing her just barely.

Trill gives a screech; she scoots closer to my neck so that I'm shielding her. Raising my shoulder, I adjust her and try to get them both to calm down and not put me in the middle of their game as a target.

"All right, I explained my predicament, even though it isn't half as spicy as what you seem to be caught in the middle of." She gives a pout, ignoring Trill as she gets us back to our original conversation.

"Spicy or confusing." I shake my head. "Though Zeek is just as confusing. Every guy seems to have an ulterior motive. Nothing is ever just a coincidence or fun."

"Yea, they seem to have that problem. If they didn't have something wrong with them, would we even be attracted to them?" Natasha massages her temples. Her short blue hair is messy and falls in front of her face.

"The siren I'm helping. He lost his siren soul and lucky me, I found it. Easy enough, right? But he also likes to shove Blaise's face in the fact that I have a choice between the both of them."

"Good, you do have a choice. You always have a choice. I like this guy. What's his name?" Natasha's fierce eyes light up.

"Domini. My worry is, would Domini even want me if I couldn't help get him his siren soul back? Blaise is sure stuck on that I'm his soul mate, but doesn't seem to want to work toward making that a reality. He has the audacity to say he will be there for me and then wasn't. He is very hot and cold, depending on the day." I hang my head in dejection. "They both care and are there for me when it matters, but it just feels like something is missing." Rubbing my head, I peer over my shoulder back to her as my horse picks up the pace, getting in front of hers. "Dumb, I'm just dumb."

Natasha picks up speed on her horse and grips my wrist in her hand. Her fingers are cold and freezing. I try to grab my hand back from her, but she holds on tightly.

"Never ignore that small part of you that is telling you something is off. It is almost always right. Something most likely is off with both men, not for the reason you are thinking, but they need to work on themselves. Everything will come to the light once you spend more physical time with them and they either have to explain or let things go."

"Your small voice must be loud and annoying to get you to run all the time." I chuckle.

"Yes, and it almost always is right. Even now the little voice is quiet with Zeek, even though I want to run." She bounces in the saddle. "Do you know how hard it is to fight my impulse to run?" Her face goes pale.

Shaking my head, I slide my wrist from hers and give her hand a squeeze.

She holds my hand, not letting it go. "Anyway, back to what you were saying." Color returns to her face slowly.

"For right now, I'm just keeping it fun and keeping my options open. The last I talked to Blaise was in our mind meld thing when he was saving me from myself and keeping the past spell from killing me."

"Talk to him the next time we stop. The day time travels have not been lasting very long. We will be stopping for another rest until the next light break."

"Yea, perhaps I should. The dark has lasted different lengths of time. The first day here it only lasted two hours, the next was longer, maybe six hours, and this last time was three. This place is weird if you ask me, but we are always so tired every time, no matter how much time we get to rest."

"This place sucks the life out of you." Natasha notices Robert and Jazmin have stopped and are conversing.

Trill, who is still at the dullest that her flame will go, tilts her head to the side and nods. "They are close." Her small voice carries to the entire group.

"Then why are we stopping? Robert?" I call out.

He holds up a hand with a finger stretched out. His eyes scan the dimming horizon. "The light is becoming bleaker and not as bright," he states.

There isn't anything in sight that I can see, but there are many hills of sand that are surrounding us.

"Which way are they in?" I ask Trill, my voice keeping low, letting Robert and Jazmin figure out whatever they need to.

She points off to our right. "That way."

I scrutinize the land ahead where Robert and Jazmin are and then off to the right. "Why aren't we headed that way?" Giving a curious look, I glance at Zeek.

His head is up and looking off to the right, then back down. After a few times of that, he stares at the dune to the right. He moves his horse quietly towards ours and saddles up next to Natasha. He taps the side of the horse's neck and then grabs at the reins of the horse, making sure it doesn't go anywhere.

"Stay silent," his low voice growls. "I think he is on to us because if we go the way we need to in order to get them, then we will run into a trap."

"What do you mean, a trap? What kind of trap?" Natasha asks. Her hand lets go of my hand and snakes up my arm, wanting to keep me close.

"A huge sand dragon is off that way, sleeping just beneath the sand. If we disturb it during the light time, it will destroy us. That isn't even the worst part."

"Of course it isn't," Natasha says.

"The only thing that would be even worse is if the light doesn't last and night takes over. When that happens, the dragon will come out of hiding and start to hunt all on its own." Zeek answers, all in stride. "Not even I have a death wish like that."

"How do you know it is a sand dragon?" I scan his cloak watching his hands I don't see any device there. What had he been looking at before?

"Being a death dealer gives me access to many things, including some powers and devices that aren't available to others. The device tells me where exactly within a ten-mile radius of me different creatures are located." He taps his chest where he hid the contraption. He doesn't move to bring it out and show us. "The power that I hold can, when I'm concentrating on a point, determine what kind of enemy we are dealing with."

"Isn't that useful?" Natasha remarks.

Robert and Jazmin make their way to us, keeping quiet and slow. "You fill them in?" Robert's eyes flick to Zeek's. He waits to see him nod once before his eyes train to our right. "Jazmin said she noticed shadows creeping up over ahead, which could mean that we are about to lose our light. Or it could be another predator, one that hunts during the light time."

Natasha speaks up, her eyes going wide. "Why would they lure us into a trap or go the way of the dragon?"

Tina bursts out of my chest in anger. "They wouldn't do that, he might, but my sister is good!" Tina seethes in anger and glares at Jazmin. "How could you even say something like that?"

"Sister your light." Trill reminds her.

Tina's flame instantly dissipates as she jumps up on Robert's shoulder. He comforts her by patting her back, hugging her close to him, murmuring to her in a calm voice.

"Could the dragon have eaten them?" I choke out.

Trill taps her foot in nervousness, dancing on my shoulder. "Our sister lives. We cannot tell on Shade, but Taz we know she lives. We would have felt her passing. That much I know is true." Trill answers, though her nervousness doesn't dissipate.

Natasha drops her human appearance and flutters her wings. Her hand slips off my arm as she rises. "I will just fly over there and see to make sure. No harm, no foul."

"Don't you dare!" Jazmin mutters between clenched teeth. Her horse crosses across the sand, bringing her right up next to Natasha. "A dragon knows its space both in the air and its surroundings. It will take you flying above it as an active threat, with how close you would have to be in order to make sure their sister is okay and Shade is alive."

She rolls her eyes and stops her wings, dropping back down into the saddle on the horse. The horse gives a small nicker as her weight comes down.

"Fine. Do you have any ideas?" Natasha waits for her to answer.

"That is what Robert, and I were discussing up there." She motions to the darkness creeping over the ridge. "There is a town close by where we may be able to make it before darkness descends, but there may just be another creature up ahead, one that may be worse than a sand dragon."

"There is worse?" I cough out, trying to cover my mouth before I can make too much noise.

"There are many worse things," Jazmin mutters. "This conversation, for instance."

"You are a necromancer. Can you detect anything dead up ahead? I know the sisters said Taz is alive, but what about Shade?" I chew on the bottom of my lip, trying to think up solutions.

"Unfortunately, I sense many dead all around us. Give me a moment." She closes her eye and lowers the hood of her cloak, letting her purple hair wave in a nonexistent breeze. "This must be the sand dragon's lair, so to speak, because even trying to sense just for humanoid type dead is a challenge. There are bones of the deceased littered all around."

"Can you explain how your power works what you search for exactly?" I twirl my fingers in the air next to my head, trying to think through things.

Jazmin's eye pops open. Her eye is a pale, lavender as if she is looking at me in another sight. A dark metal covers her other eye and is decorated in silver flowers and thorns, and draping over the side of her head. Her voice comes out in a whisper. "Bones or bodies, hold essence from when it was alive. I can then use that essence to pull or pluck a piece of that person back to this reality."

"Essence, what do you mean by that?"

"Essentially a soul." Her lips crimp in thought. "Your warrior. He didn't have a soul, did he?"

"Are you able to detect a dark spot or something that doesn't have a soul? Has that ever been searched for before? Is it possible?" My mind races in question.

Her eyelids lower and I see her eye race back and forth as if she were looking for something or a lack of something. "Soulless ones are very rare and not much is known about them, but I should still be able to sense a lack of something." Her hand reaches out as if reaching for something over the top of the hill.

Robert and Zeek move closer to one another and whisper quietly. They both shoot looks from the party to the hill and around. Nodding to one another, Robert notices my stare and turns his back on me, moving Zeek into place so I cannot see their mouths or expression.

"They will probably scout ahead or do something idiotic. What do you want to bet?" Natasha pulls a coin from her pocket and flips it into the air.

"Of course, they will, well, Zeek more than Robert."

"Taz is out there also, and that is where the unpredictability comes in with him. You know how he is when it comes to one of the fire sisters." Natasha gives a hoot of laughter.

"The question is, will we continue towards the sand dragon or away?"

"That is a better question." Natasha turns and looks both Robert and Zeek up and down, weighing her answer. "They mentioned a town, didn't they?"

I nod. "They did." My eyes flutter back to Jazmin, but she is still in her trance, searching. I worried about Shade and Taz, but we have been in this place for a while now. Maybe we needed to regroup and come back. Giving a shake of my head, I try to dispel my turbulent thoughts.

Natasha looks north to the darkness that is climbing over to us. "My money is on the town."

"That is what I was thinking, but you reminded me that Robert could throw a wrench into that plan." I remind her. My mind turns to worry about Taz and Shade.

"It is smart. They will scout out what we need and will go to town to get supplies. That or ask for more information on this place or the beasts that inhabit it. They will wait to see if Shade and the fire elemental move or if they stay. So far, they have been moving around."

"I hope you are wrong about that. Jazmin thinks we need Shade before going into the Dark Court." I stop my thoughts before they get pulled into a vortex of unsureness and questions that I have no answers to.

"You do? But you just agreed with her," Jazmin whispers. "I sense a dark emptiness hunkering down close by. They are not moving. I cannot sense more than that and my magic isn't able to touch his due to him not having a soul." She comes out of her trancelike state when her eye flutters open, her irises are a darker hue of purple.

"Boys, do we have a plan?" Natasha calls to the backs of Robert and Zeek. Tina's flame brightens before dimming back down.

Robert swivels his head to her and glares as he nods to something Zeek says. He walks up to us and Zeek stays where he is.

Trill gets up and jumps down from me, hopping over the sand, curious about what is going to happen next. She jumps up on Robert's other shoulder.

Robert raises his hands out from his body as if encompassing us. "That we do. One of us is going to scout the top of that dune to see if we can spot anything. That way we can have a better idea if this is a trap or if Shade is just that stupid."

"That's a little harsh," I bite back.

"Is it?" He bites down with an audible click. "It's not only his life on the line, he has Taz." His eyes are wide and wild looking.

"He wouldn't put her in harm's way on purpose." I fight for him since he isn't here to defend himself.

"Wouldn't he? You don't know him well. Why did he take your power? Took it with no worries about what that would do to you or how that may cause you issues. He didn't care about the danger you were in, just about his end goal." His hands close into fists at his side, barely holding himself back.

"All of this is new to him. Perhaps he doesn't know better."

"No excuse. He has something, Margret, and I care for. This is personal." He gives a visceral growl.

"Zeek, you can't be going along with this?" I look behind Robert and notice Zeek is no longer standing there. My eyes hunt for him frantically. "Where did he go?"

The rest of the group also looks around once they notice he is missing. I notice a small dot near the top of the sand pile.

"Is that him?" I point out. He had left his horse behind. I watch as he slithers up the sand hill.

"Yes," Robert answers. "He said it had to be him since I'm too emotionally invested in this. He would get a better read on everything and we would make a plan from there. All we need to do is wait."

Looking in the opposite direction, I notice the darkness creeping up closer to us. "We are going to lose our light. Natasha, I take that bet. I bet we will have to wait here while he is gathering intel and camp here. The town will be too far away to travel to."

Natasha's eyes spark as she gives a wicked grin. "What are we betting?"

"Something good. How about the winner decides at a later time as long as both parties agree on them first?"

She swishes her nose in thought. "Like an I owe you. I already have one of those for you but I could always have another. Deal!" She holds out her palm for me to shake.

I shake it vigorously. I keep my eyes on the coming darkness, hoping that it would move faster, so we had no option but to camp out.

"How long is he going to take?" Getting down from her horse, Natasha puts a hand on her hip, cocking her head to one side.

"He should be only a couple of minutes, just long enough to see what is happening. I just hope he is being careful and not going into the dragon's area or it could attack."

"Something doesn't add up. If you are so worried about the dragon attacking if we get into its space, how are Shade and them alive?"

"That is why we are saying it is a trap, because there is no way. Unless the dragon is keeping low, waiting for the night cycle in order to pounce, but that is highly unlikely."

"But it is a possibility," I intone.

The light dims and is quickly setting low in the sky. Soon there would be only darkness. It is gray and dim. Zeek is starting to blend into the sand.

"Should you go check with him?" I look at my wrist as if it had the time there. "How long has he been gone?"

The horse beneath me dances in time with my nerves. Moving side to side, unable to stand my nervous ticks.

"It will be dark soon. We will have to set up tents if we are to stay. If they do not move, then we can regroup first thing when light hits and see if the dragon is still there or has moved to a different place." I say with eagerness.

Natasha's hawk-like eyes pierce into me. "We should wait for Zeek. I think we can still make it to the town. We will have to trek through the darkness for a little bit but it can be done. Obviously, we learned that first night that we can if we have to."

"Robert, we're not really going to leave Taz out here, are we?" Robert follows suit and gets down from his horse. He pulls out some weapons, checking his stock.

"That's cheating," she hisses. Natasha gives a curse. "We can wait. The fire sisters have a lock down on one another and we can be out again searching in no time after regrouping in the town and getting weapons. We can then try to take on these monsters." Natasha tries to remind him.

"It's hard to say when there is a light cycle in here from outside the Abyss. It's best to stay in here until we are done," I argue.

Soon, Zeek is skidding down from the top of the dune, sliding down slow. He waits until he is in the middle of all our horses. His horse is off to the side where it waits for him.

"What did you find out?" Robert all but attacks him with his question.

"The dragon is hiding under the sand somewhere down there. I see a tiny tent that is off to the side, but there is no fire and no other movement. They must be in the tent and not moving."

"Could they be hiding somewhere else and not in the tent?" Robert asks.

"I don't think so. There isn't much down there. It is like a sinkhole that they are in the middle of, or a nest, and it's just a vast circle that dips."

"What is their plan?" Robert's eyes raise to look at the hilltop. "What is our plan?" He trails off.

Zeek takes charge as Robert thinks to himself in his own disquieting bubble.

"The darkness is coming on fast. I don't think we will be able to out run it and if we tried traveling through, it would be difficult to not get cut off from one another. We almost lost each other last time. I say we hunker down and wait, though I dislike how close we are to this dragon's nest. If it comes out during the dark, we could be toast."

"That determines it. We set up camp." I nod and maneuver to get down off the horse.

"You think you have won? We will see." Natasha all but seethes as she passes Zeek, fully ignoring him.

I cringe and avert my eyes when Zeek gives me a curious look. I don't mean to have her be upset with his decision. She will get over it.

My legs have been weak from all the use. My feet hit the ground, and my knees buckle. It takes all my arm's strength to keep my feet under me and crouching. I pull myself back up and stretch out my legs, trying to kick them out and wiggle them awake.

Getting the supplies off the horse, I untie my straps wiggling the weight from the horse. I don't want them to change their minds, so I work quickly to get out of the tent. My pack is just my back pack. That is all I had with me. The others had larger bags, so that is why my horse had to carry our tent. I don't have too much trouble bringing down the tent, but getting it up is a whole different beast.

Struggling with the lines and poles, I get it all out of the pack, hoping that would make a difference and be self-explanatory. I set off to wrestle with the fabric and shove the poles into it. I grit my teeth when the metal hits one other on the ground and makes a loud sound.

"Can someone go help her before she gives away our location?" Zeek states, annoyed.

Robert walks over since he is the other one that wants to stay here and helps me. Ripping away the cloth from my hands, he calmly works it into shape. Slowly, it forms a tent with just a little guidance to help when he needs it. "You have been helping and watching how to put up this tent for many cycles. How do you not understand how to put this up yet?"

I shrug in answer. "I'm usually not watching what you are doing, just worried about how I can help. It doesn't help once I think I get it, another part makes it difficult and not look right. Darkness is falling quick, and we need to hurry." The tents are reinforced and have spells drawn into them. As long as we stay in the tents out of sight, we would be hidden and safe.

I could hardly see five feet in front of me. "Done." Both tents were up and close to one another. Zeek and Jazmin took care of the horses and put them in some protective bubble so predators wouldn't mess with them.

"Why can't we use the protective bubble that the horses used to keep them safe?" I ask.

"We cannot move. It is a containment spell and something Quintan came up with to help our livestock not get attacked by creatures of the night. The spell is in their blood and is only working still because they still have it running through their system from the food. They have eaten so much with a little of it added in. On the way back, we will not have that kind of thing to help us with the horses. We may need to find a way around this place, which we would have avoided anyway if it weren't for Shade and having to get him."

"Does Quintans spell not work on humans?"

"This one doesn't, no. I bet he could make one if needed. He would have been an asset on this trip even if he would have been slower. We would have had to bring a cart."

I look to the ground, watching the other three get their stuff and start to move into the tents. "I don't know what to say."

"You don't have to say anything. I know why you made the decision you did, but he has changed over the years. We aren't all like our younger selves, or at least I hope we aren't." Robert gives a brief chuckle. "He does like power, yes, but it is because he craves acceptance where almost none was given to him. He was raised with thousands of other mages that were better than him. His only way to get ahead is to play politics. Most of us are in the same boat. He has atoned for his misgivings. If he did not, he would not be in our town."

"You haven't changed. You're still gruff, strong, and don't back down. Mother didn't much care for you when she first met you. You were young and not willing to understand."

"I have honed those skills, but I have learned that following rules isn't everything, even to get ahead in a job. I almost ruined your mother's life because I was following orders." His eyes turn sad. He walks around and pushes me toward our tent. "Go on. Just know if you blame him for those small misgivings, then I fear for others who have done worse and have asked for forgiveness or have proven themselves. No matter what this world makes you think, it isn't just good and evil, dark, and light. We are all shades of gray and should embrace our ability to have both inside us to make our own way in the world. Not everyone is given that choice." Robert turns and follows behind Zeek into their own tent. I wait till the flaps fall down before turning to our tent.

"She forgave you though and maybe I will for Quintan. One day," I whisper to myself.

Darkness has all but descended now, so I turn and hold out my hands, making my way by touch. I knew it was a short walk from the men's tent. Walking in, I stop. Since it is pitch black, my eyes have a hard time adjusting. Slowly moving forward, I trip over Natasha's legs. Sand fills my mouth as I fall face first into the sand. Moaning, I flop onto my back, spitting out the sand.

Natasha gives a quiet snicker. "That's what you get." She doesn't move to help me.

We all don't want to move for fear the vibrations will be felt under the sand. Though the tent covers us and hides us from anyone around, it can't protect us from anything coming up underneath. The fear is genuine after that first night here in the dark, Abyss. Those creatures could crawl up in our tent and easily deal with us before we even realized it.

"Did you at least set up my pallet?" I ask the darkness just laying on my back, not trying to move too much.

"Yes," Jazmin whispers near the side of the tent where I came in.

I roll slowly over to the right and find it there. Getting on the cushion, I keep my movements small and tight.

Laying on top of the blankets, I sit there unsure if I could fall asleep. I don't undress or go under the blankets. The warmth from the fire sisters will be enough once they come back to me. My thoughts drift off as my aching body slides into sleep. That is what it has been like the last couple of times. Sleep overtakes me, my body being too tired to do much else. The excitement from the times I'm awake making it too much to deal with.

My thoughts begin to slur and blend together into the dream world.

# Chapter 3

A LOUD ROAR SCREECHES across the sky and brings me into a sitting position immediately. The ground rumbles as something moves and shifts underneath. The tremors get more violent and the grounds begin to roll.

"Move!" Zeek bellows out, his angry face illuminated by a faint glow. He retreats out of the tent just as quickly.

All three of us scramble up off the blankets and out of the tent.

"What is happening?" Natasha snarks, calling on her ice magic. It flows into her palms and lights things up. Her short blue hair is tossed with sleep and wildly sticking out at all sides. Though it feels only like a few minutes, we had to have been resting for a while for her to look like that.

Jazmin is behind us, poised for a fight. "Trix! Go see what is happening. Be careful of the dragon and enemies," she whispers.

Red glowing eyes light up as he races away.

I watch the red of his eyes dance through the darkness.

"Where has he been? I haven't seen him in the last couple of days? Has he just been stowing away all this time? Couldn't we have used his help before this?"

Her glowing lavender eye stare at me as she hums. "He was not here before. He was called away. I didn't mention it before. It was not prominent information."

"He likes to run away when there is trouble," Natasha snarks.

"How did he leave? How did he get back?"

"I asked him to come back once he was finished silly," she states calmly, as if she actually gave an answer.

Shaking my head, I walk over to where Zeek and Robert are, tired of Jazmin's head games. I would not get a straight answer out of her. Both Zeek and Robert are in a close huddle. Natasha is also stomping her way over to them to see what the loud commotion is. The ground continues to move and shake. Another screech, along with fire, shoots up from over the sand hill.

"Taz? Shade?" I ask, my worry hurrying me across the last few steps. My legs wobble as I try to keep my balance as the ground shakes.

"The dragon has awakened and is upset about something. The ground is shifting and moving because it is waking up and moving the earth."

"Okay, so we should be safe, correct?" I ask.

"Normally it would be fine because the hills that are surrounding the dragon are high and we are far enough away from the base to not be a bother."

"Normally?"

"It would seem..." Robert gives an uneasy look over his shoulder back towards the hills.

"Spit it out, Robert." Natasha spits.

"Well, others in this land like the idea of a dragon around, so the sand burrowers have made their nests around here as well."

"You mean those fuckers we dealt with on the first night... The things that almost made us second guess coming in here? The things that can feel movement from the vibrations of us being on the sand." Natasha's eyes the ground under her feet. She calls up her wings to take flight, just hovering over the sand.

He gives a hesitant laugh. "Yes."

"Great, so the ones that have huge claws to slice us to ribbons and a face full of teeth."

"But they are mostly blind."

"Yeah, can't forget that. Then at least they can't see the looks I will give it as it devours our bones."

I place a steadying hand on Natasha's wrist, holding her in place. "Why did we not know about the nest that we are apparently on top of?" I ask to clarify.

Another violent roll throws all of us still on the ground to our knees.

Zeek recovers first. "They were far enough under that it didn't trigger any radar that I had going. The noise from their normal protector has brought them to the surface. They are worried that whatever has upset the dragon will come for them next."

"Great, could this night get any worse? Why did we not learn from the first time?" I ask.

Sand comes flying from up above us as some tan monster screeches above. We all dive on to the sand as fiery flames lick across our skin. The fire coming too close for comfort.

"You had to say something!" Natasha yells in my direction.

"Just because I said it doesn't mean I made it happen! It would have happened no matter what," I yell back.

"Shut up, both of you!" Zeek growls.

"Ugh what?" Natasha looks at him, stunned into silene.

"Robert, you there." Zeek's eyes travel around the group

"Yea brother." He rolls up in a crouched fighting stance.

The dragon breathes more fire up into the air. The rest of us crouch low to the ground, not wanting to make a target for the flames to get to. Both Zeek and Robert take off in separate directions but head towards the same target.

I fight the urge to change into my badger form. Last time, fear forced the transformation on me. This time I want to control it. Feeling the fur rush through my arms, I fight the change that shudders through me. I didn't want to run off or possibly get eaten. These creatures were much larger than me in my small badger form. My luck would not last, the last time I got lucky because Natasha helped me by sending ice spikes. I somehow don't think my luck will continue. I have a feeling this would be the exact opposite and I might end up as barbeque for a dragon.

Racing across the sand, I crouch down behind the tent, trying to stay out of their way. Doubling over in pain, my hands wrap around my stomach.

"Where is she going?" Robert yells out.

I ignore him as I struggle to hunker down, fighting what my body is trying to make me do. I haven't had the time to really train, so I don't think I'm ready to take on actual combat.

"Forget her for now," Zeek bellows out as the dragon flies by too close to the group. He hops on the neck of the dragon, being whisked away from the rest of us.

He rides the dragon, trying to keep and steer it away from our group. The dragon lights up the place while its fire is spewing left and right; it makes things easier to see and fight by.

My legs bounce in worry as my eyes keep track of him. Robert goes somewhere else; I couldn't track him as clearly as the light only happens periodically. Natasha calls on her other form. Her whole body turns blue, glittering with ice as sharp wings erupt from her back. She rolls her hands tipped with black fingers together, creating ice daggers that are held at the ready to attack. Jazmin's eye turns ghostly as a lavender hue seems to haze around her. She is calling on the dead that surround us to make zombie minions for her to attack with. Last time I could not see what she called up out of the ground. This time my eyes go wide in horror as I watch her call fourth creatures of all kinds, along with humanoid figures that are missing body parts. Most of the things are too grotesque to look at, being they are in different stages of decay. She throws her hoard at the sand burrowers climbing up out of the ground. The dead things do not stop or stay down. Even though they are getting chewed on, they would rip and tear through the burrower as they themselves were being devoured.

Sand moves under my boots. I carefully lift one foot up and back up slowly, trying to not disturb the sand as I move away. Knife like claws swipe out and up at me, trying to catch me unaware. Next, mouths full of sharp teeth come out of the ground covered in dark scales. Teeth and claws are pouncing on me, taking me to the ground. The thing's claws come out and dig at the ground beneath me, trying to crush me under the sand, taking me down below. Confusion and fear wrap around my throat, closing off my screams before I can even yell out.

As the sand parts, I struggle as I'm pushed down into an almost nonexistent hole. The sand rushes in my mouth; I fight to spit it back out. Coughing out the dust that I inhale into my lungs makes it impossible not to breathe in the sand. The claws dig deeper into a frenzy as its teeth snap closer to my cheek. My arms fight to hold off the creature, but they are buckling.

Seconds later, I fall into a tunnel that is small and tight. The packed ground rushes up against my back, air bursts from my lungs as they forget how to inhale. The burrower's teeth come down on top of me gnashing, my arms raise up automatically as I try to block it. Teeth tear at my arm, as pain zings through me, causing me to black out for a second. I come back to and notice it sniffing at me, as if it is unsure of my limp body. Springing to action, I don't give it time to second guess. I kick out with my feet, kicking the thing away, trying to get up. Wheezing out trying to get air, I struggle to my knees but am not able to stand up in this small, cramped tunnel. I crawl forward, down the tunnel, my hands scrabbling for a weapon, an exit, or somewhere I could hide. The creature quiets behind me as it listens to my fearful struggles; it takes careful steps. The claws come down on my legs, shredding my pants and shoes; the rubber, does nothing to protect my feet. I keep moving regardless of the fear coursing through me. What would happen if it got its claws in me? Did it bring me down here to be food for their nests? I don't want to see this things babies.

Kicking the creature off my legs and moving forward is my only hope to keep going. The air constricts tight in my lungs as my breath saws in and out.

I can barely see in front of me. I go mostly on feel alone. This is worse than the darkness up above. It all looked the same, but down here I'm very aware of the dirt and sand surrounding me.

Something tugs around my stomach, wrapping around me tightly. I feel a strong chest against my back as I lift from the ground, speeding through the tunnel. I don't feel claws at my legs anymore. A loud whine and whimper echoes behind us as we move away. Wind tugs at my hair as we soar through the dirt tunnels perfectly flying down the middle. Tucking my head down into my shoulder, I brace for impact, afraid we would hit something in this dark place.

"You should leave this place. Why are you even here?" A voice yells above the wind. His voice is scratchy, like he hasn't used it in a while.

"What?" I ask dumbly, not sure what is happening and why someone is talking to me. I thought Zeek or Robert had come down here to save me. Everyone is getting good at saving me and it is getting irritating. This voice is not low.

*Robert? Zeek?* No, this had to be someone else.

"Have you forgotten me already? Since I'm no longer at-tached to you?" His tone is serious and not joking at all.

"Shade?" His voice is a lot different from the last time we spoke. He was the only one attached to me though, so if it wasn't him, I don't know who it could be.

"Yes, what are you doing here?" He asks again.

"Looking for you, actually. Was the dragon a trap for us?" I blurt out. His arms around my stomach hold me tight against him. I bring my hands off of his arms, unsure where to put them. My body tenses up, unsure if he is friend or foe.

"There was a dragon?" He says sarcastically. "Guess I didn't notice while hunting."

"You had a tent pitched up by the dragon and everything. You knew it was there." I roll my shoulders, wanting to get away from him and this conversation.

His body shakes as he continues to wind through the tun-nels quickly.

Fear encapsulates my body and freezes me from doing anything more. I don't even know how he is flying us through, let alone not crashing into anything.

"T'was not my tent. Could be another. I was in these tunnels the whole time. These are the safest venues to travel, especially to someone who blends into the darkness and can whisk through the tunnels with magic. Draining though it is, but we rest often enough."

"We? Taz is here, then? She is safe?" I ask.

Two spots warm my back in answer. Trill and Tina are here with me, knowing what is going on and that their sister is close.

"We are all exhausted and worried, but the fire sisters were worried about Taz," I complain when he says nothing else. I hope they can converse with one another and get more feedback from Taz than Shade is giving me.

"You have your answer," Shade says.

"You mean to tell me you didn't know we were following you?" It is hard to stand my ground when I'm not facing my opponent, let alone on solid ground.

"I didn't say that. But I was not worried about any of you until now." He gives a shrug.

"Where are you taking me?" I grump, wanting to be off this rollercoaster of a ride.

"Nowhere," he says vaguely.

"It feels like you are."

"We are circling." He stops suddenly, causing me to lurch and my stomach to roll. "We are right below where you came in. Do not move." He has a death grip on my waist, holding me in place. Since there is still no room to stand, we crouch there.

"Why did you take my magic? Why did you leave me behind? You are supposed to protect me," I whisper. I don't want the creature with claws and teeth to come back to finish me off.

"Those people turned me human. I needed something that could help me, so I could keep protecting you. You had something that I could use and you wouldn't. I also knew your people were there for you, you did not need me there. I went hunting for the one that can cause you pain. Your uncle is still out there. I had lost him after I became human and have been on the hunt ever since. I was told about a creature that could help me out here. You are safe enough for now while I deal with your main issue."

"We don't even know if he is alive!" I hiss out.

"He is alive. I know, He was in terrible condition but I know what a person can and cannot come back from. He was not burned that badly, though, badly enough to keep him down for a while. We need to find him now before he becomes a problem yet again."

"What about all the problems I'm dealing with now? I didn't stop needing your protection from others."

"I had no way of knowing that," he states with no emotion radiating off of him. His hands peel away from me as he shrinks back into the darkness.

"You understand that isn't okay, right?" I ask, genuinely curious. Spinning around, my eyes turn to my animal as I pinpoint where he is amongst the shadows.

"I'm a spell, Alexia. Remember that I'm following the directive your mother wove into it. Are you upset that I'm no longer tethered to your form and no longer have to endure your presence?" He gives a look of confusion.

"Is that all I'm to you? Do you even like me? Do you even want to be here?"

"Like isn't something a spell does." Cocking his head to the side, he is legitimately curious about it. Crouching, he places his hand on the dirt. He also places his other hand up above on the dirt ceiling.

"You were more human when tethered to me. You cared about my feelings and comforting me." Backing away from Shade, I could not believe the words he is saying to me.

"I had your soul to guide me. The spell wants me to protect you, but being tied to you, I had to protect your feelings. Not so much anymore, being away from you. I do not have your soul to tether me and I do not have your feelings that I have to consider when keeping you safe."

"Why do you even care about keeping me safe, then? Just leave." I rush forward, pushing him back.

"That isn't the directive. What I feel or have a lack of feeling for doesn't matter. I know no other way." Shade lets me push him back. Still crouching, he lowers further.

"You are human, though. Go live a human life."

He rushes at me, colliding with me. Tossing me over his shoulder in a matter of seconds. He springs upward out of the sand. Giving a squeak as we rise high in the sky, he doesn't just jump like I originally thought. No, we are flying again, except this time there is no ground to keep us low. Maybe it isn't as scary underneath the sand as I originally thought. My hands tighten on their own as we fall back down to the earth. He takes the brunt of the force as he lowers me to the ground. I cling to him, unable to let go.

"The others will be back here soon. Do not continue to look for me." He tears himself away from me. Turning his back, he walks away.

My hands scrabble to find purchase on his arm. "I need my magic or you to come with me to the Dark Court," I say with conviction.

He stops and stares outward.

"Jazmin says we need to be seen as a united front in order to show that we are strong and are part of both worlds. You took all my magic. I have none left. Only the animal is powerful within me now." My hand wraps around his wrist, keeping him here with me, afraid that he would take off again.

He doesn't move forward to leave, but he doesn't say anything either.

"You took my powers from me. Just give them back if you don't want to come back with us. It's okay I get it." My face falls as the sadness deepens, feeling a tightening in my chest as my heart thumps loud in my ears. There are only a few people in my life. I never figured that he would be one that is no longer in it.

"No, I can't do that. No matter if you have just the one power, no one can take away where your blood comes from. You have both of your parent's lines alive in you. You will be fine."

"But you took the power. Why can't you give it back?"

His eyes cut back to me. The thick sand covers both of our shoes as we sink in a little more standing there. "It was written into the spell!" Shade yells, his voice cutting off part of the way through. "If I ever had to leave you or not be tied to you any longer. I was to take the magic as far away as I could."

"You mean to tell me my mother spelled you this way to take my magic from me?" I ask, shocked.

A magical orb raises from his palm hovering between us. We are still hidden behind one tent. He gives a terse nod.

I let go of his wrist. My arm hanging lifelessly next to me. "She said nothing like that in the spell when you were created."

"The spell, as I shall be referred to." He gives a snarl, making me shudder away from him. His face is scary and scowling. A part of his black hair hangs into his eyes. His dark eyes peer at me. "Was not created in that one instance. Your mother had to work on my creation for many days and weeks. I took a lot of time and patience. The final spell was to imprint me onto you and was the last part of it. That part was quick. She planned this present for you a while before giving it to you even."

"Okay then, the other option is joining our party and come with us to the Dark Court." I nod with finality. My eyes stay glued to him, taking in his form for the first time. "This is our first time seeing and talking with each other outside of when this all first happened. Don't you want to learn more about each other?"

"That isn't something I can do. I must follow this lead and keep you safe. If you interrupt my hunt again, I will have to take drastic measures. There is time for the other stuff at a later date." The shadows and darkness around the light pull into Shade. It coats him like a second skin. His green eyes all but glow in the dark.

"Like what kind of drastic measures soulless one?" Jazmin comes around the tent. Her steps are light.

Shade and I turn around quickly as he shoots the glowing light into her face.

She easily bats it away from her face, deflecting it just as easily.

"Where are the others?" I ask. Shade pulls up a hood from the darkness that is already hiding most of his body.

"Searching for you." Her eyes never wander from Shade. "You cannot harm your master. What do you intend to do with her if we try to stop you?"

"Put her in a place where she cannot. One that will be safe for her." He faces Jazmin, fully meeting her head on.

"Safe is a relative term. Keeping her trapped somewhere could still hurt her. Maybe not the way you think, but it could." Jazmin cocks her head in thought. "She will not be safe at the Dark Court if you do not come with her."

"I do not know that for sure, and this is more pressing. I know that this will bring her pain and torment in her future. The Dark Court that I am unsure of and am not aware of any threats. It is what you call an unknown."

"That is your prerogative. She will have a struggle with no magic." Her pale purple eye glows just as Shade's eyes do the same, glowing a light green color.

"As I told her, the spell as it stands wants me to keep distance from her." Shade says.

"One you can choose not to listen to, now that you have a human body." She gives a creepy smile, showing her teeth.

I wonder if that happens to all magic users when they pull on their power. Both Shade and Jazmin, their eyes almost have an eerie glow about them when they grow closer with their magic.

"She has the other two fire elementals with her, like the one that rests with me. She can call on that kind of magic."

"Elemental magic differs vastly from actual magic and you know it," Jazmin chides.

"From what I have seen and felt since we parted ways, she does not need magic in order to get into trouble. She does that well enough without access to it. She will make do with what she has."

"Were you the one that helped me out of that past spell? I felt a tug, but thought that was Blaise." My voice barely comes out above a whisper.

"Your snake isn't the only thing that slithers," Shade hisses out. He grows taller and his body begins to bend as he takes on a new shape.

"The magic will eat at you in time, soulless one," Jazmin all but cackles. "If you do not come with us, you will beg us to if you keep on using her power like that."

"Not my problem." He towers over us. The light only shows us a little of what we are looking at. As he hears the other party getting closer, he pulls away and rushes over the sand dunes, escaping.

"Shade no," I yell out. My voice scratches over my sore throat.

Jazmin's chilly hand latches onto my arm, holding me back. "Let him go."

"We got to go," Robert croons as they race over the sand. The dragon is circling high above in the dark sky, the tan hide glowing in the middle. Fire pours out of its open mouth as it rains down near us barely out of reach.

"Move your asses!" Zeek yells as he undoes the spell to get the horses and items that we can salvage. Each of us grabs our packs and moves to a horse. "Leave the tents where they are."

"What about Shade?" I call back.

"What about him? Did you find him?" Natasha's wings stop for a moment, causing her to dip to the ground, but she flutters before she can touch down.

They didn't see him? Looking to Jazmin, the tent partially hiding us. She gives a creepy smile that doesn't reach her eyes. She shakes her head silently.

"Yes, but he will not come with us," I answer.

"Right now, if we don't get out of here ourselves, we will be barbeque. We can worry about if we are going to capture him and make him do our bidding later." Natasha gives a huff as she flies over to her horse. "See, I knew we should have just kept going to the town."

"Move!" Zeek yells out.

I race through the tent to grab my pack. Scrabbling through the sand to get the items I could into the bag. I tear out of the tent, my eyes jumping around, trying to make sense of the scene. My horse is the only one left. It is waiting there patiently in all of this chaos. She dances and stomps her feet in worry as the fire again falls upon us, missing us as it chases Zeek and Robert, who are distracting and shooting off some kind of laser pointer at it.

My tired arms pull my weak body up into the saddle as I kick into gear. I hang on for dear life as she takes off. Natasha and Jazmin's horses are not far ahead of me as I race to catch up with them. I let the horse guide me; she has trained for this, so I trust her judgment over mine right now. Everything is a dark blur and shadows that live in the darkness skate by. I bury my head into the horse's mane and hold on to it with one hand and the saddle with the other, hunkering down low so nothing snatches me out of my seat.

I hear the roar of the dragon further in the distance. Looking back, the wind tears at my hair, loosening it into strands that flow around me, causing my eyes to water and not be able to see exactly where the dragon is. What I do see instead is light, burning the sky as it sends up a flare in anger. It is getting further away.

"Natasha, Jazmin?" I bellow out.

"Yes?"

"We are here," Jazmin states.

The horses are still running, so focusing on balance and speaking is taking all my strength I have left in me. "Zeek and Robert?" I ask.

No answer comes from either of them. I try to see where we are headed the dark is becoming lighter as the daylight fights to break through. I see the shadow outline of both Jazmin and Natasha.

"Let's slow down. We have gained enough distance for now. Otherwise, we may run into the hands of another enemy." Jazmin yanks on her reins, jarring the horse into a slower gait, giving us time to catch our breath.

Both Natasha and I tug on our reins at the same time and cannot see much further in front of us but a few feet. Noises and growls sneak up on us as if they were on their way to us. "We can't slow down too much and stop or else we will be food for the other creatures in this place." My head swivels around, making sure we were not about to get jumped.

"The cute little fluff monsters just want to cuddle," Jazmin giggles. A lone skeleton pulls up from the sands. It raises and shambles into the dark behind us. A yip, then growls and a thump lands behind us. Cackling and yowls can be heard in happy yips as they have tackled the thing Jazmin sent their way.

"Where is this town?" I question.

"We should come across it soon. Not that far from where we had camped. Made it faster with the quick jaunt of running for our lives, if we chose the right direction. The dark here isn't a pure dark where we can see stars, so it was a guess from the last light time."

"Will the guys at least meet us at the town if they make it? The darkness is already letting up, so that is good news." The sun peeking through the dark chasm cloak.

"They know to head to the town," Natasha says with finality, though her eyes flit behind us, a crease of worry marring her face. "They must be covering for us and will follow later."

"Let's get out of here!" Jazmin calls out. Though she doesn't kick her horse into a full out run, we just continue to gallop ahead. "Before trouble finds us."

After about a ten-minute ride, we come across signs of life that don't want to kill us outright. We pass out of the darkness shortly after into the sun setting. My heart leaps for joy when the sun hits my face. I raise my face to the heat that shines down on me with my eyes closed.

"Let's rest the horses for a little while and see if the boys follow us out before moving on," Natasha says. "We have some sun left, so let's enjoy it."

Bringing my face down to open my eyes, I notice it sinking further down across the sky. I don't want it to be night after living through so much darkness.

We stop the horses for a rest right after and wait to see if we notice Robert or Zeek come through around here. There isn't too much traffic, but there are some that travel the length of the Abyss.

As I watch the people, I notice they will not dare go near the black slash against the desert. "They fear the creatures that call the Abyss their domain," I comment.

Jazmin glares and raises a small shambling creature next to her that has rotting fur falling from its body. It growls at the horse's feet, ready to pounce if anyone comes near. "Three women like us would normally be set upon by all types of vultures, but they saw where we came out of and made it in one piece relatively. Look wild and angry. It will keep them at a distance. They worry about the power we hold." Jazmin gives a sardonic grin with teeth showing.

Some men stop to assess us, but they move on, looking for weaker prey, leaving us there at the edge. Most of the people we see move down the road to the town. It is surrounded by an enormous gate.

"Main gate closing!" A guard yells out at the top of his lungs through a horn that magnifies his voice.

"Do you think they will let us in after hours?" The horse's sides are wheezing and panting. Whispers erupt around us as people rush towards the gate. We push the horses into a slow walk as we give them time to catch their breath. A line is already forming in front of the gate as it closes for the night.

"Who knows?" Natasha shrugs.

"If they wanted to keep the town safe this close to the Abyss, then I wouldn't." As we grow closer to the gate and people, Jazmin lets the little critter lay down by the side of the road and lets the soul leave the physical body. "Rest little soul," she says as a goodbye.

Making our way to the front gate, we watch a small group huddle near it, waiting. The line dwindles some but the large gate doesn't budge or open.

"What is happening?" I stand up in the saddle, trying to get a better viewpoint.

"Let's get closer and check it out," Natasha says. "We shouldn't dally too long; the guys will meet up with us later. They will know where to look since we discussed it previously."

I nod as we all move towards the gate. The moon is high in the sky as the sun disappears behind the horizon. I slouch back in the saddle and collapse against the horse; the adrenaline dissipates, causing me to crash. "We need actual rest and not just a nap before heading out again," I reply weakly.

The crowd thins as some move to the side. We rush forward, not wanting to be left outside with no way in. As we grow closer, we notice a smaller door set inside the large gate. Entry is happening, but at a snail's pace. People with wagons or other large wares have to park off to the side and either wait for daybreak or hope their stuff doesn't get taken as they go in the town to wait. Horses can barely get through, so the door is large enough for that, but not much else.

Waiting in line, I fall from my horse, barely catching myself before the ground rushes up to meet me. I hold the side of the saddle to keep myself upright and conscious. We are only five people away from the front. The line isn't too long anymore. Many were waiting for day break due to them having a lot more items.

"How much longer?" I yawn, rubbing my eyes.

"Delicate sunflower can't handle the darkness and what it takes," Natasha says.

My face pinches with a frown as anger bursts through me. "Bite me. Just because you are used to sleeping in four-hour interval times doesn't mean we all can do that as easily." The no sleep thing is getting to me.

My body shakes from the cold, my temperature plummeting with the lack of sleep. The fire sisters start to warm and try to keep me toasty as much as they can. Wrapping my arms around my center, I hug them close to me to keep the warmth within. The line moves again and we are at the front.

*Now we are talking!*

Jazmin hands him something. A look of surprise washes over him as we are quickly brought through.

"Where is the inn to rest and get some food?" Jazmin asks the guard as we first step through and to the side, making sure others can still come through and we were not blocking the way.

He tips up his helmet and glances at her. "You will follow this main road down at the end. There is a large building that will be the inn, and it has a restaurant in the middle if you need sustenance. Take care to remember once you are in behind the gate you are in for the night and we do not open the gate to go out till daybreak. We only allow people in and only if there are many, if there is only one or two, we wait, otherwise it isn't worth the hassle, so remember that when visiting Neustaria next time." He bumps his chest with his fist and bows before moving on to the ones that come in behind us.

"Thank you, good sir." Her eyes all but laugh at him. Jazmin also gets down from her horse and waits for Natasha to do the same.

"What did you give him?" I ask.

"Just a token of appreciation."

We head down the road while keeping an eye out, towing our horses behind us all our heads are lowered as we continue down the road. It isn't long before we are at the inn and we pass off and pay for the housing of the horses.

Once we step into the giant inn, we are welcomed with heat. The room isn't very busy even though it isn't too late.

"Over here." An average-looking woman calls us over. Her eyes are pitch black and her hands are tipped in claws. Giving her a curious look, I stand back, unsure if she is going to attack us or help us get a room.

"What are you?" I accidentally ask.

Natasha pins me with a crude stare.

"You are not from around here?" She nods as she decides. "Some people who live close to the chasm of darkness decide we must keep our darkness close to the edge, so sometimes we look more monstrous. You will run into this over here. This will be true of most people you meet when heading further into the Dark Court." She makes pleasant conversation as she takes our money for the food and beds.

"We will have two men that may stop by looking for us ring us when they do. We got separated in there and we decided this would be the meeting place," Jazmin says to her before heading back to the main room where we can get a good meal.

I'm last to leave the room, so I hear her, unlike the other two. "Poor dears, doesn't know those men are probably long dead or wish they were if they show up. Will probably be heartbroken when they find out."

She didn't know Robert or Zeek, but I hope she is wrong. No one deserves to die in a place like that.

The rest of the night is uneventful. We stay in the main room only long enough to get our fill of food and water, then are up in the separate rooms to get a decent night's rest.

"Your rooms are up these stairs and to the right." The same woman that checked us in also serves us the last of our meal. "Have pleasant dreams."

"May the stars brighten your darkness," Jazmin says to her.

She gives a toothy smile, reaching out a hand to Jazmin's arm. "There are also showers and a heated bath that will be open in the morning."

"You are too kind." Jazmin pats her furry hand before dividing up the keys. "We each have a separate room, so enjoy! There should be a small bathroom off each of our rooms. We can go to the showers tomorrow morning once they open. For now, try to rest and get a good night's sleep."

All of us trudge up the stairs, leaning into each step. Each step I take is heavier than the last. Once I get into my room, I barely move before I fall onto the bed. The room isn't huge and there is only one door off the other side of the bed. Rolling to the other side, I peek into the even smaller bathroom, checking it out. There is enough room for a sink and toilet and that is it.

Hanging my head off the bed, I lay there, trying to muster up enough energy to get up and take off my clothes. I don't want to move or do anything. It is so hard, but after spending so much time in the sand and cold; I take a few extra minutes so I can actually enjoy this bed. I drag my torso up and remove my clothing, barely able to move my stiff limbs. Once I undress, I slip under the covers and pass out with little thought to anything else.

# CHAPTER 4

HE IS THERE WAITING for me in my dreams. I haven't fallen into a deep sleep lately with being too on edge.

"Where have you been, Minx?" Blaise's low voice is liquid honey in my ear. Something soft wraps around my head, covering my eyes. Before I can get my bearings and know what is around us, the dark cloth cuts off all sight. My fingers raise up, touching the delicate velvet, wanting to push it up and away. "Leave it," Blaise all but hisses, pushing my hand back down.

"I have been traveling," I answer. My body shivers as I feel the warmth of his bare chest behind me. He holds me tight against him as large bands constrict around my legs, forcing them together. "Are you tying me up?"

Roving my hands down my sides, I feel a thin dress. Muscles constrict and tighten in answer. They are thick and smooth against my legs as it grows tighter, not biting into my skin. His nails are long and thin, but they do not press into me. His long tongue makes a long slow lick up the side of my neck. I feel his tongue flick as he inhales my scent, tasting me.

"It's all me, but I don't want you to look yet... Have you talked to him, since..." His breath falls over my shoulder.

What did that mean? Annoyance flairs in me. "Not that it matters, but no, I haven't talked to either of you."

Silence reverberates around me. "I've missed you," he sounds melancholy. "After what we had been through, I was worried about you."

"You have a funny way of showing it."

"I was going through my own issues."

Turning my head toward him, I feel his cheek against me. "Why don't you lean on me like I tried to with you?"

"I don't want you to see that part of me." He nuzzles the back of my neck. "I should have been there for you when you needed it."

"What if I want to see that part of you?"

"Minx... I can't... I don't know how to." His arms come around, embracing me. "There is too much." His voice turns fervent.

"What do you need?" I breathe out.

My breath comes in hot huffs. His nearness awakens a fire in me. Molten lava pours into my center. My tiredness melts away as the excitement pours into me. He surrounds me completely as I struggle to keep my mind on our conversation.

"Minx, I need you." His hips push into me as a large, hard cock presses up against my back, rubbing against me. "I need more than this dream can give," his voice cracks.

The sadness in his voice tears at me. "I have no magic. There would be no way to bring me to you or you to me, even if I wanted to." Sinking back into him, I try to console him and give him the touch he craves. "I take it you are not mad, from what I told you. We have not talked since then. I thought you were upset with me."

"Minx, I know what you are to me. I'm not upset with you. Domini though…" His hold tightens on me as he rages.

"With me, he is more than upset." Domini's voice sounds directly in front of me.

Heat cascades down the front of my body as he comes closer. My nipples harden in response, my body eager with anticipation.

The wrapping around my legs tightens in response almost painful.

"What is he doing here, Minx?" Blaise whispers in my ear.

"I'm always close to my Flower. She holds me near her heart." Domini chuckles his thick hands skate over me, sending goose flesh across my arms where he touches. I stretch my body to meet his in response, wanting more.

"You brought him with you on this adventure?"

"He needs what is his. I will not keep it from him. He is a siren and you want to keep something that is so deeply ingrained into him away from him?" I answer, shocked at how cold Blaise is being.

"No, but you do not have to keep him so close." Blaise moves his hands to my waist.

"How and where I choose to keep him isn't up to you," I bite back.

Blaise rubs his lips against my neck. After nuzzling, he opens his mouth to rub his sharp fangs against the side of my neck as if in warning. Warm hands brush against the thin fabric on my nipples, rubbing against them. I push back against the thick hardness that is still nestled near my butt. Blaise's hands remain at my hips, so it must mean Domini is the one that is torturing my breasts.

"Flower?"

"Yes?" I answer.

He pinches my nipples lightly, rewarding me for the answer. I arch up into his hands, craving more. "Do you need him as much as he needs you?"

Blaise moves his thickness, so it isn't up against me, but in between my thighs. It brushes against my fiery center as he massages himself against me.

Domini's hands wander away from me, causing me to cry out. "I want fun. I want physical connection. We are too far away and I'm growing tired of nothing being real," I say the last bit dejectedly. Slumping into Blaise, I give in to the depressive thoughts.

"You are amazing!" Domini brings back a hand, hefting the weight of my breast into his hand, massaging it. He grabs my chin with his other hand and though I can't move much, my head comes forward, slamming into his mouth. His hand slides up my chin to wrap around the back of my neck, massaging there and holding me as his tongue slips between my lips, hot and searching. Blaise's hands tighten on my hips as he holds me tight against him, continuing his slow hip rolls, bumping his cock against my sultry heat.

Both of them are tempting danger and my animal is here for it.

He finishes nibbling at my mouth, kissing the tip of my nose and a peck on the cloth that is covering my eyes. He brushes a thumb over my sensitive peaks that are pulled painfully tight. "You have been so patient and good with your answers. Where are you, my sweet? Somewhere safe? Alone?"

Blaise stills his body, waiting for an answer. He holds absolutely still, but a part of him can't stop twitching as I move against him.

Anticipation and need burst through me, making me feisty. "What do I get if I tell you?"

"Yea warrior, what will you do if she tells us?" Blaise almost growls out.

"I have more pull than you think snake. But this isn't about you. Remember that."

Something happens where I feel a shudder go through Blaise. The thing around my legs loosens at the same time as he retreats, the warmth of him stepping away from me.

"I do not like to share," anguish tinges his words.

Is Blaise in his snake form? Did his tail hold me prisoner? Why was he pulling away? Sharing is that a possibility? A thrill runs through me as I pause to give that some thought. I never thought of it like that.

"Even if it is what your other half craves, you will deny her when you could make her extremely happy? You have shared others you care nothing about before. What makes it different now? Is it because you think she is yours?" He laughs as he gathers me into his heated embrace, keeping me company when Blaise would not. Though his body is fully clothed, I still feel the warmth and the smell of sea water in his clothes.

"I want something different," his voice sounds further away. I turn my head in Domini's arms so I can better hear, but keep the blindfold in place.

"Do not bring that here. Another time, but not now," Domini says to Blaise.

I shake my head and try to dissuade from a fight; I did not need this after what I have been through. Not wanting this to be a problem. The heat of the moment chills. I only want this if all parties are interested. I do not want to force anyone to be a part of something they are not comfortable with.

"If he doesn't want this, that is okay. It is his decision." His lips caress my hair as he kisses the top of my head. "Though I think the snake will regret his decision."

"You are correct, Domini. That also means he will have to respect my decision then. If I want something more than he can offer, we can either come to a compromise or move on." Slipping the mask up over my head, my eyes land on his, making sure he knows I'm serious.

I feel Domini's gaze on me. He runs his hands up and down my back, massaging the tension that shudders through me, melting at his fingertips.

Blaise's lower half is large and that of a snake he is curled up on top, his top human half perched there, looking down at both of us.

"I understand Flower, but he doesn't yet and even he needs to follow the rules that are set forth."

"You are all about rules, aren't you siren," Blaise sneers out. "Did you tell her the rules you have to follow for your master?"

"I said not to bring that here." Domini turns me from Blaise. He gives him a haughty glare as he goes still.

"Then leave," Blaise says.

Holding still for fear of making the wrong move. How did this go from hot and heavy to this in just a few minutes? This could have been everything, and yet here we are all in pain.

"I did not harm you, snake. Do not lash out because you do not know how to keep your pain in check."

"I know," he seethes behind me as the intensity builds. "I..." Blaise's voice breaks as emotion takes over him.

Domini bends down so his mouth is right at my ear. "Stay here, Flower. I will be right back." He waits for me to nod. He pulls the soft cover back over my eyes. "No peeking." He taps me on my nose before walking away. I hear his boots echo off the floor to move behind me.

The sharp mark of his boots stop; stopping in front of Blaise. "I could make this easier for you, snake. I normally would not, but I will do it if you ask me to. You are a warrior yourself. Do not pretend you're not. We each have our own battleground. Do not let that person ruin a good thing in your life."

Blaise whispers something back, but I don't catch what he says. It is a good thing this is just a dream. I'm braver in here. Out in the real world, I don't think I could be with either of these intimidating men without my animal being a part of this. I'm still too new to have any confidence outside of the bedroom, let alone in it.

"Do you want what we can offer?" Domini waits.

Blaise answers clearly and no longer in a whisper. "Yes, I do. Please help me through this."

"You understand you will still be in control of your anger and the darker thoughts. They will just be further away than they usually are." Domini is careful in his words and his voice is tight. "I will not do a full siren call, not with this."

"Understood and I accept."

"I do not do this lightly. I like people to understand me, to know they are doing it at their own will. None of my past lovers have heard my song as you and her have. Understand that?"

"I do know what it means. Thank you." Blaise heaves a heavy sigh.

"If it wasn't for the bond riding you so hard, it might be easier. That being said, the other rules will be explained on your way to this place." Domini hums his tune. It shies away from my ears, circling on one in particular. The song and tune are nice but have no hypnotic power over me. His song drones on as if it takes more power than when tempting me to take the ruby.

"Thanks." Blaise let go of the tension and breath he is holding. "After this, we will talk," he whispers.

"I will come to you before I start our journey to make sure it takes. We can talk then," Domini says.

Domini's hard steps come back to me, taking my hands in his. He brings them up to his mouth and kisses each digit. He lets go of my hand that he has already kissed and places it in Blaise's. Another mouth sucks on the tip of each finger. A shiver races down each arm, shuddering me to my core. Fueling fire back to life.

"Flower, you are doing such a good job making sure that stone stays with you. The power you have come near in order to get what I need is amazing." His tongue brushes over the pulse in my wrist. "With that power, I can make this dream a reality with a favor, if it is what you truly envision."

Blaise places my hand on his naked chest and pushes closer to my warmth. His hand seeking my body. I fight to lower my hand and keep it there on his chest. My mind tries to remember what Domini asked of me. Blaise's hands skate over my hips, rubbing up my back, pulling me into him. His nails slide back to their short human form.

"Both?" I squeak. "I ... I ...but."

Blaise's hands tweak my nipple closest to him, hoping to sway me.

Crying out, I struggle to not push away. Domini boxes me in from the other side. It all seems too much.

"Answer the question, Flower," he growls in my ear as his fingers travel low and slip under the dress I'm still wearing. His fingers are slow and tantalizing underneath, but they only tease. I feel my lower body flood itself as it craves the touch.

I swallow a couple of times trying to find my voice through the pleasure and my mind. "That would be fun, yes." As that sinks in, my mind comes to a screeching halt. "But we can't... I don't know... can we?" My mind races, as questions flood my mind, making me unsure of myself.

He grips the back of my neck and guides my mouth to his, brushing his lips against mine in a teasing kiss. "It will be fun. Don't worry, we will go slow." His mouth turns up as he smiles. "Would you allow someone to tell you what you already know feels right?"

Licking my lips, he twists my head the other way and another's lips are there. Blaise's mouth is bruising and demanding where Domini's lips are sweet and tantalizing. His tongue strikes in and tangles with mine. My mouth clashes with his and soon his fire consumes me.

"Your animal is thrilled with this, isn't she?" Domini circles to my back, letting Blaise mold himself to my front as he barely lets me up for air.

Fire scorches my throat as my hands come up wrapping around him, keeping him close. My animal is there. She brushes her fur against me. I feel her twirling in the heat and friction that both of them bring me.

"We will all have to let go for a moment. I will be quick and then you will be pulled physically to somewhere else. It is out of space and time, though it will seem longer there than in reality. This will not be a dream and nothing will be able to be brought here that is on your person." Domini's hands turn me toward him, lifting a side of the eye mask up. One eye opens as I see his face. "That means protect what you wear and make sure it stays hidden. Be ready." His lower hand tickles and plays with me under my dress.

"Your soul will be safe," I pant, knowing this is important.

His thumb rubs over the back of my neck, brushing me there. "Blaise push her out of this dream. I do not think she has the power to herself."

Blaise hisses, gripping me to the front of his body. He must decide it's for the best and ultimately shoves me out of our mind space.

I'm thrown back into the darkness and hear a door slam as he kicks me out. I fall back into my body and wait there to catch my bearings. Not too long though, so I do not waste time. Taking the chain from around my neck, I hide it there under the pillow. Glancing around the room, it is still pitch dark. Not much time has passed that I could tell.

Would the fire girls feel or be with me, or would they worry? "Fire sisters?"

Sluggish voices answer me. "Yes?"

"Where do you guys go when you are here with me inside? Do you feel what I do or hear my thoughts?" I should have been more worried about this before, but them being so young and not around that much. I just didn't give it thought before this.

"We are in a deep sleep, one of deep rest. We do not feel anything that you do unless you die, of course, or get close to death. Hearing your thoughts, no, we cannot do that either. We can travel to an area of our making kind of like a happy place while we are waiting." They both yawn, but Trill just listens as Tina explains things.

"It's okay, we can discuss more later. You sound really sleepy. Just know that if I disappear for a little while, I'm okay and in a safe spot and will be back soon. Do not get any of the team, including Robert. You mustn't tell him."

"If that is what you think is best. We will not worry," Tina answers.

"Yes, we will," Trill answers instead.

"But we will be with her most likely and be able to help if there is a problem."

"And if we don't get taken with her?"

"Then we will wait a while before getting help?" Tina hints at a question.

"A long while," I whisper, not sure how long things will last. He said there is a time limit on it but didn't give how long it could last and how the time works differently. "Though Tina is probably correct, you will just come with me, but please do not come out at all."

"We will only come out if you are in danger."

"Yea, like the time your body went haywire and your temperature skyrocketed to unsafe levels."

"That was because my animal came out forcefully and I was going through a cycle. Nothing like that should happen again, but if my temperature does rise, still don't come out this time. Please." My bases are covered, just in case. I knew I would be in safe hands with Blaise and Domini. I didn't want to be nervous about the girls peeking out unexpectedly.

They give sleepy agreements and pass back out into their own dreamscape.

My body thrums in answer to the need flowing through my veins. While I wait, I use the restroom and splash some cold water on my heated cheeks. Laying on top of the covers. It isn't long before I hear a popping sound; I open my eyes. Eight enormous arms descend from my ceiling. Holding in a scream, a small sound escapes my closed lips. They fall upon me, gathering me up into its arms. I lay still, unsure if I should just go with it or try to escape. The arms were very muscular and are a deep purple. It will be tough if I have to escape.

The ceiling crawls closer; I turn my head, worrying I would be a smashed Alexia up here. 'Alexia didn't have a chance. She got stuck to the ceiling.' That would be my eulogy.

As the ceiling comes closer, it fades away from space. I slip through as if it no longer exists. Colors surround me, all of them everywhere I look. It is blinding, as the arms carry me through the colors, not stopping for a moment. Is this what it looks like out of space and time? Another wall appears, this one the color of red picking up speed we push through, this one not fully in existence. It is more like a bubble that refuses to allow us through for a time. Once through, the whole place is in reds of all colors, dark red to light red. The arms wrap around me tightly as we pass through a blinding light and then he loosens them, helping me to stand up fully. They let go once I'm standing and fade into a smoke like figure that towers over me.

"Welcome to my abode." His top half pulls together to his chest is naked. Anything below his stomach is fuzzy and faded, still into smoke as he floats there.

"Hello?" I looked down and do a double take. I'm completely naked. Domini was right about that. "Domini?" I cross my arms in front of my chest, trying to hide parts of myself.

"He is through there." He nods his head. Four of his arms are pointing down a hall.

I look down the hall and head that way. "What are you?" I ask turning back to him, wanting to know how we came to this place.

"A djinn."

His accent is thick. "Like three wishes?" I ask, unsure how close djinn and genies actually are.

"And what wish do you have, little badger?" He asks, his arms bulge in answer as he crosses them across his smoke body.

My mouth dries out as it hangs open. I'm saved by someone who walks up behind me. Their warmth surrounds me.

"Thank you for this," Domini says.

"It is to your liking, then." The djinn bows low.

"Yes, it will do for what we are needing."

"She is a lot milder than you are used to." The djinn swirls around us, his form whisking close to me.

He gives a half smirk. "For now. She has claws she likes to use, though."

"I will get the snake, then maybe take my time to play with him." The djinn all but disappears.

"Flower, never give a wish to a djinn. Do you hear me?" Domini quickly turns me in his arms, his eyes serious as he shakes me, his strength barely restrained.

"Why?" I whisper out.

"They are tricky in nature and will always try to get the upper hand, no matter what it is. Just don't."

"Okay, no deals with djinn."

"He owed me this favor, but that isn't how it usually goes. He will do what he needs to, to get more favors on his side. Now come with me." His husky voice lowers as he walks with me back to the room, his form just as naked as mine.

"He went to go get Blaise?" I ask as I follow him, my hand in his.

"Yes, he will join us in a moment. In the meantime, I will go over the rules while we play here."

When he opens the door, I'm hit with a blast of heat. The room is hot but not stifling. There is a pleasant breeze blowing in from the open windows. The sheer curtains flip through the wind. Sheer cloth hangs over the bed and looks silky to the touch. There are toys lined up on a sturdy-looking table along with a couch. My mind is already thinking of ways we could have fun.

"This is my domain. What happens in here doesn't happen without my say? Ultimately, you are the one that controls the temperature. Meaning if something is too harsh or rough, you let me know. Do not endure something you can't. There is no judgment here. While here we will have a light system in place which I will check in routinely to make sure. Green, you are good, yellow, unsure maybe change something up and red, we are stopping."

"What about our signals?" A jolt of something wild cascades down my back.

His eyes pierce me. "Those are for another time. This is a bit different." Dropping my hand, he walks over to a dark couch that is set up in the room along with the bed. On the left side there is a roaring fire with a soft fluffy rug laying in front of it. I take it all in, not even watching what Domini is doing. Walking back, he pulls a soft brush of cloth across my throat. My eyes follow him as he hugs it tight across my throat.

"For later."

My fingers reach up and brush the velvet cloth strip that is thick around my throat. A metal loop hangs in the back, as if waiting to be clipped to something. I brush my hand down my throat on to my chest as I take the weight of one of my breasts in hand.

"I feel your excitement and your apprehension all at once. Remember, you are in control of this overall and I'm your back up control if you let it slip. I know you are new to this and may not be in control as much as others will be. We will go slow and just be open and honest about what is happening, okay?"

My eyes drift around the room to the toys and outfits that are left out. This room seems to be fully stocked with every-thing a person may need for one of these sessions. Though all the tools seem to be sweet and lighter than what they could be.

My feet move on their own accord, being drawn to the sheer clothing that is black. "This would match the collar." My fingers brush over the soft fabric. It feels so nice.

"Try it on." He looks at the clothing, but his eyes dance to the other toys that we may be using tonight.

I slip into the sheer see through dress as it pulls tight on the girls. My nipples push tight into the fabric, but the cloth feels so nice, making my nipples pucker. My own fingers brush down on one in answer.

"Perfection," he utters as his eyes zero in on my actions. He fists his hands at his sides but refuses to touch me or himself. "One question we have danced around tonight is yes, you want to be with both of us, but have you thought about the logistics of it?"

I nod, my cheeks heating with just the thought of it.

"And you have never been with another that way, correct?"

My eyes shoot down to the floor, but I shake my head.

He tips my head back up to meet his eyes. They are intense and angry. "Judgment free zone, remember that, Flower."

I stare at his eyes. They are stormy gray, as they hold mine.

"I see you. Never forget that."

He makes me feel seen and doesn't judge me for any of my faults or what I thought of as failings.

"No, I have not, but I want to try," I say back to him.

"Then we will have to prepare your body for it and even then, there still might be pain and again you will stop if it is too much." He wraps his hand behind my neck and grips the hair at the knap of my head. He pulls it so I'm looking up at him. "You will not be hurt in my domain because here you are mine, and I like you just the way you are."

A thrill goes through my body as I stretch to get closer to him. Though his words were harsh, they were hitting all the buttons of making me feel safe and wanted.

"I understand Domini. Please help me get ready, will you?" I stick out a lip in a pout, wanting him to come closer.

He leans forward, nibbling on my lips, holding my head in his palm as he loosens his hold. Again, his lips are soft, as if asking permission before continuing to do what he wants. I open up to him, our kiss deepening. The heat in the room is making me already hot with want.

He tucks me into the side of his arm as he moves to the table with multiple toys on it. He looks at the selection and picks a couple, laying them out in front of me. "Which do you like? These are the ones that would be good for first timers."

They were all pretty in their own right. The one that caught my eye is a red and yellow jewel. It reminds me of Domini and Blaise. This is for all of us, so it feels right. I pick that one up. "This one... Now what?"

Grabbing a jar and something else, he leads me over to the couch sitting down. "Lay across my lap." He leans back, smacking his thighs. His cock stands straight up so he forces it down so I can lay across him fully. The dress rides up only slightly, barely hiding my ass, though it is still see through.

Rubbing my back and lower, my muscles unclench, I relax against his touch and lay my head on my pillowed arms.

Gently, he moves the silky cloth up as he rubs the cool metal against my heated skin. I feel his hand skim over my butt; he tantalizes me with the cool metal in his other hand. His hands go away as I hear something rustle, he moves back and forth as if doing something, my body grows tense as I struggle to not look. My head starts to turn and a loud pop smacks across my ass.

My thoughts turn lusciously naughty after that. Shivers race across me as the sting burns into my ass. I shove my head back down into my arms, not even thinking of looking. He pulls the cloth against the sting and pets it with gentle fingers, rubbing the warmth that is growing there. He spreads my cheeks as his fingers dance there. They are light and playful.

"Give me a color, Flower." His thumb sits on my entrance to my butt, while his fingers massage my center, dipping a finger in feeling my wet heat.

"Green." I breathe out, trying to sit still and not get into the movement or scoot away from it.

Pushing the tip of his thumb, something slippery and wet slips in as he moves it around.

I make a sound but one that I'm unsure of if it is pain or pleasure. It dances on that careful line. He slips a finger in as he continues his careful work, which turns it more to pleasure.

"You are already so wet. I can't wait to lick you sweet, delectable honey."

Wriggling across his lap. "You want a taste, so do I," I challenge.

"That may actually work better, but first." He moves my hair out of the way. I feel a click of something fasten on to the loop at my neck. Looking over my shoulder, I see a leash that connects to the collar. He moves it to the side, making me have to follow. I quickly move off his lap. A tingling sensation starts to heat near my ass, but I easily ignore it. He grabs the rest of the items on the couch and has the leash in the other. "Crawl to the rug for me."

He watches from behind; I feel his eyes on me as my body moves forward slowly. The carpet is soft on my knees and the rug looks even softer. The fire is hot, making moisture bead up on my skin. He sets the items out and lies beside me.

I wait for him to guide me up on top of him. He brings me over his face, facing me away from him. I then bend over, showing him everything he wants. He holds the leash tight, keeping me from my prize as he takes a long lick of my clit all the way back to my ass. Though he has control of my throat, he doesn't have control of my hands. So, I slowly tickle my fingers down his chest to his thick cock that is waiting for me. I cup a hand around his balls, massaging them first.

He gives a long, sensuous lick to my hot, throbbing pussy. Tasting me, his tongue tortures me. I continue to massage him with my hands as he holds me. He pushes his tongue into me and flicks against a spot that has me trembling, soft and light pressure at first. He loosens the leash, giving me some length so I lower my head some more, but all I can reach is the tip so I lick it and do what I can, swirling my tongue around the head of his penis teasing him as he teases me.

He lets go of the leash, completely laying it on my back so he can use both hands to play with me, spreading my lips and cheeks for better access.

Letting me loose, I fall upon my prey and swallow him inside my mouth, forcing my mouth down to the base of his cock. He scrambles for the leash and yanks it back. The collar digs in, forcing me off.

"Greedy little thing."

I laugh around the tip of his cock that I still have in my mouth. Which causes it to kick.

"Did no one teach you not to gobble your food?" His mouth moves to my clit as he sucks and flicks his tongue. Pushing a finger in slowly, I push against it, wanting more. Thickness fills my entrance as his tongue continues to play with my clit. He again holds the leash, keeping me from swallowing him.

Using my teeth, I brush them lightly against his head; I feel a shudder go through his body as he releases the leash. Going slower, I learn his body as he does the same to mine. I run my hands up his thighs, scraping my nails against him lightly as he again gives a shudder. Grinning to myself, I realize he likes a little pain with his pleasure. Oh, how I see this being a lot of fun.

As the thrumming of the toy vibrates inside me and his tongue wonders, his fingers toy, and dip into my ass, bringing a new sensation that my body isn't ready for. I scream my pleasure around his cock as I tip over the edge. He pushes his hips up into my mouth further, choking out my screams.

He stops licking at my clit and quickly moves his hand, sitting a warm metal against my ass entrance. I rock back and forth as the orgasm works its way through me.

"Come back, my Flower, slowly keep that rocking motion."

Trusting him, I rock back into his hands as he helps me through the motion. I feel pressure, but my mind goes fuzzy, and pleasure is the only thing that surrounds me. I continue to nuzzle and nibble at his shaft, curling my hands on his thighs. My body has a mind of its own and wants to rub up and down the thing that is giving it pleasure.

I feel a sharp pang as something slides in me. My body freezes and tenses with the solid mass. He takes the vibrating toy out of my vagina and replaces it with his tongue. His hands trail over my lower back, massaging me there, trying to loosen up the tightness that sits there. The pressure doesn't go away totally, but the pain dissipates as heat warms through my body. He would flick the ending part with his tongue, causing it to move as I begin to ride his face. Pleasure floods through me, leaving me wanting and needing more.

"What color are you at, Flower?"

"Yellow... maybe green," I say, unsure.

"Give it some time, sit with it a moment, and let your body adjust." His tongue continues to flick against me playfully but holds himself from the heavier petting as his hands grip my legs, wanting to do more.

I allow myself to rest against him, letting myself just feel and enjoy what he is doing. My fingers trace the dips at his hips, learning the contours of his body. The feather light touch has me clenching and opening to the sensations he is causing.

The collar tightens around my throat as I feel the leash being picked up, pulling me off him to the side. Domini gets up with the leash in hand. "Sit."

Sitting there on my knees, I bring my gaze up, seeing where he is looking at. The vibration is turned down low, but I still feel it there in my ass. The long buzz of it makes shivers of excitement race over my back.

Blaise is standing in the doorway, slight anger rages through his body. Though he is naked, he isn't enjoying the scene. The veins on his arms stand out with the strength he is showing at keeping back. "This is hard for me... but I'm here and I want to... try this." His hazel eyes turn more vibrant green of his snake.

"Crawl for us, Flower." He walks slowly so I can keep up the plug that still sits in me feels different as I move my body, making it awkward. After a moment, my body pulses around it, causing me to forget what I'm doing. We stop in front of Blaise. "Sit pretty for him." Domini angles his head to Blaise. "You know the rules."

Sitting back on my knees, I sit with my legs apart and my hands on my upper thighs, pushing my breasts together. I look up at both of them with large, wanting eyes. Hoping he could move past this.

"Your djinn friend explained them before we got here. See-ing as he had to wait a bit for me to finish up."

My eyes travel up the length of Blaise, the chord pulling tight between us, begging me to touch him. Domini's back is to me, but I dare not move. I want only pleasure in this session as much of it as I could get. My body is already being pleasantly pushed past its normal boundary. I don't want to try more new things by acting out.

"Good, again I will just reiterate this: you both have the light system. If at any time either of you say red, we will stop. Understood?"

I nod, but Domini's eyes stay on Blaise, waiting for him to nod.

"In my domain, I will not make this easier for you, snake. Like I did in the dream. We talked before coming here. We both decided it best not to siren song you for this part, and nothing is done here that isn't wanted by all parties. Remember that."

"I will," his voice comes out rough and angry.

"Flower, will you treat our snake here with what you were treating me with?"

Hesitating. "I can move?"

"Yes," he groans.

I crawl the few steps it takes to get to Blaise and look up at him, rising on my knees. I wait to make sure he doesn't turn away. Domini grabs the back of Blaise's neck with his hand and brings his face forward to kiss him as softly as he kisses me. Another zing flows through me at how entranced I'm at seeing these two powerful males come together in such a way. At first Blaise stands still, Domini's left eye slits open and looks down at me. His arm comes up, caressing my cheek, and then pushes me forward to Blaise's body.

I cup Blaise's balls in my hand and take him into my mouth, since he is soft. Licking and kissing, begging for him to raise. I keep my eyes open wide and focus above me. Blaise's body responds to me and Domini all at once.

Blaise's hand cups the back of my head, feeling my hair and his other wraps around Domini, deepening their kiss. I moan into him as he becomes harder. This causes my throat to vibrate around him.

Blaise tears his lips away from Domini. "Fuck Minx." His head kicks back in ecstasy.

"She is a greedy little thing. I think she dreams about stuff like this all the time. Naughty little Flower."

Grinning, I give a long slow lick till I come up off Blaise's penis and then lick Domini's just the same, all the while keeping eye contact, daring him to have a problem with my naughty little thoughts.

He pulls the leash tight, forcing me up off him into a standing position. I give a little pout as he faces me away from him, his hands on my breasts pinching them into hard nubs until I gasp out and then Blaise's mouth is on mine, taking all the air I have from me. His mouth dives into mine, his tongue toying me into submission. I fight back, not making this game easy. My hands wrap around him, leaving only enough room for Domini's hands to continue pinching my breasts, raging the heat higher.

"Take the dress off before it becomes ribbons," Blaise gasps out as we come up for air.

Raising my hands, I wait for Blaise to remove the clothing that upsets him; he does so effortlessly. He molds back to my body, his body hot to the touch.

Domini's cock bumps against my behind, knocking into the plug, pushing a new sensation into me. He also pulls me back with the collar, tugging me back towards the bed. Not letting Blaise go, I pull him with us. The anger that coursed through him earlier is dying down as things heat up.

"Climb up on the bed and hang your head over the side with your arms up. Blaise, there is a jar you will need later, as well as a remote. Bring both back with you, they are by the fire."

I do what is asked on the bed. He leans over and removes the leash and choker; he positions me with my hands hanging off the bed, my face up. The only part of me on the bed is my top half and down. He crawls over me, pinning me to the spot with his own body between my thighs.

Rubbing himself over my entrance, he feels the moisture of how wet I am. He covers himself with my scent. "She isn't quite ready for both of us to be in her, but soon she will be. That remote there will help her get there. The plug inside her can grow bigger and move depending on the buttons that you press. You will have control over her. You will fill her in other ways until then."

My hands being over my head, causing my nipples to rise high in the air and beg to be touched. Which both men do not disappoint. They each take one after Blaise puts the cannister down on the floor next to the bed and keeps the remote in hand.

Domini pins me with his lower body as he wraps a hand around Blaise's cock, pulling him on an even shorter leash than mine. He brings him forward to my mouth, pushing the tip of him to my lips. I keep my mouth closed at first and then open up, but I keep my mouth small, so it is hard for him to push in too fast. Domini controls the speed, but once Blaise keeps the motion, he brings his hand away. Blaise has let go of my breast and only concentrates on the motion, and still has the remote in his hand.

Domini slides back down my body and on the upstroke of Blaise pushing into me at the same moment Domini pushes into my core. Filling me as I have never been before. My hands spasms out and grip onto Blaise's thigh. He lets me stop the motion and hold him there. Domini also holds his position, letting me get used to things.

"Flower, are we still green?" Domini growls out. Grounding his hips against mine.

My tongue whips around Blaise's cock as he is fully in my mouth. My grip on his thighs refuses to let him go. He kicks back his head and lets out a moan all his own. I roll my hips into Domini and take one of my hands off of Blaise and hold up an okay hand sign, letting them both know I'm perfectly fine with where this is going.

Domini moves inside me, and Blaise picks up the same rhythm. The sensation is intense and almost too much to keep up with all at once. As I handle the rhythm they are setting, Blaise looks down at the controller as he himself slows down. Domini picks up my hips, thrusting deeper into me as my throat angles onto Blaise even deeper. A moan slips from me as a rumbling comes from the plug, sucking in on Blaise more as my fingers scratch at his thighs. Concentrating on anything but what I'm feeling is impossible. Breathing isn't something I worry about in the moment, but Blaise makes sure to watch and listen to my body and knows what it needs before I even do. Pressure gains as they move as one. Blaise clicks buttons and the thing moves, the vibrations operating at a different pace now. I can feel it against what Domini is doing to me as he pushes deeper into me.

This one comes on so fast I'm screaming over the edge as Domini reaches something deep inside me, making me orgasm. My body spasms around him, my body and mind are in a blissful haze as I lose feeling. He slows his pace. Blaise removes himself from my throat as Domini slides out of me. He stands to the side of the bed. There, with Blaise, I watch as they come together, kissing and holding one another close. A small moan escapes my lips. Domini lets go of Blaise and gathers me into his arms, and holds me close to him.

"Blaise, give me the remote. Let's move this to the couch now." He walks with me in his arms over to the couch. Sitting down, he drapes me over his lap.

I move into a better position with one leg on each side of his straddling him.

"Slide in behind her," Domini demands.

Blaise slides behind me, his cock jutting between my slippery legs. Domini reaches down between us, playing with both of us there at once. Blaise comes closer, sandwiching me between the two of them, pushing himself against me, giving a guttural moan I can tell he likes the touch of Domini's hand and my juices on him. Domini pushes Blaise inside of me, his length hot and throbbing with need.

Moaning, Domini captures my lips with his, kissing me into submission. There is no teasing this time and no asking. There is only giving and taking. Blaise sets the tone this time first softly to build me back up. As Domini tweaks my nipples, he rubs the remote against them. The coolness of the plastic taking away the stinging heat. He ups the intensity of the plug and increases the size much larger. Blaise's increasing thrusts raise the intensity as he feels the vibration through me. He thrusts hard and deep in a slow pace that about does me in. I scream out, fighting myself for everything I feel. Bringing my hands up to Domini's shoulders, I dig my nails into his skin. My animal wants to lose control as he thrusts into me over and over again.

"A color Flower?" He stops kissing me and moves to lick and nuzzle my nipples.

"It's fucking green!" I yell. I include some other things that sound like words but definitely are not.

Blaise laughs behind me. "I think she wants us to stop."

"Very vocal, this one. We may have to think of other ways to torture and punish her if she is going to continue with such a mouth on her." Domini rubs against Blaise as he is pumping into me. He rubs against my clit ever so gently, which sends me into another tailspin. He grinds deeply into me as he rings out my orgasm.

"I think she is ready," Domini says in response.

"For a nap?" I respond, my eyelids already dropping.

He laughs as Blaise pulls out of me, still hard and throbbing. "Soon, Blaise go grab that jar. You will be first, but you will follow my directions."

I use Domini's chest as a pillow, as I'm too tired to pay attention to what they are discussing. Their soft murmurs continue, but I'm in a soft, warm cocoon of pleasure. The vibration from the plug still rumbles and is nice, but not over-powering. Rubbing my breasts against Domini, he rubs my back and his fingers dip down to the plug, thumping his finger against it, causing it to press into me. I nuzzle down further and bite against his nipple.

His chatter with Blaise stops there as his attention zeroes in on me. I try to lick the nipple in apology, hoping to take away his sting like he did to me.

"My little Flower is like nightshade. She isn't too tired to play, is she?" He growls out as he slides his body lower on the couch. "Ride me, Flower, as if your life depends on it."

My eyes follow up his chest, his eyes hold me captive. They are hard and demanding.

He grabs my neck as I'm about to turn to Blaise to see what he is doing, but he stops me. "No, look at me as you take me into you."

Slowly, I push myself up and position him correctly before sinking down onto him. His thickness seems even more snug as I feel all of him. He holds on to my throat tight just enough for me to breathe; I dig my fingers into his shoulders as I hold myself there, riding him slowly, finding my rhythm. I don't break eye contact as his other hand moves over my ass, gripping it in hand and moving it. He brings his other hand down away from my throat, but I still hold his eyes, never wavering as the pressure builds. He spreads my butt cheeks apart as I go fully down on him, massaging into him. I feel fingers there at the bottom of my ass. Blaise is playing with Domini's balls and me at the same time. He grips the sides of the plug and as I pull up, it gets pulled out. My breath hitches in, but Blaise's face is there, his tongue soothing the ache, as I continue back down on Domini.

Blaise slips behind me and rubs against me with his member, long and slippery. Domini continues to move below me, making sure I feel every inch of him. He tightens his hold on my ass and holds them open for Blaise; I feel him at my butt as he pushes in slowly. Shivers rack through me and pain begins to sizzle.

"You are so tight here." Blaise hisses through clenched teeth. He pushes into the hilt, and I curl my fingers on Domini's chest.

"Breathe, easy," he whispers.

Blaise retreats. My face crumples in answer.

"Stop, snake."

He freezes in answer, but I hear a hiss come from him and his nails bite into my hips as they grow.

"Flower color?"

"Yellow... red... yellow," I hiss through teeth, trying to breathe through it. Not wanting our game to end.

Blaise pulls me closer to his chest, easily picking me up and pulling me off Domini. I'm still seated upon Blaise as he sits down on the couch with me in his lap. His cock twitches within me at the slight movements which pools warmth into my abdomen. I lean back on Blaise as he spreads my legs, inviting Domini in.

"I'm going to mark you like you marked me the first time," Blaise whispers into my ear just for me as he moves feather light fingers over my clit, stimulating me there.

Domini stands and watches my face carefully. He comes to kneel before us, his tongue darts out, starting on Blaise's penis and following it all the way up to my sweet center. His tongue laps at the golden honey I hold. Soothing the sting, I relax against Blaise as he continues holding me and making sure I stay seated fully on him. Between Blaise rubbing me and Domini's slow, sensual tongue. How could I not enjoy myself? My fingers snake into Domini's hair as I grip him there, holding him firmly against me. My legs shake as the pleasure begins to build.

His tongue goes back down as he licks Blaise and me where I'm seated, making it even more wet and delicious. He soothes the ache there. Standing up, he towers over me, pointing straight at me. He rubs himself against Blaise's hand and my lower lips.

"Color?" his voice shakes.

"Better it's green."

Blaise grabs Domini's cock and rubs him against me, pushing him into me ever so slowly, his hand right there touching both of us together.

Moaning, I throw my head back as he begins his slow descent into me, my juices coating him thoroughly. As he sinks into me fully, he grabs the back of Blaise's neck, smooshing me in between them. Giving a harsh kiss to him he doesn't hold back. His movements pick up speed. Blaise mostly grinds against me and only moves slight movements out and in as his hands hold my ass in place.

Domini's fingers brush against my nipples, them being extra sensitive with all that is zinging through me at once.

"Too much, not enough." A hitch in my throat comes out as Domini continues to hit hard and fast right over the spot that is making me see stars.

"Minx, take what you need and I will supply the rest. You are so beautiful," he says in awe.

Blaise's hands push my ass up further, slipping further out before bringing me down fully on top of him. My legs and arm spasm, curling around Domini, bringing him closer to our web.

The pain subsides as the salve that he used takes effect. I move in between them, finding my rhythm. My own claws continue to make their self-known as I scratch at Domini's back, them coming out more and more. His body jack knifes into me with each cut. Making it harder and harder to stay in rhythm. Blaise moves more in and out, picking me up easily and maneuvering me between them both where I'm doing nothing but receiving both of them. With my mouth open wide, I feel the fangs descend over my teeth. I strike as I feel myself tip over the edge. My mouth latches onto Domini's shoulder, causing him to lose control almost instantaneously. He hammers into me with no control left. Holding on, I roll into another as he tips over himself. Blaise is last but joins us as he strikes into me with fangs and cock as he unloads into me.

The last strike sends a third rolling through me, my limbs and body no longer responding to anything that I send it. We lay like that for a moment, coming down from the bliss; I continue to lick and nuzzle at the bite I created, and Blaise does the same to me as he grinds against me.

Domini slides from me first, which makes me pout, but my eyes droop close, regardless. Blaise turns me in his lap, also sliding away from me.

"Is she okay?" Domini asks, his voice further away than I would like.

"She seems fine, just tired," Blaise answers as I curl into him for warmth.

"Bring her over here," Domini demands.

Blaise holds me close as he brings me to where Domini is. He pushes me down into the soft bed from before. My eyes fly open as I feel something against my tender skin. A wet cloth is in Domini's hand as he cleans them from me. Once I'm clean to his satisfaction, he motions for Blaise to join me on the one side. Domini puts the stuff away and then cuddles into my other side. I'm surrounded by both of them, their hard and warm bodies a comfort to me.

Blaise's tongue runs over my shoulder where he bit me, soothing me. My claws and teeth melt away in the afterglow. All our legs twine in and out of one another as we hold each other close.

"Is that what you were thinking it would be like?" Domini asks.

I just rumble a lot of m's through my closed lips. Talking seems like too much energy to spend.

"Let her sleep, warrior."

"I will always push for her to answer because her thoughts must be heard. Too many voices are silenced in this world. Flower's will not be one of them."

Struggling against sleep, I mumble my reply. "Yes, I liked it very much. No grumpy talk to ruin the bliss." I touch both of them, running my hands over their chests, stomachs, anything my fingers could find and reach. Both of their holds tighten, coiling us into a tighter ball.

"How long do we have?" Blaise asks.

"We still have time. The djinn will come get us when needed. Time moves different here. She should be able to get plenty of rest, all of us should before needed again."

"What about us?"

"Hush snake, the djinn has us covered. Rest now. You will be back to reality all too soon," Domini growls.

"Thank you," I croon, falling into slumber.

"No, thank you, my love." Blaise curls protectively around me, his arm wrapping around us, including Domini.

Could we have something like this? Could we all accept one another? Time will tell.

# CHAPTER 5

MY SLEEP IS DEEP and uneventful. The bed turns less warm during the night and the comfort is not there when I wake. My eyes are bleary in the early morning, but I hear birds and livestock stir. My body is pleasantly sore in all the right places. I would definitely need that soaking bath they promised last night.

After getting my necklace from under the pillow and changing into some new clothes. I grab my pack, leaving the room, and cross the hall to Natasha's. She should be up this early in the morning.

Knocking on the door lightly, I try to whisper through the wood. "Natasha."

I can hear a quiet murmur through the door, then something skitters against the door. "Fuck," she says next to the door but under her breath. The door creaks open so I can see her mussed hair and her eyes that are laden with sleep, just as mine are.

"Did you want to come with me to check out the baths? I can't remember exactly what they said about them?" I say, my voice keeping quiet.

She leans her head against the door frame. Looks back into the room and then shakes her head. "Yea, give me a moment. I will meet you downstairs."

Scuffing my feet, I head down the stairs to wait for her. The fireplace is lit, and some patrons are already up and eating breakfast. My stomach flip-flops at the sight and smell, making me aware I could not hold food down right now, maybe after waking up.

A few minutes later, Natasha is dressed and coming down with her pack. We head over to the counter where we checked in.

"The woman that checked us in last night stated we could wash up somewhere this morning." Natasha bangs her hand down in greeting. The male that is at the desk stands up straight and his dreary eyes blink open rapidly. His shoulder-length brown hair is tangled and needs a brushing badly. His clothes are mussed and have splatters of dark stains.

"The baths and showers are down that hallway." He directs us. "Breakfast is served till ten," he calls out as if reading from a script.

Natasha salutes the man and heads off down the hallway. We come across a door, one for men and the other for women. We make our way through a locker room type setting that holds some showers and changing rooms along with a huge soaker type bath. There is enough room for multiple people. I rush to the heated bath, craving the delicious warm liquid to soothe me in ways I desperately need.

"Oof, they need to invest in a better morning person. Did you get a smell of that guy?"

"No, I was too afraid." Undressing quickly, I make my way over. "Did Zeek and Robert make it back?" I ask knowing she would have the answer.

Natasha's cheeks heat and turn red. I avert my gaze, hoping she doesn't see that I caught it. "Yes, you were out for the count, so we let you keep sleeping when you didn't answer your door."

"He was there. Wasn't he in your room? You didn't have to come down here with me."

"Perhaps he can get some rest now. Every little move I make, he wakes with a start, worried I'm running out. I did it one time, and he's going to hold it over me from now till he dies." She tosses her clothes to the side, diving into the deep waters.

My descent is slower as I slide into the waters. "Can you blame him?" I hiss as the heat kisses my tender flesh, letting me know that everything we did last night was deliciously real.

"What's up with you? You seem in more pain than horse riding would cause." Her eyes zero in on me questioning.

"You spill first every time we speak about my sex life. Some-one leaves out the tidbits to her own." I groan out as I lean back into the water, my head the only thing just above it.

"That is because there is none. It is just teasing and sexual tension that is thick enough to get stuck in."

"That sounds...not fun," I hesitate.

"It's frustrating as hell!" Natasha runs her fingers through her hair, grabbing at the strands. "Let me live vicariously through you. Was yours fun at least?"

My eyes roll back in my head as I think back over last night. "So much fun."

"With who, which one?"

"Both," I giggle.

"The siren and the snake. What?" She splashes forward, causing warm droplets to drip onto my face.

My eyelids pop open as I see her stand over me, her hands grasp at me. "Yes?"

"I thought you said you didn't have any magic. How did you work that?"

Smiling, I give a wicked grin. "By doing this new thing called asking."

"And they were both down?"

"Well, Domini was more so, but Blaise got on board soon after they talked. I caught some of what was said but not all of it."

"Aren't animals possessive when a mate is involved? At least that is what the readings usually say."

Giving a shrug. "Yes, but this is still all new to me and I like them both for different reasons. I have a pull with Blaise that seems almost unnatural, but I feel Domini balances both of us out in ways we both need."

"Not all animals are the same, I guess." She shrugs, shrinking down into the warmth of the water relaxing back. We both sit there in silence as we let our worries scatter away.

Rubbing my legs and arms helps loosen up my stiff limbs. "Shade will not help us with what we need. How far away are we from the Dark Court?"

"Jasmin stated you are going to need your magic to help you traverse the court."

"Yea, I don't really think Shade cares. Also, why do I need my magic that I never really used, anyway? At least I can shift things when I get angry or scared."

"Have you been able to shift on command?" Natasha peeks open an eye and gives a ruthless look.

"Not really. When did I have time lately? When I get to practice, it's not a full shift, but I have been practicing on my claws and teeth."

"Shifters will not like it if you can't control things. It might help with you being related to Flit, but he isn't the alpha."

"He's not?" I ask, confused. "But isn't he the leader of all the dark side or something? King of the darkness?"

"Yea, but that doesn't mean he is the alpha of badger shifters. Depending on the lay of the land, there could be multiple alphas." She dips her short hair into the water.

"I have never been to a Dark Court party. What all transpires there?"

"It is so deliciously evil and dark. It is full of sex, blood, and death. All the great things the dark side brings." Jazmin walks in a long purple dress covers her. In one smooth move, she whips the dress over her head, never stopping her stride. She tosses it to the side and steps into the pool we are in. We both pull our feet closer to ourselves until she is fully in and sitting down.

Pulling myself up, I sit up straight, intrigued about getting some time with Jazmin away from the men. "Tell me more about Flit and the Dark Court and why Shade is so important. Unless you have a way to capture him and make him do what we want." I say, hoping she had thought of something since last night.

"I pushed to get Shade to make things easier on you. If you go there as just a badger shifter, you will not be able to pretend to be anything else. You will be a badger shifter and that is all you will be and you may have to deal with the alpha questioning you, where you are from, and which pack will speak for you. If we had Shade close by, at least Flit could claim you as the heir from their past, and then he has familial bonds to pull from to protect you."

"Can't we just explain what happened?" I ask.

"Why can't Flit claim her as his granddaughter unless Shade is there? That doesn't make sense," Natasha sputters out.

"First, it's not that easy without being able to prove that you have both sides. Second, it isn't in his best interest to make ties to you until you have at least proven yourself. Depending on how things are received he may speak openly about claiming you or keep it more like a secret. It also means you have no protection there. These can get dangerous and he would have no power to stop it. He is as tied to the court as everyone else. There are too many variables to dictate how this will go. Having Shade there would have been easier."

"How were you planning on us making it through the Dark Court?" Natasha asks, her face screws up in a nasty scowl.

"Honestly, I was hoping we would be needed elsewhere or would find a reason not to go or to go at a later time, not during the festivities."

"Flit is the only one that knows what happened to my parents. He knows where my brother is. Why is he not here instead? Who are you to him?" My rapid questions leak out of me. I don't want to tell her how I knew for sure he had all this information. "Are you my grandma?"

Jazmin cackles, kicking out her leg, spraying water at both of us. "Goodness gracious dearie, no. Look at me. I'm one cuckoo short of a henhouse. Do I look maternal at all? No, I ensure you, children are not for me."

"Then why do you know so much about him?" Natasha asks for me.

"I'm Flit's consort, at least for now. I have kept favor with him for the last couple of years, though the way court life is that will not last. They say I'm the only one bat shit crazy enough to have fun with all the politics and backstabbing."

"Sounds like love doesn't get to be a part of court life. Is that also why my family fought so hard for their own space in between? They didn't want to have to lie, cheat, and steal to get where they wanted."

A tear falls from Jazmin's cheek. She flicks it away with a long nail. "What your parents had was magical a once in a lifetime kind of love. To think that it may never have happened if it wasn't for you."

"Why would the light and dark side not accept their union like they would have if it were Ivan and Jade?" I ask, needing to know for sure.

"I thought she went back into the past to see all the memories from her mother." Jazmin asks Natasha as if I was not there.

"She did."

"I did," I say, louder frustration leaking out of me. Being right here, she could talk to me. "Some memories were disjointed; others were very clear. But the ones that I'm confused about were in times where my power was waning and I came close to dying. My mother also went through trauma of her own, which confused even her and reliving through made it easy to forget some things."

Jazmin nods still not looking my way. "Both sides feared what would be created from your mother and father. The test clearly said that Ivan and Jade were the match of choice that would create the perfect union. Your mother failed that test. It was public record, and after what Ivan did, it made the people restless? Things were supposed to just go back to the way they were until another power couple could be found. Ivan would not wait. He refused to be a part of this anymore. He had his heading."

"Did they hunt him?"

"Like a rabid badger. It took all of Flit's cunning just to keep him ahead of things."

"Your parents never played by the rules and they would always ruin a good plan somehow." Natasha chuckles. "Or so I heard."

Somehow swirling through my mother's thoughts and past, I still knew very little about them. Their true love wasn't till the end where things were taking a turn for the worse.

"Did Natasha let you know the boys made it in last night?" Jazmin changes the subject.

Giving a curt nod, I raise up out of the water before plunging down deep into the waters. Wanting to hear nothing for a moment. I want the warmth to wash away my fears and troubles. Holding my breath, I lay under the water for a while before bursting from the water; I gulp in the air.

"Trill are you with me?"

"Yes," a small voice speaks to me but doesn't come out.

"Very dramatic, that one. Tsk, tsk, tsk. The fire flame will not come out surrounded by all this water." Jazmin says.

"I do not need her to come out, just some answers. Trill, is Shade and your sister still nearby?"

"They are still in the Abyss, close to where we left the dragon." She pips up with mention of her sister.

"Why was he there in the first place?" Natasha asks.

"He said he is hunting down my uncle, Tom. Said that he is an enormous threat to me and one he must eviscerate."

"He seems like he has a handle on your magic with no problems," Jazmin says. Swimming closer to me, she slides beside. "He has a human form, I'm told. Why did he look like a shadow creature and then change into that of a snake at the end?"

"It is what he is comfortable with, I suspect. He has been traveling through the caverns left by the sand burrowers. He says he didn't know he was under a dragon, but he could have been lying."

"Then who was in the tent that was near where the dragon slumbered?" Natasha's hands move through the water, stirring it in front of her. coldness slips from her but she is quick to rein it back in before she freezes us in the bath with her.

I felt the chill of water linger before the burners turn back on to heat the water.

"Could it have been your uncle hiding there? Are they in league with a dragon? If so, then Shade might be correct in taking care of him as a problem." Jazmin stands up walking back to the front of the pool to get out. "That changes things then. Let's leave this Shade to his work of hunting down your uncle. He will come find us when he is finished yes?" She turns back, waiting for an answer.

As if I had an answer. "Yes?" I ask. "He didn't say he wouldn't, but his spell is still in place to keep me safe. If he took out a threat, I would guess he would come back to reassess. He must be happy to be away from my tormenting thoughts and emotions. When I'm hurting, if there isn't something he can go after, he has problems figuring out how best to help."

Jazmin nods and walks out, forgetting her dress on the floor. Both Natasha and I leave our jaws open, waiting for her to scream or others to make noises, but nothing comes.

Locking eyes with Natasha, we sit there stunned, not sure what just happened or if the whole inn got an eyeful as she walks back to her room.

"She did say she was not all there, didn't she? That could be what court life does to you. It makes you crazy and not act right anymore." Natasha sticks her finger in the air and circles her head, rolling her eyes. "You know the strangest people, Alexia."

"Hey, I don't pretend to know any of you, not really. I was just dumped into this life and am just along for the ride."

"Robert will be upset we are not going for Shade; he thinks Shade will end up hurting Taz, who he carries with him."

"Taz is fine. I doubt Trill and Tina would stay with me if they thought their sister was in any sort of trouble."

"We would not. Taz assured us she was doing well and helps keep him balanced. Her soul is replacing his missing soul for now. She is helping him learn this world and what it takes to be in it," Trill whispers to me.

"She has a lot of work to do with him," I mutter. "He still is very cruel."

My stomach growls in answer. Both Natasha and I go through the motions of scrubbing down before exiting and getting into clean clothes. We decide to just keep quiet and give each other space to think through our own issues.

"Alexia?"

"Hmm?" Brushing my hair out, I look in the mirror over my shoulder where she is looking into the steaming bath.

"What do you really think about Zeek? Would you give him a shot?" She looks lost.

I stare at her without turning, judging by her lost in thought gaze and her hesitation. This is bringing down her confidence she needs guidance. "How does he treat you? I don't really know him, just that he helped me when he didn't need to. I know you think it was for the ulterior motive of getting to you, but still." Continuing to brush my hair, I wait for her to say more. Being thorough and making sure I brush every tangle through.

"He is kind enough, not in the blunt way most people would suspect, but he has my back regardless and is there for me when it is important. He doesn't put up with my bullshit and sees through me more so than anyone else has in the past."

"That terrifies you, doesn't it?"

"Unbelievably so, and if you say anything, I will deny it all." The temperature drops as we continue to talk.

Continuing to brush my hair, I look away as I see tears gather in her eyes. "I would expect nothing else from you." We are quiet once again, but I could feel the tension still there. "Perhaps this deal is good for the both of you and gives you time to come to an understanding of sorts."

"I don't want to waste my time."

"Don't you? Are you more afraid that he will like what he sees and accept you?" My throat catches on a feeling that rushes through me. This talk is a little too close to home and why I worry I will one day have to choose between Domini and Blaise.

"That and that he still will choose to leave or made to leave in the end. Either way, it all leads to being alone at the heart of it."

"Would that be so bad?"

"Dang, Lexi, I didn't think you would be so dark."

"I meant, would it be so bad to at least have felt love and been through it? Rather than not know it at all? We all meet our maker in the end. Why not enjoy what we have while we have it?" Turning around, I give her a sad look. "If I didn't think about it this way, I could fall to the darkness inside me. Fall into the hole that fights to consume me and make me go down the road of vengeance and death for all. I have endured and been through too much. It is time to live and enjoy the time I have left."

"That doesn't help me. I can't stop thinking the worst of people." She gives a grimace.

"Do you want to end up like your parents? Or do you want to have what they never could? What do they deny each other from having? We have to find our own way, even if it is in the steps of our parents or another treacherous road that we pave all our own."

Natasha lets out a deep breath and nods as if having decided on a final thought. She gathers her things and races out of the now empty changing room.

"Well, that conversation is done," I say.

"Finally," a smooth feminine voice swirls around me.

"Whose there?" My head passes back and forth from the bath to the changing area and around me, near the sinks and toilets but no ones there.

"An admirer of sorts." The voice breathes down my neck, making me spin around.

"What are you? What is your name? Show yourself."

"I don't think I will," it whispers.

"Then what do you want?"

"I hear you are coming to the Dark Court. Good. You have something that belongs to me and you will give it back."

"I have nothing." Again, my head shifts back and forth, trying to hear where the voice is coming from, but it sounds like it surrounds me.

"You carry more than you think. Be careful before deciding to double-cross me," she drips disdain.

"Tell me who I'm speaking with and I will take care to not mess with what is yours." I give a scowl, thinking the exact opposite.

"All you need to know is I know who you are, I know what you have and I know how to get to you wherever you are."

A small cold current flow through my body as if a cord is being pulled around me and tightened.

"I hope you enjoyed yourself, because that is all there will be."

Something pulls on me, but nothing is around. I catch my reflection in the mirror. My eyes swirl to a different color, almost as if glowing a gray light. "Come to the Dark Court, little badger. Make your way to our midnight, showing it will be something you will be particularly interested in."

"Midnight showing?"

"It's called Beasts After Dark." The voice gives a chuckle. "Don't be late." My eyes glow brighter.

"Beasts After Dark," I repeat.

"Make your way there in two days." Her voice lulls me.

My eyes light up almost blindingly so before they dim back to my dark brown. I shake my head.

"What just happened?" Glancing around the room, I try to remember what I am doing.

"You coming deary?" Jazmin's voice rings by the door. "You did not come out shortly after Natasha. We worried something happened."

Opening my mouth, no words come out. Her shoes click against the hard floor as she comes back to find me staring at the mirror still.

My eyes tear away from it as I see her in my peripheral. "Is it time to head to the Dark Court?" I ask, but feel no authentic emotion in my voice.

"It is what we are discussing now." She motions me over. "Let's go get some breakfast and go over that."

Gathering up the rest of my stuff, I quickly pull my hair in a bun, not trusting any of it to be down. My first night out here, these bird-like creatures ripped and tore at the strands of my hair. Since then, I don't leave it down or even in a ponytail while traveling at least.

Before leaving out the changing room, I slip on the necklace and tuck it back in my shirt before leaving the room. It holds Flits black stone, my flower pendant which is useless now and the heart-shaped ruby. As it rests there on my chest, I feel a beat against my chest in answer to my own thumping heart. It is his way of letting me know he is there if I need him.

I keep my eyes on the floor and my head tipped down as I walk in behind Jazmin, who goes over and sits down with the rest of the gang. I slide into a chair a glass of water sits before me. Gripping the cold chilled glass, I down it in a matter of minutes. My stomach in answer rumbles for all around to hear. Their eyes pin to my stomach and then slowly pan up to mine.

"What? We didn't eat much yesterday and we could barely keep our eyes open last night," I defend.

"Glad we ordered for you. It should be out soon then. Meat lover's platter thought you would need it from all the riding we have been doing," Zeek calls out. His eyes travel back to Natasha in worry, but stays on me afterwards.

"Yea, I'm surprised that your badger hasn't taken over at all with the lack of food that you have been living on," Robert says.

"Perhaps her appetites are quenched in another way." Natasha says under her breath next to me. She is on my right, furthest from Zeek.

Both Robert and Zeek eye one another and give a questioning look, clearly having heard the comment. I can feel my face turn red.

"I already filled the boys in on what was discussed between us earlier. Robert wanted to continue searching and persuading Shade, but he knows how useless that would be now." Jazmin steps in and changes the subject.

"Zeek and I discussed it while you were gone. I can head back in search of Shade alone. Zeek will take you the rest of the way to the Dark Court."

"That is preposterous. How are you going to track Shade?" Jazmin asks, her mouth open in shock.

"Trill or Tina, I was hoping one of them would come with me just for the time being to help me in this endeavor." Robert's gruff voice is laden with worry.

Tina rises from my arm, a small hot sizzle crackles up my arm as if her anger sparks something. Her voice is louder than Trill's has been. Her flame like body hovers over my arm looking up at me. "You do not need the both of us right now, and have not called on us to practice with either. Let me go with Robert to search for our sister and keep tabs on him."

"You are free to do what you want. If you would like to go, that is up to you. I have not called on you both because we have been traveling and there has not been time for practicing."

"You call on your animal when attacked and run when needed. This isn't the kind of adventures I wanted to go on. I need motion. Movement forward, not just staying stuck with the same problems. I need to do something. Trill is more lenient with you and you are alike enough that she understands why you do the things you do. I do not have her patience." She skips across the table to Roberts waiting open palm. "Maybe when you are up for more fighting and disaster, we can work something out. Until then." She moves down into Robert's arm. He winces as he feels her blazing anger scorch him. A red mark spreads out on his arm.

"She is going to need all the help she can get at court life." Jazmin's eyes fade to a light lavender color.

"You said it yourself. We cannot help her with everything she does or else they will think she's weak. She will have Zeek a death dealer with her, so that alone will instill fear in the people we need. When you get there, you probably will head to your lover's room to update him. So, we can't count on you while there since you play a part to the king of darkness. Natasha will be the other guarding her when out mixing with the others." Robert shakes his head. "Two guards are the perfect amount to not say I'm weak and vulnerable but also to let people know don't push or we will obliterate you."

"This isn't smart."

Showing his teeth. "I didn't ask for your opinion. Plus, my skill set isn't needed here at this time."

"And what is your skill set again?" She barks back. "You're not like Zeek, so what is your skill set?"

"No one is like Zeek. I am a death dealer like him, though." He gives a half cocky smile.

"Death dealer is just a fancy title for assassin. I asked you what your certain skill set is."

"One of his skills is dealing with other plains of existence." I lean my head on my arm in front of me, tired of their game already.

"Doesn't sound important to me. You are right, you will not be missed." Jazmin all but huffs looking around the room for the waiter. She spots him coming through the door with food loaded in his hands. He moves to our table and passes out the surrounding food.

Perking up, I pick myself up off the table. Wiping my mouth with the back of my arm, I feel wetness from where I'm salivating. The food smells wonderful and steam rises from the hot, fresh food. My hand grips the fork and shovels it in as fast as I can eat.

Silence falls upon the table for the next half an hour as we are all famished and really need all the food that is around us.

As we near the end of our plates, the chatter picks back up. "I apologize for my sharp tongue. I get that way when I haven't had a proper meal in a while."

Robert nods to Jazmin but keeps his mouth shut.

"We will head out after this meal and make our way towards the south where the Dark Court lies," Zeek responds, pulling us all full circle.

"Will this be as bad as the Abyss?" I ask, nibbling on the bacon that I save for last. It is thick and crunchy, all of it is delicious. I wish I could have this kind of food more often.

Zeek hesitates. "Not as dangerous as it, only because we should be able to see what is coming at us. There are still parts we will head around because of tough terrain or dangerous monsters, but we will be able to see what is coming."

Nothing much else is said other than wishing Robert well as he goes back the way we had come. He let us know he would check in if he is not going to be able to meet up with us later.

Before leaving, he takes me to the side. "Take care of Trill, please. She is the oldest, but she is just as young as the other two, no matter what she wants you to think. Ask for her help even if you don't think it will, create that bond that you are so badly needing."

"Bond?"

"Shade left a hole. Did he not when he got ripped from you?"

I let that sink in and wonder why it doesn't feel as if there is something missing. Blaise is my anchor to this world. Maybe that is covering for Shade's loss. I shrug and nod, letting him know I would keep it in mind.

We first stock up on weapons, Zeek end up getting me a knife since I can't rely on my shifting abilities. Robert picks things that would help him with a dragon. Zeek gives him a few trinkets to help him. Soon after, we wave goodbye to him as he rides away. We ready ourselves by packing and getting the horses to go to the opposite gate of where we came in.

Unlike the first couple of days being in pure darkness, this part is mostly uneventful. Zeek took us around the dangerous spots which would make us get into town later.

On the second day, my agitation ratchets up. "We need to be there. I should be there by now," I whisper fervently. "She said two days and we should be there." Pacing around the camp, I bide my time before rushing into Zeek's tent, yelling at him to get things going.

Jazmin's gaze follows my fevered movements as I pace in a circle.

"We will still reach the town by nightfall. What is so pressing that we get there by tonight?" She asks.

My wild eyes dance around her form but chase back to the horses, wondering if I could just make it out on my own. "No, I would become lost," I whisper. Louder for Jazmin to hear me, I say. "I have a bad feeling if we don't make it there by a certain time that everything will be lost."

"Have you had these feelings before?" She beckons me to her.

Dancing away, I do not move closer to her. "Feelings about people yes." Quirking my head to the sky. "Not places usually."

"Eat something." She tries to get me to come sit by her.

Shaking my head, I take off for Zeek's tent. "We should get going, should we not, if we want to make it before nightfall?"

I hear a low whisper. "Why is it imperative that everyone wakes me up before I'm ready? Four hours, that is all I ask and yet I'm not even getting that!" Natasha screeches.

"You talked long past your hour, Ice Queen." Zeek chuckles. "Why must we get there by the end of today? I was planning on stopping once more to not push the horses so much." His head pokes out of the tent.

I make a low growl in the back of my throat.

"We will make most of the trip today, but stop a couple miles out and trek in, in the morning," he reiterates as Jazmin walks up.

"I think that is for the best. The worst of the festivities is tonight. None of us should be in attendance," Jazmin states, siding with Zeek on this one.

"Great, more sleep than to make up for the lack of it today." Natasha seals the final nail in the coffin.

Clenching my fists tight, I stomp over to the horses, trying to calm myself.

A horse knickers and stomps the ground with me, shying away from my touch. Another's head whips around as it tries to bite at the sleeve of my shirt.

My frustration swells. I walk away from the camp and horses so no one can hear me.

"I will get there tonight, one way or another. I will wait till everyone is asleep and will take off on foot. Zeek will stop early tonight then, since he wants us and the horses to rest. It would be an early night should give me plenty of time to get there still. The show isn't till midnight."

Shaking my head, I hope he will not be too far away from town, where I will have to walk many miles. Why am I cursed with being a badger? Why couldn't I have been something bigger where I could carry a pack with me and run fast? Shifting into a badger would not help me in this endeavor. I spend my time circling around through the trees, trying to calm my racing mind and heart.

"Alexia!" Jazmin calls out to me. "Let's go. They are ready now."

"Finally," I grumble, trying to get in a better frame of mind so none of them suspect anything. Louder I say, "coming!" My voice is cheery. Breathing in deeply, I hold it before letting it go and calming my shaking hands.

We pack things up and are out of the woods in no time. We are soon in a mountain over pass before we push back into the trees.

Many hours later, the sun starts to set behind the trees when we stop for the night. We were on the edge of the tree line next to some very tall grass and wide open space.

"There is no other suitable cover on the way to the city. It is only a couple of miles down that way." Zeek points as he pulls his horse back into the cover of the trees and sets up camp. Making sure I know how far we are from the town.

Yawning, a few times during the trip, I again increase the frequency and sluggishly make my way to help them. I need them to believe how tired I'm, so it doesn't look bad with me going to bed early.

Jazmin's eyes follow me as she tries to help. "I see what you are doing, girl."

I worry my bottom lip, unsure if she would stop me from doing what I need to or if she is just lying so that I will cave and tell her everything.

"Jazmin leave her be she is just tired and not feeling well." Natasha comes to my defense.

I spoke to her earlier to let her know I'm feeling drained.

"Go lay down and rest. Hopefully, you are not coming down with anything." Natasha feels my forehead before letting me go. "You have a bit of a temperature, but it could be from the very hot day we are having."

My skin feels hot to the touch as obsessive thoughts keep swirling around. I need to get to the city before midnight. I lay down for a while before I hear the others gather around the campfire to rest and relax. Their quiet murmurs can be heard as they chat.

I reach for the ruby under my shirt and check to see if heat is coming off it. It isn't warm to the touch. I clench my hand around it, searching for Domini's power. For the first time, it sits dormant and cold to the touch.

"What if there is something wrong with him? See, I will know more once in the city. He should be there by now."

I gather my pack in case. The dagger Zeek got me lays nestled in the clothes in my pack. It jostles as I move and the glint of steel catches my eye. My fingers itch to palm the blade but I fear carrying it on my person.

I move the blankets to look as if there is a person sleeping in my space. Hopefully Jazmin will drink too much tonight, like she usually does before going to bed. Last night she came to bed really late in an almost hung over state. Then they wouldn't notice my absence till the next morning and I would already be in the city.

I scuttle around, making sure not to leave prints in the dirt. Moving to the back of the tent where Jazmin usually sleeps, I pull the tent up next to her bedroll. Sliding underneath, I pat the ground, making sure there is no disturbance from me. I swipe the dirt from the blankets that my shoes carried in and slide everything back into place. Crouching down, I hold my breath, waiting to hear what the group is saying and doing. I hear all three of them speak in turn to each other.

I won't have to sneak away while someone is patrolling the woods. With Robert not here with us, Zeek is always patrolling and making it hard to do anything without notice.

Doing a crouch run, I sneak past the trees. As I'm about to slip past the tree line, I crouch even lower in the tall grass. Hiding my form from view. I walk like this for several minutes. Soon my back is aching from the harsh toll of leaning over. My thighs scream in mercy as I crouch lower. I sit back on the wet earth and rest both my back and legs for a moment. The grass bristles as the wind whips through it.

I struggle to call on my badger eyes as my vision goes in and out. Searching the grass, I look around for anything my human sight can't pick up on before my vision fades back out. I peek my head above the blades to see if anyone is following me or lay in wait as a trap. The woods are a ways away from me now, and the ravine is just to the south. Picking my way through the dirt, I crawl to the ravine and slide down into it. There is no water. The bottom is dry and barren, but it is deep enough for me to stand in and not be seen over the tall grass. I follow the dried ravine for a while; it follows the path to the city.

Setting out, I start with just a normal walk, but soon my feet itch to pick up speed, so I jog, wanting to get there faster. I wasn't sure of the time, but the nervous energy I feel keeps increasing as time wore on.

Lights and tops of houses peek in between the grass in the distance. They circle around a large black castle that reaches for the heavens.

Stopping to look, as I cress the hill, I see the town looks huge. There are many homes nestles around the castle. Both towns that I have seen were on the smaller side. The town we started in there were mostly houses with only a few buildings that held business. The town we just left was busier but was easily surrounded by a wall and gate to keep people safe. Other towns on our journey still did not compare to this magnificent sight.

The stillness only lasts a couple of seconds before I'm racing down the ravine towards the town and castle. I bet the show would take place there. I hope there will be someone around to ask to know where to see it.

As I race down, I slip in shallow puddles that are spread out. This place has seen some rain recently. We had not come across any yet on our travels. The further into town, the ravine seemed to grow bigger and deeper on the sides.

Racing up the lower side is tricky with the slick mud. It's a better idea than trying the deeper parts of the ravine. I pull myself up and out of the ravine, struggling to calm my puffing breath and make sure I'm on the correct side. Patting my hands down the length of my body, I try to clean the dirt and grime away as best as possible.

This city doesn't have a wall built around it like the last one did. There were just a few houses with lots of room in between and as I kept walking, the number of houses increased and the amount of space between them decreased. The moon, by this time, is high in the sky, only a sliver of it able to be seen. I slow my jog to a brisk walk, not wanting to scare anyone if they saw me running. The streets are bare, and no people are about.

Keeping the castle in sights I make my way toward the center of the city. I could hear sounds from inside the homes and down alleyways, but I don't want to stop to check things out. The castle is soon looming over me, much bigger in person. There is still no wall, but there is a fence with guards sprinkled around. I notice people walking around inside near the castle, but on my side of the fence, most are making their way to other parts of the city or to their own homes.

There is a line by the guard's house where most of them are stationed. Creeping closer, I hesitate at the end of the line, wondering what this is for.

"Is this the line to get into the castle for the show?" I ask, tapping the shoulder of a plump lady in. Her dress is beautiful and her hair hangs in ringlets around her face as she turns to me.

Her eyes gaze at my attire as she scrunches her nose. "This line is to be let in for the festivities at the palace. They will not let you in looking like that, though."

Looking down at my dark baggy pants and my loose shirt that may or may not have some stains from my travel. "I don't have a dress or any money." My eyes travel back to the town thinking of another solution. "But I need to get in to see the midnight showing."

"This is the show of the year that everyone will be talking about. They only put on one of these shows once a year."

"The one with beasts?"

"The very one." She nods. "Tickets for the show sold out really fast. The only other way to get in to see it is if your name is on a list." She gives a toothy smile.

"A list?"

"Yes, a special list." She gives a cackle. "Did you get a ticket?"

Shaking my head, I continue to stand in line as it moves forward.

"You can't be hoping your name is on the list, can you? I have never seen you around here before. Are you new to town?"

"Just made it here." I peer around her, hoping to spot something in line or see something that I could use. Keeping my ears open, I strain to hear the conversations further up in line.

"Well, the best of luck to you, lassie. If you find yourself in need, come by my place later tonight. It's a building with a red roof on it and called the Red Dragon." She gives a smirk. "I will make it worth your while." The lady then turns back to the front, done with the conversation and not willing to help further.

I felt a tugging sensation pulling me forward, but I hang back and make sure not to push my way to the front. The line feels so slow as it takes many eons to finally get there. The guard lets the voluptuous woman in front of me right in when she shows him her ticket.

"Have a good night, Mistress Penny." The guard salutes her.

He turns back to me, his eyes skip over me to the next couple waiting. I move forward, bouncing on my toes.

Seeing the top of my head, he finally looks down and wrinkles his nose in disgust. "You do not look as if you belong here."

Not looking down again at my attire, I keep my chin raised and my head up. "Can you check your list for my name?" I ask trying to sound confident that it would be there.

He is taken aback and grabs a metal clipboard with several pieces of paper on it. "You street urchins are all the same. Your names are never on here, no matter what some pretty person promises you." He holds the clipboard in front of him as if he is going to ward me off with it and looks at me expectantly.

I hold my ground, waiting.

He gives a huff. "Name?" His voice drips with annoyance.

"Alexia."

"Alexia…" He scrolls through the paper. "Alexia what?"

"Is there more than one there on your papers?" I ask as he continues to flip through the pages.

He gives a snarl as he flips to the last paper. "Look at that. No one on my list. Great for me…" He does a double take and squints at the bottom of the last paper. "Peculiar Alexia, no last name given." He crosses off the name and throws the board on the desk next to him. "Come with me." He doesn't wait as he briskly makes his way across the grounds.

Using my nervous energy, I skip to keep up with his long legs. He doesn't wait for me to catch up, just keeps walking the same brisk pace. We make it across the courtyard and head inside one of the many doors. The people are all making their way towards the center, but the guard brings me down the left hallway and away from the others.

"Aren't we going to the show?"

"Soon. There were special instructions by your name." He opens a door to a room. Hesitating, he waits a moment before pushing me inside. The room itself is bare other than a dress hanging up next to a screen and as we come further into the room behind the screen is a bath sunk into the floor of the room.

"Get yourself ready. You wear that dress and exit out that door." Another door opposite to the one that we entered through. The walls are covered in a deep honey gold wall paper with a swirling black pattern.

Looking at myself in the mirror, I notice how much dirt is smudged on my face. I wipe the back of my hand across my dirty cheek, trying to wipe it away.

A snick of a closing door shuts behind me. I peer around and the male guard is no longer there.

"Well, I guess I will get cleaned up then." I set my pack and my clothes on a dresser in front of the mirror near where we came in. Dipping my toe into the water, it is lukewarm nothing like the sultry heat I felt at the previous place.

I move the screen into place so that it covers me fully if the door opens. I double check both doors and they do not have locks, so I will have to be quick.

I sink into the warmish water and go underneath, scrubbing my face and hair to get the dirt off of me. The rest I can hide with the dress for the most part.

Sinking down, I relax in the water for as long as I can. My fingers cage the ruby and necklace I still wear, hoping to feel warmth spill from it. It still lays cold and dormant. Pushing my feet against the black stone floor, I spring out of the water, flipping my hair back, taking a gulping breath of air. A rustling sound nudges something close by, but I can't tell if it is in the room with me or outside of it. I hurry and scrub through my hair, wanting to be into some clothes soon.

Getting out, I spot a towel behind on this side of the panels. I rush to one and pat myself dry, wrapping it around my quickly cooling body. Going over to the dress, I touch my fingers against the fabric. It is tough and has an itchy feel to it. I grimace in thought and contemplate putting on my previous clothes from before. Looking back over to where I set them, I notice my pack and clothes are not where I left them. Making sure the towel is secure, I move across the small room and look behind the dresser to make sure it didn't fall between the wall and it. Nothing, nowhere.

"Where the hell are my clothes? My stuff!" I screech.

Rushing over to the dress, I quickly throw it on before it all but disappears. I tighten the strings myself, which causes my breasts to perk up even more than usual. I hide the ruby down in my cleavage, only the chain can be seen around my neck. There are flats sitting below where the dress is. The small shoes are black. I put them on before anything else goes missing. I'm glad I keep the necklace with me, otherwise they would have everything of mine.

Going back to the first door I came through; I test the knob and it is locked there are no locks on this side to try. Jiggling the handle, nothing happens. "Great, this is just great."

Throwing myself against the other door, I hope that this one to isn't locked. I'm surprised by how easily it opens and am sent into a cascade of people. Someone pulls the door from my grasp, closing it as the movement of people catches me and keeps me moving forward. Another set of guards stops the line from progressing further than some velvet curtains than some velvet curtains that are draped against the wall. They ask for names and then take them away through the curtains. My fingers play with the neckline of the dress, my fingers eager to play with the necklace in a time of stress.

My eyes catch another man staring at where my fingers dip. I force my hand to stop and put it down at my side. Edging away from him, I switch to another line to get away as far as possible. In a matter of no time, I surge to the front and am at another guard.

This one looks at me and waits. He is patient with me since he knew everyone that is here is meant to be.

"Alexia," I whisper, since he would not speak first.

The guard nods and gives me his arm so he can show me the way. He takes me through the curtains. The dimness of the next room hides things from view. There are hardly any lights and only very dim ones to help people see so they can get to their seats. We pass many people and groups of seating that is around tables. I spy a couple warming each other, not waiting for the show and another group that are having the time of their life laughing and being loud.

My hold on the man's arm tightens as fear kicks in. "What am I doing?" I ask myself. "What do I do about lost personal items?" I ask louder so the man that is guiding me could hear. His arm feels solid under my touch and his physique is thin and tapered.

His eyes slide down to me, letting me know he heard, but he doesn't answer. We turn a corner, coming closer to the stage. We keep going till I'm right in front. This section is divided into privacy booths that have high walls, plush seating, and a clear view to the stage. The guard stops and grabs my shaking hand to help me up the step into the booth area, making sure I settle in before leaving me for the next guest.

Looking around, I can't see much, so I slide to the far left of my seat, trying to look around the walled edges. But all I can see are the booths next to me, which are empty for the moment. The fabric of the couch is velvet and plush, the color is dark gray.

"You made it." A woman with dark hair pokes her head out of a door marked 'stage'. There are a couple of tall, hunky men that have no shirts on that follow her through as she makes her way to me. Gray, glowing eyes meet mine as she walks up to my booth. A small frown emits from her pouty lips.

The well chiseled men stay back in the shadows but are there.

"I did." Unsure of what to say to this person who acted like I'm meant to be here. Her voice sounds familiar.

"Did you bring what I asked?"

Confusion etches itself over my face, unsure of what she is talking about. "What you asked for?" Something in me yearns to give her what she needs.

She gives a light laughter. "Of course, you did sweet little thing. We will get to that later. Until then I will leave you with..." She looks back, her gray piercing eyes no longer holding me entranced. "Thorn, keep our guest company throughout the show." Her gaze comes back to me. "Make sure you pay attention to all parts and let me know how you enjoy it after the show. I'm open to criticism and would like some honest feedback."

"I've never been to any shows before, so I don't know how much I will be able to help you."

"Then this will be a great one and not easily forgotten. All the same, Thorn will make sure you are well taken care of in the experience. Some people enjoy seeing this show with other senses." She breathes in deeply, scenting the air.

She turns on a sharp black booted heel and her short red dress follows her thin form back to the door. The other man with her holds the door open and makes sure she isn't waiting for him.

I sniff the air like she did, wanting to know if I can smell what she had. The place has a sweet smell with undertones of sex. The smell adds to the appeal of what this show offers.

Thorn comes closer, his white blond hair catches in the low light. As he comes closer, his muscles bunch together. He towers over me, making me feel small and feeble. His long black pants are molded to his legs. A bulge already sits in the middle of his pants. My eyes quickly travel down and notice his bare feet on the ground. He stands at the right of the booth; I scoot further in, making room for him. My fingers fidget with the feel of the couch, trying to keep my mind off this behemoth of a man.

"Friend or foe," I murmur before I can bite my tongue.

His skin is very pale compared to the dark shades surrounding us.

"Don't worry, I don't bite." Thorn smiles, his dark eyes hold laughter at my unease. He prowls forward, his hips rolling as he walks. Taking the seat closest to me, he makes sure to pin me to the side of the couch so I can't put distance between us.

The hair on the back of my neck stands on end, the wet ends still damp from my bath earlier. The cold draft along with the heat coming off Thorn sends shivers up and down my back. Music starts and the lights blink on and off.

"What's going on?" I shrink down in my seat.

"The show is about to begin." He leans his arm around me. It splays on a lip on the back of the couch.

His warmth surrounds me, seeping into my skin. After a few more minutes, the lights die all the way out and everyone quiets down, waiting, eager, and expecting. Small sounds of pleasure can be heard around us, but no loud sounds. Everything is in hushed, quiet tones. Music clashes and begins a smooth dance of tantalizing delight.

The stage lights turn on and the curtain parts as the woman with gray eyes takes the center of the stage. Along with a couple of huge and powerful white wolves. Giving a loud, long howl, they race around her and dance in and out of her arms and legs as she dances around the stage. Her short dress showing more of her as she twists and turns in time with the music. Other animals join her and leave in turn showing the audience that she has control of many animals. A djinn ghosts up to the ceiling. She shoves her body through his smoky trailing form, throwing the smoke and controlling where it moves with her hands. Her eyes never dim or lose their power as she continues with the show. A large snake slithers onto the stage in full cobra form with his hood fully engaged and a spear in his hands. His long body where legs would usually be is only a tail and the powerful muscles that move him around the stage, he stands fully up on his tail. No clothes cover him. His dark skin is black, only his underbelly is a beige cream color. Nothing hides the length of his cock that lays flat and down.

"I don't think that is anatomically correct for a snake," I whisper.

Thorn pulls me in closer to the side of him and whispers into my ear, my eyes can't leave the stage. "A strong enough shifter can choose what body parts change and which one's stay more human. This one is in his beast mode. The wolves before were fully shifted to their animal form, being weaker. They do not yet have a beast form." His hand wraps around my shoulder, keeping me tight to his body, purring in my ear.

The other snake dances and plays with the woman on stage. She touches and teases him, making him excited. His soft length rises to attention as they grow closer in each other's arms.

I lean away as much as possible, but he would not let me leave the circle of his body. I continue to watch as another snake saunters onto the stage. This one rattles his tail and hisses as long venom teeth descend. He has a spear in hand and dashes over the stage. Where the other one is all snake other than his penis, this one is more human in form from the waist up along with his already hard cock. My eyes travel up the length of him and come to rest on his face as realization hits me in the chest.

"Blaise," I whisper as I recognize the snake that just appeared on stage.

"You know the star of this show, well, other than the Master?"

"Master? What's her name?" I look at Thorn sitting next to me. Fur ripples over his upper half in white soft fur.

"Pet me first. It's all a part of the experience."

My eyes continue to be mesmerized by the fight the two snakes are going through with the woman dancing around with scarves, weaving them in between to hold and tighten all three of their bonds. The slice of the spears cut through strands of gauze tempting and tantalizing the dance into more motion. Thorn picks my hand up and brings it to rest on his soft chest; the fur covering it well. My fingers dance in the softest fur I have ever felt. They caress and touch him. He purrs in response, letting me know he wants this even more than I do.

"The name." My dry throat cracks as my voice leaves me.

"We are not given one for her. She is simply, Master." His hips gyrate in time with my pets. He wants to meet my fingers before they come down to pet him. He stretches up to keep my fingers lingering where they touch him. My fingers stop moving, not giving him what he wants until I get an answer to what I want.

"She has to have a name for when dealing with people that are not her slaves." He gives a mewling sound like a cat would, begging my fingers to start their pets again.

Waiting a moment, I start to pet him again when he would not talk. His eyes slide shut, opening his mouth. I see sharp teeth descend as I move my hand lower down his abs.

"We are all playthings to the, Master."

Thorn slowly turns into that of a cat as the show goes on. The same for the performers I'm watching. Some animals were animal and others start in human form and turn to their animal counterpart but most of them were in a half state that shows their huge masculine bodies in the best light. At the center of the surrounding scarves that hold both the snakes and the woman. They take turns kissing the woman in the middle. They were all part of a snake sandwich. Each snake twines their tail with one another and she comes down between them. The lights turn on as the curtain falls over the stage, hiding the sexy scene that they had built up to.

"Is that it?" I ask, looking around.

"Oh no, my little pet, there is much more to come. The next part is where things start to get interesting." He pushes my hand down further across his abs, the only thing hard in the soft fur until my hand covers the huge hard bulge that is camping in his pants. The button is undone and must have come undone sometime between the start of the show and now.

Now that my attention isn't distracted by the show, I have to fight my revulsion to him and not snatch my hand away.

"Master says you like pain. You will be pleased with the amount I can cause." He purrs into my ear.

"I think your master has the wrong idea about me."

"Either way, I take on the pricklier part of my animal form. Barbs included." My hand freezes as he pushes his hips into my open palm, holding my wrist there for his own pleasure, rubbing himself against me.

Wanting to run screaming, the music comes back softer this time and the lights dim back down, the curtain rises and the two snakes are with the woman on a bed entwined. They are giving pleasure to the woman in more than one way. Blaise holds the woman in a loving embrace as he pumps into her with his cock, twining his tail around her leg, capturing it. The other snake is twined around the other leg of hers, playing with her breasts and letting her play with him in her palms.

Feeling something tighten on the back of my neck as Thorn lowers his hand, massaging me, making sure my head doesn't move from the display on stage before me. I couldn't look away even if I want to. Watching Blaise do the wicked things that he had only done to me just days before. I know he is a slave to someone, but he never explained what he does exactly while in slavery or what it meant. Both snakes scratch the other when they want a turn with their master. It is rough and bloody and hell of fucking hot for all parties included. They all look to be in complete pleasure, even with the blood spilling.

Thorn moves his pants down, letting his cock spring up. "Careful, don't prick your fingers." He lays my hand back up on his soft fur as he palms himself. My eyes freeze on him as I see little barbs surrounding the base of his penis. His other hand continues to hold the back of my neck, keeping me in place so I cannot run away.

Sounds of moaning and pleasure can be heard from all around us, not just on the stage. I do not want to be in this booth with this cat, so I focus my attention on the stage. My heart crumbles with every stroke. I watch her as she rides Blaise him on the bottom and the other snake coming up behind her as she leans down, letting the other snake penetrate her; she pushes Blaise's head back off the bed that they are swaying on. His eyes look out toward the crowd and at that moment, the house lights flip on.

Thorn wraps me up in his arms and sits me down on his lap, taking care not to prod me. He spreads me across his chest as the light's beam down on me. Blaise stares at me as I stare at him His eyes turn from snake to pitch dark, his adam's apple bobs in front of his master. She kisses his throat, making him continue to look at me. Thorn takes my body freezing as a good thing and hikes up the dress. Feeling my supple legs quiver in fear. I feel another pinch at the back of my neck tighten. Thorn brings a hand around my throat, so I stay in place. The dress is so slow to rise, I almost hope that he is only kidding about doing this to me. My eyes flick to my animal, making everything become sharper and clearer. My mind screams out for Blaise as I search my mind for the pathway to him, needing him. I never had to find my way while such terror consumes me. My body freezes and plays dead, hoping the body beneath it would take the hint, but Thorn continues to roam and touch and prod his way to me.

There, the door is in my mind. I touch it and am shocked by how cold it is; snatching my hand back I blow a warm breath over my frost covered fingers. A red string wraps around the door between us and pulls tightly. I feel that choking feeling once again and a pinch at the nape of my neck. As the snakes and their master finish as one, the string pulls taut and breaks the door in half, severing mine and Blaise's connection. A burst explodes in my mind, causing pain to radiate through my head.

Darkness billows up inside me and screams for release as I retreat into my mind. Though Thorn's hands try to tease pleasure from me, it only feels like knives scraping the inside of my stomach. He whirls me around to face him, wanting to play with me and take our own pleasure like so many others around us. I let him manipulate me into a better position. Moving my hips forward, I brush the dress that is between us on his fur scrubbing at him with the itchy cloth. Hoping it would scrape him raw, as it is doing to me. The lights still shine on our bottom section. I let my head fall back to see what is happening on the stage. The snakes were removed by others and other creatures are brought in, in return. A new game starts anew, but one where she is the master manipulator of all of them.

The cat beneath me purrs as I curl my hands onto his chest in his soft fur. This is the only thing soft about him. Everything else is uncomfortable and something I don't wish to be a part of. My badger eyes notice his head thrown back in pleasure. He relaxes his hold around me as he takes his own pleasure. I stroke my hand against him, going cold inside and out.

My inner darkness begs for me to hurt him as he is harming me. But I knew that would get me nowhere. He is just a pawn in this game of hers, and I don't need another enemy. I'm accumulating too many enemies and not defeating any of them.

Pressing my chest down on top of him, I whisper into his ear. It has gone pointy, with tufts of fur around them. "I need to use the little girl's room before we proceed. Mind telling me where that is?"

"I will show you later." He circles my hips, pressing me down more firmly onto him. I feel the prick of the barbs and fight to not tense.

Nipping at his ear, inflicting paint back to him, I nuzzle him. "I can't hold it. I need to go now."

"The only restroom near here is the one that the warriors use in their downtime. Their show was earlier today. You are my plaything tonight," he pouts.

"Would your master be happy if I did not get to have the proper fun I was intended to tonight, all because you didn't give me the break I needed?" I try to manipulate him the way I need.

Licking the side of his cheek, I tease. "I can make it worth your while." He ignores me, hiking the long dress up more, wanting to play. Taking a breath to not yell at him, I stop his hand before it goes too high. "Thorn."

Giving a huff. "Through that door you saw the Master go through, go there, and hang a right. Once in there, it is the second door on your right." He moves his hips up again. "Don't make me wait too long." Screams of pleasure echo around us. His eyes have gone wide and dark as he picks up my wrist, sniffing there. "I have your scent now and I love a good chase."

"Don't worry, you will not have to come hunt me down." I smile sweetly, swaying my hips as I pick myself up off him. I head down the little ramp. The lights dim back down, focusing on the stage now as things heat up even more. I take care not to fall or trip over anything as I make my way to the door.

The door handle turns in my hand easily. I slide through and close the door quickly, so the light doesn't escape out, ruining the experience for the other people who are actually enjoying the show.

The door opens up to a beige wall; the hall splits both left and right. I follow the black tile down to the right as Thorn stated. Pausing to listen, I hear a rattling and a loud hiss. Thumps and a colossal bang can be heard from the other way, towards where the stage is. Clenching my hands together, I keep walking till I get to the correct door and head in. Peeking in before I walk through the door, there is a large pool that is empty. Going in, I walk around, heading to the room beyond.

Wheezing in and out, I fall to my knees before I can make it to the sink. I grasp at my chest, bending my head down to the cool ground. Barely able to catch my breath, I pound my fist against the cement. The necklace slips out as I hit the floor. Squeezing one fist around the ruby, I cut my palm against the harsh edges. My chest feels tight but so empty all at the same time. Racking sobs cough out of me as my body crumples the rest of the way to the ground. I keep my other hand near my stomach. The ruby continues to dig into my palm, the pain the only thing I could feel at the moment. Yanking on the chain, I pull it forward hard, but it doesn't break. Welcoming the pain, it is better than the quiet darkness that is seeping out. I need to feel something, anything. How is this possible? Our bond just disappeared? I thought we had to reject it or accept it together. I feel frozen and ripped in half, a part of me no longer there. How could someone remove it as easily as she did?

A cold, numb like feeling descends around me as my mind retreats into itself. I don't care if Thorn comes to find me; I don't care if anyone finds me like this. I just don't care.

My mind gives up, and my body will not get with the program. I scrape the red ruby further up my palm towards my wrist, needing more pain to ease the numb state.

"Flower?" A thump and a whisper echo.

I stare straight ahead, not moving. Not willing to acknowledge what is happening or stopping what I'm determined to do.

The top half of my body moves, and half of it is picked up. My eyes stare blankly up at Domini, who is holding me tight. He is wearing a long-sleeved black shirt with holes in it. I barely feel him. My eyes slide to the side, not wanting to latch on to him.

"Flower stop. You must stop." He tries to pry my fingers away from the stone. When he can't get me to let go, he brings my face back to his.

Tears roll down my eyes as I stare up at the worry written on his face. "I can't," I strain to whisper to him.

"This is what she does. She can control ties and break them. That is all your feeling is the break of a bond. It doesn't mean it is still not there." Noticing the blood that comes from my palm and wrist, he works at it again, trying to free the rock from my grasp. His hands slip over my blood, making it hard to get a good grip.

He grips the chain around my neck, hauling me up closer to him. Bringing another hand up to cup the back of my head, he crushes his mouth to mine and bites at my lips, forcing his tongue between my lips. The chain tightens and my hands loosen. Pulling the ruby from my grasp, he swivels it to my back so neither one of us can reach it. He uses it as a collar to force me in place.

Struggling against the changing of emotions, he loosens his hold on my head, calming the intensity of the crushing weight of his mouth. He is barely hovering over my lips, brushing them against mine. His sincere touch calling me back from the dark and cold.

As the pain leaves me, the numb feeling crashes into me. I no longer have the stone to help tide the emotions they begin to build inside me. Fighting to be free, looking for a release. I struggle against Domini's hold. My hands punch out at him, shoving him away. One moment my hands are human and the next they are in the shape of sharp claws, my fingers spread wide for maximum damage.

Anger crawls through me, gaining traction in my numb state. My animal eyes pick up on Domini's bare feet and ragged pants. He isn't dressed to be on stage. Why is he even here? Would he hurt me like Blaise did? Why does everyone I get to know leave or hurt me? He wouldn't know, he wouldn't understand. None of them would. It would be better if it would all just stop. Shade doesn't even want to be connected with me, and he is a spell specifically made for me. What help is there for me if I couldn't even keep anyone around? Blaise never wanted to be with me in the first place, and he especially didn't want to be with the both of us. What is wrong with me? Why couldn't I just be normal or want one person? Why couldn't I be attracted to a normal person? Not some snake that isn't even supposed to have a soul mate in the first place. Why me? What did I do to deserve this?

My thoughts collide with each other, giving the pain in my head more energy to live off. They make me doubt everything I have ever done or been a part of. Picking small things apart in my mind zeroing in on how it is all my fault every part of this journey, every part of my life. It is all done by me.

Screaming out, I grip my head as the rage burns bright.

Domini raises his hands, trying to calm and cage me.

"All you want is this!" I yell as I swing my neck so the ruby swings back around to my front. I get my legs under me, into a crouch in front of him.

Gripping the red ruby back in my hand, I hold it out to him. "Go on, take it."

He shakes his head, standing up and backing away. "No, not like this."

"Trill, it's time to come out and play. We are going to make this castle burn!" Fire erupts around me, licking my hands and ankles. Walking closer to Domini, I hold the ruby out, going for his chest with claws and fire.

He bats my hands away, shying away from the stone. Coming in closer, he dodges my hands. Holding onto me. His clothes burn away as the flames take light on him.

I try to scramble out of his hold, but he holds me close, not caring that the flames grow higher and higher. I open my mouth in a scream as the heat radiates out of me. Picking me up, he races to the pool and dives into the center with me in tow.

I shut my mouth, but don't have any time to take a breath. The flames douse quickly. Trill hides back under my skin where she is safe.

I hope she is okay and isn't hurt by the cool water. I still clasp the jewel in my hand and force my elbow down between us, pushing the gem against his skin. Most of his shirt is now gone, burned away by the fire. Blood continues to run from my palms, turning the water a pinkish red hue.

A pulse emits twice and then releases from the jewel, diving into Domini. A high-pitched screech whizzes through the pool and more blood flows into the water with me.

My arms reach up above me, scrabbling for air. My mind races. Bubbles cover my vision and rolls of water pulse against us. His hands release me.

I claw my way back up to the surface. The pool is so deep and we still haven't reached the bottom. I paddle my way to the top and reach the air, gulping it in my lungs. The waves pulse and swish back and forth, causing my stomach to roll. Water splashes about the room and a magic pulse hits; causing the lights to flicker out.

Kicking to keep my head above the rolling waves, I stay in the center, catching my breath. Unsure of what to do here in the dark. My hands hurt and I'm so tired. I kick to the side, but something slides between me and the side of the pool. I feel hard scales push me away from the ledge as cold, slimy hands hold my legs in place.

Anger quickly turns to fear, and the dress swirls around me, dragging me down. It is heavy with the water soaking it through; it carries me down my arms alone can't keep me afloat. His hands also guide me down. I take a deep breath before my head submerges. The hands let go, but something still holds me there; I open my eyes, but the water is dark red, and I can't see anything clearly. Something swims in circles around me and razor-sharp points flip past. The current sloshes me back and forth with the power of this thing's movement. A dark shadow comes closer and looms over me. Sharp talons emerge from his hands and sharp spikes at a tail that flips through the water. The darkness and water hide him well with no lights to see with. My animal eyes only help me see his shape. He grips me and pulls me firm against him, the top of him still feeling like the Domini I know.

"Are you with me?" His voice rings out under the water in a song like voice.

Nodding is all I can do since I'm not a siren and can't talk under the water. My anger halts and though fear tingles through my body, I know this is ultimately Domini. Who I feel safe with every other time.

"When we come to the surface, I want you to put your palms against mine and breath, look me in the eye and hold my gaze."

The darkness caresses me with doubts once again, but I wait till Domini moves us back up into the air. Once I break the water, I take a breath and keep myself facing him, struggling to raise my hands when he still has my legs trapped. I dip down. He wraps his tail around my legs, pushing me up and his palms capture mine.

My eyes shy away from his, not wanting him to see this part of me, not wanting him to see the monster within. I already lost one. Do I want to tempt fate and lose another this night? Holding my palms out to him, I place them against his scaled hands.

"Flower? Look at me." His voice holds a hint of melody but doesn't call me to him as he has in the past.

"I can't," I all but choke out.

"Do you fear the monster you will see?" he asks softly.

I shake my head vigorously; my eyes raise to his. "I fear you will not like the monster you see before you."

"I've faced many monsters in my time, and you are not one of them." His hand slides down my wrist and moves the hair that is in my face gently behind my ear. "Do not hide from me, Flower. Let out whatever is hurting you." He draws me closer, his other hand wraps around my waist.

I gasp for breath, not able to get enough into my lungs. "Every time I think of it..." Tears flow down my face. Domini's eyes continue staring at me, waiting for me to find the words. "He was up there with her," I bite out the ugly feeling slithering through my chest. "How did you know I was here?"

"I could sense my siren half close by. I followed it to you. Here."

My arms finally drop and catch in the dress that floats around me, my fingers snag in the cloth getting caught. It drags me down into the water. "I want my own clothes; I don't even know why I came here."

"Weren't you headed this way last we spoke?"

"Yes, but I wasn't supposed to be here tonight. I left Natasha, Zeek, and Jazmin back in the woods. We weren't supposed to be here until tomorrow. Something called me to this place, but I don't remember what it was." Shaking my head, I try to pull myself to the side of the pool.

Domini holds me firm in his grasp, not letting me dip any further. "It's what she does, especially to those who have an animal to call. She makes you do what she wants. She can unravel a tie if you have it. That is why they call her The Beast Master. She collects others that are not animals such as me, but we usually are for other things and not for the show you saw tonight."

"What does she need you for?"

"I fight. I'm a warrior." The water sloshes and is the only sound that echoes around us. "She has many enemies and many more beasts that need to be kept in line. I'm either fighting her own animals or those that try to come up against her. Some fights are just for show, kind of like the performance that you saw of the snake."

"Will she know that you have your siren side back with you?" I ask.

"I will not allow her to find out. I will stay for a time, but will focus on finding a way out. After I take care of some things to make it less likely for her to follow. You could always come with."

"Where?"

"Anywhere, I could show you my world or you could go wherever you want. It doesn't have to be this world."

My back hits the side of the pool. His body is close to mine, holding me there. A soft light comes from the pool. "That sounds nice. What are you doing?"

"Giving us light since you smashed all the lights in here." He chuckles. His skin is smooth as I brush my hand down his arm. Pulling my fingers back up, they catch on the scales. His blond hair stands out against his dark tan scales. His eyes are piercing blue, but more of an oval than a round pupil. He pulls away from me to swim around in the pool. It feels a lot smaller with him in here with his siren form. There are jagged fins scattered down his spine flowing down the back of his tail. As he flexes, the spines stiffen and retract down. Sharp dagger like prongs protrude from the tips of the tail, waiting to slice at something that gets too close.

He leans back and just floats there in the water. "Have you missed it?" I ask.

"If you couldn't breathe, would you miss air?"

"Good point."

"Sorry." He stretches his body and tail; I curl up into a ball in the corner to give him plenty of room. "It has been so long, yes, I miss it. It is so much a part of me that without it, I feel lost and mad."

A loud crash echoes outside the room. "What is happening?"

"Us warriors were called to deal with Blaise. He went rabid after... I felt the pull of my siren soul and came to investigate. You only knocked the power out in here." We both see the small light still coming through under the door. "Otherwise, people would have come in here to check on things."

"What do you mean, went rabid?" I ask.

"Most shifters are not the same if their tie with another is destroyed. Even if they choose to not keep together willingly, things are tense. Rabid means an animal shifter has chosen to live as their animal would. They don't want to bring out their human form or they want to forget their human counterpart. Most shifters that go rabid get put down, eventually."

"Blaise didn't even want a mate." Shaking my head, clearing the water that is trickling down my face.

"He may not have wanted one at first, but it is what he needed and a part of him craved to have you." Domini turns sharply in the water and makes his way over to me. The fins and tail grow smaller, as if constricting around him.

"Why, other than the outburst before you found me, am I not acting like that? I feel emptier than before, but it isn't so severe that I lose myself, I think."

"One could argue if I did not find you in time, you could have lost yourself as well. But you do not rely so heavily on your animal as others do. You only just met her, did you not?"

"But if you hadn't come in here..." My eyes swivel over to the door, reliving what happened moments ago.

Domini crowds around me. His scales and fins are nowhere to be seen, but the glow continues. He slides his hand over my cheek and tilts my head back to him. His thumb is on my lips. He brushes them with the pad of his thumb. "Your animal may have taken over. Since I was here and you felt comfortable enough to let me in, she relaxed. Don't get me wrong, what is between you and Blaise, I will never be able to touch that, but we have our own special bond, of that I'm sure."

Relaxing into his hand. "I'm glad you are here."

"I'm as well."

Our eyes lock onto one another, our bodies drawing closer. His heat envelopes me. His chest is broad and strong; my fingers beg to inch their way up his lean stomach.

"Flower..."

Three loud knocks echo around the room. We both jump and stare at the closed door.

"Alexia, are you decent? You missed the best part of the show. Master would like to have a meeting with you. Have you eaten?" Thorn asks through the door, his voice muffled.

My mouth opens, but no words follow. Domini's light winks out. "Flower, are you listening?" he whispers. His hand is still on my chin, so I nod to let him know I'm. "This next part is crucial if we meet outside of here pretend we have never met. I will be asked to deal with the snake, so I will check on him once you go with Thorn."

"Alexia?" Thorn's voice comes out rougher.

"I can't do this," I barely whisper out.

"Yes, you can." He grips the back of my neck, pulling my body into his. The dress blocks me from his delectable body. "Tell him you will be right out."

My mouth opens, but no words come out as my eyes flick to the door.

"Alexia, are you all right? I'm going to come in." The doorknob turns.

Domini's hand runs up my side, tickling me. "Now!" He urges quietly into my ear.

I laugh out, not being able to stop what his hand is doing to me. "Thorn! Don't worry, I will be out in a moment. If you rush me, I will not be able to play."

The doorknob clicks back. "Perhaps after seeing the Master, we will still get to play, but she must come first."

"Of course, I will be out soon. Go sit back down and I will be right there."

"I will wait at the door." Silence fills the space. "Oh, and Alexia?"

"Yes?"

"The Master said if you try to leave that I can use any and all force needed to deal with you. That means I get to decide how I see fit. I like to work up an appetite before devouring a meal, just so you know." He chuckles as he moves down the hallway. His laugh echoes back to us.

"That is, one messed up kitty," I say quietly, not wanting him to hear me even though he has moved away from the door.

"We only have a moment, so we need to make use of it. You will exit this room and go with Thorn to meet the Master."

"Looking like this?" Picking at the wet clothing glued to me. The darkness almost squeezes around me as I huff out, trying to calm my shaking body.

He calls the green light back up so we can see. He moves back and swims to the stairs, exiting the pool. "I command water. Did you forget?"

I stare at his backside as he swims away from me. "How could I?" I all but grin, making my way behind him.

We both exit the pool of water. Him with no clothing on and me with the miserable dress. "I'm going to pull the water from your dress and hair, so it doesn't look as if you were trying to drown yourself." He bends down and gathers the forgotten necklace. He holds it out to me so that I can slip it on.

"Why do you think your master wants to see me? She had a special viewing seat for me ready. What more could she want from me? Was I supposed to bring something for her?" I wait till he places the chain around my neck and then back up. The water lifts from my skin and dress, racing back to the pool.

"Most likely about Blaise. Why do think you were supposed to bring her something?"

Shaking my head, I bring my eyes back up to his. "What?"

"Did she ask you to bring her something?"

Thinking back, I try to remember. "I don't think so."

"Think carefully. She is called The Beast Master for a reason she can get inside your head. Also make sure you don't lie to her or any shifter. They will be able to smell a lie on you. We can help throw them off by enticing Thorn and making it seem as if you want him, but make sure you stay as close to the truth as possible."

"I will need every advantage I can take." I latch onto his hand, wanting to prolong our time together.

"Flower?"

"Hmm?"

"Did she ask you to bring her something?" He emphasizes.

"Didn't I answer you?" I look around, not understanding why this is so important. "I said I don't think so."

"You're not sure?"

"She did say when I first met her today if I brought something, but then she said of course I did. But I just had the dress and my necklaces on me, so she must have been mistaken."

"Or she could see that you clearly brought it." He stares at the necklace sitting around my throat. "Flower, I'm going to pour a tiny speck of myself into the heart jewel."

"No! You can't." I step away. "I will not keep you from your siren soul."

He holds his hand up. "Don't worry. It will only hold a tiny bit of my power so it can fool her into thinking you still hold my soul inside."

"Won't she just take it from me and be done with it?"

"Do not underestimate her. She plays many games. I do not even pretend to understand her reasons for what she does." He places his palm over the red heart ruby, his hand comfortable.

My heart races as he pushes against me. "Domini?"

His lips rush to reach mine as he backs me up against the wall. My arms raise up around his neck, hugging him close. Reaching for more of him as they search his body, hugging him to me. Our tongues dance together, my leg inches around his. He pulls my leg up, trying to get it up his waist, but without his other hand to help with my other leg; it keeps sliding down, bringing our bodies deliciously close.

A vibration pushes against my chest where the jewel lays.

Our lips part as he pours more of his power into the jewel. He bumps into me. "Yes?" He whispers out as he leans his forehead against mine.

"Never mind, you read my mind." I give a breathless laugh.

"Did I?" He gives a chuckle; and let's go of my leg to let it slide down his.

His legs are strong and solid against mine. I rake my nails lightly down his chest, feeling him solidly in person. "You are real."

A shiver runs through him. "I am." He smiles as he stops my wondering hands. "You have to go, or Thorn will come back in here to see what is keeping you."

"Let him," I dare.

"Disobey me again Flower, and you will not like who you meet next."

I pout, but nod my head in acceptance.

"If you need me, we can still communicate through the jewel if needed. Make sure it is touching your skin and think of me," he whispers letting his hands fall back to his side.

My fingers curl around the warm jewel and I feel him still there, not as strong as before, but still there. I nod to him and walk over to the door, not wanting to put this off any longer.

"Flower, you will need all your wits about you for her. Be careful in how you play this. Everything here is a game for somebody. I don't know how I will be able to help."

My smile fades and my eyes darken. "Let the games begin." I open the door and glide through it. If everyone here has an agenda, is Domini any different? How can one woman be in control of so many people and have them wrapped around her finger? Giant butterfly wings flutter through my stomach as I walk down the hallway towards Thorn, who is waiting to take me to my doom.

# Chapter 7

I FOLLOW THORN DOWN a bunch of hallways as they twist and turn into themselves. I quickly lose track of which way I'm going and have no idea how to get out. Sticking close, my short legs struggle to move fast enough to keep up with his long stride.

Thorn takes in a deep breath as we make another turn. "Something smells delectable. Good enough to eat." His tongue peeks out, licking his canine.

My eyes slide to the left, peering up at him. "Are we almost there?" I try to give a coy smile, hoping to entice him. Nervous energy runs through me, begging me to run in the opposite direction. If I knew Thorn wouldn't catch me, I would already be gone from this place.

"She wanted to meet you in her sanctuary," he states, as if that would answer all my questions.

We continue down some more stairs that end with a door; it is large and ornate. Silver metal entwines into the wood. Three large swords cross in front of each other on the door, barring our entrance. Thorn strains as he pushes it open. He holds it open for me as I walk through. The room is large and is the center of many corridors that connect to it. Four of the eight paths have gates and are barred from us. There is no way forward. Only one path is lit. Thorn takes my hand as he lets the door fall silently close, ushering me down the path that is lit.

"This way." He pulls my hand close to his face, nuzzling it and smelling my hand.

Struggling to keep up with his stride and the awkward position, I stumble against him. "Thorn, you silly kitty." I wiggle my fingers at his nose, wanting to boop it, yet shooing him away at the same time.

He purrs loudly as he rubs against the arm; he holds captive. "You are nice to Thorn. I could get used to this. Perhaps you would not scream as others have." He turns his wicked eyes towards me.

I smile to cover up the fear that zings up the back of my spine. A part of me dies as I continue. "I might even like it." I give a dangerous wink. Whatever my future holds, I knew for sure it would not be with Thorn. Something in him is twisted and not something I can fix.

Thorn calls out as we walk into an opulent room. There are doors lining the walls, but sheer cloth hangs from the center, a few are tapered to the wall hiding the doors. "We are here, Master. We have made it."

"What took so long? Did the little critter run of fright?" The woman that had been up on stage now sits in a large chair off to the side as others stand or lie around her. Her long legs are free, but two large cats lay next to her, their eyes and ears alert, ready to pounce. She has boots on now, the black leather climbs up her legs and stops right before her knees. Another short skin tight dress replaces the one she had worn on stage.

"She did not, no," he whines as if sad he didn't get to chase me. "She just had to use the little girl's room after seeing you with the snake men." He pulls me along as he makes his way closer to his master.

Holding back from him, I dig my heels in, hoping not to grow too close. Whatever she does to these people, I do not want to be a part of it.

"How did you like the show, little badger?" She coo's as she leans forward.

Biting at my lip, I worry I may say something wrong. "I have never seen a show quite like that."

"I bet you haven't."

"Is there a name I can call you by?" I ask, raising my head more, wanting to feel more on even ground with her.

"You can call me, Master," her soft voice flitters in one of my ears, calling to me. She stands up, her gray cold eyes meet mine as she walks to me. "All my pets do." She motions to the men and women that have gathered around her.

"But I'm not your pet, and you are not my master. So again, I ask, what can I call you?"

She glares at me as she purses her lips in thought. "A pet that isn't housebroken yet. How rude." Her eyes cut to Thorn, her boots make a sharp sound as she walks, when her heel hits the cement floor. She turns on her foot as she passes by and circles around behind Thorn and I. "Your part is done for now. Go fetch the warrior."

A loud thud and bang echoes behind a door where two wolves are sitting at the ready. "The snake has not calmed down yet?"

She stops directly behind Thorn, her height matching his. They were both tall. Though she is slimmer than him, she still feels like she is standing over him, waiting for him to cower. She crowds behind him being silent. "The warrior?" Her calm demeanor is deadly.

"Yes, Master." He looks at me a second before dropping my hand and walking back the way we came.

"If you won't tell me your name, why did you want to have a meeting with me?" I move away, looking up at the cloth draped from the hook hanging in the middle. Checking out the room, trying to keep away from her and out of reach.

"You have something that is mine."

"What is that?" I toy, keeping an eye on the animals and people around the room. Most were in a half and half form. There were some that were full animal though.

"The snake he is mine, and you were distracting him from doing what he does best."

"I did not have him; he was not with me." A lion opens its mouth wide at me, showing me their very pointy teeth. I pause and turn back to their master.

She towers over me; I didn't even hear her come up behind me. "You know very well how you had a hold of him." She smirks as she looks down at the necklace. "Two birds, one stone." Another loud screech echoes from a distance. "Doesn't matter anymore, I guess, since the binding is broken. It's too bad a half rat like you cannot feel what they have lost. You do not belong here. You do not deserve him."

"I'm very aware of that."

Snatching my hand, she grips it in hers, staring at the palm and wrist. She gives a cruel smile. "So, it affected you. Good."

Ripping my arm away from her, I hide both of my hands from her. "I may be a lot of things, but I'm not heartless. You do not know what I have been through or how I feel about certain things."

A look of shock runs through her. She hides it with a coy smile. "Would you like me to help you?" Her gray gaze meets mine as they soften and pull me in. "I can make all of this seem like a dream. All you have to do is give me what I want."

"Give you what you want? What could I possibly have?" Her voice is hypnotic. My eyes flutter, having a hard time staying open. My body sways to her, shaking my head. I try to dislodge her voice. Wasn't I trying to stay away from her?

"Join my menagerie and work for me. All will then be forgiven. You just need to say that I'm your master and a simple blood ceremony to finish it." She gives a wink.

My hand wraps around the ruby red heart, jiggling it on the chain in worry. The flicker of her eye catches me off guard as a hum flows into me.

"Interesting. So that is where you put it," she purrs. Her gray eyes glow as she moves closer to me.

"What are you talking about?" My fingers let go of the chain, letting it lie on top of the dress.

She taps at the ruby heart; it thuds into her chest with each tap. "Nothing important." She meets my eyes and grips my chin, forcing me to keep looking at her. "You can keep it for now." Her eyes turn liquid silver as an eerie pulse pulls me in. "Prance about him and show him what he can't have. You will not give it to him, though."

"I will not give it to him," I repeat. My mind fogs over, confusing me of where I was in this conversation. Were we talking of Blaise? Sharp claws scratch at the back of my forehead. Rubbing my hand over my forehead, I break our eye contact. "What did you say?"

"I said you should join me." She gives a wicked smile.

"Sorry I'm taken," I say.

"Excuse me?"

Dancing to the swaying song in my head, I pass around her easily. A few of the animals rise from their lounging and are at the ready.

One girl that is lounging by a wolf gets up. "I don't think she is all there. Something has to be wrong with her. Are you sure she didn't break from the bond? She could be rabid just like him."

"No matter, no one other than us knows she is here. We will make her go away without a problem." She flicks her hand away. "There you are, my warrior." Her eyes watch Domini very carefully.

Standing in all his glory next to Thorn is Domini, he is clothed in jeans and a black fitted shirt. His eyes ignore me as he walks in, only having eyes for her.

"Master, how may I be of service?"

"We have a bit of a problem with the snake getting out of control. He could be hungry. We should give him a proper meal. It has been a while since his last feeding."

Her eyes roam over Thorn as she nods and points her head and hand in my direction. Thorn slides up behind me, keeping me close.

"The snakes are cold and temperamental."

"Yes, but I don't think his tantrum is going to just go away until a problem is dealt with. Thorn, bring her over here." She snaps her fingers as her heels hit the ground. She makes her way over to where the thrashing noises were coming from.

"Is he restrained?" Domini asks.

"No, I need you to go in there and restrain him for the time being."

"The way he is going, the restraints won't matter. He will be out of them within an hour."

"Good. That will be just enough time for this little badger to think things over or face the consequences of her actions, whatever they may be. We will pick up the pieces after and see what we are working with. Then Thorn can have what remains if there are remains."

Domini nods in acceptance. The door opens, it leads to stairs that spiral down below. It is dark and cold.

Thorn whispers to me as we watch Domini disappear. "Down at the bottom is a large room with bars on one side and cold stone on the other three. So far, the snake stays in the cage, but that will not even hold him when he is at his worst. They say a snake will wrap around its prey before it eats them to make sure they have enough room for you in their stomach." Patting my shoulder. "Do try your best to live, I would like to have my fun with you before you expire."

Giving a shudder, I walk forward as Thorn crowds behind me, making sure I walk down the stairs. I hear a clang below echo up to us. My feet move slow not wanting to go down there. The sounds echo around us and are horrible as fist meets flesh. Growls and snaps can be heard along with grunts. A soft jingle toys with my ear.

"Those will be the chains. Do you like chains?" Thorn asks as he holds my hand, petting it absentmindedly.

As we walk down to the dungeon, it grows colder the deeper we go. The fighting and yells get louder the closer we get. "Someone will come looking for me," I say, just above a whisper.

"Who would come looking for you, little badger?" The Beast Master cajoles behind me as she follows us down, the sharpness of her heel hitting the stone with each step. "No one knew of you when you came here. You don't even really exist."

"Flit…"

"Doesn't even know or care about you at all. You are some long-lost thing that may or may not be related to him. What does it matter? He is the vilest and most hated person on the dark side; he doesn't need you. Knowing him, he would sell out his own sons if they were both still alive. He will be glad that I took care of this problem before he had to."

Sell out his sons? They aren't alive? With my mother, Sera being alive and having a brother, I never thought that Ivan, my father, wouldn't be alive as well.

Trying to swallow it, catches in the back of my throat. She could be right for all I know. I don't know Flit and only have the journal to go off of. When did he write that entry? It could have been many years and he may have changed since. Clearing my throat, I keep my head straight and holding on to Thorn's hand, trying not to show how much this woman unnerves me.

The stairs continue to circle around for many turns, making my stomach uneasy. A part of me wants to run in fear, but another bigger part of me is frozen and only continues forward because of Thorn. No one is going to save me this time. I couldn't even trust that Blaise or Domini would help at this point. The only thing I can rely on is Trill, who I still hold inside me, but how can she help me? We won't have enough power to burn everyone here to a crisp. My badger form, if I can call upon her, wouldn't be better. I still don't know how to fight properly in that form, let alone the half and half form.

Grunts and signs of struggle can be heard as we make it down the stairs. I stare straight ahead, trying to find my balance, knowing I would not have Thorn to lean on soon.

"Put her in there," she snaps a demand. Her voice reverberates around the small enclosure.

Blaise strains against the metal chains, Domini stands far enough away so Blaise can't reach him, gripping the chains tightly. His forearms bulge from the strain.

Thorn goes to the bars. They look like a jail cell. I wonder if that is what each door up above leads to. He pulls it open easily and pushes me into the cell with Blaise. The room is a rectangle in shape. Sliding to the far side, I try to stay furthest from Blaise that I can. You could probably fit four people length wise and one and a half wide. There is plenty of room for the snake shifter to move, but not so much room for me to get away.

"It looks like storms may be gathering." I laugh to myself.

"The weather will not save you here, little badger," Beatrice says from the steps, not coming down into the room fully. "Unless, of course, you have changed your mind and would like to be a part of my collection."

Domini struggles to lock the chains down into the cement to hold the snake in place. His eyes flicker to mine, giving a look of worry. Blaise is still in his half and half form. In a blink of an eye, he shrinks down into a full snake form. Eyeing the door, Thorn stands in the middle of it. My heartbeat is strong and thumps wildly in my chest.

"Don't fret yet, my dear. The chains shrink and expand with his shape."

My wild eyes snap to The Beast Master, then back to the snake, who switches back to his half and half form. Domini takes his time with more chains and locks. Once done, he walks back to his master all without giving me another look.

"I would worry more about what happens to you when he gets out of those chains." She all but laughs as they walk back up the stairs.

A few lights stay on where we are, but the stairs turn dark as the door up top closes with their departure. Blaise continues to bite and fight against the chains. His eyes zero in on me. Anger radiates around him. Looking around, there is just stone and the chill of the underground that answers us. There is no exit, not even a hint of freedom in this dark and unfriendly place.

Crossing my arms, I hug myself for warmth. Nothing about him reminds me of the man I once knew. His hissing is ragged and the metal collar around his neck chokes him as he exerts pressure. I can feel the hatred coming from his eyes as he glares at me.

"I didn't ask for this. I didn't reject you." My voice booms in the small space, echoing off the walls. His tongue flicks out in answer, but the straining doesn't let up as he tries to escape.

He hisses at me, showing me his fangs. His surrounding hood is wide and erect. Scars crisscross over his chest and shoulders. Blood drips down his wrists and anywhere the metal meets his skin. Coming forward tentatively, I reach my hand out to calm him. Rage pours around him as he ramps up and moves around in a frenzy, trying to release himself. His tail thrashes back and forth.

Side stepping, I cross to the side of him on the same wall, but down a little way where he can't fully touch me. Putting my back to the wall, I hunker down into a crouch. Keeping my sight on him, I wait to make sure I don't have to bolt away quickly. After fifteen minutes, my legs grow tired of the strain. I stretch them out and sit down on the cold floor. The cement is dry and not too gritty feeling. There is a drain in the middle of the floor.

"Easy clean up, at least," I say sarcastically.

The fear in me fizzles out as I grow tired. With the amount of days it took to get through the Abyss and always having to be ready for an attack at any moment, things have taken its toll. I lay my head against the wall as I sit there, resting my eyes.

"Do you mind if I rest before you kill me? I have been going all day, and the night is finally hitting me."

He growls and snaps quiet as his movements grow slower. My eyes peek open, but he just continues to watch me. I close my eyes once again, relaxing my mind and body. I knew he could talk even in this beast form, but the human mind might be too fractured and gone. Silence surrounds us as I wait for him to calm down. I move closer by a few inches. If I reach out my right arm, I could touch the scales on his torso.

He tests the strength of the chain once again, but not as harsh this time it is just a test, and then pauses, holding his breath. The silence again is deafening. My mouth moves on its own, accord not being able to stand the silence. "I miss our link," I whisper out. "Something in me feels missing. No matter what has happened with Domini, I enjoyed the bond I had with you."

He thrashes about, only responding in anger.

"So that is what you do for her? Have sex with her and other people? Why couldn't you tell me all of this? Why did I have to find out this way?" A small sob escapes me.

The chains strain to hold him as he rattles them. His tail kick at the wall hitting against it. Dust falls from the bricks but it holds, for now.

My eyes flutter as his tail moves swiftly over the floor. Looking up at him, he looks away towards the door of the cage. My gaze falls to the floor. "Fine, if you won't talk about that. I know we hadn't decided yet on if we wanted to strengthen the bond or disband it. But I never thought that choice could be taken away from both of us. How did she do this?"

"It can't be gotten rid of, not really. Our bond will go back to the state it was in before we joined," he says in a scratchy voice. His tail slithers over the floor and wraps around my waist. "We are mates. No amount of magic or manipulation can change that. It is just back to normal before we joined together."

My eyes raise to his in surprise. "Then why... Why are you like this?"

"My animal took over; we can't feel you and we know what pain we have caused you. Rage took over. I had to get to you, needed to reach you. Beg you to take us... back." His claws work on the chains and the lock at his neck again. His voice is gruff as his animal slips through. "I didn't think they would bring you here to me. I didn't think she would do this. Seeing you with Thorn, after what we had with Domini... I couldn't listen or see reason."

"They thought you went mad and wouldn't realize who you were attacking, even if it was me." I bring my hand up and caress the scales along his tail.

Silence encompasses us once again as I pet him more to comfort myself than him.

"I will always know it is you. Why did you not run away while you could? Domini could have made sure that you were safe and away from here?" He curls his tail around me, hugging me to him.

"I'm not leaving either of you behind with her. Domini made sure I knew my options. I needed to know and see for myself if you no longer want this. Thorn was an added problem to the mix he would have given chase, so I'm not sure how Domini could have gotten me away."

"I could never say I don't want to be with you." He pulls on the chains, struggling to get free. "Thorn," he growls.

"You kind of did say that."

"When…" He thinks back to our time together, shaking his head. His serpent eyes turn back to human, but his dominant form remains more snake like.

"You would throw me out of your mind when you were in this form. You did not want to show me your darker, colder side. Or if you were with others, you would block me from it. You even stated you never thought you would have a soul mate."

"I don't want you to know this side of me, the side that is with her. Or the others, I wanted to be perfect for you. Be what you deserve. Be a mate you could be proud of." Parts of him slowly change back to human. His chest and face turn back to, man, only his tail remains and his fingers that are tipped with long nails.

"Back when we first met, I didn't even know you. My animal responded to yours. Do you think she would have allowed that if she didn't think you were worthy? I didn't ask for you to change and only wanted to know more to better understand. I didn't judge you, wouldn't have dreamed of it because I didn't want you to judge me for my lack of a past. Lack of anything, really."

"Domini has been good for you." He gives a sad smile as he hangs his head. "More so than I have."

"He has been good for the both of us. I don't know if we would have talked otherwise. He balances us. We have both been hurt. That will take time and patience to heal."

"You still want to be with me?" He gives a hopeful look; his hands release the chains.

"Do you know of a mated pair that has allowed another in? Will it work for us?"

"I have never even heard of a snake charmer getting a mate, so this is all unfamiliar territory." He tightens his tail around me, drawing me closer to him. Scooping me up and facing me towards him. "As long as he treats you decent, I don't mind him being our third."

I nod my head, not knowing what else to say.

His coils do not restrain my arms. He twirls me around as more coils loop around me. My feet leave the ground. I am eye level with him. "Until we have a plan for dealing with getting the siren and me out of here, we should not remain close to one another."

"Why not?"

"If we join like before, the mating will take hold again. I don't think there is any part of me that could stand waiting for you to decide if you want to bond with me for fear of being ripped away again. It is hard enough with it just being like this." He winces like he is in pain, clawing at the chain. He claws and scratches at the lock and metal around his throat, slicing himself. "When you are close like this, I can think through things easier and keep my animal at bay. I don't even want to think about you not being here. It will not be good." He uncoils his tail from me, lowering me onto my feet.

"Are you in actual pain from it?"

"Nothing I haven't dealt with before," he says carelessly. "You have changed from the first time we met." He gives a wolfish smile.

"How so I don't feel like I have changed at all? I'm just more lost in this world."

"Your actions were more animalistic, or you let your shadow protector guard you. You don't have a shadow protector anymore, so you are having to handle things on your own. Your animal and you are starting to listen and come to an understanding. You have found your voice. You're not settling for what life throws at you anymore." He gives a glancing smile.

"I grew tired of things happening to me and not having a say. Others treating me fragile when I need answers." My eyes zero in on him. Waiving him away with my hand, "Don't you think I'm the best person to understand what I need and how I feel about things? I need others to respect my barriers and my feelings on the matter."

"I'm sorry I should have been a better mate and helped you through that process. My plan after our joining, since I was called back. My hope was that the distance would weaken our tie and you could forget about me. I thought it could be something we could ignore." He hangs his head in defeat.

"What did you know from that time about me? Did you know who I was?" I ask.

"I still barely know who you are... Other than what you or Domini have told me. He has started to spend time with me when he can. I was meant to only monitor you when things progressed as they did. I asked to be recalled. Which I stopped by to give my report to your uncle, and he used that against the both of us, as you know."

"Yea, he tricked me into saving you. You were gone by that time, or he said you were."

"Beatrice took me after that... I had another appointment to keep." His voice thick with emotion.

"Why did The Beast Bitch call me here?" I ask before losing him to the anger again.

"Beast bitch? You mean the Master? She only became interested when you distracted me or tried to protect me from her wrath. She could not control me as easily as she had in the past. She didn't like that another had more pull than she does."

"Do you know her true name?"

"No, she hides it, says names have power."

"Talking to you like this almost feels nice." A cold draft blows up the back of the dress, causing me to shiver. "If we weren't locked up here, you know freezing, it could count as normal for us."

"I wouldn't know what that is like."

"How long have you been with her?"

"Too long. Much longer than your siren."

"What kind of debt do you have with her? She trapped Domini and said he must pay off a debt before he can get his siren form back. What does she have on you?" Wrapping my arms around my body, I huddle around myself to keep warm.

"Let's just say I will be here for a good long while," he snaps. His hands go back to struggling with the collar. He elongates one of his nails and flicks it into the lock, trying to unlock the padlock.

"It's not like you or I have anywhere to be. Might as well talk. Would you rather I found out some other way?"

"I'd rather you not find out at all," he growls, his anger rising.

Rolling my eyes, I turn my back to him and walk to the other side of the cage, stretching my legs and trying not to listen to his struggles. "Come on, it can't be that bad."

"It is that bad. I'm a traitor to my own kind." He gives a hiss in warning. "Stop!"

"How so?" I turn abruptly, eager to know why he is here. "Stop what?"

There is terror in his eyes. He shakes his head; his eyes lock on to me.

"A snake charmer can charm other shifters, and especially other snake shifters. That is why she hunted us, all of us. With her powers and snake charmers in her back pocket, she could do no wrong."

"Were the other snakes on stage charmers as well?"

"No, those were just shifters. She only has one snake charmer and can only ever have one. That was the deal we made. She will not hunt us all down if I work for her and keep funds and people padded in her pockets. If I'm ever to leave, the next one to stand in is one of my siblings and I would not wish this on my worst enemy, let alone my family." The chain and lock crumble from his neck in his scramble. Wisps of something comes off his nails as if it is acid eating through the metal.

"Well, we can think of something else. You can't stay here with her."

"I will not burden my family." His voice booms as he raises higher, standing fully up on his tail, pushing him across the floor towards me. His face contorts in rage. The chains snap at his wrists as he lunges.

"I wouldn't ask that of you," my voice waivers. My back hits the wall as I again try to get the further from him. He crosses the floor in a matter of seconds and pins me to the wall. "Your eyes have gone snake again." I try to point out.

"You do this to me! Stop moving away," he snaps. "I crave you and yet you poke at sore spots in my life that should be kept in the dark." He stares down at me; his arms extend next to my head. Cornering me.

I stare back at him but can feel his breath mixing with mine. He is so close I only have to push up on my tiptoes and I could kiss him. What is wrong with me? We are finally talking through things and all I can do is wonder how his lips would feel against mine. It feels as if I have not been with him in so long. It feels as if those other times were only a dream compared to what this really could be. I give a quick shake of my head. My mind wants me to move, but my body is all too happy to stay in his arms.

"We will think of something," I say breathlessly. "Something that will keep you and your family safe." I raise my hand up to caress his cheek and raise up on my toes, diminishing the distance between us. At first, he stands rock solid against me. The touch of my hand caresses him to bend and break against me, pushing me into the wall, he holds me there firm. Kissing me.

The fire that usually comes with us touching isn't as hot and sultry this time. Despite that, I can feel the burn there under the surface. One of his hands skirts down the dress, bunching the cloth, inching it further up my leg. He deepens the kiss.

The chill of the wall behind me moves, I sink into it, slipping away from Blaise. My eyes spring open as my hands scramble against him, trying to latch on. Two dark shadows stand behind him at the ready as I continue to sink further into the wall.

Blaise takes a moment, wondering why I'm scared, and moving away from him through the wall. "What... No!" He bursts out, his free hand not sinking into the wall that I'm. He grabs my wrist, holding me, not wanting to let go.

The shadow warriors are like the ones that my mother had dealt with in her past. "These are Flit's shadow warriors, aren't they?"

"No, it can't be. He wouldn't know you are here. Don't leave me." A guttural cry tears from his lips as I slip further from him.

Wrapping my hand back around his neck, holding me there. "I'm not leaving you, but I will not be able to get us all out of this place from inside this cage. I will see you soon, trust me. Do not worry, I must go now."

"Then promise me you will get out of here with the siren if you guys get the chance. I may not be nice in the future. My animal will consume me."

"We will see."

"Promise me." He urges by squeezing my wrist.

"No, I have made my decision and we are going to see it through." I pull him toward me one last time and kiss him. I sink further into the stone being whisked away from him.

"Alexia!" He yells out. His rage shakes the walls. As the darkness swallows me whole. I see the shadow warriors drop down into the floor before all the light is cut off. Air cuts off from my lungs as I'm being pulled from behind.

# Chapter 8

IT DOESN'T TAKE LONG before I'm in another room. This one isn't anything like the dungeon I just came from. I'm deposited into a lavish bedroom. The bed has one of those frames with surrounding curtains. Pink silk is tied to the posts on one each side. There are soft comfy rugs covering the hardwood floors and a gigantic fireplace that takes up one side of the wall it is lit and making the room cozy and inviting.

"There you are!" Jazmin exclaims. "How did you get mixed up with the likes of her?"

I gasp in surprise, meeting Jazmin instead of Flit. My eyes narrow. "Where are Zeek and Natasha? Where is Flit? Her who?" I ask.

"Her who? Who her?" Trix zooms in through the crack in the doorway behind Jazmin.

"The one that doesn't like to be named. I call her Beatrice. It goes with the beast who she says she is master over, and it irritates her. It also helps that it isn't a bad ass name." She gives a giggle.

"I like it. Finally, I have a name to call her because I sure as hell was not calling her master. Now, where are the others?"

"Calm down. You are the one that ran, not us. We were where we were supposed to be. You, on the other hand went looking for trouble, didn't you?" She raises one of her eyebrows. She is in a purple dress once again, no longer in her riding clothes. A steel band sits over her bad eye it is tied back into her hair with a chord that weaves through her hair.

"I had to answer the call," I try to explain.

"She answered the call that had her in grips. She almost got chopped to bits, yet here she is throwing a fit." Trix interrupts, howling in laughter. Weaving in the air, dancing to a song only he knew.

"What are you wearing?" She looks me up and down, noticing the dirty and damp dress that I have on. It is dull and no longer pretty to look at. "Zeek and Natasha are settling in. They will meet us after I get you cleaned up and ready to meet everyone. Flit is where he should be nowhere near you or this problem you have brought to his doorstep. Foolish child."

"Excuse me." I take a step back, unsure of which Jazmin I'm dealing with. She had never spoken to me in such a way before. "Are you okay? I have never heard you speak like this before."

She gives me a hard stare. Picking up her dress, she glides over the floor to me. Keeping her voice low, she whispers. "Keep your voice down." Pivoting, she motions her head towards the open door. Trix rushes around the room and bumps the door the rest of the way close. He gives a shriek of laughter. "Remember, there is always someone listening. The dark side is made of secrets and power moves. I will act and be not as I really am, so will others. Do not hold it against them, they do what they must, to survive. Know how to spot the difference.

You put us in a predicament, coming here without backup and getting captured."

"What are you talking about?" I say, still in a normal voice.

"We need to get you changed into something else and try not to say too much when we get there." She looks around the room and spots the wardrobe. She walks over to it, throwing open the doors. Looking at the garments there, she gives a grimace. "You are much shorter and leaner than I. Such a little thing." She searches through clothing to find something. "No, this just won't do." She eyes me once again, then goes back to the clothes.

"Hold on." I rush over to her, delaying her hands from looking for clothes. "Are we just going to meet Flit, or are there going to be other people there also?"

"Flit is the Lord of Darkness for a reason. You will be in the presence of multiple people. Most likely Beatrice also, or when she hears of you escaping, she will not like that. Flit helped you."

"But he didn't. You did." She shakes her head. "Why did they deposit me here in your room, then?"

"Who do you think warned him?" Her eyes return to the clothing in front of us. "If I didn't get here in time, he still wouldn't have known you were here. You wear a part of him even if it is useless," she flicks the obsidian stone that hangs from my necklace. "And to think what that snake could have done to you?"

"I was safe. He was fine," I remark, waving her away.

"I may have the dark one's ear from time to time with my position, but he still has to think of everything as a whole and not even I'm privy to all the games he is playing, nor do I want to be."

"So, those were his shadow warriors?" I ask.

"Yes, of course they were his. He didn't want you harmed down there. There is a thin line between Beatrice and Flit. They have been at war with each other for a long time now. Secretly or not so secretly, but it is well known."

My eyes scan the clothes in Jazmin's wardrobe. Most were in the color purple or black. "You have a theme going on here."

She smiles to herself.

"Here, this is simple and plain it will help you blend in." She takes a black dress out that is long. "Though it may be a bit too long on you."

I shake my head. "I don't need to trip and fall my first night here. What do we need to say when everyone sees me for the first time? Do you want me to blend in? I thought we were going for powerful. At least that is what you said before."

"Yes, we need to make a statement, one that says you have power since we don't have Shade here. But showing power might bring out Beatrice or others. Beatrice will not let things go and will definitely point you out. She will wonder why you are not down in her dungeons. I'm hoping to hide you and not make it too much of a pressure point."

"I think we need to put up a strong front. Push her buttons and stir some things up. Don't hide me at all, use me. Let's show them I can't be messed with. I will also need training with my shifting. I'm tired of being the weak one in a fight and am not taking chances anymore with this."

Jazmin lifts her head and nods in agreement. "I like where your head is at." She pulls out a bunch of clothes and pushes to the back of the wardrobe. There are many short and slinky looking dresses along with some see through garments.

"Do you own anything that isn't a dress?" I ask, uncomfortable with some of the choices before me.

"No, not really."

My cheeks heat at seeing the wicked garments, but I stand firm in my decision. "Knowing my luck, Beatrice will be there. We can't avoid her."

A ghostly chill enters the room as Jazmin drops the clothing that she is handling into a pile in front of the dresser. "She is already there."

"How do you know that?" I meet her eye, seeing that she is no longer looking at me, but through me.

"The dead are speaking, dear."

"Right. Necromancer. I almost forgot."

"You will be staying in the room across from this one, so if you ever need to leave, that will be your safe space. Trix will be floating around. Call on him if you need help to navigate around here. We will help you as much as possible, but I'm not sure how this will go."

"I think this will make a statement." I pull out something that is small and slit up the side. The fabric is dark green and velvety to the touch.

She is silent for a moment as she listens to something else not of this world. Shaking her head, she comes back to the real world as the color in her eye becomes more vibrant, the purple lightening to a lavender. "Sorry." Giving a look at the piece of cloth, she nods her head. "I think you're right and this will cling and accentuate some of the curves your slight frame is hiding. "

Making quick work of getting out of my current dress, I'm soon in this snug one. Jazmin circles me like a shark. She pulls at the treads, pulling some through others, making the threads wider and more stylized across my body. As her fingers roam across me, she notices the necklace and touches the black shard carefully. She makes sure there is no cloth hiding it. "Keep this out."

"Okay," I say breathlessly.

Her eye roams up to my hair and gives me a frown. "What a rat's nest!"

"I usually wear it up. What's wrong with that? You have never said anything about it before."

"Before you weren't in front of the masses that will judge you for your appearance alone, let alone the power you symbolize and the plans that others will start plotting once they see you. I feel you are correct. Wearing it in an updo is a more powerful statement. But it needs something more…" Her voice trails off as she looks around the room, rushing to a table with a mirror. Many powders and pendants lay strewed about.

"What is all this?" I ask, fiddling with a bottle that is half empty.

"A little of this and that." Her fingers snatch the bottle from my fingers to place it back. The next thing she pulls out is a chain that crisscrosses a few times, making a net. She places it on my head as she fiddles to get it into place. Walking behind me, she tugs at my hair, focusing on raising it up and gathering the tendrils into the net that will hold it secure behind my head in the little chain net. She brings out a small piece forward to frame my face.

I watch her skilled fingers make simple work out of my hair and clothes. In a matter of minutes, I'm done and ready.

"You are amazing!" My eyes bulge at my appearance as I walk in front of the mirror.

She waves her hand at me. "I'm a woman of many talents." She stops for a moment, cocking her head to the side. "We must go now. She has beat us to the punch, so to speak." Jazmin ushers me out of her room.

Trix rushes by in a flurry and zips down the hallway way ahead of us. He rounds the corner and is gone.

"Trix will be around for me to call to him if needed, correct?" My voice whooshes out as I get pushed down the hallway at a breakneck speed.

"He will be around, yes."

We make our way towards the extravaganza; on the way, I get a proper look at a much more unique part of the castle. This way had lush carpets and hallways of rooms, along with statues and decorations littering the walls. "How big is this place?" I ask.

"Good question. This place is always changing and hiding rooms that were there one moment and not there another. This is Flit's favorite place to stay when there are many people gathering in one place."

"How come? Why doesn't he have his own place and make others travel to where he is?"

"He loves this place because there are always hiding places if he needs to get away. This is where he spent a lot of his earlier years. He knows this place better than anyone, even the owner. He moves around so it is harder for others to have a lock on him. It also keeps enemies and friends at a distance."

"If they can't get a lock on him, then it's harder to make a plan to get rid of him."

"Precisely." Jazmin gives a smile that is almost a snarl. "Many people of the dark side like it here and do not want to combine sides because they feel like they can live by their baser instincts and don't have to hide who or what they are. No matter what, you still have politics regardless of what court you are in." She gives a sad sigh.

Staying silent, I think over her words. Giving real thought to some issues, I have seen these same issues in each place I have gone. People are so worried about what others think of them. I can only imagine what the light side holds. I have only met people from that side, but have never been to any of the towns or cities on that side. But they can be just as dark as any over here and be nice to your face. How do you fight something like that? How did mother and father plan to help people come together when they are so good at hiding who they are from the womb?

Before too long, we come to the back of a large group that is focused on the front of the room. We hedge towards the side and make our way closer, catching snippets of conversation as we do.

"Beatrice, you are always a pleasure. I hear your performance was top-notch, as always. What can I do for you?" Flit's voice booms over the crowd, making sure all can hear.

Whispering to Jazmin, who is guiding me, "Flit calls her Beatrice also?"

"All of us that view her as an equal or think of her as a lower call her that. Since she will not give us a true name to call her by, we make do."

We stop once we make it to the front. None of the others are really looking my way, only a few that we have bumped into. But their eyes snap back to Flit, entranced by what is about to happen.

She gives a grimace at the name. "I have word your shadow warriors were seen sneaking around my rooms," she calls out.

"Did you not put up wards or spells to counteract that sort of thing? Seems silly to me if you were trying to hide something, would you not make sure that thing is protected?"

Jazmin gives a hiss of laughter into her hand that she brings up to cover her mouth. "Nice one."

My head remains high to see over the other people's shoulders that are in front of me, but my eyes slide from her back to Beatrice.

"There was an unruly guest that we were dealing with, tis all."

"Perhaps you should not keep guests hidden away. Why not bring them into the fold and let their peers deem if they are worthy of such punishments? Or were you worried about their ties?" He is stoic and is standing straight with his hands in front of him, framing his body. His black straight hair is down and loose. It falls to the middle of his back much longer than I last saw him.

"That's our queue," Jazmin whispers to me, grabbing my hand as she walks me forward through the throng of people. They turn to us as we make ourselves known and muscle our way through. Once they see Jazmin, they part ways for her.

"Here they are now." Flit gives a small smile as Beatrice turns.

I meet her eyes straight on, not shying away. As the crowd parts, they make room for the both of us, so I quicken my step so I'm next to Jazmin, meeting her stride. Beatrice's hard eyes bore into me, her anger clearly written there on her face.

"You should have stayed put, little badger," she grumbles out under her breath as we pass by. We pull up short before Flit and are directly in between Beatrice and him. "Yes, that is the culprit. She tried to take something that was not hers," her voice booms louder for all to hear.

"What did she take?" His eyes meet mine but are dull, as if he is bored with this meeting. "It doesn't look like she could hide anything with what she is wearing." He clasps his hands behind his back, waiting patiently for Beatrice.

"My snake charmer, he is beyond useless now. They mated."

"And you broke the bond as soon as you found out," he says shortly.

Her lips purse in thought. "No, not at first. I didn't think it would get in the way with them so far apart from one another. I broke the bond more recently due to her distracting him from his job. He ended up going rabid because of it."

"Perhaps if you would have broken the bond when you first noticed it, we would not be here today," he chides. "It is funny how you let a mere slip of a girl best you without you even knowing."

"She was caught red-handed and must be taught a lesson. She took the lure out of her protection and must deal with the consequences of her rabid beast. I did not hide her, just made sure she delt with the cost."

"Should I look into what else you hide?" Flit asks Beatrice nonplus.

Her eyes glare at him, shooting daggers, but her smile is soft. "I'm an open book to you, my lord. There is nothing I hide from you; I merely made the mistake. I did not know she was under your protection. All I knew is she mingled with one of my snakes and thought she could take him from me. I just wanted to play and toy with her a bit. No harm done."

The masses roll on that. Many speak in hushed tones, talking to one another. "Protection," I hear, thrown around with questioning looks. "Who is she? What is she?"

He laughs. "She isn't under my protection, but she is a guest and one I intend on getting to know more. Remember Beatrice, we all have a place, remember that." He holds her gaze for a long time but doesn't back down.

She breaks the contact first. "Very well, I understand. I will get back to my problem at hand and let you know if anything is needed as a guest." She gives a smile. Turning on her heel, she walks back the way we came, not looking at the crowd. "But if she isn't careful, I may have to claim her, her being a beast and all with no alpha to answer to." She cackles. "Have fun, little badger."

I give a low snarl and Jazmin holds me back. Since she didn't look over here before passing, she doesn't see my movement, but Flit does. My eyes close in on him after she walks out. He gives a small shake of his head.

Flit speaks up in a loud, booming voice. "For the rest of you, have fun this week with the festivities and cause chaos wherever you can. Alexia here will be our guest for the week. She will stay here. Tread lightly, that is all."

Most glare at me and give me looks that could kill. Still others gossip in hushed voices. Some stick around, others get out while the getting is good. The looks and the whispering cause me to fidget and lower my head. Jazmin pinches me at my elbow before she links our arms together, making our way towards Flit.

"Get out of your own head, girl, and pay attention. They don't matter, remember that," Jazmin whispers close to my ear. "Those two right there." She points out.

I notice two men gaze at me, eyeing me up and down. One has a dark stripped mohawk down the center of his head, and the other is stockier with reddish brown hair. They whisper to one another.

"Those are two of the badger alphas. There are four in total, but the others didn't come to the festivities. With whom is here now, you may need the backing of one of them, but let's worry about that later." She gives a pat to my arm as we walk up the two little steps to where Flit is.

"I have a feeling growing up human and hidden away is going to make these things tricky for me," I whisper back.

"It gets better with practice." She gives a sad smile before slipping away from me. Flit turns before we reach him, turning back to a door that leads off to the side and into a small enclosure.

Following behind him, he wears dark slacks and a dark shirt, with his dark hair flowing behind him. He is the epitome of the darkness. "Jerome, Niles. Please give us a moment."

Both men that have been giving me a look nod in agreement, going back to their conversation.

He shuts the door after we clear the doorway, hiding us from prying eyes. Jazmin launches herself at Flit, embracing him. He sinks into her arms and kisses her passionately. They lose themselves in one another.

Looking around the room, it is decorated modestly with a few seats and tables. Clearing my throat. "Is this just a go between or a meeting room of sorts?" I ask. Both intrigued about this place and what happens next, but also nervous about interrupting their warm welcoming.

"Yes, it is a private room used for many reasons," Flit answers me, but his eyes stay on Jazmin as he looks over at her. His hands cup around her face.

"I'm okay, you big brut." Her hand curls around his hip, holding him there. She presses her forehead to his and they take a moment to rest like that.

He gives a sigh of relief and turns away from her. "Alexia, I presume."

"Yes."

"Jazmin told me you were coming. Her and Trix both have had many things to say about you and your situation."

His cold, calculating gaze doesn't hold the affection I'm expecting. "I'm your long-lost granddaughter."

"So, they say." He looks me up and down.

I give him a quizzical look. "After reading Sera's journal, I read your message. To come to your domain and that my mother is here. I will learn from you what I need to in order to find my brother and the rest of my family."

"Do you want to know how many others have come before you? Pretending to be my lost granddaughter. Many have gone to more exuberant lengths than you have."

"You wrote that you have watched over me. Wouldn't you know who I should be this entire time?"

"There were many journals scattered around here and there."

His voice sounds tired and already disappointed. "I wear this." Raising up the sliver of obsidian, the chain pulls on the tension at the back of my neck. "This is from a memory of my past. I picked it up there from when Sera called on a favor to help her protect me. If memory serves, I thought she had died." Forcing my eyes wide, I try really hard to not cry out in frustration. "But then I find out she is not from her journal."

"Again, those trinkets are far and few between, but can be stolen. It is but a shard. You could have gotten that from anywhere. It holds no power from me anymore, if she used it. Now it is just a rock, or a piece of jewelry."

"But you have seen me before in the mirror from Sera's past. You must remember me." I grab at the chain thing in my hair and yank it off. "I may have changed a little from then, but I am still the same person. Going through the Abyss will change a person." I shudder.

"Yes, you are correct. You look like the girl from back then, but there are creatures out there that can pull even that off. No, you will have to pass that hardest test of them all getting by a truth witch."

"Are you sure?" Jazmin asks.

"There is no way around it, my love. She is here and must be the one to claim her. Even if I knew I could not do the claiming."

"Why am I here then if you don't believe me? Others are sure about me being who I am even when I wasn't. The first time, I'm up to claiming who you guys say I am, you now all have doubts," I yell in frustration.

"Shhh." Jazmin tries to calm me. "What about the alphas? Will they help?"

"No, I want to know what is going on." My anger peaks as I throw the chain that I pull from my hair. "You said you would protect your family. I guess you are right. I'm not your family because if someone was supposed to protect me, they wouldn't let me go through what I have. No good person would have let me be caged and drugged with people that wanted to kill me. The only thing that kept me alive was Sera's spell that made it impossible for them to kill me without killing Jade."

He did not reach out to catch the chain, just watches as it hits his chest and slides down to the floor. "Now," he utters.

Two shadows burst from the floor and fall on me in seconds. They grasp at my hands and shoulders, forcing me down to my knees. They easily keep me there even while I struggle. Growling, I try to summon my powers, but they do not budge.

"Little more than a pup you are." He gives a side look to Jazmin, who just gives a polite smile. "Do not pretend to know what goes on here or how I conduct business. You will not lose your temper around me or throw a tantrum. If you want to leave there is the door, otherwise we will go back to the fes- tivities and wait for the truth witch to arrive. You can try that with one of the alphas out there. I doubt they will be happy with your performance." He glances at the door to where we came from, almost daring me to leave.

Glaring at him, I bite at the inside of my cheek, holding my tongue for now. I would show him, show all of them. But how? First, I needed to find someone to teach me how to handle my shifting abilities and how to fight. I'm always at a disadvantage, and I'm tired of these people judging me for it.

He gives a tight nod and turns on his boot, going back to where we just came from. He cracks the door and I can hear the crowd of people talking and having a good time. "Jazmin, get her ready. The truth witch will not be long. I need to speak with the alphas."

"Very well."

He walks out the door but pauses before closing the door. "You were missed." He closes it softly, not looking back at either of us.

"Let her go now." She shoos away the shadows, frowning at me. "Why did you go and do that? You couldn't hold your temper in for a moment, could you?"

Getting back to my feet, I stomp at the shadows as they dip down into the floor. "Does anything hurt the shadow creatures?" I ask, wanting to shred them with my claws or teeth.

"Actually, quite a lot does. The shadow creatures are bound to him and have to do what he says for a reason. Hope you are never made into one."

"What was that? He didn't act like he knew me at all."

"He has a point. He doesn't really know you; you are a stranger. Just because you may be family doesn't make you or him able to claim anything. I would warn against disrespecting him like you did in front of anyone."

"Let me guess, or else."

"Your funeral," she says in a high-pitched voice. "In his position, he has to tread lightly, so he isn't interfering with others he may be making deals with. There have been many before you where they have tried to say they were family. You do not wish to know the games that go on here. This is one of many, and you will have to keep up if you wish to survive."

"Welcome home," I say dejectedly.

Dusting myself off, I fix the dress, making sure it doesn't rise or show anything.

"He missed you regardless."

"Where did you get that from?" Giving her a curious look.

"From what he just said." She walks over to the door and places a hand on it but doesn't open it.

"Didn't he say that to you? That he missed you? You two seem really close."

"Not as close as we would both like." Another sad look comes over her, but she shakes her head, brushing it off. "That is one thing you will have to work on. It might not look or even feel like something is a message for you, but it could be. No, that you were missed message was for you. He and I have between the both of us many messengers that hold our secrets. That was not for me."

"But how do you know?" I walk closer to her, waiting for her.

"You listen and not just with your ears, girl." She rests two of her fingers on my forehead and then moves them to my chest. "Don't just take things as they are with your ears and eyes. If something in here is telling you different, listen to it."

"Fine." I hold my tongue, not wanting to ask any more questions, unsure if I would just get more cryptic answers or actual help.

"Now let's go meet your mother." She tucks the hair back behind my ears, patting the fly aways down.

She opens the door slowly for us to exit. When the door opens, I notice a woman that is skipping around Flit. Her brown hair is down and in waves as she moves around him. She is wearing a white summer dress that cuts off right below the knees. Her feet are bare, and her face is beaming and happy as she continues to skip around him.

We only get a few feet past the doorjamb before a vine encircles both of us. Sharp thorns grow from the dark green vine as it circles around us, cinching us tighter together.

"Why is she here?" She bites out.

"Sera, we talked about this. She is here for the festivities, same as you are. For this week, you will see one another and then we can go back to business as usual."

"Dead men tell no tales, yet her ghosts hide her secrets."

"Stop being jealous that you can't read my secrets like the rest of these numb skulls, truth seer. Trust me, you don't want to see these secrets." Jazmin pushes against me hard. "She doesn't much like me," she whispers.

Struggling to not be thrown into a thorn, I push back just as strongly. The thorns continue to grow and tighten. Stopping just before piercing skin, if I relax at all, I would snag on many thorns that are pointed in towards us.

A cold wind whips at my back and Jazmin's voice fades. "If you want to play witch, I can play every piece here is but a graveyard waiting for my touch to wake the dead. Just say the word."

Sera skips to the vine holding us prisoner. "Bring the dead. They will go nicely with the drapes." She holds a fist up and loosening her grip, the thorns retract back in to the vine. She whips her arm to dissipate the vine. They crawl back into the cracks of stone. "Who's your friend?"

Taking a deep breath, I finally relax and look at all the people who are still watching us. Those who have left filter back in. Music begins in the back of the room, playing at a quiet tempo.

Servers bounce from group to group, offering refreshments and food. The room is still not as busy as before, but it isn't totally devoid of people. The alphas were there off in the corner, waiting and watching the events unfold.

"This is..." Jazmin looks between Sera and I.

Sera looks at me and smiles a little too widely.

"Mother," I whisper, tears prick my eyes. The time has come! I have been waiting to meet her for so long. "This is surreal. I didn't think I would ever get to see you in person." I hold out my arms.

Her arm raises, and before I know it, she swipes it across my face.

I stand there staring at her, shocked by what has occurred. My cheek burns and stings from the bite of her palm.

"You are no daughter of mine... You are just another thief come to steal what isn't yours. Begone from my sight." She raises her nose in the air, done with my presence.

"What... I'm your daughter..." I look around, seeing we are surrounded by others who are looking to see what happens. Lowering my voice. "I found your journal. I have a brother."

"You found one of my journals!" She says in a high-pitched tone. "Well, good for you. No wonder you know so much. But you cannot fake or hide from a truth witch."

Grimacing, my hands tighten into fists. No one is listening to me or accepting what I have to say. Taking a breath, I try to think through things. Looking around, I see Sera's concentration on the group of people as if she is entertaining. "If I'm not your daughter, then tell me who I am. See the truth if you dare."

"Oh, look Flit, she dares me. I have to do it now if I want to win the game." She gives a twirl and moves her arms in a swaying motion. "Why don't you alphas fight over her first?" Her fingers wiggle at them, bringing them into the spotlight.

She is acting strange. This was not how she acted when she was younger. A lot of time has passed, but her changing this much? I don't know. "What is wrong with you?" I whisper, not loud enough to disturb Sera.

"Becoming a truth witch when you are not born, one can, let's say, alter your personality." Jazmin steps up beside me, patting my shoulder.

My other hand raises to pat hers, accepting the comfort.

"Sera, what do we do when we are challenged," Flit asks in a bored tone, clearly not enjoying this as much as Sera is.

Her dark eyes meet mine as she gives a big creepy smile. "We meet them head on and make them wish they never challenged us to begin with."

"Surround yourself with enough blood thirsty minions, and you yourself do not have to be the one people fear," Jazmin whispers.

All eyes were on Sera and the people in the front area step back a healthy distance from the few steps up to where we were. Like they know what is coming next.

"You badger's will have to wait. Perhaps one of you can pick up the pieces after. Or you can pawn her on one of the other two that didn't come. She might be damaged goods by the end and would be more trouble than she is worth. We will see the truth of it now," Sera says.

"How do you see the truth? Will it hurt?"

The alphas take a step back into the half circle that surrounds us, looking on as spectators shaking their heads. "If she wants to call upon a badger pack, she will have to ask properly," Niles says.

*Rejecting me already.*

Sera lets out a bellow of a scream as she launches at me. Her long fingernails dig into my skin, pinching my shoulders.

Pushing against her, I match her force so she doesn't take me down to the floor. I bring my arms up to block her hands; she continues to scream at me with her mouth wide open.

The scream cuts off and, on an exhale, a whisper comes through. "The truth always hurts, my dear."

Soon radiating pain climbs through me. Her dark eyes turn even darker, and I can't pull my eyes away from hers. Her hair falls forward, creating a curtain, but my arms brace against her chest, keeping her as far back as possible with her fingers still gripping onto my shoulders.

It feels like my skin is peeling off in strips and pieces. I scream out, but it cuts off mid scream due to her pushing down on my chest. When I try to inhale, fire ignites in my lungs as they try to pull enough air into them.

Shoving me, I fall back; she slides me over the ground; my eyes fly open as ice starts to crawl up my body. Kicking my feet, I try to dislodge the ice, trying to find purchase on a way to stop the slow progression. Air saws in and out of my lungs, my heartbeat thuds in my head. So very loud.

"Remember this?" A voice echoes around me.

My thoughts jump from panic to sheer blown terror as I stop and realize why this is so terrifying. Sweat drips down my back as the ice makes its way up my legs, trying to grip at my fingertips. I pull my hands up further, creating a fist and pounding at the ice. "Not again. I thought I was done with this. I'm no longer caught in the past. It has no hold over me," I yell out.

"It always has a hold on us. We are but a byproduct of our past." Circling Sera appears from the darkness. She is now dressed in a dark green dress, instead of the white summer dress. The crowd of people fades to darkness, and it is only her here with me.

"Is this what it's like to see the truth?"

"You are like a brand newborn baby, a babe born with no truth. Your past is obsolete, but your future is still unwritten."

The ice pulls up tight over my stomach, creeping its way up my arms and encasing them. I put my arms over my chest, hoping to make it easier to breathe and possibly warmer. The cold bites at my skin, but it doesn't reach my heart yet.

"If I have no truth to find, what happens?"

"We can't see to help or know what harms. If we can't help, we ourselves become frozen in fear. What's this? Could it be your truth, your source of strength?" Sera spots something off in the distance and walks away.

The ice locks me into place. "What is it? I can't see. What is my source of strength?"

Words trickle in from where Sera disappears. "Hey, Alexia?" Jack waits. "Things will make sense, eventually."

"Jack? What is he doing here?" I ask as the ice climbs up to my chest now and closes around my arms.

"I know that much is true. Many will help you, but four people will be your pillars. One is made of ice and can be just as fragile. Two are made of shadows and the fourth is hard to see clearly, but is the strongest pillar and most needed. It is one you get to choose freely."

"Wait, this is from a memory has to be. Jack?" I ask, shaking my head, frustrated. I struggle to see what she is doing.

"Jack, is that the young prophet's name? We will have to meet this strong prophet that could read you when a truth witch cannot. Who are these pillars? They sound important?" She strolls back over to the ice as it curves up over my shoulders.

Her long nails click against the hard ice prison as they dance over the surface.

Biting my lips, I force them to stay close.

"Oh, come now you wish to not tell the truth to little old me?" She sways her dress forward, covering the ice as she leans into me, hugging my freezing statue.

Feeling no warmth from her, the ice is too thick. There is no risk of it melting from her heat.

"That's okay. We can go one by one, so you will have to tell me the truth. Who is your ice pillar?"

My lips loosen and speak with little sway. "Natasha." The ice is right below my chin, creeping up so slowly. Will it be enough to cover before she can get to the other three?

"How could you not know that? She is the only ice Fae traveling with us right now?" I blab, trying to keep the conversation going.

"That was an easy one, wasn't it? Will they all be this easy? Who is your shadow pillar?"

"Shade." The answer gets pulled out of me as if it is right there waiting for her. I could not keep the answer in for even a second against her truth power.

"Shade, is that what you call the shadow creature?" She gives a smile of glee. "I knew that one, him being a present from your father and I. I don't sense him. Where has he gone?"

"He is on his own adventure of sorts, dealing with his own problems at the moment."

"Weird. Though it must be to protect you." Her eyes narrow as she concentrates.

"So you're my mother?"

"Tsk, tsk, tsk. I know you read one of my journals. Stick to the truth that I am searching for."

"Isn't that what we are doing?

"Perhaps that is what I wanted you and them to believe." She waves her hands. "Truth is subjective, isn't it? No, you have other information I need to prepare for a future of my making. Stop derailing the conversation."

The ice tendrils inch up over my bottom lip as she paces away. Looking down, I try to rush the ice with my eyes. Looking up, I check on Sera, then back down at the ice. Just a moment more. One... more... second... There! Ice crawls up my top lip and I relax into the ice cocoon, happy that she can no longer get the answers she craves.

"The third and fourth pillar? Who is it?" She turns around and stops as she sees my lower face encased in the ice.

My lips move of their own accord, but the sound stays trapped in the ice. I wriggle the few inches I have given myself in success for not blabbing about my other two pillars. They were still new to me, and I didn't want to put them in more danger than we already were.

Sera races over to the ice, trying to pull at it. Her long talon fingernails scratch at it to try and pluck the ice away. It doesn't budge or stop its slow climb up the rest of my face.

"Get me this Jack person. He is a prophet and can see what she is!" She yells at someone in the background. "Even if you won't tell me, I bet he will."

The ice climbs up the rest of the way and fully encases me. The cold seeps into me, but soon I can no longer feel it. I can no longer feel much of anything. Sera slides down in defeat but climbs back up my body and peeks in from the side. "Do not look for your brother." She looks away, back toward the darkness. "Or is this the time to look for him? Where are you right now?" She taps the ice. "Answer me." Her face relaxes, taking on a calm curious aura, the anger falling away.

My lips move as I try to give her the answer she requires, but the ice stops me and keeps the answer hidden.

"I should have trusted Flit and let him kill you." She gives a sad look and walks away.

Why would they want to kill me? I remember this from her memory back in the past. Did she have these truth powers at the time I saw this? Did she see this scene back then? Can she see snippets of the future? If so, how does she keep it all straight?

*I guess she doesn't.*

Part of me wishes to answer her truthfully, only if she can do the same for me. A loud crack breaks the silence and soon the cocoon around me bursts into glittery shards.

My eyes blink and I'm back in the big ballroom on the dais. The light's beam into my eyes. Blinking back the black spots that dance in front of me. Slowly, I move my arm in front of my eyes, giving some shade to my eyes so I can properly see. Sera is over near Flit, whispering into his ear. I try to work out how to use my lungs.

Jazmin bends down, her dress pours beside me. "Are you okay?"

"I feel like an enormous truck has run me over," I croak out.

"It will be like that for just a moment. She did not look too happy. What happened in your truth vision?"

"Have you ever been through one?" I ask.

Her eyes rise over my head as they flick to Flit. "Once yes. It was painful, but my truths were nothing compared to the dead that surround me. It overwhelmed her power to know so much truth through one conduit and backed off after that."

"Flit, just let that happen to you."

"He doesn't interfere directly. He is more of a shadow guy working behind the scenes, if you will. Plus, she and I had to work ourselves out or have an understanding at least. We still have our squabbles if we are around one another too long. He trusts me to handle things how I see fit."

"What if things head a bad way? Where he didn't want it to go?"

She lifts her shoulder in a half shrug. "Even I do not know all that goes on in his head."

Looking Jazmin up and down, I really look at her. "Do you love him?"

Her purple eye turns back to me as her face pulls tight. "It always starts off that way, but hardly ever concludes that way. When you are in power like he is, and do what I do, you get used to hearing stories where it doesn't work out more times than not." Raising her head, her eye catches on his face, and she softens. "I, like the ones before me, will most likely be gone before too much longer."

My mouth comes open as I feel the anguish coming from her. Before anyone can see her face and gaze, she schools it back into one of calm serenity.

"Jazmin," I whisper, shocked. "What do you mean, gone?"

Shaking her head. "It is better that I have lived with a love as great as his rather than to not know it at all. That's enough of that. Come on." She stands back up and reaches out a hand to help me up. "We all die in the end."

Taking her help, I slowly get to my feet. "But what if he feels the same?"

"Doesn't matter if he does or doesn't, the power and people come first. The plan needs to be followed, and every consequence needs to be thought of. Every possibility needs to be accounted for." Fixing the skirts of her dress, she presses it flat and dusts it off, even though there is no dirt to be seen. "Now what did the truth witch learn?" Her voice is louder so all could hear. "Or did she fail again?"

"Not much was learned from this viewing. So, for now, she will be treated both as family and as not. Until this Jack prophet can be located and brought here to help with the connection. Now I think our brothers from the south have something they would like to show us, so if we could please make our way outside, we have a festival to get back to." Flit gives a clap of his hands to dismiss everyone.

Many move right away, heading towards the doors to outside. Only some freeze in fear of doing the wrong thing. Their eyes are on a constant swivel to keep everyone in sight.

Touching Jazmin's hand, I get her attention. "I'm going to go back to the room. You said the one across from yours is mine, correct?"

She gives a nod. "That's right. Do you want Trix to come with you? He should be around here somewhere."

"No, that is fine it wasn't to many turns I think I have it."

"I will have someone deliver some other clothes to your room, ones that suit your style more. I have already put your bag and your gear that you brought here with you in the room." Turning to the side, her purple eye lights up. "Quiet Maurice, that is quite rude of you. Do not interrupt me again."

"Thank you." I back away slowly. I don't think I will ever get used to her talking to the dead.

# Chapter 9

NATASHA GRABS ME BEFORE I can make it back safely to my room. "That was crazy!"

"You're telling me," I say.

"Do you want to blow off some steam? They have a great workout place here and I feel like tossing some ice shards," she says flippantly as she creates an ice knife.

"I do. Maybe they have some shifters that can help me with getting my abilities under control. But I don't have anything other than these clothes."

"We will just borrow some."

I nod and follow her down a couple of stairs. "Jazmin explained she is going to stock my room with clothes I like later, and my items should be there already. Are we going down to the dungeons?"

She shakes her head. "Almost, but not quite, and we will be on the opposite side of the castle."

"This place is immense, almost like a miniature city. How do you not get lost in this place? How do you know where everything is?"

"Mother and I would come here often. The guy she fell in love with kind of ran this place in the past."

"Is your mom here? Who owns this place?"

"There are a lot of stories about who this place belongs to. No, they had to go into hiding. Flit has taken over running it for now. Father has been hunting them down when he isn't busy ruining my life. It is a centralized place that can be used when needed. Flit makes sure it is well stocked and taken care of. All you have to do is reach out and let him know if or when it plans to be used." Grabbing my arm, she yanks me closer to whisper in my ear. "When I was a little girl, I used to think that I would come across a secret room and find the owner of the castle and he would reward me and take me away from my family to live happily ever after in this castle."

"Like a princess?" I giggle.

She gives a happy sigh. "Yep, I was full of hope back then." Her arm tightens, almost as if she were hugging me.

Stopping our stride forward, I unclasp her hand from my arm and give her a proper hug. She holds her breath, but after I don't let go, she unleashes it shakily. "I feel like this place is spooky," I admit.

"It for sure is. But I like the dark charm. I wanted to be a dark fairy princess, one that is lethal and pretty." She bats her lashes at me. "Come on." She waves her hand forward, so we continue walking down the corridor.

"Of course, you would want to be a dark princess. One that feasts on the blood of her enemies."

"How else do you expect people to leave you alone? Be nice to them? Wrong!" We laugh at that and carry on.

We hear grunts and sounds coming from a room up ahead. The doors are thrown wide open. Stepping in, we notice a dirt floor where tile or flooring should be. Looking up at the ceiling, we can see the dark sky above, but it is covered by a glass ceiling. That is domed into a pyramid shape. There are rings where people are fighting and off in the corner is an archery corner. Weights are scattered around, along with some other equipment.

"There is also a pool. It's back across the way we came."

Looking back through the doors, there is another set of doors, but they are closed.

"Where are the changing rooms?" I ask.

"This way." We make our way around a few rings. One fighter is in beast mode. "Cheater," Natasha whispers.

"Can they not fight with their animals?" I ask, looking over at the lizard shaped man. He sticks his tongue out at Natasha then continues beating up the other man who is just getting back up.

"You can, but usually when it is friendly competition, we all stay in human form unless we are doing it for training, or someone ran their mouth."

"I guess that happens quite a lot." Heading through a big wide open doorway, there is a path to follow. As we come across the lockers, I stop and stare at a half-naked man that is covered in sweat and muscle. His face is down, and his hair is loose and wet, which is covering his face. My mouth hangs wide open as I freeze to the spot.

Bumping into me, Natasha tries to get me to move.

Not moving, my eyes are glued to his back, that is covered in tattoos.

"It's not polite to stare," she hisses in my ear as she finally pushes me to the next aisle that is clear of people.

"Does everyone share this changing room?" I whisper back, my eyes roam around. The lockers end in a dead end in this aisle, so I keep my back to them, watching for who else may walk in.

"Yea, shifters rarely have a problem with nudity. Those are the ones that usually use this area. Most other creatures don't mind the different species or if the different sexes share. If you don't want to share, you can always head back to your room to shower and change there." She gives a shrug, opening a locker after she places her palm in the middle.

"How did you do that?"

"It is spelled to me. I have had my stuff here since the last time I visited. I told you I visited a lot, so I get to keep a locker when others have to check in and out one." She sticks out her tongue, grabbing a change of clothes. "You can go check the closet for clothes to fit you. Head to the right out of here, away from the tattooed man. It's the door on the left before the bathrooms."

Hushing her, my eyes glare daggers.

She points at me and then points down the hallway.

"Don't make me call Zeek on your ass," I hiss at her before jogging away, not wanting to hear her comeback or whine session.

After ten minutes of rifling through the closet, I find a shirt, a sports bra, and shorts that I fit. I change into the clothes in the closet since it is hidden better than an open locker room. I don't feel as comfortable in my skin as some of the other people in this castle. Not yet, at least. Holding the dress to my chest, I peek out the door, making sure no one is waiting to attack me. I don't know if I would ever feel comfortable here.

"Done." I walk back into the row I left Natasha in. She is sitting there leaning back against the locker with her leg kicked over her other one, swinging as she makes ice daggers in her palm.

"Good, I thought you got lost or eaten back there." She throws a weak made ice stick that breaks on contact with my arm.

"Hey. Haven't I gone through enough today?"

"Yea, I was thinking about that, and maybe your family is as fucked up as mine is. What was up with Sera slapping you?"

"I have no clue. That reminds me, do you still have contact with Jack back at Morning Star?"

"Yea why?" She sits up fully and places both feet on the ground.

I give her a look of desperation.

She gets up and walks forward. "Wait here." She pushes me further into the little section we are in before she checks the rest of the room. "Okay, we are alone. What is happening?"

"Flit and Sera might send someone after Jack and bringing him here."

Natasha shoves at my shoulders. My back slams into the locker behind me. "Why didn't you start with that?" She huffs.

"Honestly, I didn't think."

"That's right, you didn't think." She interrupts, pacing back and forth. "Tell me what happened. He is in that place because he will not work for either side. He is a strong prophet."

"I don't know what she did, something with the truth magic, but she overheard my conversation with Jack and him talking about how I have four pillars in my life."

"And she got all the names? Why do they have to get Jack?"

"No, they didn't I got frozen in an ice sculpture thing like in a memory I lived and it kept me from giving all of them away. It must have been a safety precaution or some latent power I have that protected me. I don't know." I twist my fingers together trying to calm my nerves.

"So, which ones did you give away?"

"My first two pillars."

"Who are?" She asks, giving me a pointed stare.

"You and Shade."

"Me? Why me?"

"You were the first person I latched onto when getting here. The only one that has helped me through things, you under-stood what I'm going through."

Shaking her head, she stares at me in bewilderment. "Doesn't matter. I can protect myself. Shade she most likely knew because he is the byproduct of the spell she created. But the other two, she wouldn't know who those are or how to use it against you." She gives a hiss as her fingers massage her temple. "Jack better come out of this, okay," she states.

"How do you know she would use them against me? Maybe she would want to help me." I try to think positively.

"Has she done anything loving and motherly yet? You are talking to someone who has parents that use her in their own feud. I know a thing or two about this."

"No. I guess you're right."

"No, that's right. All you have gotten so far is slapped and pain." Natasha's hands turn blue and when she touches the metal of the locker or wood of the bench, a cold sheen of ice appears out of her hand. Shaking her hands, she dances away. "It is probably too late. His shadow goons will be there soon, if not there already, in other magical ways. Jack has been keeping two steps ahead of people like Flit for a long time. If he is meant to be here, he will. If not, we know he is safe somewhere else."

"I thought his power doesn't work like that. I thought he gets confused about what timeline he is in. How can he keep two steps ahead when he is unsure of what time he is in?"

"That is only when he is talking to others because he sees so many parts. With himself, it is a little more linear and he will be in a place where he has to be. It's hard to think about it logically. All you have to know is he will be where he needs to at any given time."

"Will he tell them what they want to know?" I ask, worried, waiting for her to calm down enough to change.

"He might. It depends on what he sees from them. I would think since he is avoiding both higher ups from the light and the dark side, he would help neither, but that is the bad thing about a prophet. They are working towards what they want this world to be. They work toward the best version that they think the world could be, unfortunately it rarely works out for them."

"They won't hurt him, will they?"

"Flit usually doesn't have to use force, I hear. Not his style." Hurrying through the motions, she changes into some work-out clothes and makes her way back to the front. I follow behind. "After this I will ask around and check back with Quintan to see if he can get back in touch with that place and Jack."

Giving a nod, I see the man still sitting there on the bench. "Do you know who the strongest person here is and would be a talented trainer in shifting?" I ask the guy with the many tattoos as I walk with Natasha to exit the locker area.

He gives an angry grunt and looks up at me. "Who wants to know?"

Raising my head and looking him directly in the eyes, I put my hands on my hips. "Me."

He gives a low chuckle and shakes his head. "There is a trainer out there in one of the rings he can help you. Just ask around for the warrior that helps train, and you will find him. The shifting part he should know someone that can help you with that."

Nodding, I leave him in peace.

"I thought we were going to train together?" Natasha asks, waiting for me at the doorway. Her skin changes to a darker hue of blue and her fingertips are tipped in black as she makes weapons with her ice power.

"Sorry, but no. I have been training with you and the most I have learned is how to dodge and avoid attacks."

"Well, yeah, that is the first thing you should learn."

"Well, I need to learn either how to shift better or how Trill and I can work as a team to better fight and help protect myself with the power I have."

"That's fair and I can't help with the shifting thing since I'm not sure how one really does that, being Fae myself. The elemental is another weird element that I don't really have any direction on." She twitches her fingers. "Oh well, have fun I will be around." She states before running off to a ring that has many people surrounding it, causing a large commotion.

I head in the other direction away from all the people, not wanting to get dragged into any more drama. It sounds like there is a fight going on that people are taking bets on.

There were a few women fighters training with metal poles and spears. "Do you know of a warrior trainer?"

They wave at a lone fighting ring at the back of the gym. It is well stocked with items needed for a fight, punching bags line around the ring on the outside. Two men were in the ring with Domini circling them and correcting them as they fight.

My eyes widen in surprise. I didn't think I would run into him here.

Walking over slowly, I watch him and the fighters. His black pants mold to his physique and his tank top is already sticking to the muscles of his back and stomach.

Clearing my throat, all three fighters stop what they are doing to look at me. I climb up onto the wooden fence sitting on the top bar. "Do you know where I can find a warrior trainer? Some others have pointed me in this direction."

The two fighters look at Domini.

"That would be me."

"Would you be willing to help me learn to fight? My last teacher only taught me how to dodge and evade, along with take a beating."

"That is an important part to learn. The entire part isn't to get hit, but you should know how to stand up even after being dealt a punch. What kind of power base are you?"

"huh?" I give a confused look.

"He means what kind of powers are you working with, sweetie?" One of the fighter's pops in.

"I bet she doesn't last long." The other fighter claps the one that just spoke on the back.

I give them both a look of ire. "I'm a badger shifter with an elemental that has fire power."

"Shit, elementals can be strong." The first fighter speaks up again.

The other fighter is silent, judging by the way he is studying me. He is trying to guess how much of a threat I pose with my small stature.

"I will have some time after training these two if you can wait," Domini answers. "It's best to sit on the benches around the rings. Sometimes our fighters get out of hand and ram into the sides of these rings."

Giving a nod, I climb down from the ring and find an empty bench in the corner. They wait, watching me until I sit down and then resume their training. I watch over them, trying to study their techniques and listen in to learn all that I can.

Next to my bench, there are some women that are whispering and looking at me out the corner of their eyes. They are coy about it as they continue their whispering.

One gets up the courage turning to me fully. "You're that girl that might be related to Flit, right?"

"Yes, Alexia is my name." My eyes flick to the side. I turn back to the fight, concentrating on the fighters.

"You're new here, aren't you?" She lowers her voice as the other two behind her argue over something.

My face turns fully to her, taking in her and the other two women behind her. One woman keeps shifting her fingers to claws and back again. Her canines dip out as she talks in a furious tone.

"To this place and to this world, yes," I answer honestly, not sure if telling the truth would be more helpful or not.

"Well then, you should know that my friend over there is having a meltdown. Her guy is in the ring, and we need you to keep your eyeballs to yourself."

Looking between the shifting claws and the two fighters going head-to-head. "I didn't know. Which one?"

"The one that called you sweetie." She winces as another wave of snarls starts up.

I stop myself from looking back at the fighters and pissing off the shifter. "Well, maybe you can help me then."

"I can help her into an early grave." The one with claws throws over her friend's shoulder.

The other one gives a light chuckle as she holds her friend back. "Girl, I don't get what you see in my brother."

"What do you need help with?" She ignores her friend.

"I'm trying to learn how to shift to help me with fighting and defending myself."

"Celia quiet down! She is nothing but a pup." She throws back at her friend, which makes them both pause mid argument and stare at me.

Their gaze bores into me, making me uncomfortable. I shift on the bench and bounce from looking anywhere other than them to back at them.

"My friend here would be the best one to ask since she is the shifter out of the three of us." The girl comes forward, sniffing me.

She looks me up and down before she walks over, dismissing me. "Just focus and concentrate on the body part you want to shift. Works for me."

"There you go." The woman covers up a laugh.

Looking down at my hands, I stare at them over the next several minutes, trying to focus on shifting them to claws. I try to keep my eyes away from the fighters, not wanting to start that up again; I lose track of time as I focus on my hands and sit with my thoughts, calming the noise running through my mind.

"How are you liking the weather here on the dark side?" Domini asks, standing in front of me, the fight done.

My eyes flick to his, then back at my hand in concentration. "There are a few clouds here and there, but right now, it looks clear."

"Looks can be deceiving at the best of times. What are you concentrating so hard on?"

"Trying to shift my hand at will. I was told to concentrate and focus and that would work."

Domini looks over at the fighters and the three women. They are all laughing and snickering.

"Though it takes concentration, I don't think those women were trying to help you." Domini blocks my view of them.

Letting my hand fall in my lap, I look up at him. He is relaxed. "You can teach me, right?"

"Not really in my wheelhouse. What's your name?"

"Fl... Alexia." I almost let slip the name that he calls me. "What's yours?"

"Dom."

"The shifting I won't be able to help you much there, but I can teach you how to fight and you said you have a fire elemental with you, correct? How old?"

"Trill can you come out?" I ask.

The little flame raises up from my wrist, dancing down into my palm. "I miss my sisters." She looks at the ground a little forlornly.

"I bet they miss you as well. This here is Dom. He is going to help teach us how to fight and get stronger."

Her little flame body stands a little straighter and gets brighter in the palm of my hand as her flame raises higher. "He is? We can get stronger than and can unite back with my sisters. Then eventually mother, maybe?"

"Maybe? Dom here wants to know how old you are."

"Does he?" Her fire hair curves up around her, making her form bigger. She grows in size, gathering energy and power to her. The heat coming from her intensifies but doesn't burn me. "Mama taught me to be weary of those of the opposite element." She all but stomps her foot.

Don gives a slight smile but doesn't laugh. I give him points there. "Did she? She sounds like a smart woman."

"She is." The steam all but deflates out of her.

"I bet you have her smarts." He tries to cheer her up.

"Yea?" she questions.

"You chose a great host to help you on your journey. I just want to help you both get back to your family."

"I'm not the strongest of my sisters. I'm not even the most adventurous, ask Alexia."

"If you ask me, strength can only get you so far. Having an adventurous streak just gets you into more trouble most of the time. But intelligence, you can use that to your advantage, calculate your opponent and think of every outcome and how to use your surroundings to help you."

"Yes! I need to learn that. My sisters and I had to leave Mother before we could learn all that we could from her. We have little knowledge of our world and kind."

"I think you and Alexia here have to have a long conversation on how to best blend with one another to really and truly become one, but I can help you both learn how to work together to help one another out." He opens the palm of his hand so Trill can jump to him. "Each time you blend Alexia will lend you some of her strength and you will grow stronger as she gains power, so, too, will you?"

"I must get stronger." Her hair flares around her, covering her like a cape. "I'm only a little flame right now, but my mother, she could be a huge flame as tall as you and change into human form and back to her flame self, if needed." She kneeled in his hand, fitting there comfortably.

It is hard to think of her being any bigger than she is now. To think she could be my size is unimaginable. She's just a little girl. She didn't need this kind of pressure on her at such a young age.

"Having an elemental within you is an interesting power. You can both have Trill's power and not have it at the same time. The first thing you will need to work through is silent communication."

"Why is that?" Trill asks.

"Do you want Alexia to announce what she wants you to do each time before doing so? She would tell her opponent her moves so they are ready for her."

"No, no, no, that would be bad."

"Very." He shakes his head. "Second, you will learn to be a part of a weapon. Which will be challenging for you, Trill, because you have to surround the object without burning it to ash and if it is crashing into something, not harming yourself in the process."

"Sounds like it could be painful." I wince. "Margaret and Robert will kill me if that happens."

"With practice, we can avoid that," Dom states.

"Third?"

"Yes, the third and final thing that we will go over will be Alexia using your power as her own, borrowing from you, and knowing the amount of energy and power you can give and hold at one time."

"I'm the biggest, so I should hold more, right?"

"In theory, that is correct, Trill. Alexia, remember that her power does not come freely. You will need more fuel to access her power along with the practice to wield it."

Getting up, she dances around in his hand, ready to start the training. She jumps down off his hand onto the dirt floor growing as large as she could. Her flame rose to my shin. It is the largest I have ever seen her.

Dom races over to the corner and ruffles through a box there. He comes back with a couple of metal balls. "We will just start with the one right now, but eventually we will work on splitting yourself over two or more items and calling yourself back together."

Taking the weighted ball in hand, it is heavy for such a small size. Trill jumps up and hops on top of the ball at first, stomping her little feet on it.

"The surface is very smooth."

"That is right. Eventually, we will work up to that one." He takes the ball back from her, waiting for her to hop down into my palm. His other hand comes around with a smaller blue ball that still has some heft to it, but not as much as the other. "This one has holes and divots, so you can hold on easier to build up your strength as you learn."

Trill wraps her flames around the ball, her flames struggle to surround the whole thing. She makes her flames higher at first, then spreads herself over the ball.

Testing things, I throw the ball up in the air only a little at first and higher after I notice her staying on the ball as it goes up in the air. Each time the ball comes down in my palm, I wait to give her time to get her footing.

"Again," she yelps.

"She has to remember to keep her fire body away from the places the item will connect with other things," Dom warns.

Each blow against my hand as I catch the ball causes her to tumble partially off. The cries of pain between the two of us trade back and forth as we continue to practice.

We practice this a few times, with Dom correcting us. We try communicating wordlessly to one another, but neither one of us could get through to the other. The last thing we try is me borrowing her power and using it as my own. The most we could do is light my hand and arm on fire. He had me go through different motions with my body to stretch and move. Trill's flame diminishes down as we spend the energy to train. Her flame almost goes out as she puffs out tired breaths.

"Again," she calls out weakly.

"That's enough, little one," Dom says.

She stands up and calls her flame back to her. "I can go again," she sputters and dies down, her heat giving out.

"Do you want to hurt yourself now? What if Alexia needs you later when she is in danger, and you are too tired to answer her call?"

Trill shrinks down and looks up at me in my palm. "I didn't think about it like that."

"Trust me, sometimes the smallest or slowest movements are for the best. It adds up in the end. No matter how little the movement forward is, it is still traction you didn't have before. Alexia, after training, you will need to replenish energies you used. Your animal will push you if you do not. You may find yourself more hungry than normal."

"You're all right for a water person, I guess." Trill gives him a shy look before dropping into my arm and getting some much needed rest.

"Thanks for that." I blush.

"Anytime. I mean it." I give a firm nod of my head before turning to some commotion that is going on in the next ring set up beside ours. Climbing the boards of our ring, I hop up to see over the group of people that have gathered around.

"Where are...?" Dom cuts off as he notices the group.

Blaise is in the ring with the tall, very muscular guy that is covered in tattoos that I had talked to earlier. He gets tossed and pummeled, trying to keep away from his enormous fists. Blaise moves quickly around him and lands a few good taps, but this guy moves just as quickly and hits even harder. As Blaise moves past him, trying to circle around back the mountain of a man, swings his beefy arm around and hits him in the back of the head, causing him to stumble forward.

"Blaise!" I call out automatically.

His face is in the dirt, but his eyes rush to where I am. They move past me, catching on something over my shoulder. He gets back up to his feet slowly and turns to face the behemoth of a man. Blaise goes full tilt at him, jumping and clinging to his upper torso, hammering punch after punch. The other fighter keeps blocking him at every turn. He slithers further up the fighter's back, attacking his head, making the man stop and stutter as he falls back, trying to dislodge Blaise.

I try calling out a warning but am ignored. Soon my cries are swallowed up by the cheers that are hoping for the giant to win. Calls come out in the crowd as they take last bets. Blaise moves out of the way and is soon back up, hammering at the guy's face. His arms are slow to defend as Blaise gets more of an adrenaline boost, keeping him light on his feet.

"We have more to go over," Dom states next to me in a quiet demeanor.

"We do?" I ask, but don't turn to him. My eyes stay on the fight in the next ring. "Why is he doing this?"

"If he can't perform how the Master wants him to and doesn't want his family to take on his burden, then he will try to find another way to serve out his sentence."

"By becoming a fighter?" I give a look of exasperation.

Dom tugs at my hand to help me back down into our ring. I follow, allowing myself the small touch and comfort that he can give in this instance.

"He is trying to survive as he knows how. Now we will start with hand-to-hand combat. It is good that you have some weapons to fall back on, but sometimes those are not at your disposal, and you will still need a way to protect yourself."

Looking him up and down, my cheeks heat up. "I have to fight you?" I wheeze out. "Last time I fought someone I was attracted to—" My eyes roam over to the other ring as I think about my first time with Blaise. "Let's just say it didn't end too well." The worry in my voice cracks as I try to keep it low.

"No. If you fight me, how would I help you correct your stance or fighting technique?"

"Then who?" I look around the ring, not seeing anyone close by other than the two fighters from before and the three women.

"Suzanne," He calls out, crooking a finger at the group of girls. "May I borrow you for a moment?"

"Get your own girl, Dom." One of the male fighters calls out.

Dom just stands there staring at them, waiting for the woman to come forward. She comes forward. Her hair is curly and tied up in two pigtails, almost making pom-poms. She is shorter than the other two women. This one is not the one that talked to me earlier but had consoled the girl with claws. She lowers her eyes to the ground as she meets Dom.

"How can I help?"

Low grumbles come from her group, but she ignores them.

"Will you help with training? Your brothers over there need to rest and stretch while cooling down."

"I don't know how much help I will be. Are you sure you wouldn't want Celia? She is the shifter?"

"No, I don't think it best she gets in the ring right now." His eyes stay trained on her turned down head. The red streaks in her hair are very prominent.

She turns her freckled face to me and nods as the distance closes between us. She sticks out her hand. "Suzanne."

I immediately shake it. "Alexia." Giving a firm shake, we release and back up a few steps.

"If she gets hurt, I'm coming for you, boss." The larger of the two fighters calls out with his arm hanging protectively around his girlfriend's Celia's shoulders.

Suzanne gives an irritated look. "Alexia, do you have any brothers?"

Her one question sucker punches me in the stomach. "Yes, I think so. We don't know one another, though. I hope to one day."

"Well, pray that he isn't overprotective like those two big lugs." She sticks her thumb at them and crouches into a readying stance. I follow suit, getting my fists up near my face, ready to protect. She hangs back, watching my feet and center. Her eyes never come fully up to meet mine.

"They can't be all bad."

Chuckling, she rubs the back of her neck. "Their not, but most days they are free to a good home to whoever will take them."

Circling one another, we do a dance back and forth, neither one of us wanting to make the first move. Dom moves around us, watching us with scrutiny but keeping quiet as we figure things out.

"Come on." I growl to myself. Lunging forward, trying to catch her off guard. She easily blocks and pushes me to the side, causing me to tip to the side and almost trip. I catch myself before going down, circling back to our starting point. I walk the embarrassment off. Dusting off my hands, I get them back up. She again doesn't make a move, as I have seen others. This one is careful.

I step into the center of her body; She stops me with a block. I sidestep out of it and get my leg behind her, pushing her back, making her fall backward.

"Good," Dom announces.

She rolls back and is up before I can come at her. She hangs back, studying me.

"Suzanne," Dom warns.

Her eyes flick to his feet and then back to me. She keeps on the defense, not coming at me. I study her as I jump back and forth on the balls of my feet. Blowing out a breath of air, I make a beeline for her, moving into her space. She is ready for me to do the same thing as before, so I continue to move into her space and throw my elbow up, catching the bottom of her jaw.

Her fist comes out of nowhere and punches directly into my ribs, that are uncovered. Air gets knocked out of me as I back up. Her steps are quick as she moves forward. Her hands are even more swift and decisive as she beats at my tender flesh. The jabs hit at weak points, bringing me down to the ground. Rolling into a ball, I cover my head and wait for the worst to come.

"Hold," Dom says in a clear, deep voice.

No punches come down on my back. Peeking up, I see Suzanne mid punch to my side. Her breath saws in and out of her lungs as her eyes stare straight at my side where she would have hit.

"I knew it." He comes between us and makes Suzanne back up. "Your family doesn't know, do they?" She shakes her head, keeping her eyes on the ground in front of her.

Uncurling my sore body, I look over, but the group is talking to one another and only checking on us occasionally.

"You will not be able to keep this a secret much longer."

"I'm working on it. I know the risks."

"If you talk to your mother, I bet she can help." His eyes are soft, though she doesn't see them.

"Don't," she says.

"Very well." He backs away.

I struggle to get back to my feet, holding my ribs.

"Can you continue?"

Whipping my shirt off the sports bra covers me, I check on my ribs, noticing a red spot already blooming across my pale skin. That is going to bruise. I chuck the shirt in the dirt. "I can continue, yes, but maybe let's just stick to learning moves."

"I think that's for the best. Suzanne, can you continue? She will need a partner on some of these."

She gives a worried look, glancing at her brothers, they are enthralled with one another. Looking at her fists, she squeezes them and stretches her fingers. "I can, but no actual fighting will be good for me."

"What is going on?" I whisper to both of them, trying to not be too loud.

"She has the heart of a champion inside her, one she will have to deal with sooner rather than later."

"That's a bad thing?" I ask, so confused.

"For the women of her family, yes." He holds up his hands, facing me. "It is her story to tell if she so wishes."

Looking at Suzanne, she shakes her head. I guess her story would remain a mystery to me for the time; I doubt I would ever run back into her, so it isn't horrible to not know. Rolling my shoulders, I stretch out the side that she hit to loosen it up for the exercises that would be coming.

"We will run through a couple of drills and then practice on one another. Be prepared to be sweating by the end of this and feeling as if someone has ripped out your lungs."

Giving a chortle, I shake my head, not knowing how much it would cost me.

An hour and a half later, sweat drips down my back, coating my already wet sports bra. The shorts also stick to me. Having just finished with an intense session of learning how to work with Trill and learn how to use her powers in a fight, I thought it wouldn't be too difficult. Wrong. The hard part was the combat.

Heading to one of the shower stalls, I notice most of everyone is gone for the day. No other beings occupy the area, so I take my time enjoying the alone time.

Heavy footsteps come up behind me. Turning quickly, I see Blaise before he pushes me against the wall.

"Do not wear something like this in my presence again. Do you understand?" Blaise hisses out, his eyes already turning snake. His body is hard against mine, pinning me to the wall.

"Why? Can't stand the sight of me snake?" I blurt out, not being able to hold my ire. "If you can't stand this, then just wait till you see what I change into. Have your feelings changed?"

His throat bobs. "You know I can't and haven't," he barely gets out. His tongue flicks out, tasting me.

"Why not?" I ask, confused. I did not expect him to agree with me. Let alone what he was doing to me.

"I can't stand the sight of you anywhere other than with me. Can't stand that you get to be close and touch others. Can't stand that others have that freedom with you." He raises his head slightly and inhales deeply as he rubs his cheek against my hair. "Watching you fight, learn and become who you truly are, I crave a part of that."

My animal is right there with me. I could feel her this time and knew we had the same thought. This man, though broken and dealt a tough life, is still ours. He is something we crave.

Something dangerous and wild, like me. "Blaise," I wheeze out.

He pushes against me, melding his body to mine, trapping me there against the wall. "It is something I need to deal with myself. I am working on it. I want to be better with you. For you…"

"Where is Beatrice?" I interrupt.

He freezes as if I dumped cold water on the both of us. Better that then continuing down this road where we get stuck with the same issues, or worse.

"She is resting, getting ready for another performance tomorrow. I will not be performing." He clenches his teeth together.

I feel him tense up against me. "Why? Because they are worried you have gone feral?" I stare at him and see his eyes change to snake and then back to their human shape.

"I'm one step away from feral, yes. You being here is the only thing keeping me intact. This performance will be more for the alphas who have not joined with her yet."

"Is that so? Then why did you choose to ignore me and just go on beating up that other shifter?" The shirt he is wearing is loose on him and ragged. It looks like it has been through a lot. The cold wall against my back cools me down, helping my body keep under control.

"Trust me, if you weren't around, I would be worse off, and I think she knows it."

"Who Beatrice?"

Blaise's hand rushes over my mouth and holds me firm against the wall, silencing me.

"Do not say that name to me," he hisses out. He breathes in and out in quick succession, his chest heaves with every breath.

Licking his palm, I probe him with my tongue, trying to release his hand from my mouth.

His eyes go full on snake. "Don't start something you don't intend to finish."

My own eyes meet his as they lower into a glare, daring him to not remove his hand. He keeps his hand firmly in front of my mouth, not letting up.

"No, let me say something while you can't speak, makes it easier. Without the mating bond to tether me, I'm a ticking time bomb, and she knows it. Hell, everyone knows it. She will put me to work in more dangerous situations with clients who like that sort of stuff until she cannot control the situation anymore. By that time, I may slip into my full snake form to retreat. Her next steps from there will either to give me back to my family and take someone else or kill me off. You said before that you were working on something. That you didn't want, Domini, and I stuck here with her. I want a way out of here, a way forward with you, so I will entertain the idea of leaving with you and the siren if you guys figure a way out of here."

I bring my head forward and his forehead meets mine. His hand comes free of my mouth as we sit there, just taking in each other's energy and thoughts.

"We will all make it out of here. We have to," I whisper, not wanting to disturb the peace that has come over him with making this decision. "If she knew this could happen with you becoming feral, then why did she break the bond in the first place."

"She didn't know how far it had gone. You were here as insurance to make sure I didn't go fully feral. I was, for the most part, still doing my job and sleeping with her clients. She didn't know we shared more than just our bodies, but our minds as well. We both have pulled one another and shared a part of ourselves that we don't always share with the world. That kind of mind meld doesn't require us to know one another. Our souls register one another on a deeper level. A part of her thinks she can control that with her pack ties alone."

"Pack ties?"

"It is the magic she wields that helps her to be The Beast Master. She cuts all the ties with others, so you only have the tie that she gives you with her own pack to rely on. Sometimes that is a blessing in disguise if you come from an abusive pack, but for most it is a deal with the devil you don't know." His frown deepens as he pulls me away from the wall and against him into a crushing hug.

My arms go around him, automatically lending him what comfort I could. "You were younger when you made the deal and she didn't really give you an option, it sounds like."

He curls his body around me. I hold on tight, not letting him go, knowing he needed me more than I did at this moment.

"Snakes already don't have really strong pack ties. It is why she sticks with animals like that. The snakes she keeps with her, have deals in place that hold us there more so than any tie."

"Does she have badger shifters?"

"No, she leaves them alone because of Flit, mostly. Though they are invited to the show tomorrow with the other alphas and that could all change. How is your badger handling things?" He uncurls from me and stands back, looking me up and down this time.

Giving a small shrug, I look away from his questioning gaze. "So far, I have only shifted fully on a couple of occasions by accident. One was when I was going through the mating season, or whatever you call it. Margaret, who I stayed with, helped me through that and explained I needed to make sure I was giving my animal what it needs or else it will take what it needs. So, I have been trying to listen to her and make sure she just doesn't take over. The other times were in fear or defense when traveling to get here. It is hard for me to partially change or fully change when I want to. Usually, I have to be in danger or angry."

"That is how a shifter first learns. In time, you will be able to communicate with her and she with you. Is that why you were with Domini earlier?" He brings his hand up and runs his hand through my hair, smoothing his fingers over it, almost petting me.

I let him, knowing he needs the physical touch. Every time his fingers skim over my scalp, it sends tingling tendrils along my back; I lean into his body more.

"Yea, I asked around for someone to train me and they pointed me in his direction. I knew he was a warrior, but I didn't know he trained others."

"Yea, he is a good guy that has a bad rap sheet. Most creatures stay clear of sirens, because you can't trust them. He has paid his fair share. More so than most, he has the respect of most of the warriors."

"You seemed to be really against him when we first met."

"I didn't really know him before. The warriors differ from us, who take care of carnal desires. We don't run in the same circles. She has many people she surrounds herself with. We all just either try to keep to ourselves or keep to our own circles. She has so many ears it is hard to know which ones are friends or are just going to rat you out to move up in the pecking line. I only knew he was her most seasoned and favorite warrior. I didn't know he hated her as much as I do. He gets to be close to you. I don't like that; it can't be me. That kept me from really getting to know him. I have opened to him about it."

"Sounds like you guys have been talking."

He gives a small chuckle as he rubs his cheek against mine. Hugging me close to him. "You could say you brought us together. Or at least got us talking. I'm learning he means well and is not trying to steal you away from me. I don't think we would work if he was anyone other than him."

"Well, he couldn't help me with my shifting problem, but he is still teaching me how to fight and use the fire elemental I hold inside me. Is your snake coming to accept the both of us, then?"

"You didn't have the fire the last time we met."

"No, Trill is newer. I had another of her sisters with me, but she went with someone else to track down the third sister."

He nods. "I could teach you," he whispers into my ear, easing me back against the wall.

"I don't think that would be best. You can barely control your own animal, let alone mine, to teach me to shift."

"Do you want me to stop?" He freezes next to me, careful in his actions.

"I have heard it takes concentration and focus to learn to shift, and I don't think I could do that with you. You would not leave me alone enough to achieve that."

Blaise raises his head up, towering over me. Keeping his head raised, he looks down at me. "Answer the question, Minx. Do you want me to stop touching you?"

"I like your touch. It is comforting, but very distracting. Right now, my shifting only seems to be controlled by my emotions, either when I'm scared or angry."

"You shifted when we first joined, no problem. You were neither scared nor angry then."

Laughing, I push at his chest, giving us a little more breathing room. He lets me push him back. "I don't know how true that is. One could say since it was our first time that I could have been scared. Another could say I was angry at you. We started things off in a fight."

"I want to try something if you will allow it," he states.

Crossing my arms in front of my chest, I lean away from him, unsure. "What?"

"I think it is in any highly emotional state that you would be able to shift. Where your head gets out of your body's way and lets you do what feels right."

"So, what are you saying?"

His hand hooks behind my neck, pulling me forward as he firmly places his lips on mine. Ravishing my mouth with his. The kiss lasts a good, solid minute before he releases me from his hold, letting me catch my breath.

"What I'm saying is sexual tension might be a good way for you to learn. When you're not scared or angry, there will be times when you need the help of your animal."

"So, we are just adding horny to the mix?" My heart beats wildly with him so close, I bet he could feel my racing heart in his finger where they hold the back of my neck.

Smiling against my lips. "It's a start. We will go slow enough so you can feel how and where your shifter power comes from, so you can learn how to always activate it."

"What if we can't stop? Or don't want to stop?"

"We are in a public enough space we will get interrupted. It also gives us more incentive to figure out a way out of here. Have you decided if you would like me as a mate?"

"I never stated I didn't want you. Just that we hardly knew each other. I also worried when you shut me out. With Domini being an added complication, I wanted to make sure we were all in agreement."

"I felt I had to, to keep sane. To protect you. To protect me. I had to understand things for myself before I brought you into it. I now know that was not a healthy way to deal with things, but I'm learning too." A couple of footfalls echo into the locker room. He pauses to listen.

Keeping quiet, I keep my eyes on him, unsure of what he wants to do.

Grabbing my hand, he pulls me into one of the shower stalls that is big enough for the both of us before closing the shower curtain. He turns on the shower to hot and lets it fall over the both of us in the small space. He kisses me harshly, trapping my screams from the first few blasts of cold water before it turns balmy.

"We can't be caught together. She has eyes and ears all over this place. If you want me to leave, tell me now."

I watch as the water coats both of us, his shirt molding to his body and becoming almost see through it being a white shirt. His pants mold to him but are black and soft.

The water rolls over my body, wetting the black sports bra with the black shorts, getting them soaked. My hair is thrown up in a messy bun and gets partially wet with the spray. His hair is fully wet, the soft hair falls into his eyes. I move a few of the strands to the side, really looking at him.

"Teach me," I whisper to him, trying to keep quiet. The animal within me brushes up against my insides, urging me closer. "I feel her fur."

He crowds in next to me, keeping his voice low. His eyes take on the green sheen of his snake as they turn. "Good. Keep her close, get to know her, what she feels. Move how she moves. Let her help you through this. Let's start with just the claws, and we can move from there if you want."

He brings my hand up in between us and nibbles on the pads of my fingers before his fingers skate down my arm. Everywhere his skin meets mine she bats against my insides, wanting to touch and be touched. I focus on my fingers, trying to change them or at least lengthen the nail. She moves away as I continue to stare at my hand.

"You will not stare it into existence. Get out of that head of yours."

I glare up at him. My animal sends a picture of bared teeth to me. Which I mimic. He isn't Domini. I could challenge him all I want without consequence. "Why don't you make me get out of my head?" I test.

He looks up at the ceiling, closing his eyes, letting the sultry water fall over his head he smiles to himself. Scales dance over his skin and disappear back to normal skin. His own fingers dance down his torso. I watch, hypnotized at what he is about to do. He raises his shirt, chucking it into the corner of the stall. Standing there before me, his chest and stomach bare for me to see.

My mouth opens slightly and my eyes go big as I can't believe he has taken my dare. He takes my hand that he is still holding and places it on his chest. It is firm and hard against my fingers. I can't move my eyes from where I'm touching him.

"Be careful when teasing a charmer. Your turn. What does your beast want? She may learn to listen to you if you listen to her."

She sent me a picture before maybe I could send one back to her. I send her a picture of my hand turning into a claw. Nothing happens and nothing is sent back. My fingers skim down his chest, feeling his abs as I move south, my hands growing bolder.

With each move, my chest heaves as the band of the sports bra digs into me, constricting me where it hadn't moments ago. Claws scratch at my sides as a picture comes to mind, one of her slashing the clothes to pieces and running free.

I send back my hand, turning into a claw and doing just that if she would help me with what I want. The warmth of her fur disappears as she moves away from me, not happy with being asked without receiving anything. Picky little creature.

I huff out in frustration, letting my fingers fall from his flat stomach.

"It's okay. We can find other times to try again," he says calmly.

I quickly twist and yank off the sports bra in a hurry, throwing it in the same corner that his shirt went. Blaise scoops me up so fast, my legs automatically close around his hips as he holds me there against his stomach. My back hits the side wall as he leans into me, kissing me. He begs for more as his lips devour me.

My animal rolls into me, the fur thick and pleasant. She is there, lending me her claws as my hands rush over his back, toying with the muscles there. I nix the claws, enjoying the feel of him there under my groping hands. He massages my thighs as they climb up him, wanting more. Hugging him close, I want to feel his hot skin against mine. The badger brushes up against me, urging me to do more to feed her more. She likes the feeling of him and how this is going.

He holds me and changes direction, taking me away from the wall and placing me in the warm spray. The warmth of the water and him were rocketing me up a notch. I deepen the kiss and rock my hips against him.

The spray turns ice cold on my back and makes me sit up and unlatch from him. I give a silent cry and scratch at his back, the nails coming out just as quickly. He holds me up still, so I don't go too far away, but pushes me back against the wall so he sees more of me. "Sssstop that," he hisses at me as he takes one of my arms and holds it against the wall. "Now try to ssssshift." The snake in him is closer to the surface.

I glare daggers at him as his body slowly heats mine back up from the cold spray. He slides us further away from the spray, so he is blocking me from it. Looping my legs back around him, I clench his warmth to me. My animal sends an image of her clawing at his face until he gives us what she wants. My chest rumbles as the laughter works its way up.

"I ssssee her there in your eyes. I know she is close. Ask her to shift this hand and only this hand." He squeezes his hand around my wrist. His other hand has a hold of me, keeping me tethered to him.

"I think she is also saying make her," I whisper out the challenge.

His head dips to my chest as he flicks one of my nipples with his tongue, sending an arc through me. My body pushes into him of its own accord, pushing my breast into his face, wanting him to take more than just the tip. He doesn't let me push him as he flicks and licks the left breast, going agonizingly slow. "Ssssshift, Minx."

Trying to break his hold on my arm, I stretch, push, and pull away from him, but he doesn't let me get very far. He bites the tip of my nipple before he blows on it with a warm breath. A loud, low moan bursts out of me as lava heat races across me. He jerks me forward, capturing my mouth in his to muffle the noise. My legs constrict around his waist so he can easily maneuver his other hand. He pinches the right breast between his fingers, keeping up the torment.

I try sending pictures of my hand shifting and then pictures of me joining with Blaise for her to understand his needs and mine and that they align with what she wants.

Her fur pushes more into me, and I feel her travel down my arm. Warmth seeps into my skin as she buts against the hand that holds me there. Wanting more pets from him.

As if in answer, his thumb brushes against the underside of my wrist as if answering her call and knowing what we need.

His lips mold to mine in my fever of heat, needing his kisses as much as my animal needs his pets. He matches my strength and heat with his own.

Needles spread over my hand as it changes to the claws he asked for. Whining into his mouth, I feel the pain of the slow change. Without anger or fear pushing up the speed, it hurts a lot more than I'm used to.

His other hand lets go of my nipple, and he stops kissing me. He holds me close and rests his head on my shoulder. "Good, there's my Minx," he barely whispers out. Raspy breaths puff in and out of him as his hard chest presses against my soft skin. His touch ignites a hunger I didn't want to curb. "The pain will be more, but it will get easier each time. Now ask her to take the claws back," he growls.

Before even sending the thought to her, she arches back up my arm, taking the heat of him with her. Not taking any time to move away, he sets me down, unwrapping my legs from him. Annoyance cascades around me, wondering why he didn't want more from us.

"Call on her one more time, but this time feel how she moves. Feel how you both move as one to make the shift happen. Understand what goes into it and what is needed for the exchange," he whispers into my neck, breathing in deeply, nuzzling me there, bringing tingles against my flesh.

She bounds back down my arm, wanting to please him and for him to please her. The shift went quicker this time, but I pay attention to the movements and how she moves with me to shift my hand into a claw. Each time, I swear I could feel more of her than before. Like I could understand her, maybe even understand myself.

"You're doing amazing." He continues to speak into my shoulder, his breath coming in spurts now.

"Thank you." I bask in the euphoria of being able to change so freely with practice. Maybe I could even shift on command without any emotion needed to bring it out.

"I'm glad I could help." His teeth scrape against my neck.

"Blaise?" I ask. His skin turns cool against my hot skin.

"Minx?" He throws back at me.

Blaise shifts into his snake beast form so quickly, bringing me up the wall with him. He continues to hold me against it with my clawed hand. He backs up in the small space and crashes against the other wall. Releasing me, I drop down and back away to the corner near the cold spray. My claws at the ready in case I need to hold him off.

The cold water breaks over my toasty body, freezing the warmth I felt moments before.

Blaise holds his head as he moans to himself, shrinking further into his animal and away from me. His arms transform into those long, pointed sharp nails that hold poison on the tip of them. He looks down at me and gives a silent cry as he falls to the floor, wheezing. Scales erupt over his back and body as his legs meld to one, tearing the pants away from him. His snake body takes over.

"Blaise, what can I do?" I whisper, unsure if others were still around or not. "I have not heard anyone come in since we came into the stall. Did I push too far?"

His mouth and nose take on the snout of a snake as he morphs fully into that of his animal. His arms combine into his body, creating a hood instead. I had never seen anyone become one with their animal. I had done it, but I had never seen it happening before my eyes. A snake with a hood and sharp fangs sits coiled up in front of me. The top part of his body rises and dances side to side with his hood fully out. His mouth comes unhinged and opens wide. The two fangs descend and drip poison down them as the green sheen of his eyes lock on to me. He is brownish green all over and is very large for a normal snake.

He moves back and forth. My eyes lock on to the shine of his as he sways, making his way forward to me. My claws sink back into my fingers as my soft fingertips reach for him through the cold water. As he dances from side to side, he rears back, calling me forward.

A loud bang reverberates as someone slams their locker closed, the sound bouncing off the walls, breaking the power he has over me. Looking at the wall, I wait to see if there are any other noises. Looking back over to Blaise, his huge snake snout is right at eye level. He hisses at me, making me yelp and spring back from him. I fall into the cold spray and sprawl over the ground.

Blaise takes off in his snake's form as fast as he can. He zips away, his body slithering across the smooth tiles. My body shakes both from fear and the cold. I reach up and turn the water to hot. It takes a while, but the water warms back up. I wash away all the emotions I have been keeping bottled inside me. Turning the water even hotter, I melt into it, letting it all go for just a moment so my mind can calm. Tears run down my cheeks.

As Blaise leaves, I hear screams just outside the locker room screaming. "A rabid is on the loose." After that, no other people or noises come back here to check things out. I'm alone in my misery. My body continues to shake as I break down, letting out a quiet sob.

# Chapter 10

HE LEFT ME WOUND tight after he left. After I shower, I turn the knob for the water, as far right as possible to make it arctic cold. I shove myself under the water, trying to quell the fire that burns inside. Yelping, I can only stay under the spray for a couple of seconds before jumping back out. Shivering, I wrap my arms around me trying to huddle around my center for warmth. The frenzy was worse than what I'm feeling now, but it still consumes me. I can't concentrate on anything but the needs of my body.

He didn't want to combine again unless we both had an out, and I'm a hundred percent invested. Which I could understand. Shaking my head, I focus on the task at hand. I push myself back in the cold water and do a quick rinse.

Rushing, I go to the locker with my clothes and change, not comfortable with who could come across me in such a vulnerable state. I need to get back to my room and rest for the night. "Or is it morning now?" There are not many windows in this section of the castle. I'm careful with the borrowed dress as I shimmy it back on sluggishly after the intense workout. Relaxing and sleep are what I need, but my mind is racing with where my body wants to go. If I knew where Blaise had run off to, I might just follow him, consequences be damned.

Making my way back to my room, there are little to no people out. That told me either there is something going on in some other part of the castle or it's late, and people have retired to their own rooms. My eyes scan from left to right as I try to keep the directions that Natasha and I took to get here firm in my head. I don't want to get lost and end up in a dungeon again.

After a few turns and another set of stairs, I make it back to my room. Before going in, I knock on Jazmin's door that is across the hallway, but no one answers. "She must not be back yet or is with Flit."

Opening the door, it is a room that is laid out much like Jazmin's, just with calmer tones of blue instead of her intense purples and pinks. The bed is massive but plain a good place to sleep. My body doesn't want to move anymore, not wanting to mess with anything further until I have actual sleep. I don't flip the light on when coming into the room. Closing my door, I make my way to the bed, careful not to run into any of the other furniture. Only a slice of moonlight can be seen through the drapes that are covering the windows. I leave them closed as I pass them, begging for the warmth of the comforters. Smoothing the blankets down, I roll onto the bed and yank them back up over my cool skin. Immediately, I sink into the soft mattress and give a sigh of relief.

Closing my eyes, I imagine myself falling asleep in no time. My body doesn't listen, though. I toss to my other side and kick my feet out, trying to get more comfortable. The fire and temptation continues to war in my body. The dress still clings to my curves, but I don't want to get out of bed to take it off. I move some straps and brush my fingers across my sensitive nipples. Sensations dance through my body, making me to arch up from the bed; I desire more. I growl in frustration.

"How can someone that has two men still crave more?" I whine. "Maybe if I actually could have time with them and enjoy them as I was intending to, it wouldn't be so bad," I reason with myself.

A soft knock comes across the door. Holding my breath, I wait to see what happens. Not sure if I want to know who is at the door.

Another soft knock sounds.

"Yes?" I whisper.

The door opens a tiny bit and closes. Raising up my hands scramble to cover myself with the blankets and make sure I'm properly hidden in the dark room.

"You need me?" Domini's low voice cuts through the dark.

I stare blankly into the darkness, not sure where he is and not trusting my voice.

"Flower answer?" He comes closer, holding a dish in his hand.

"Yes." My voice comes out husky and low. "Blaise..." I couldn't finish the thought. My mind is racing a mile a minute.

"He told me he thought it better I visit you." The blankets stir as he pulls them back. "Delectable as always." He sets the dish down on the table next to the bed.

His voice rumbles over me, awakening me even more. Desire burns through me. I stretch, not hiding myself from his prying eyes.

His hooded eyes watch me as I writhe in front of him. "Are you sure? What if she finds out you're missing?" I tease.

"She will not be a problem right now. I usually sleep around this time. She will not look for me till later."

"What if there is a fight or a show? Not sure how that works."

He gives a chuckle before he slowly lowers himself on to the bed with me. "The fights are always scheduled in advance, same as the shows. I'm her dominant warrior, but she has others she likes more than me."

My hands shake as he grows closer. I scoot further back to make more room for him.

"What's wrong?"

"It feels like this is all new you know? The other times it was mostly water or whatever and the last time it all felt so dreamlike."

"The djinn's world is kind of like that, but it definitely happened." He sinks down into the bed clothed in a black tank top and dark slacks. "We can just talk. But you need to feed your animal." He pulls the dish off the side table. "It's just meat, cheese, and crackers. Remember, if you don't want your animal taking over, you need to keep her satisfied. That can require more than just food." He gives a wicked smile.

I roll over to my side facing him, moving the straps back in place to cover myself more. "Do you have a family?" Reaching for the food, I nibble on it.

"I do."

"Can you tell me about them?" I brush the edge of his tank top up his stomach, running my fingers over his hip.

"I have a vicious sister named Star; she is younger than I but don't let her think that means she is weaker. She can take me on plus some. I know she cares, but she has had to fight for her spot in life in more than one way. It has changed her." His smile slips. "Both of our parents weren't around much, at least then they weren't."

"How long has it been? Have you been able to communicate with them to tell them you are, okay?"

He shakes his head. "Not directly, no, but there are clues I leave or messages I have gotten to them to let them know I'm alive. They know it is a contract they can't fight against and since there are rules and stipulations involved, they view it as fair." He rolls on his back and scoops his arm around me, pulling me into his side. "It has been…" It is quiet as he calculates.

I hold my breath, not sure which would be worse numerous years being held against your will or a smaller number. Either sounded horrible. Grabbing a piece of meat from the plate, I pop it into my mouth.

"About five years." His fingers mess with the strands on the side of the dress, running his fingers in and out of the holes. "I had lost hope until you came along."

"Tell me more." My own fingers curl around his hip, scooting him closer.

"I was captured because I'm very dangerous in the water. After a lot of training, I became just as good or even better out of water." As he talks, his fingers continue their sweet torture as they skim my side to just under my breast.

"Now a question for you to answer, my sweet. What do you want out of life? Why help return something to me without much push? What do you want out of this?"

"That is more than one question." I wriggle as he tickles my side. "But answer them I will." Flipping to my back, I stare up at the dark ceiling better than Domini's searchable gaze. Giving a deep sigh, I sink into the bed. "When we first met, I was going through a mating cycle, so of course I called others to me with little say over it. My animal started to take matters into her own paws. You were very rule driven, and you have kept to those since we have been together. What drove me to you even more is we are similar. You are in a cage of your own. I wish someone would have helped me out of my cage, but am just glad I don't remember most of it. I think the badger inside of me is in tune with my wants and needs, more so than I am."

"That is only because animals don't worry about the moral dilemma and consequences that may happen from it. They do what is needed or wanted at the time and worry about the fallout later."

"I have a hard time with that. Growing up or remembering mostly human memories makes that part hard to understand or listen to. You gave her a voice; you believed in me more than any others have. When we first met, you explained what you wanted from me. You didn't hide it or try to make me do something I didn't want to... I like that." The last part catches in my throat.

He curls into my side, leaning on his arm so he is perched over me. He moves his leg in between mine but settles there, waiting for me to continue. "Another bite." He pushes the small plate, wanting me to have more.

I pick a few things from it. "That answered why I helped you? The first question is hard to say. I'm not yet sure what I want out of life. As soon as I achieve one thing, there is more to still accomplish. I want to control my shifting power and to be of help in a battle. I know I also want to find the rest of my family and bring them together, if possible." He moves the plate back to the side table, watching me with intense eyes as I finish up my snack.

"And what do you want from this?" His fingers caress my cheek.

I can only see his outline and parts of his face only because he is that close. Feeling more so than seeing. I know his whole body is trained on me. His legs entwine with my own as he holds.

"I want to see where this goes." My voice starts out small. "Do you?"

Pushing my chin up, he lays his palm on my throat and tightens his hold only slightly. "You could be dangerous for me," he whispers against my lips.

My tongue swipes against his lips as he breathes.

A sound rumbles out of him, vibrating against me. The temperature rises under the covers, making it hotter than just a moment before.

"In all these years, someone on land has not once tempted me. I understand why the snake now refers to you as Minx. Part of me is grateful for you returning what is mine with no qualms and that is refreshing in these parts. You had all the cards and yet you chose not to play them. Over here we learn from a young age there is always a game of some sort going on. I like that about you." He brushes his lips against mine as his voice breaks. He lingers for only a heartbeat and then pulls back only far enough for our lips not to touch. Releasing his hold on my throat, he skates his hand down my side, his fingers come to the bottom edge of the dress.

"So, we are on the same page." I bite my lip as his fingers toy with the hem.

"Looks like it." He moves his hand up my thigh, going so slow raising the dress higher up my legs. "What does that mean, though, for Blaise?" His hand stops moving and just draws circles in a waiting pattern.

"I have already talked to Blaise, so now I will tell you. You are my choice; I want to see where things go with you, but I have this bond with him. Beatrice broke the tie, but it is still there, if him and I unite again it will resurface stronger than last time. He wants to be sure that is something we both want. We are still working through that part. Would you be okay with that?"

"He listens, so that shows he cares. I don't think he likes the idea of sharing, but seems to be working through that on his own. At least that is what I get when we get the time to chat."

"You said before you have a way out of here, can you make it a way out for all of us?"

"Let me look into a few things and I will get back to you on that. It might be a last-minute kind of plan, though. That way no one really knows what's going on, including us, so it will be easier for us all to get out."

"What we had before with all of us together showed me what we could have if we can work through everything. It was nice, thank you for making that a reality if even for a little while. His views on a mate were not quite ready for me."

"We each chose in that moment to make it a reality. We just have to want that again and keep choosing things that move us towards that future. You only dared to voice what you thought up, but I think that night moved all three of us in a way that we were not expecting. Him and I will have to work through things ourselves, but if we are open and honest about things, I don't see the harm."

"I don't want Blaise hurt, but I also don't want to hurt myself in the process by keeping my animal caged up. She has been locked up for most of my life. She and I need to be free." At that, I pull the band of his pants down lower, freeing him.

His hand moves up, shoving the dress up to my stomach. His hand rests on my hip, teasing me there. "I don't think he hurts. He is just having a hard time with what he thought his life would be, versus what he pictured his life with somebody, versus what it is like with you and I." He kisses me as my fingers skim the underside of his cock.

"Domini," I whisper against his mouth. "I need you."

"Put your leg over my hip."

Letting my legs free, he waits for me to comply. He rubs himself against my lips, creating delicate friction. He pushes against me, barely entering, and then retreats. "I will show you..." His voice stops as his lips meet mine. He adjusts himself, holding him and himself still. He licks my lips with his tongue, asking for entrance. I allow his tongue in and at that moment, he makes his strike. He slides into me with ease, opening me up. He stays still as I adjust around him. His tongue dances with mine.

As our mouths continue to move, my body grinds against him. He moves slowly out of me before he slides back in, holding there. He pushes all of himself into my body each time as he slowly exits. Giving me all of himself and showing how much he truly needs me.

He keeps the rhythm building in those slow, strong movements. Each time he hits home, I gasp a little as he hits the spot. It knocks the wind out of me as liquid fire pours over me.

"What are you doing to me?"

"Seems like a certain kitty has an itch that needs to be scratched."

Wrapping my arm around him, I hold him close, needing more of him to hit it just right. Sliding out, he hits home and holds me there. Moving against him, we make slight movements to brush against each other's body. My nipples harden against his hard chest, my fingers play with the short hair that is at the nape of his neck.

He pulls my arm over his head and brings my arms together, keeping them in one of his hands. He pulls my leg up to get a better angle before diving into my center, slamming home. Rolling on top, he grinds into me; I stretch to meet him.

Little moans come from me as he hits the spot I need before pulling back away. My hands fight to break free and take over so I can get what I need. Nuzzling at the dress, he nips at my breast that comes free, which causes me to pause; he gives it a few licks, stirring another fire all the same.

Pinning me to the bed with his weight, he fills all of me. "I'm going to retreat and release you. Do anything other than flip over and get on your knees will make this last a lot longer than you ever wanted, plus a punishment of my choosing."

I give a nod. He presses more into me for good measure, then slowly retreats. Pulling out ever so slowly. Once he is fully out, he slowly lets go of my hands and legs, fully retreating but letting his fingers dance over my hot skin, causing more delicious tingles to shake me to my core.

Once he is fully away, I waste no time flipping over and getting to my knees. I shake my ass at him to signify I'm ready.

A loud slap and a happy yelp bursts out of me. He smacks it one more time on the other cheek. I lean down my face, feeling the softness of the blanket giving a happy mumbling sound. I feel him slide his cock straight into me, going deeper in this position. He pushes all the way into me, and we both sigh in contentment.

"I'm going to go slow but hard, do you understand, Flower?"

"Yes," I agree greedily.

He slams into me hard but goes deliciously slow; the fire ignites on the initial hit and burning with each slow torment. After the third slide into me, I curl my fingers into the sheets, not sure if I could take the slowness. The edge is right there and getting closer each time, but I back up just short each time.

He would swivel his hips, hitting that spot, driving me mad. Moaning into the bed, I try to smother the sound coming out of me.

Pulling fully out, he rubs the head of his cock against me, teasing me. "I brought something for you." His voice travels away as he gets up.

Staying in the position; he left me unsure of what would happen next. "What is it?" I ask my body craving to get back to what we were just doing.

"So impatient. I brought some toys for us to play with. Would you like to try some?"

My voice goes husky. "Yes, Domini."

"Good girl. Stay like that for me for just a moment." He comes back behind me; his palm grabbing my ass as he pets me. I feel something slick and cool against my opening as he plays with me there, then slowly trails it to my butt. "Come back to me slowly."

I press against what is there very slowly and then rock forward.

"That's it. Do that rocking motion till you can manage. Listen to your body."

Coming back to him a bit more, it works its way into me. He also massages my opening and me, distracting me from the job at hand. Coming back toward him, I sink on to it all the way. He holds me still as I feel it sit there. Soon, a buzzing starts, and a thrum goes through me. I trail my fingers down my side to feel back there. I feel a gem on the outside pressing on it, causes it to push into me more. The pressure mixes with the delicious rumbling I feel.

"Leave it for now. How are you doing?" He commands, moving my hand away. He rubs his cock at my main entrance, entering me. The feeling of him and the vibrator together sends me spiraling down. The feeling unbearable I feel so filled and unable to contain the pleasure that is happening to my body.

"It's fucking amazing. Bright and sunny."

He starts up that slow hard motion, reaching the peak faster than last time because of the new sensation and I'm already worked up.

All too soon, he is slipping back out of me before I can go over the edge. Crying out, my fingers turn on their own to claws, shredding into the sheets.

"Stay like that or we can't have fun with the next toy."

Freezing, I try to stay still and calm down. I retract my claws back into fingers, but one entire hand stays transformed. He places something at my entrance, pushing it deep inside me.

"Now take off that dress," he puffs out as he lays back in the bed, ready for his part of the show.

Turning around, I notice him there with his hands behind his head stretched out, with no clothes on at all. I take the dress the rest of the way off, following his orders. Crawling over to him, I sit there, ready for what he wants next.

"This next game is a sort of matching game. The amount you give to me is the energy you will get back."

Cocking my head to the side, I wait to see if he will give me more. He closes his eyes in answer and rests against the pillows.

I crawl in between his legs and touch him there. Though his body seems relaxed, he is hard and erect. Grabbing him gently, I kiss him there. Taking him in my mouth, I take my time enjoying the feel of him and learning about him. As I get into a rhythm, his arms move, and another vibration answers, the one still going off in my backend. A vibration in my vagina also starts up in answer. When I stop to bask in the pleasure, he stops both vibrations. Giving a happy lick from base to tip, he causes both to go off simultaneously.

I keep moving on and around him, wanting the energy to keep building. I pour over him everything he gives back to me. The rumbles vibrate quickly through me as I move against him. I slide him down my body to my breasts, wrapping them around him. I feel a happy answer as his cock bobs against me. Continuing rubbing him against my body all the way down, I sit on him with him between his belly and my crotch. He can feel the vibrations of both things and the slickness coming from me. I move my hips as I sit upon him, wanting him to feel exactly what he does to me. His hands are still on the remote as I lean down to kiss him. Playtime is over. The rules are about to change for him.

"Take the one out of my vagina slowly." I bite his lips. Leaning up so he can reach between us, he grabs at a loop that is still on the outside of me and tugs at it. The vibration pulls against me. He lines his cock up with me so I can spear myself down onto him.

Pushing fully down on him, I feel him fill me up even more so. He is fully engorged, and I take the time to sit up fully on him, sinking down even more on him.

A gasp comes from him as I lift my hands up, swaying my hips on him. I ride him thoroughly, dancing and taking what I need. He hits a button, turning up the other vibrator. He lifts his hips up, meeting me fully before I make my way back up his length.

Letting out a happy little gasp, I come forward to feel him fully by moving him in and out of me in time with his hips. He matches it with gusto. He hooks my leg with his and rolls me to the side, switching positions. Strong, firm fingers dig into my waist as he moves me into a better position, pushing pillows under my hips, after he dives deep into me. Gasping, I feel him fully there where I need him. He speeds up the rhythm, but the hard tempo stays the same.

"Don't stop," I rasp out my arms, move up above my head, pushing against the soft headboard. Making sure I stay in place so he can hit that sweet spot repeatedly.

"Don't stop," I breathe out, arching up as I race to the edge, not wanting to be brought back down.

He keeps it up, understanding what I need and not backing down this time.

I lean into it and him letting my body take over. I arch back a loud moan quakes through me as I throw my body and soul over the edge, not worried who would catch me. He rocks against me, moving with my grinding pelvis, pulling me into his arms. He brings me up to his kneeled form. My arms wrap around him, tight my nails scour his back wanting all of him. The claws slice in more than my normal nails. My body is heavy and blissfully unaware. He kisses my neck, cheeks, and then my lips.

He rolls his hips one last time and spasms into me, holding me firmly to him. Happy spasms race through my body, bringing me gently back to him and reality. We hold on to one another for quite a while as our panting and breath get back under control. Fumbling for the control he turns off the thing we both forgot about for a moment.

"Fuck," I breathe out.

"Damn," he answers back in time. "How's your ribs?"

"What ribs?"

"You will feel it tomorrow." Leaning back towards the back of the bed, there is a tendril of light that falls across him. "Or later on then, since it is tomorrow already."

I sprawl out on top of him, content to lie there in a blissful state.

He nudges me from my partial slumber. "Come on, let's get you cleaned up and then we can rest."

Yawning. "I want to talk and know more about you."

He pats the right side of my thigh. "Come on, there will be time for that if you don't fall asleep first."

My eyes spring open at that, glaring down at him. "Is that a challenge?" I move with very deliberate movements.

"Not at all, darling." His eyes light up with mirth.

Grabbing his hand that is still curled around the control, I press his finger against the button turning it back on. The vibration moves through me as I give a happy purr in his ear. Kissing my way down his body, I flick my tongue against his nipple. "Who says we are done yet?"

"You need to rest after all you been through."

Striking out, I bite down hard on his nipple.

He picks me up easily and dumps me back onto the bed as he gets up. Cold, hard eyes pierce me. "Follow me."

"Domini, I didn't."

"Now!" He growls out, walking away from me. His penis already hardening.

I follow him to the ensuite that is connected to this room and get to work on my diabolical plan. The vibrations turn to a different rhythm, stopping and starting in different intervals. It also stretches me, growing larger. Giving a low moan, I stop behind him, surveying the damage my claws did to his back. One side is bloodier than the other.

His back muscles bunch as he turns the knob and watches as steam rises.

"You are in my element now, Flower. One thing you have probably learned being with me is pain helps push me over the edge. What you forgot to take into account is it also pushes me to my limits." Pulling a soft bench away from the wall, he drags it in between the shower and the mirror.

"Domini, please," I beg as I wrap my arms around him, molding the front of my body to his strong back. One hand rests on his chest, holding him to me as my other hand wraps around his partially stimulated penis. Squeezing tightly, I feel him thicken in my palm answering the harsh tugs. "You can make me sleep so sound and for so long, believe me I can handle it."

"Bend over the bench and point your ass towards the mirror," his tone is low, as if he is holding something back.

Doing as he asks, I peel myself away from him, crawling over the bench, I bend over it. Looking back, I see the jewel shining from my ass in the fogged over mirror. His soft steps retreat.

"Feel yourself, play my little wicked flower."

A flip of a switch as he walks away causes the mirror to defog. Soon I can see myself crystal clear. My fingers roam over my ass as they tease, getting closer and closer to the jewel. Pushing on it, I feel it sit deeper. Pulling at the jewel, I watch as my ass stretches a bulb peeking out. A bit of pain comes through, so I push it back in. Quick vibrations reverberate through me in answer, licking away the pain. The thickness diminishes as it returns to a smaller size. Moving it around in small movements sends happy gasps through me. My other hand delves down to my core the dual sensations edging me higher.

"You will not come unless I tell you to," he says back in front of me.

Looking at him in the mirror. I give him a smile. His eyes darken as they watch me. Feeling myself getting slicker in excitement. "Only if you do not go until I tell you as well."

"You will not win this game, Flower."

Turning my face back to him, I open my mouth. Taking him into me, I scrape my teeth against him. A shudder runs down him. He slams into my mouth, hitting the back of my throat. I moan around him as I use more teeth as he leaves me. My fingers pause in my pleasure as they come to rest on the bench.

"What do you crave, Domini?" I ask, wanting to know more about what makes this man tick.

He walks around behind me. "Drag it out slowly and show me." He wraps his large hand around his thick cock, manhandling it as he watches my hand dance over my sensitive skin.

A part of me knows he craves me, but I want to know more and want to hear him say it. By the end of this, I will get him to answer me. I just hope I can outlast him. Wrapping my fingers around the jewel, I slowly pull at it. It is smaller now, so it doesn't stretch me as wide. My other hand slides back as I dip a finger into my hot, snug pussy, wanting more of the slickness covering me. Slowly pulling out the plug, I fight, wanting to push it back in. Once it is out, I leave it pressed there as my ass greedily asks for more. Putting the toy aside on the bench, I give Domini a wanton look.

"Back at the djinn's, we had a special cream that helped you. It would help takes away the pain, but without it we have to train your body up to taking us." The tip of his cock is a deep red as he squeezes himself hard. He comes forward leaning over me, the head of him bumps at my fingers. I spread my lips for him, letting him in. He spears forward into me, letting go of his penis at the last second.

He inhales deeply as he sits fully in me. Stroking in and out of me four times, he pulls himself back. All the while, I am looking back at him, watching him intensely, feeling every inch of him. Kissing down my back, he spreads my ass to him and licks me thoroughly. His tongue lashes at me twirling inside. He takes his time.

Pleasure cascades around me, begging for me to fall over the edge into a beautiful orgasm. Fighting my animal back, I show her there will be more. She stops, intrigued enough. Soft fur erupts over my body and pulls back in.

"Losing already, Flower?" He laughs.

Shaking my head is all I can manage.

He slides the plug back up where his tongue leaves off, sliding the tip into me. He rocks it into me; it slides in easily. Pressing the switch, he turns the intensity up on the speed. The blub increases in size. I watch as it stretches me. He holds it there, stopping it at the widest part; he gives me time to adjust. Vibrations start small and crescendos into larger ones, picking up tempo. Pinching my nipples as pleasure rocks through me, I ease back on the toy, feeling it all in me.

"Such a good girl," he purrs.

Domini caresses my lower back as he walks back around to my front. Grabbing my throat, he pulls me up to him. He captures my lips; my hands are free; they dance down his stomach to his cock, his hand still gripping tightly around himself. Going lower, I cup his balls. I squeeze his balls as I push my tongue into his mouth. Deepening the kiss, he holds me tight against him as he pushes against me just as strong. His hand pushes my neck back, breaking the kiss.

"You will crawl to me in the shower and please me as the water rains down on us. Do not lose your bite." His hand drops as he plays with my breast, pinching the nipple. Turning away from me, he grabs a pillow off the cream-colored bench and takes the few steps to the shower. The water cascades over him, wetting his hair and body immediately. He drops the pillow in front of him.

Lowering down to the floor, the toy rubs against new sensations for me. Breathing through it, my eyes feast on Domini, naked and ready for me. His palm releases his cock, letting the blood flow before he constricts his hand around again. Crawling to him, I feel the toy more than I ever have before as I get into a sitting position in front of him.

Since he has a hold of himself, I lick his balls, sucking them into my mouth. Pulling at him, I rock on the pillow. His hand slides up his cock, giving me more room. He flexes his hand, not stopping the motion. Bringing my own hands up, I touch, feel, and caress him. Mixing up the harsh and light touches his body bucks against me.

"Flower," he gasps out.

Moving his hand away, I pull him into my mouth, giving his poor cock the warm release it needs from his harsh hands. Sucking and licking, I take away the pain. The heat of the shower raises the heat in us. My skin becomes extra sensitive when the water droplets touch me. His power radiates around me as I continue. Holding his balls, I squeeze in an upward motion as my mouth pushes all the way down on him. I struggle to take him into my mouth but force as much as possible. As I come up, I scrape my teeth against the underside of his cock and release some of the pressure on his balls, massaging them. Keeping with that rhythm, I have him losing control in a matter of minutes.

Rocking back and forth, the movement and vibration of the toy increases. My body stutters and stops, not wanting to ratchet my pleasure up anymore. I am on the precipice of going over. His hand comes down on my hair, he pulls the hair tie from it. Freeing my hair, it tumbles in wet ringlets down my back. He gathers the tendrils in his palm and controls the speed and depth I go down on him. My tongue curls on the underside of him, rubbing against the ridge of his vein.

"Flower, come for me," he yells out in passion.

My hips begin their rocking motion once more, not questioning his motives. His hips shove forward into my mouth. Moaning around him, my hand that is not holding his balls hangs on to his thigh, my nails making half moons in his skin as I hold on as he rides my face.

Shoving himself all the way to the hilt, my throat constricts around his cock and threatens my stomach.

"Flower, tell me I can go!"

He grinds against me, making it impossible to tell him.

"Bite down if you want me to."

I hold out for a few seconds, but air is precious, and he has his hand on my head keeping me locked on him.

"Please," he sighs.

Hearing that, I know he is not one to say that very often. Shaking my head, my tongue swirls on the underside ridge. I would not give in.

Pulling out of my mouth, he quickly grabs my upper arms to help me stand. He yanks me up. My legs automatically cling to him. Pushing me against the wall, he crushes me between him and the wall. His arms pull my legs wider, as he kicks out each of my legs on top of his arms so I am open to him. He fucks me senseless as he presses into my hot sheath.

Moaning out, this is what I crave. Pulling him into me, I bring his lips to mine.

"Didn't I tell you to go?" he growls.

"Tell me what you crave?" I barely get out between happy hiccups of pleasure as he thrusts into me.

"You, I want you!" he yells out passionately. His hands inch closer to my butt as he pumps into me hard and fast, pulling at the gem in tempo with his strokes.

"Domini! You can go!" I yell out, no longer able to keep the orgasm back with the double sensations.

He lets out a rough yell as he lets go; he slows his pumping as he grinds us into the wall, the warm water keeping us comfy as our heat abates.

"Now don't you feel better?" I smile at him, panting.

Giving a half smile of his own. "Oh, Flower. We are far from over."

We continue as I get to learn more about him as well as his body. He did not win, or perhaps we both did in the end.

# CHAPTER 11

A FTER OUR FUN ADVENTURE through most of the day, I
do little other than rest and speak to Domini. He had to
leave after a time, which left me to my own devices. I slept the
rest of the night and continued until late the next day. Domini
was correct. The bruise on my ribs welts up and is very sore
to the touch. He doesn't come back to check on me, though I
didn't expect him to either.

I dress in loose clothing and leave my hair down. After wearing the dress, it feels nice to wear pants and a shirt again.

What is concerning is that no one checks on me. I poke my
head out of my room. In the bright hallway, there is a bustle of
people moving about already. I step out and keep my back to
my closing door, pulling it tight behind me. Waiting for a few
of the staff to pass, they trudge down the hall with their carts
of cleaning supplies and dirty laundry. Most of them are in a
dark button up long sleeve with black slacks. I make my way
across to the room directly in front of me and tap on the door
a few times. A few seconds go by with no answer.

"The mistress isn't there."

"Mistress? That must be Jazmin." Giving a cursory glance around. "Do you know where she is?"

"With the Lord of Darkness himself, of course," she answers sharply.

I wince in answer to her high pitch cheeriness. "And that would be?"

"Oh, I can't tell you that." She shakes her head. "No, no, no." She wrings a towel in her hands nervously.

Shuffling my feet from side to side, I give a glance around. She smiles and continues on. "Wait," I call out. "Do you know where I can find Natasha or Zeek? They are friends of mine."

"I don't know who that is, miss. Do they stay here regularly in the castle? The guest hallways will be on the third through the sixth floors in the west wing." She tries to point me in the correct direction.

"Natasha said she visits here often. Would that mean she has a permanent room here?" I should have asked her yesterday where her room was.

"Not sure, miss. I have not heard of her, but I'm new here and getting the people figured out." She gives a sweet smile as she blinks.

"That's okay. Never mind, I will just have a look around then."

She gives a curt nod and waits a moment longer than last to make sure I don't need her for anything else. My stomach growls so loud it is enough for her to hear it. "It's late for lunch, but if you head down the main stairs just down this way and head to the right on the first floor, you will come across the dining hall. There is always someone around they can get you something to eat."

"Food would be good." I head the way she is walking to the main staircase. It is a grand center stair case I am on the second floor but it goes up three floors from here. The ornate rails are wooden and detailed with swirls and what look like clouds. "Thank you. I slept most of the day away yesterday and wasn't able to get much in the way of food."

Then I might run into someone I know. At the stairs, she continues down the hallway to wherever she is meant to be. I descend the stairs. There are a few people walking around and talking with one another, but not as many as I saw last night at the show or when seeing Flit and Sera. I take a right down the hall and make my way to some food. This hall is warm and inviting, but no one is down this way. Soon I find myself in a large room with many tables and seating. There are people cleaning up from the lunch rush and only a few sitting down and finishing their meal.

"Excuse me," I call lightly to one that is cleaning up a table. The man ignores me until I repeat myself, coming around so he can see me fully. "Hi." I wave to get his attention.

He gives me a questioning look but remains quiet. His rough hands slow their cleaning but continue to wipe down the table.

"A lady said I could talk to someone about getting something to eat." His blank eyes meet mine and just continue to stare at me as he walks around the table wiping things down. I act like I have a sandwich in my hands and am taking a bite, then grab my stomach and show a look of pain. "Do you not speak English?" I ask, unsure.

He gives a polite nod and walks away, heading through a door. Looking around, I don't see another person who works here and all others seem too enthralled with what they are doing to notice me. I give a hesitant look at the door he went through. Waiting a few moments, hoping for the man to walk back through. I head over to the door, testing it; it opens into a bustling kitchen with people moving around one another.

"Pardon me," I call out. Someone carrying a large plate that has many other dishes on it walks up.

"Can you open the door, please?" Her eyes glare at me.

"Yea, of course. I was looking to see about getting something to eat." I let her know as I open the door.

She comes barging through, breezing past me over to a table, ignoring me.

"Okay, I guess you won't be taking my order," I say to myself. Turning back to the kitchen, I jump back, startled, noticing the man that had been cleaning before. He gives a creepy smile as he hovers in the doorway. There is no way around him to get to the kitchen. He raises his hand, and that is when I notice something wrapped there.

"Is that for me?" I ask, unsure if I should take it or not.

He pushes the wrapped item to me. Taking it from him, the contents are warm in the wrapping. Unwrapping it, I notice a burrito. Taking a bite, I sink into it, not caring if there is human food in it or not. The taste is unbelievable, and I only slow down after the third bite to inspect what I'm eating. The contents look like there is bean, cheese, and meat.

"Thank you," I say around a mouthful.

He holds out another one. I take that one also, bowing as I take the amazing food he has provided. Moving away from him, I head back the way I came. Not wanting to sit down and dirty another table that the man would have too eventually clean.

After devouring the first burrito, I rip into the second one, trying to slow down enough to savor it and make it last longer. I didn't know which way to go when coming back to the main stairway, so I just walk around and see where my feet take me. After a few turns and going down another set of stairs, I get turned around a bit. Some hallways double back and others feel like they go on forever. Wandering, I find myself in a different part of the castle than I had seen the other night.

Turning down a hallway, this one is darker than the others. I back out immediately, unsure of wanting to head down this way. People stick to the main areas, and I wondered down a hallway where I thought the west wing would be. Hoping to run into Natasha, Zeek, or hell anyone I knew at this point. There are no signs pointing me in the correct direction, so all of this is a guess.

A hissing sound emits further down the spooky hallway along with a thump.

"Is someone there? Are you okay?" I call out, but not too loud. Looking back, the way I had come, I search for someone to help. I don't want to go into the darkened hallway, unsure of what lay there in the shadows. I freeze, not wanting to move forward.

A large snake moves into the light, zipping down the aisle so quick he comes to a stop just in front of me. The hood of the snake isn't as erect as last time, and there are scratches on its underbelly as it stands up, eyeing me. He moves back and forth as if trying to mesmerize me.

Staying weary. "Blaise is that you?" It looks like him, but I have not seen any other shifters shift fully into a snake, to know for sure.

The beast nods its head as if it understands. Moving away, he heads into the shadows. Stopping only before disappearing fully, and looks back at me, waiting.

"You want me to follow you?" He nods again, still waiting for me to move.

Taking one small step forward, I make a stand. "You're not going to attack me this time, are you?" A growl slips between my lips. "For that matter what are you still doing in your snake form and why are you all scratched up?" Forgetting my firm stand, I walk forward, my hand stretches out to his hood to pet him.

He rises, meeting my hand, letting me caress his scales. A few pops and cracks, his body bows into itself as he gets even larger. He twists into himself as a torso takes shape out of his snake like body.

"The beast is easier to handle when you are near," he hisses out. "I'm not doing very well, Minx."

"Why are you not resting, then?"

"I had to come find you and show you something. You must know." Taking my hand, he pulls me to him as he slithers down the hallway into the darkness.

Falling to his side, I try to match his stride. The way his body moves is weird as he slides back and forth over the carpet.

"Domini said he is going to find a way for all of us to get out," I whisper to him, wanting him to know that freedom is within our grasp. "That is hope you can use to keep you human."

"That isn't something the snake part of me cares for at the moment," he bites back.

Taking my hand back from him, I stop. "What do you want, then? And where are you taking me? I can hardly see." I fumble to make out the shadows in this dim lighting. We stand right in front of a picture of a forest with butterflies sprinkled around.

"You know what I want and need. The man will only ssshow himsssssself to you." His beast takes over, making the S noise more prominent. Gripping the side of the picture, he pulls it open, showing me a passageway beyond. Another pop and snap comes from Blaise.

Placing my hand on his arm, I reach out to steady myself. He freezes. The scales ripple down his arms. "What can I do to help you?" My face softens, my heart pounding. "I know you are only dealing with this because of me. If we would just complete the union, you would be better off."

Placing his hand on mine, he stretches his neck as if settling into this half beast form. "That is only a part of the problem. If we did combine, that would be a for sure death sentence for me and you. The Beast Master would not allow me to live and if she did, she would make my family pay for my happiness." He pulls me into the secret passage next to him. "Your touch and closeness help, believe me."

"But it also tortures you because we can't finish this."

"That isn't important right now." He shakes his head, walking me forward. His tail latches onto the side of the painting as we make our way through and pulls it close behind us. The tight corridor barely allows us to walk side by side. I have to walk in front of him, but I keep his hand in mine so he can guide me while also keeping him calm with my presence.

"What is important?" I whisper, unsure if others could hear us moving within the walls. "Are there passages like this all over the castle?"

"Yesss, we will need to keep quiet as we move into this next section." I nod, being guided into a series of twists. Ducking down, we push through a smaller walkway where we must walk one by one.

My fingers touch the walls, having a hard time seeing. Cobwebs catch on my fingers. I cringe back into Blaise. Shaking my hands in front of me, I try to dislodge the sticky web. Keeping my mouth closed, I let out a quiet squeal, not wanting spiders to be crawling along my skin or hair. Shaking myself, I can't stop my body from shaking. Blaise's hands travel over my arms and pick at the web between my fingers, removing it. He waits for my fear to settle back down.

Turning in his arms, I rest my forehead against his chest. I wait there till my nerves are calm. He leans down next to my ear. "We are almost there, Minx; you can do this." I step away from him, leaving one hand for him as I make my way back down the creepy hallway.

He tugs my hand back, stopping me when we get to an opening where there is some room for us to spread out. Bringing up his hands, he pushes my hair back behind my ears and holds my face as he looks at me. He takes one of his hands back and taps his finger against his ear. We wait and listen.

Looking around, I have a hard time keeping my eyes off of him. The silence is almost deafening. Murmurs can be heard from in front of us. He moves us closer to the wall.

Glaring at the wall, I try to make sure there are no spiders or webs on it before getting my hair or head anywhere close to it. The murmurs are muffled but I hear the sounds a bit clearer.

"Did you tell him?" I hear Beatrice yell out in a fit of anger.

"Calm down," Sera hisses in response. "No, I did not tell him about your nasty spawn."

"Then how did he know? You said you would keep my secret if I helped you. Are you lying, truth witch?" Her voice lowers.

"You know...the truth...I'm... on your side..." Her voice goes in and out.

The rest of what she says cuts off because she lowers her voice even more. Staring at the dark, rough wall, I check before laying my ear against it.

"Sera and Beatrice?" I mouth the words to him; afraid they could hear us.

My eyes flick to him as he nods. Closing my eyes, I try to not think of how much dirt and grime are built up on these walls. Blaise still has his hand in mine as he brushes his thumb over mine.

"Flit has his ways of knowing things besides me." Sera picks back up.

The words become clearer as I lay against the wall. Hopefully, they don't step away.

"Then why this meeting? It isn't good if we are caught together." Beatrice's voice becomes hard.

"I think we can help each other out."

"How so? With your possible spawn? Who, by the way, has taken out my best money maker," Beatrice snaps.

"Again, you are thinking too small. Think larger picture," Sera says mysteriously.

"I could kill her to solve all our problems. Thorn has been wanting to get his claws in her ever since he met her," she cackles.

"You want to be in charge of things and Alexia out of your hair so you can get back to doing what you do best. Is that about right?" Sera asks.

"That's right."

"I want this prophet Jack brought to me for answers and if this girl is who she thinks she is then I will also need a shadow creature to be dealt with. "

"What about the girl?"

"If she is my daughter, then we use her as leverage. Flit won't be able to resist his own blood. That is something he cares about," she bites out.

"Not to save his own boys...How can I help?"

"I'm told that you have ties to the institution where Alexia met your pet snake. Is that still true?"

"Yes…"

Something tickles my neck. Swiping the side of my neck, I catch tendrils of dust and little hairs. The dust stirs at the wall, my hair, and cheek having disturbed its resting place. Holding my breath, I try not to breathe any of it in, not wanting to stir anything further.

My leg jiggles with impatience, waiting for it to die back down before placing my cheek against the wall.

"Procuring the boy for you is easy enough, but how are you going to get him to tell you what you need to know?"

"I have my ways. Making sure he can't resist is what I do." Sera's shoes tap against the hard floor as she takes two steps to the side.

Sliding down the wall with her, I try to keep her close, adjusting as she continues to talk.

"I also hear you were in contact with my half-sister's husband," Sera says.

"Who?"

"Jade's husband, Tom. I heard he hired your snake to get close to the girl."

"Who told you that?" Beatrice's voice shrieks as she herself backs up, her voice fading from Sera's.

"Truth witch, remember. There isn't much that goes on that I don't know."

"You sure seem all together for one that is plagued by the power."

"Do I? Must be a good day. Wait to see what tomorrow brings. Anyway, Tom?"

"Yes, I was in touch with him. He had to go deep into hiding to heal, said he was on the run from something." Beatrice gives a laugh.

"Tom could never do anything right. Why Jade married him, I will never know. The only dreams he could make come true was the fake kind. If this is the girl, then it could be the shadow spell that is coming for him."

"Couldn't be anything to do with this girl. She isn't scary at all. I will get with Thorn and send him out to find Tom and this shadow fellow, if that is who is following him."

"We will know more once the boy Jack is here, but good to have Thorn on call to take care of the other problems."

"How will this help me take down Flit and for Alexia to leave my snake alone?"

"Flit will, like I said, do anything for blood, so he will follow this girl and help her with all his being. It will be his only tie to family. Easy to take advantage of someone distracted. With the shadow in trouble, she will leave at a moment's notice to try to save him, only later to find out he has already been taken care of by your cat."

"Thorn can finish another on his way back if you so choose. Like the girl," Beatrice comments.

"Perhaps," Sera says cryptically.

"Deliciously evil for a truth seer."

"Once you let it in, it takes root and grows."

"And to think you started off as one of light?"

"The light is easily darkened by the toxic sludge that we house here." Sera gives a giggle.

"Why do you hate Flit so much?"

"He took and hid something that belongs to me. I think the rage inside is palpable to what he has done to me over the years."

"What did he hide from you, pray tell?"

Silence covers the area like a blanket. Quiet words utter out of Sera in a deep tone. "Just because we are working together doesn't mean we are friends. Careful what questions you ask me. I hear your snake got out of its cage," she fires back.

The silence thickens. Beatrice breaks. "Yea, some warriors thought it would be fun to poke the snake and wanted to battle it to see how they would do when it comes to a rabid. Thought it would be more of a challenge than what they are used to."

"Cute."

"We will find him soon enough."

"I'm surprised he doesn't go straight to his desire, could be he is too messed up from all the years with you?" Her cruel intentions wrap around her words, hitting with finality.

"He is too far gone for that. If you sat her in front of him, he wouldn't even know she was there. We found the cage in tatters. It is a good thing Flit's goons whisked her away while they could."

"Do you think he will come back to sanity when Alexia is gone?"

A big sigh releases before Beatrice speaks. "Honestly, I don't think he will come back from this. We will most likely have to put him down. I will use him as cannon fodder for the fights until he is too far gone, then put him out of his misery."

"No more snake charmer then."

"He has a cousin that is on my list that would be a perfect snake charmer to my den of creatures."

"And what will you tell Blaise's family?"

"Why do I have to tell them anything?" Beatrice says haughtily.

"What they don't know won't hurt them?" Sera's questions.

"Exactly. They will think he perished by normal means or tried to escape. The story doesn't really matter. He will just leave a space for another person to fill his contract."

"If they want your protection from being hunted, they will fulfill it willingly."

"Correct. Score one for The Beast Master."

They both give a hoot of laughter. Continuing to chat, they move onto different topics, one that didn't seem to pertain to us or anyone I knew. Pointing, I signal to him we need to move back through the way we came. He moves to the side and waits for me to slide between him and the wall, keeping a hold of me as we move through the maze-like walls. Only stopping when we come to a split in the road, I follow the way we came. He pulls me back and to the right side.

"Didn't we come from this way?" I keep my voice down, unsure of who else could hear us in this in between space.

"Yessss. But that way is blocked now. We must go this way," he says easily, leading me to the right.

"Is it safe to talk?" I ask, since he knows more about the passageways and what is behind the walls.

Shaking his head. He slithers through more twists before stopping us at a dark nook. Giving a knock. The wall opens and slides back, opening to a large empty room.

Looking around, there is a grand bed, but everything else is empty except for three doors. "Is this how you have been getting around and avoiding getting caught?"

"Yes," He rumbles over my hand as he brings it up to his cheek, rubbing it against his face. His voice is more human-like. The scales disappear as he pulls himself together with my closeness.

"Have they talked like this before?"

He gives a small nod. "I knew you would want to know."

"This changes things. I must get with Natasha, her and Zeek have to warn Shade."

"Natasha won't leave you by yourself here."

"I will have Jazmin, plus we have a friend out there that Zeek is close with. She will want to go with him to make sure they are all right. Thorn, from what little I know of him, is a sadistic psychopath. They will need all the backup they can afford, especially if Thorn brings friends with him."

"What's the rush?" He eases me back into his arms, stopping me from walking away from him.

"You, you." Pausing, I swallow, trying to get rid of the dryness in my throat. "Need to go find Domini and tell him his plan needs to be sped up. For all of us, it looks like things are about to hit the proverbial fan. We need an exit strategy for all three of us, like yesterday."

He gives a sad look to the bed and then back to me. His tail taps at the wall, sending it back into place behind me. I feel the firm wall at my back as he pushes me closer to it, trapping me. Dropping my hand, he places his arms around me near my head, looking down at me. Caging me in, but not forcing anything more. He leans his head into his arm and closes his eyes.

Pulling himself together, his snake form fades. My eyes almost pop out of my head at his naked form standing over me. Heat from him radiates against me. He is so close, almost touching. I could feel all of him.

"Blaise." I barely forms his name.

"Just a few more minutes, Minx." His words tear out of him with pain. A small tear trails down his cheek.

Staring at him, I can't look anywhere else. My heart breaks in two from what this man has gone through. He deserves to be happy and to have a mate that doesn't give him any trouble. "I'm sorry you got stuck with me," my voice breaks. "You shouldn't have to deal with my trouble on top of what she puts you through."

A corner of his mouth lifts in a grin as his eyes open slightly, looking at me from the side. "No, I'm not. I would choose this all over again if it led me to you and the moments I have spent with you. I'm far from perfect and will be challenging at times which is good because you challenge me to be better."

"Clearly you are in a huge amount of pain, which I'm causing. The stress I'm putting on you. I can almost feel how much you are hurting."

"I would rather feel that than the emptiness and numbness I have been feeling the last ten years. Feeling or caring is not something I come by easily." He lowers his lips to mine and brushes the softest kiss against my lips. "When someone is at the point of feeling nothing, you would think they are safe from being hurt, but in truth it is the opposite. They will do anything to feel, which means they will most likely hurt themselves and others around them just to feel or experience something real."

My heart breaks for him as he confesses what he has been dealing with. I stare into his eyes, not looking away. "Blaise you need to go find Domini so we can all get out of this place. I will go get with Natasha and Zeek right now. One of you find me later to explain what is happening."

His arms don't budge, and he doesn't move to do what I ask. He stands there, our eyes glued to one another. His arms shake as if he is holding himself back.

"I'm not the only one affected by this. I can smell your excitement."

My mouth is dry as I rest my head against the wall, leaning my body back. Trying to put some much needed distance between us. "Did you want to do this now, here? Where we could be caught, and our plan exposed. She would not let either you or me out alive. We have grown closer to one another, but I still think we need time."

"She is keeping an unyielding hold on my tether. I feel it. She would know the moment we come together," he whispers out between clenched teeth. "I don't know how long I can last before going full rabid even with you around." His eyes turn back to that of a snake and his skin takes on a greenish brown hue.

"Hold tight a little longer."

"I think before it was easier knowing you weren't around to tempt me. It is harder now that I know you are here. You are real and physical. No longer just in my thoughts and dreams. I know I want this, and yet we still have to wait."

A part of him is no longer fighting things and standing at attention for what he wants. Licking my lips, my eyes move from his eyes to lower and then back. My heartbeat thumps in my chest as a low heat burns through my body.

"I have to go," I say halfheartedly.

"Do you?" He presses into me, pinning me there to the wall.

Feeling him thick and hard against me turns the warmth up and the flames begin their ascent up my body. "There has to be a way to ease this without..." Nuzzling my neck, his fangs scrape over my pulse, sending tingles through my body.

"I need more," he says almost feverishly. He nibbles and kisses his way over my throat.

My fingers raise of their own accord, lightly brushing against his side. They slide over him and over to my chest. I yank on the chain around my throat, fumbling for the red heart ruby. "Domini," I utter as I grip the stone in my fist. An answering thrum pulses in my hand.

Blaise's hand moves quickly and pins my arm to the wall with the stone still being held. "Bad Minx." He throws me over his shoulder and quickly crosses to the bed, throwing me on the comforter. The sheets and blankets smell of him and the rich spice he always smells like. The smell is intoxicating as it surrounds me. I scramble to raise up, but he is there. His weight smothers me, holding me there. He pushes a knee between my thighs, rubbing against the fire, edging the flames higher.

"Domini," I whisper out before the heat and feeling consumes me.

He kisses me, robbing me of the chance to call for help or logic, both of us out of this decision. My fingers unclench from the stone as they crave to grip on something else. My arms twine around him, pulling him closer.

He raises up enough so that his weight isn't restricting my movements as my hands move south. His body moves in time with my hands as he gives a happy purr of excitement. Looking up at him, the restraint is clear on his face, but his body is in total bliss with what is happening.

Strong arms wrap around Blaise and pull him back off me. He slides from my fingers back towards the bottom of the bed. I come up finding Domini there, straining to hold Blaise still.

"Go," he utters. His muscles are flexing as they restrain. Sweat pours off him as he tries to hold him still.

Hissing comes from Blaise as his teeth and nails elongate, getting ready for battle.

"Stop!" I bellow out in a low tone. Both men look at me and freeze. My eyes flick to Domini. "He needs something... We have to hurry with our escape." I lower my voice, making sure we are not heard. My eyes flick to the closed door.

"No one knows I'm here."

Bringing my eyes back to his, I crawl forward. Domini pulls Blaise and him back to the bedframe post, leaning against the round thick wooden pole. Using it to help keep Blaise contained. Crawling to them. "Let me put him at ease. Keep a hold of him so it goes no further, though. Blaise? Will you be able to work with Domini after? Work with him on how we will get out of this place?"

His fangs and nails return to normal, only his eyes stay that of a snake. He nods in answer, his body still strains to be free.

"What is happening?" Domini asks.

"We overheard a conversation. I have to go warn my friends so they won't be attacked. I will work on that, but both you and Blaise have to work on an exit strategy she plans to end his life sooner rather than later, especially if he continues to degrade to a rabid." My fingers skate over Blaise's lower form, caressing the soft skin there. He opens his legs so I can kneel there in between his thighs.

"Train with me later tonight in the gym and I should have a plan worked up by then," he throws my way before turning his eyes on Blaise. "Okay snake, this is how things are going to go. If you are a good boy, we get to continue with Flower there doing whatever she wants. If you are bad and don't listen to me or keep fighting me." He puts emphasis on this by tugging at his still moving arms. "Then she will walk away right now."

Blaise begs me with his eyes to stay, but he releases the tension that he is putting on Domini.

"Good, now put your hands behind your back so you won't be tempted to touch the delicate Flower," Domini whispers next to Blaise's ear, his voice rumbling in all the best ways possible.

Blaise moves slowly, but puts his hands behind him. Domini still has an arm around his chest. He eases back so Blaise can lean on him but still has him held if he gets out of hand.

"Relax fully snake. Once you do, I will allow her to really touch you," he says.

His legs were curling in towards me. He kicks them back out and lets the tension go. He also fully leans on Domini, making him take his weight, releasing himself to what is about to happen.

"That's it." Domini unclenches his fist and lays his palm flat on Blaise's hard chest. His fingers brush against him in a teasing manner.

Domini nods at me.

Eagerly, I make my way down to his very firm and throbbing member. Grasping my hand around him, he isn't as wide around as Domini, but he is longer. Pushing down on him, I push my hand down around him to the base as I flick my tongue over the tip and kiss the top of his cock, sucking it into my mouth.

Blaise bucks his hips and hisses, straining. Domini flicks his nipple and pinches it hard. "What did I tell you, snake?"

Blaise throws his head back on Domini's shoulder and continues to push into him. "Easy siren, I'm not going anywhere."

Pausing in what I'm doing, my eyes follow the two men. Blaise's hands move behind him as if he is petting Domini.

Lowering myself, I lick from the base of his penis to the top before I open my mouth and take him into me, wrapping my tongue around him.

I hear a sigh of relief and a shudder go through his body as I continue my examination. My other hand wraps around his balls and rolls them between my fingers. I look up to see what they are doing. Both men are staring at me, fire in both of their eyes.

"I bet she is wet at her center, ready for you," Domini whispers to Blaise. Domini's other hand encircles his waist and trails up to his other nipple, squeezing and toying with him there.

Blaise's eyes close. A small moan slips out.

"Do you want me to tell you how your little Minx is training to take you?" His hands stop pinching and instead brush lightly over the swollen nubs.

I take this moment to take him further into me, pressing down where he just brushes the back of my throat. I come up quickly, bobbing a few moments before taking another breath and pushing back down.

"Yesssss!" He moans, his hips wanting to buck forward, but he holds still.

I keep up the rhythm, needing this to be done quickly, even though I crave this time with them. Shade, Robert, and the fire sisters, they all could be in trouble.

Domini whispers things in Blaise's ear where I can't hear. Whatever picture he is painting really works him into a frenzy. Domini's left hand comes down and cups my cheek.

Easing back, I slow the motion; he moves my hand from around Blaise's balls, cupping them himself. Wrapping both hands around him, I put everything into licking and sucking Blaise.

Domini pushes into Blaise's back, firmer, as he rolls his balls in time with my rhythm. Looking up at them, I see Domini nibbling on Blaise's ear. Blaise's eyes are half lidded, enjoying the pleasure rolling through him. I run my nails lightly down his inner thighs as I sink down on him, holding there, trying to swallow around him. Coming back up for air, Domini's hand follows, rubbing him and keeping the motion with his hand.

"Come for me," I whisper to Blaise as I look up at both men. Domini mouths the word go as he plays with Blaise helping him. Edging away

Blaise fights to get to me. "What did I tell you, snake, if you don't listen? This all stops." Domini holds a tight grasp on his cock.

I crawl back and lick the tip of his cock; it is swollen and very thick. He relaxes as Domini releases the pressure but continues the motion to work him back up.

"Blaise?"

"Hmm?" He moans as I caress his stomach.

"Come for me and next time you will get what you desire most."

"No, you can't possibly keep that promise," Blaise whispers, fighting his body, wanting this to last as long as he can push it.

"Listen to me, snake. We make the rules here, not you. Do as she asks. Have faith in your mate."

Moving over his leg and perching next to Blaise and Domini, I hold Blaise's head as Domini continues rocking his body. I spot Blaise's hands, massaging Domini as best he can behind his back. I brush a kiss against Domini's lips. "Now," I utter before I mash my lips to Blaise's, forcing my tongue into his mouth, wrestling with him. Domini attacks him in other ways, and only a few moments go by before Blaise is bucking against us. I release him as Domini takes him fully in his arms. I slip from the bed, listening as Blaise lets out a cry of both anguish and relief.

"Shh. I've got you," Domini whispers.

Making my way across the room as quiet as possible, I open the door and look back at both men one last time. Domini stares at me with a half-cocked grin on his face. With white stuff coating his fingers, he dares to lick one as I stare. Blaise turns into Domini's cradled body and sobs into his shoulder. He would be safe and cared for. They both would be fine for now.

Shutting the door, I make my way down the hallway, trying to find my way back to the main room. Since he took me through the tunnels, I'm not sure which part of the castle I'm in.

The rest of the day passes in a blur, trying to find someone who could lead me to Natasha or Zeek. After a few dead ends, I finally make my way back to the dining hall. Needing to get a snack since my stomach is tying in knots. Flint, Jazmin, and Sera were all busy, and I'm not worthy enough to know where that is or interrupt them. "Trix," I say under my breath, hoping to call him here to me. Jazmin said he would be around, but that might have just been yesterday.

I don't see him fly past, so he must be off doing something else. I knew no one else in this castle that could help me. "Maybe they will find me instead if I stay here. They have to eat sometime, right?" I mumble to myself.

# Chapter 12

"WHAT THE HELL ALEXIA!" Natasha bellows.

My body shudders awake, her voice making me jolt up. "Hey," I say sharply. Wiping my face, I push up from the table. Looking out the windows, the sun is setting. "How long was I out?"

"How am I supposed to know? I just got here." She gives a critical once over. "You have a mark on your cheek from sleeping on your fingers." She gives a hoot of laughter.

Giving a glare, I wait for her to stop. "Where have you been?"

"Is that why you have the entire castle looking for me? Chill Alexia. Why didn't you just ask for directions to my room? Or ask Jazmin to give you directions?" She gives a look of concern and confusion as she pulls out the chair next to mine to take a seat.

My sleepy eyes zero in on her, trying to tell if she is being serious or not. "Are you kidding me? That is why the whole castle is looking for you, because every time I did ask, they wouldn't know or didn't have a moment to help a nobody like me. Jazmin wasn't in her room and was with Flit. No one would help me there. They couldn't possibly be bothered to disturb the King of Darkness, no," I say sarcastically. "This whole place is a maze and as soon as I think I'm going the correct way, I get turned around. That is why I ended up just staying, knowing someone would find me or I would spot someone I know. I know how to get to my room and here, that's it. Shoot, I don't even remember how to get back to the gym we were at last night... or was it the day before? Also, why are there not a lot of windows in this place?" My chest quickly rises with the huffs of breath I take in between my talking. "It's hard to keep my days and nights separate if I can't see outside much."

Natasha's mouth pinches as she looks around. "When this place was built, our half of the world was in eternal darkness, at that time windows were not really needed unless you wanted to look up at the stars. You will notice some of the more modern built places or addons will have more windows." Giving a shake of her head. "I forget that Sera and Flit have not claimed you as their own yet. In my eyes, it's a done deal."

"Yea, that is kind of weird. Do they get many people saying they are me?"

"Anytime you are dealing with money or power, you deal in secrecy and plots. Unfortunately, some of them have been pretty good. Or at least that is what Zeek could uncover."

"Where is Zeek? I wanted to talk to both of you?"

Giving a frown her eyes dart away, looking at the entrances to this room. "He will be down in a moment. He is wrapping something up."

Placing my hand on hers, I wait till her attention is back on me. "How are things with you two?"

The stress and worry are clear in her face. "He is always there. No matter how I try to lose him, no matter if I ask for his help or not, he is always there."

"Like a stalker?" I question. "I didn't think..."

"No, nothing creepy like that." She gives a quick shake of her head before patting my hand back and sliding away from the touch. "To be honest, he is growing on me. The time we spend, I like it. He makes me feel safe without even asking."

"I'm confused. Then what is the problem?" Really studying her. My eyes meet hers and I see the unshed tears in her eyes.

"I don't know if I'm strong enough to let him in. Let myself be that vulnerable, to end up hurt in the end. I almost..."

"How do you know he will hurt you? Wait you almost what?"

"They all do at some point." A corner of her mouth kicks up. "Nothing."

"Are you going to be able to last a year?"

"A year and a day." She gives a sickening look.

"Can't you tell him to go away? I thought he let you make the rules."

"You overheard that, didn't you?"

My cheeks heat up as I look down. "Yea mostly."

"Great. Yea, I can tell him to go away as long as we converse for an hour each day and I don't try to get with anyone else."

"Seems simple."

"How many times have you had sex since we left that place?"

My mouth puckers, not wanting to answer. I stutter, not sure what to say. "That's a different story."

"Is it?" Natasha gives a wicked look.

"Yes, I went into a heat cycle.... Also, I had never really experienced anything like that, so..."

"Easy to become addicted to, am I right?"

My face falls as I give her a dead panned look. "I also had the mating frenzy to contend with."

She waves her fingers in the air, bypassing my statement. "Yea, yea. The thing is, people like me like to have the freedom to be with whoever I want and go wherever I want."

"So, you think you traded one prison like Morning Star for another like Zeek?"

"Sometimes it feels like that. Sometimes I wish I could not let my past ride me so hard. Where I could be carefree and just let myself be happy for once."

Biting my lip, I let my fingers fidget. "I'm not sure what to say. I don't know how to make this okay for you."

"I don't think there is anything you can say or do to make this right. It's just something I have to work through with him. I guess. But I'm glad you are here and willing to hear me out and not judge me for it."

"That's what friends do."

"None that I have known of before," she gives a scoff.

"Good thing you have me now." I give a smile.

"What is this I hear of a little pup that has lost her way?" Flit raises an eyebrow in question as he makes his way into the room with Zeek right beside him.

I physically see Natasha mentally stuff her emotions back down. A mask comes down over her face as she hides her true emotions. "You too?" Natasha asks, her eyes flit to Zeek before landing on Flit.

"News travels slow around here, it would seem. Because that was hours ago," I complain.

Flit's eyes flicker to both Natasha and Zeek as he stands off to the side. "You guys don't need me then since you have her, right?"

"You are correct. I don't need you," I say directly to him, looking him in the eyes, making myself known. "Also, why would I need help from you? You can't even tell who your family is." I give a sneer.

Natasha sets her hand on mine. "Alexia," she murmurs.

Giving a snarl. "No, he needs to hear this." Standing up from my chair, I come around the table to stand up to him. He is quite taller than me, but I don't let that dissuade me.

He looks around the mostly empty room. "This isn't the time or place for this."

Biting my next words off, I hiss out. "Then take us somewhere that would be better if you don't want others over hearing." Keeping my temper in check, I hold off on the anger that is coursing through my blood.

His dark eyes bore into mine, staring me down.

I hold his gaze, not backing down. This is the last straw. I have been more than courteous dealing with others running my life and doing and saying whatever they wanted to me, no matter how rude they were. "I refuse to be treated like this anymore and you will listen to what I have to say, regardless of who I am to you."

His eyes widen in surprise as he raises his head and gives a slight nod. "Very well." Moving to the side, he makes room for me. "Follow me then."

Following him down the hallway, Zeek, and Natasha follow behind us, whispering something I can't make out. Keeping my head level, I pay attention to the turns he makes leading us to a room. That way, I know how to get back to the main area. Flit holds the door open for us as we pile in. There is a large desk with papers draped across the wood. A large screen set into it like the ones we used in the library when Natasha was showing more of this world. There are books and relics that fill the sides of the room, with only a few chairs to sit in.

"This isn't a large room, but it will be comfortable and safe enough to get whatever you feel you need to off your chest." Flit walks in after us and closes the door, locking us in.

"Is that necessary?" Zeek asks his eyes fly to the corners of the room searching.

"Yes, very." A muscle in his cheek twitches as his eyes land on mine. "If you do not wish to be retaliated against for whatever you are about to say, and do not wish for plots to ensue. Then yes, the lock enables a barrier around us so that what we say here stays hidden from prying eyes and ears."

Natasha interrupts my pent-up outburst. "Why do you not claim her as your own?" Crossing her arms, she cocks her hip and leans against the desk. "Why not help her and protect her through all of this?"

Closing my eyes and breathing in deeply, I slowly release it and wait for the answer. I walk over to the desk and look through the papers, keeping my hands busy. Most of the things on the desk are in a language that I can't read.

"Since Sera is here to do the claiming, it has to be her. I could if Sera stayed away like I had planned, but she has other tactics." He gives a pinched look.

"Even though she has gone crazy?" My hands stop as I look at him, refusing to believe that.

"The power that Sera has gained has..." he gives a pause. "Changed her, but she is still in control of her faculties."

"Did you warn her of the troubles she would have with the power she gained or did you just let her dive head first into power regardless of the outcome?" My anger boils back up, not wanting to stop. "Did you even try to stop her?"

Flit walks to the front of the desk and places both hands face down on the papers resting there, leaning into it, getting closer to me. "No one tells Sera what to do or not do when she puts her mind to something. Be careful in how much you push, even I will not tolerate being accused of things you have no understanding of."

Putting down my own hands on the desk, I mirror his stance and glare right back at him. Looking him over, I see his hair isn't as smooth as it had been a day ago. It is loose and looks as if he has been running his hands through it nonstop. On closer inspection, his eyes look tired, and he isn't as put together as he would have us think.

"Why were you looking for us, Alexia?" Zeek asks, trying to diffuse the situation.

Hanging my head, I say under my breath. "I just want my family back together."

"I want that too," Flit says.

Looking back up at him, I catch a glint of emotion. If I didn't look up for it in that instant, I would have missed it.

So, the dark one has feelings. He to just stuffs things down like Natasha. These people have otherworldly powers, but they are still people at the base of things. If you know what makes someone tick, you can figure out their end game.

"At first, I wanted to find someone because this place is a maze to me. I have found a few places, but this place is huge, and the hallways turn into themselves, making it easy to get turned around."

"Some rooms and hallways are spelled that way to keep the guests always guessing." Flint gives a chuckle as he stands back up right. "It is why I spend most of my time here in this place than some others. It is both more comfortable for our more human like side and it also has defenses built in."

"And the second reason why you wanted to find us?" Zeek asks, keeping us on track.

"I need you and Natasha to go find Robert and Shade and protect them?"

Natasha falls back into the chair, plopping down. "What do you mean, protect them? Did something happen?"

Zeek comes up behind Natasha and braces his hands across the back of the chair. "Alexia, please explain what happened." He becomes very calm and freezes in place.

His lack of movement worries me. "I overheard a plot. They plan to go after Shade. If Robert is there, they will take out anyone with Shade. If they aren't there yet, they will be close, and Tina will pull Robert to Taz if she feels her sister getting hurt."

A scream wrenches out of me as my wrist engulfs in flames. They quickly separate from me, pulling into one tall flame on top of the desk. Tears spring to my eyes as pain spears my wrist.

"What is happening with my sisters?" Trill stands there, her flame dancing high with her long hair fully spread out around her.

Holding my wrist, I cower away from her heat. Glancing at my wrist, it is red with angry welts surrounding it.

"That is what we are trying to figure out." Natasha puffs out a chilly breath as she brings down the temperature in the room.

She stomps her foot, causing her flames to burn higher.

Raising my other hand in protection. We all back further away, giving her some space.

"Why did you not tell me, Alexia?" She looks at me with hurt in her eyes.

"Sorry. I just found out today I was just getting everyone together before we do something about it."

"You never use us! I could have done something about it. Could have at least gotten these people here faster, if nothing else."

Natasha shakes her head. "You know better, Alexia."

Biting my tongue, I give a low growl. "What do you want from me? I'm trying. She isn't Fae, so I can say those words to her. Trill I would have told you sooner, but I didn't want you to worry until we had a game plan ready to go."

"Well, what's the plan, then?" She gives another stomp, scorching the screen beneath her foot.

"I was just getting to that. I need Natasha and Zeek to go find Robert and Shade and protect them."

"Excuse you. I'm not leaving you here alone. Hell no!" Natasha interjects.

"You have to go with Zeek. I'm not sure how long it will take to find them, and he may need help."

Zeek stays quiet, letting us squabble.

"He can handle things on his own and we can communicate another way."

"I will be safe enough here with Jazmin, if nothing else. It would be better for both of you to go and deal with Thorn. That is who is working his way towards Shade as we speak," I urge.

"Who is Thorn?" Natasha asks.

"Beatrice is behind this?" Flit growls. "He is a white tiger shifter that has a thing for causing pain and enjoys watching people go through it. He has been with Beatrice the longest and is loyal to her."

"Not only her," I stop, unsure of how to pursue things.

"It doesn't matter who goes. I'm coming with." Trill belts out. She shakes her head, not waiting for our excuses. "I will be able to zero in on both Taz, who is with Shade and Tina, who is with Robert. It will be faster to find them, protect them, and then get back here to Alexia." Trill puffs, but her flame still holds tall.

"She does have a point," Zeek states. "She would be able to help us more than without her."

"You said Beatrice isn't the only one in on this plan. Who else is?" Flit asks.

"Yea, I came across her and Sera, conspiring together, discussing how to get rid of me and the people I'm close to."

"Why would she do that if Alexia may be the final fate?" Flit asks himself, more so than anyone else.

"What about the fact that Alexia is her daughter? Why would she want something to happen to her?" Natasha throws out.

"Wait, that sounds familiar, the final fate. How do you know that?" I ask.

"What don't I know?" Flit cocks his eyebrow. "Sera is my daughter-in-law. Of course, I know about the prophet who talked about her and foretold of the final fate." His eyes zero in on me, pausing. "As long as she has a tie to this world, all will be fine. If she doesn't, she will begin her descent and become the final fate. This world will no longer exist. I feel she will be the justice this world needs regardless of which way this shakes out." Flit rushes back to his desk as he sees cinders start to light on the papers strewn about his desk. "As for why Sera wishes Alexia to be out of the picture, your guess is as good as mine. She could have seen something or heard a believed truth from someone else that is tipping her over the edge."

"Didn't we read something on that, Natasha?" Staying far away from the flames that lick the desk, I baby my wrist. "Can you make some ice for my wrist?"

"Yea, I showed you a couple of pages on this." She rubs her fingers over her lips, thinking. "It said something about if two sides come together and combine their strongest people, a savior would be born." Her other hand reaches out to me, covering my wrist in a thin sheet of ice.

Shivering, I wince in pain as the ice hits directly on my skin. It cools the heat climbing up my skin. She stops before it gets too thick.

"Let me know when you need more."

"Sure," I shiver. The heat already melting the ice, making it a watery mess. My eyes scan around, looking for a cloth.

"Here." Flit pulls a silk cloth from his pocket, waving it in the air.

Snatching it away from his fingers, I bring it back to Natasha, handing it to her. Her finger skims over the buttery cloth, coldness imbues the entire cloth holding stiff.

"There you go."

Taking it back, I retreat to a different chair furthest from the flames. Pushing the cold cloth onto the arm of the chair, I wait for the ice around my wrist to finish before placing the cold compress on it. Flit gathers the paperwork from his desk, shoving it into a drawer.

"Have any of you learned self-control?" He barely contains his ire as he turns. "Here's the thing about prophecies. The simplest thing can make that prophecy come true and something no one even thought of can bring about something else. Regardless of who is the final fate or the savior, why would Sera want the final fate to happen?" Flit crosses the room pacing.

"How much of a lead do they have on us would you guess?" Zeek's dark eyes are busy looking off into thin air. He mumbles to himself, trying to get a plan together.

"Later in the day, after lunch. It's later I know, but not sure how much later." Shrugging, I walk over to a lone covered window that is in the room and bat at the covering. Outside, it is pitch black, and the moon is only partly full.

"They have twelve hours or more on us. We should get going. The good news is that this Thorn guy won't know which way to head exactly."

"Beatrice had a place to start looking said Tom was in a place she knew of and was hiding," I say.

"We will have Trill here to help guide us to her sisters, and that will pinpoint them quicker than a hunch that Thorn has to go on."

Turning back to them, I watch them hustle around the office. Trill jumps down, shrinking, but her flame is still fierce. She launches herself onto Zeek's shoulder.

Giving a growl, he blows at her fiery flames. "Tone it down. You will not burn a hole into this coat."

She tumbles from his shoulder, giving a shriek. Pooling down into a ball on the floor, she dims the intensity of her flame.

Hopping back up on his should, she avoids his eye. "Let's go then. We have to make up some time." Trill pulls on the collar of Zeek's black coat.

Natasha gets up and steps toward me, away from the others. "Are you sure you are going to be okay? You won't have Trill anymore, just your animal to call." Giving a glare to Flint, she talks louder. "You don't have family here."

"Jazmin will help and look after me. I'm not alone here." I give her a heavy stare till she understands what I'm getting at.

"Will either of them be of any help to you in this place?" She whispers to me.

"I will be fine. Have been so far."

"Barely at that," she curses but leans in and hugs me tightly. "Don't think I won't come hunt you down after this. Stay alive if you know what's good for you."

"I'm betting on it. We have more to talk about you and I." As I lean into hug her back, I whisper into her ear. "Don't be afraid to let him in, either. If nothing else, we can bond over hunting him down and killing him if he messes up," I say louder at the end as we come apart.

She gives a hearty laugh and shakes her head.

"Flit," she prods him with a finger into his chest as she turns to leave. "Even if you don't think she is family, she better be in one piece when I find her again. Or I will be coming for you."

"Is that supposed to scare me?" His eyes glare as he holds his head high and stands straight. Shadows lengthen in the room, climbing up the walls. Zeek pulls in tighter to Natasha, his eyes turn red in retaliation.

Zeek waits beside Natasha, studying the situation. My eyes flit back and forth, curious as to which one will make the first move.

"Careful who you mess with," she says in answer as she turns her back and flips her short blue hair at Flit and leaves the room. Not looking behind to see if Zeek would follow.

He gives one last hard look at Flit before following behind her. Trill hangs on as he makes haste.

"She means well," I try to diffuse. "Well, if we are done here can you tell me where the gym is from here? I have to meet someone there for training."

Waiving his hand, he dispels the shadows; the light comes back to the room in an instant. "Why of course you will head down this hall all the way till you come to a staircase, then take that all the way down then you follow that till... You know what never mind I will walk with you and we can talk along the way."

"Sure, if you must. If it doesn't inconvenience your Highness."

"What do you mean by that?"

"Forget it," I grumble. Going to the open door, I wait beside it, waiting for him to pick the direction we are meant to go.

He passes me by but stays to the side on the left, waiting to make sure I follow.

Accompanying him, he sets a leisurely pace that is of no rush. His smooth calmness irritates me with his cool demeanor.

"You know what? No, I won't forget it. I tried all day to get people to interrupt you or find you or Jazmin, but you couldn't be bothered. Or more importantly your people couldn't be bothered to help me."

"You can't fault them for that. You are of no importance to them and after the show that Sera put on, everyone knows that you are not under our protection, so why would they waste time on a nobody? If it's any consolation, I would have come sooner if I had known."

Keeping my head turned away, I roll my eyes. "Why is that?"

"Though Sera doesn't claim you as family. I do not need the definitive answer she does."

"Yet you can't treat me as such."

"That is correct." He folds his hands behind his back as we walk beside one another. "So, there is no real help from that."

"She is just so different from the last time I saw her. There were bits and pieces that were confusing." Shaking my head, I try to dispel the past cobwebs. "What was her confusion versus mine from the spell? I'm still not sure if I'm misremembering or if I can even trust what I saw from the past spell."

"I might be of some help there." He angles his head toward me as we move. The plush carpet coats the hallways, softening our steps. "Trust the time when we talked to you in the mirror. That was real."

Keeping my eyes on the turns we make; I try to remember this in case. Parts of this place are solidifying in my mind, becoming less of a labyrinth.

"Once she lost a part of herself." He gives a pointed look. "The one babe was not enough for her. She withdrew into her truth dreams, believing other truths happened, ones where she could be with people she couldn't. Then she had to give up everyone to stay safe. She did not have an anchor in this world. She spiraled."

"Like a coma? She had you, you could have been her anchor."

"Not for many years. She had to be hidden and put under for her own safety. She has only been back with us this last year. Her truth power corrupts her mind with her hiding such a big thing like this."

"And of course, you don't fix it. Would coming clean make things better for her? Would she get her mind back?"

"Why would I? It helps for this purpose not to," he says with ease. "It is easier this way. There is no telling how far her mind has gone and if it would be able to come back."

"What about the light side? What do they think happened to her?"

"Everyone is looking for an earth witch and she is more dark than light now. She takes on and embodies her truth powers here far from the light. She is safer here."

"What would make her work with Tom, though?"

"That is something I still don't understand. Perhaps she has seen something I have not. I will say for someone who never enjoyed playing games and politics, she has become very good at it. Ivan would not recognize her as she is. I hope he doesn't blame me for this." His face falls as he retreats into himself.

We walk in silence; I'm unsure of how to console him. Do I even want to? The silence is kind of nice after learning more information without having to demand it from someone. I felt that is all I'm doing lately is trying to force people to tell me things I should already know.

The next few minutes skate by as my mind races to find something else to talk to him about. What did you say to the ruler of darkness when they were your grandfather but couldn't acknowledge it in any way?

"Here we are," he says.

Giving him a nod, I make my way into the gym, unsure of how to leave things.

"Alexia..." he calls to me.

Looking back, he lets me see the anguish written there on his face. "I'm sorry for what you had to endure. I watched over you and I know who you are, no matter if I can claim it or not."

Learning from Natasha, I know he would not say such a word unless he really meant it. Taking a few steps back to him, I really look at him, weighing my words. "Was this the only way?"

"Yes."

"Do you plan to be there in the future?"

He hesitates for a moment before saying, "yes."

"Then Flint, I accept your apology and all it entails." I feel a weight come to rest around me. Settling deep in my core.

His eyes widen. "Be careful how you use that."

"Hopefully, I never have to. But it tells me something of you I am guessing not all know."

His face falls as he hides what he is thinking. He pulls away first and I watch him walk with measured steps back down the hallway. I wait till he turns a corner and is out of sight before I relax. The apology sits heavy in my stomach like a large round ball my animal bats at with her paw. Playing with it as if it were physically taking up room, and she doesn't like it invading her space.

"It's there if we need it." I try to calm her, making sure she keeps the favor. Turning back to the gym, I don't see Domini anywhere in sight. I head to the locker room to change. He would be here any moment.

Going back to the closet, I search for more clothes to borrow. The closet is not too large, but it is bigger than a normal one. It has many clothes for different creatures and sizes. Wandering amongst the shelves, I search for something like I wore the day before.

"There you are," Domini's voice whispers out as he comes into the light from the back corner.

"Am I late?" I look around to make sure no others have followed me in here. Seeing as I'm alone other than Domini, I think we are safe.

He hugs me close, holding me tighter. "No, we didn't agree on a time, but I have been waiting for a moment. We need to get going?"

"What about Blaise?"

"We talked. He will meet us on the beach."

"Okay, how do we get out?"

"Through here." He pulls one shelf forward as it swings open on a hinge. It leads into a dark, tight hallway, much like the ones Blaise and I crawled through today.

"How many secret passages does one building have?"

"That is the dark side for you." Domini urges me through the door, monitoring the doorway to this closet. It doesn't have a door to close, so anyone could walk in. "Let's go before someone becomes suspicious."

"Yes, let's I have a lot to go over. I'm hoping once you, Blaise, and I are all free, we can go help my friends. They may be in danger."

"You mentioned that to me before. I wonder if that is why Beatrice is so distracted lately. Either way, once we are free, we can discuss the next steps then. I will need to check in with my kin for I have been away a very long time. Other than that, they will understand."

"One step at a time." Racing through the tunnels, I keep quiet as I match my movements to his, keeping up with him. My heart is beating fast and my mind is racing at all of us, being free.

*Our dream is becoming a reality!*

My heart soars.

# Chapter 13

"WHERE IS HE?" I ask. My lungs burn as they struggle to catch up. We had run from the tunnels, too excited to see all three of us together.

"He must have not been able to get away," Domini responds. The moonlight catches on his frown and worrying look. "He said he would meet us here."

"We have to go back for him." I stop and stare at him, my mind locking on something I remember Blaise talking about. "His family, he said he wouldn't leave if there wasn't an out for them. He would not betray them a second time. He already thinks of himself as a traitor to his kind."

"But he could have taken care of that once he is free. Why would he lie to me about coming? Why not just tell me?" Domini asks.

"He wanted me to get free. I wouldn't leave if it wasn't with both of you. We have to go back, Domini. We can't leave him in the hands of Beatrice."

He kicks at the sand and looks to the ocean that is right there inches from our shoes, then looks back at the castle off in the distance. His eyes do not stay long on the castle before they are called back to the lulls of the sea, the water breaking on the sand. He inhales and lets out a slow breath. Kicking off his shoes and socks, he lets his bare feet sink into the sand. He is wearing dark shorts with another black tank top.

"You can't... can you?" I ask. Part of me doesn't blame him.

"It has been too long, and my freedom is right there. My contract terminated the instant I got my siren soul back. I stayed only long enough to make sure you could be free. I owed you that much for all that you have done and have become to me." He motions with his open palm. "Come with me. Let's be rid of this place. We will take some time to regroup and come back for him later." He grips both of my hands in his and backs towards the rolling surf, begging me to follow him.

I stand firm, not moving with him, and my palms fall away from his. He stops there between me and the water. Hesitating, I can see the conflicting thoughts and emotion written all over his face.

"I want all three of us to be free now. We all deserve that." Rushing into his arms, I latch onto him one last time. My body melds to his as he catches me, holding me tight. "I will get him free and then we can all be happy. He is mine and I will not let her hold what is mine."

"So, you have made the decision to claim our little snake then," he chortles.

"Yes, I don't think there was ever really a question about whether we would be together, but when and how? I had to work through what I wanted before I was ready. Let alone him being ready himself. Sad to say, but it was probably best that our bond was broken so he could realize what he truly wanted." Hesitating, my face scrunches up in confusion.

"He does seem more open now with us than he used to be. I didn't have to use my siren song on him after you left. It's probably for the best that you get him now."

"Wait, what do you mean that is for the best?"

I slide down his body, but he holds me close to where we are still touching, not letting my feet hit the sand. "If you don't go back for him, she will most likely kill him. She has no use for him if he cannot be the pawn, she needs him to be."

"Why wouldn't she just try to find another job for him?" Placing my forehead on his shoulder, resting there exhausted with all that has come with this day.

"Did it sound like that from the conversation you over-heard? Either way, Blaise would not stop trying to get to you even with your tie broken as it is." Shaking my head, I sob out. "Don't worry, though. If you didn't wish it, he would respect your wishes. It is only because she keeps him from you."

"It's not that. My heart breaks for him and you both. You guys have put up with her for so long."

"You will be good for one another, but don't forget about me." He sets me back on my feet his hand smooths over a tear that falls onto my cheek.

My fingers clench in his shirt, pulling him closer to me as I raise up on tiptoes to kiss him. I pour everything into this last kiss, wanting to tell him what I could not.

He wraps his arms around me, dipping me back as he deepens the kiss. Moaning into the kiss. "I will miss you, my Flower." He brushes his lips against mine again.

I try to memorize the feel of his lips and the way his body fits against mine. "How will I contact you if or when we are free and can be with one another?" I whisper out.

He wraps his large hand around the ruby heart that I still wear on the necklace; it warms against the chain. A red-light beams into it and diminishes as it leaves Domini's palm. "This, if it touches ocean water at all, it will call to me. I or someone close to me will come and get you. It still holds a small part of me, so please be careful with it, but it will help me find you when I need to."

"What part does it hold?" I ask, staring at it as I hold it carefully in my palm. "Will we be able to communicate like we did previously?"

"Not as well. We will have to test it later. It holds a little of this." He spreads his palm over my chest. "And this," his fingers tickle my side, causing me to laugh out loud. "It's all the best parts, don't you think?"

"Tell me everything will be all right." I let the jewel fall and nestle between my breasts. My hands come back to his, holding on to them and rubbing my cheek against him, not sure if I could ever get enough of him to let go.

"You know I can't. We do not lie to one another like that. I'm not sure what the future holds, but I know it needs all three of us in it."

A squeal and a few clicking sounds echo from the dark waters. Domini and I both turn suddenly our gazes scan the rolling ocean. Listening and waiting, "I have to go." He moves forward without thought.

"That is the reason you can't come back with me to get Blaise, isn't it?"

"One of them, yes. When I was taken it left a hole for my people, one that they will fight tooth and scale to get back. Once they knew that I had my siren body back, they will stop at nothing to break me out. I don't want a war to break out."

"Why, it might make The Beast Bitch back down," I say with a bite. I notice a couple of heads pop out of the water, their features hidden in shadows. Some had frills and others had more sharp angles. None of them looked like another.

"If there was a war, it would be the ocean against the people on land. We would be against everyone on land, including you. I'm pretty fond of you and would not like to see you as a victim of war. Even if I went back on my own accord my own people would view that as a threat there are rules that need to be followed."

"I remember Domini." I take his hand in mine and pull him closer to the water. "Come on."

He seems shocked at first, but then trails behind me. My bare toes hit the cool water. The warmth of the surrounding air mixes well with the cool water. Walking in, I let the water stop right below my knees before I stop. A few splashes happen as some move further away or dive under the water, kicking their tails at me. One moves close, heading for us at a fast pace.

As she gets closer, I can see more of her features. She is a sea-foam green color and where Domini's angles were sharp and more shark like hers are softer and rounder. Her eyes are jewel like, and her scales reflect a shiny hue to them as she moves through the water begging for you to lean in and touch her.

I stand firm, letting them see both of us together, hand in hand. A lulling song starts up as she sings. The beautiful tune hits my ears, calling me deeper into the water. I notice Domini's frown and his hand tightens on mine. "Star," he barks.

She splashes at him, getting the rest of his clothes wet.

I crouch in the water closer to Star, getting closer to her. She swims up further and continues with her singing. Leaning in, my eyes envelop her size. Her hand reaches for my face as I lean even lower. The waves bump into my chest. My animal to call comes rushing up my spine, pouring in to my arms and eyes. Everything becomes crystal clear as my arm strikes out. My claw catches on the netting that is around her chest. I pull her closer to us, holding her there. My teeth sharpen as I drop Domini's hand to get a better handle on the fish in front of me. "Your kind understands rules correct."

Star gasps as I haul her out of the water. The gills at the side of her neck flutter in the air. Her scared eyes zero in on Domini, who doesn't move a muscle.

"Answer me, Star," I growl at her.

"Yes," she says through clenched teeth. Her mouth is lined with a double row of sharp teeth.

"Then listen to me carefully. He is mine; I claim him."

Audible gasps can be heard around the group, not just Star's.

"His soul is made for the water. I will not hold him captive, but his heart is here." My sharp, pointy claws tap my chest. "I will trust you with him for now. Do you understand?"

Many heads swivel to Domini in answer. Even Star doesn't know how to respond. Giving her a shake, I lower Star back into the water, her form shaking. She makes little gasps of breath. Crouching back down, I push her back; the water comes up to her neck.

Domini walks up beside me, his fingers trailing up my arm. "Are you sure you don't want to come with? I think you would make a grand siren. Or siren like person." He smiles. "You are amazing, you know. Growing into your own."

"I had some help in realizing what kind of person I want to be, but yes between you and Blaise you guys make me feel amazing." Leaning my body into his, I lay my head on his thigh, happy to just be there. "I know they would most likely beat me in a hand-to-hand combat, but I think they see me now at least."

Giving a little cough, Star's eyes are downcast. "You will not steal him away?"

"No, there is nothing to steal."

"You are stronger than you even know, little badger." He taps his forefinger on my nose. Wrinkling my nose, I let go of Star. He pulls me up, making me stand in the surf with him. He gives me a peck on the lips and then on the forehead before walking further into the ocean, leaving me there.

"Bye," I whisper, the chill of the water finally getting to me without Domini's warmth there to combat it.

"Until next time, my deadly Flower." As he walks further into the surf, he waits till it is up to his chest, then takes on the change. His sharp fin on his back can be seen in the moonlight. He circles in the water, waiting, but he doesn't poke his head back up.

Tears roll down my face uncontrollably. Star is still close by. Her head swivels back and forth between us.

"But he hated humans." She watches as the other people who have come dip back down below the water's edge, swimming to meet with Domini and welcome him back.

I shrug as I slowly back out of the surf, not sure what she wants me to say. I didn't know him from before, and he didn't share that part of his life with me. All I can go off is what we grew into and what we are now.

"Human?" Star asks.

"Huh?" I ask, wondering what she still wants.

Star's eyes keep to the horizon where all the others have disappeared. She sits there; her pink colored fin splashing in the shallow water. "Can I know your name? Please?" Her head swivels back to me, but her eyes dodge down.

Coming out of the water, I sit down in the sand at the edge of where the water hits. Curling my legs up, I rest my head on my knees and sit there a moment, letting the sadness surround me. "Alexia."

She swims up as much as possible, lying on her front as the waves push her further up the beach. She lays there flipping her fin in the air but doesn't change to human. The silver and pinks color nicely around her tail where Domini's is sharp, she is what I expect a mermaid to look like, more pretty than lethal.

"Thank you, Alexia, for getting my brother out of that place."

"He's the one that got us out of there, but I suppose he couldn't have done that without his siren soul." Looking at the beach, it is a little nook set behind the castle, away from the town. The sand is nice and fine and soft enough to squish your toes in. Taking off my shoes, I do just that. "Shouldn't you get back to the others?" I ask, not sure why she stays here.

"I—" her tail swishes back and forth in the water harshly. "It's just."

"It's okay. I don't really feel like moving on yet either. If you would like to, we can sit here and talk," I offer. "My clothes need time to dry out some, anyway."

Pushing herself back into the ocean, she moves back, hunkering down. Pushing herself back up out of the water. "You don't hate me?" She squeaks.

"No. Why do you stay here with me?"

"I want to better understand why he would like you." She gives me a full look; her eyes scan me up and down. Her face is full of confusion as her eyebrows pull down and her mouth tightens. "My brother has had dalliances with others for fun, but never anything serious. The land has changed him much."

"I don't think either of us knows how it really came together. It just happened, we both needed someone at that point. It just worked."

Giving a dreamy sigh, she places her chin on her fists as she gazes at me. "When did you guys know it was something more?"

"I'm not sure if he is there yet or when it was for him. I would be curious to hear his answer. But I can tell you when it was for me."

Star nods excitedly as her tail flips backward in the air, hanging there in suspense. "Yes, please tell me. I have not had a brother for many years. I would like to know more about him. No sisters either."

"I just had my tie severed from my mate and things were rough. I felt the loss and my animal reacted, leaving me lost, confused, and scared."

"Your mate he died? We of the sea do not have mates. It is a weird concept to us, but we know what they are."

"Oh. No." Shaking my head, I back pedal, forgetting she did not know about Blaise. "It is why I must stay here. The one who kept your brother also has my mate. I must go back and free him. She destroyed our tie, but we are both hanging on. Our tie to each other was not solid, so it made it possible for her to break it. Domini did not care about his siren soul, and just wanted to help me with what I was going through. That was the moment I knew I could count on him."

"He did not take what was his?" She hisses. "How could he?"

"Do not worry, I gave back what was his even as I went through the pain."

"He played a very dangerous game. He did not know you. You could have played him much like the one that captured him."

Looking up at the stars, I lean back on my arms, stretching out. "I guess you're right. I could have. But that is what you do when you care for another. You gamble and hope that it is reciprocated. You do play a dangerous game when it comes to love. Have you ever been in love?"

Star smacks her tail down on the water, her tail hitting it flat and hard. Shaking her head vigorously. "No, I have had fun with some other sirens, but nothing outside of that. I do not come to the surface very often, but for my brother, nothing could stop me. We are all that we have left of this family."

"What about your parents?"

"They passed recently. Domini doesn't know yet." Her pearlescent eyes glance at the horizon. She hums a tune. "They weren't around much, anyway."

"If you want to sometime in the future, you can come to see what the land people are like. I will show you around."

Giving a happy nod, she pushes back into the ocean as it pulls her out. "I might take you up on that offer. Careful what you wish for. I will see you again, human Alexia." Her sharp teeth snap at me. She twirls around in the waves, diving and using them to help carry her back out to the sea.

"Until next time." Giving a shake of my head, I stand up and brush the sand from my butt, trying to clear it off my legs. My pants are still damp, but enough time has passed that I won't be sopping wet when I return to the castle. It is time to get back to business.

I would miss him, but I would see him soon enough. Turning back to the castle, I study it closely. I had a snake to save, and I had to do it in such a way that would not hurt anyone I care for or make waves for my family. "But how do I do that? I'm going to need to talk with Flit or Jazmin. They may have some ideas. I'm still not sure where Flit lands for us." I speak to myself, calming my nerves as I make my way back. They would try to blame someone for Domini's absence. I don't want it to be me. I couldn't let Beatrice know it was me or I would not be able to get Blaise free.

I make my way through the tunnels that empty out on to the beach. There are a few twists and turns coming out this way, so it is easy enough to backtrack to the gym closet.

"Where is that door?" I question as my hands search along the rough ridges of the wall. Searching for a lever to push against or slide open. I didn't see what he had exactly done to get the door to open. Pushing against different parts of the wall, it budges slightly. It swings open, I slide through before pushing it back into place.

"There is the culprit, mistress. I smell him all around her," the young boy whines.

My eyes pop open as I'm face to nose with a wet snout as he continues smelling me to make sure he has the scent correct.

My claws that I had all but forgotten about swipe at the young boy's muzzle.

He whines when I make a connection.

"Oh, goodie, look who came back for more trouble," Beatrice berates. "Winnie, thank you for being such a dear and locating the person who helped my warrior escape she will be held punishable for this. Please restrain her."

Winnie is small, but his strength is impressive. His long skinny fingers circle my wrist easily as he captures me there by his side, making sure to close off my exit by closing the door to the tunnel. Grounding my teeth together, I curse myself.

Trying to rip my wrist away from his hand, I struggle against his hold. He leverages my arm behind my back, twisting up. The pain that radiates up my shoulder tears my animal away, making my arm sink back into human form.

"I shouldn't have come back this way," I wheeze.

"It wouldn't have mattered, dear. Winnie here has the best nose around. He is of pure wolf blood descended from the greats. He would have found you one way or another." She runs her fingers through his short hair, hugging him to her.

Staring at her with disdain. "Start them young, don't you? Or is that your thing?"

Her hard, gray eyes burrow into me with pure hatred as her hackles rise. Putting distance between the boy and her, she comes to my other side, peering down at me as the tapping of her high-heeled boots echo across the hard floor. She pushes a couple of fingers against my chest bone and presses me into the shelves behind.

"The snake wasn't enough for you. You had to go and steal my warrior? Be careful when throwing stones when you yourself live in a glass house. From where I'm standing, you are the slut invading my home, and I demand compensation for my losses. I have a snake that is beyond useless and now a warrior that has left. I'm guessing you found his siren soul for him and that is why he is no longer under my command."

The badger is right there under my skin, wishing to rake our claws across her face. I hold back, knowing it would just cause me more trouble. "They were never yours to begin with. If I'm a basic human with hardly any powers. How could I sway them from your care? What does that say about your power? How would you fare against some of the other people in this court when you can't handle me?" My eyes light up as anger consumes her. Her whole body shakes with rage as her face turns red.

"I knew you were stupid but this—" Giving a sharp bark of laughter, she turns from me, walking out the doorway. "Knew his soul was with you the whole time. I asked you to come here so I could watch while I broke the chain between you and my snake. I wanted to dangle you in front of my warrior, but I did not expect you to collude with him while in a mating," she grumbles. She snaps her fingers and in answer, Winnie pulls me along to follow. "In the end, you would have been under my power just to be close to the snake in hopes of a brighter future and I would have the siren's soul back in my possession. If I knew you were going to be such a problem, I would have finished you myself. Unfortunately, there are certain obligations that must be followed. Soon you will be no one's problem, even if it is a longer process for me to go through."

"What do you mean by that? Because you sent Thorn for Shade?"

She stops dead in her tracks before coming out of the locker room. Jerking back to me, she whispers. "How did you know about that?"

"You have your ways. I have mine," I say.

"Do you?" She studies me as she tries to discern what else I may be holding secret. Her piercing gaze stays steady on me, dissecting me.

Shifting my weight from foot to foot, her stare bothers me. Trying to hold my comments to myself. "At least I don't have to force my people to be around me," I blurt out.

Giving a tight lipped smile. "Perhaps, but who is here for you now? No one is coming to save you, little girl."

"The alphas may help me." I try to think of a way out of this. I thought I would have more time to come up with a strategy.

"Have you talked to them at all?"

Giving a cock of my head, I give a look of confusion.

"Of course, you haven't. Well, if you had, you would find out that both alphas have joined my lot and the other two will be easier to persuade. They will not help you hide from my wrath, no matter what you choose."

She turns on her heel and walks away. Winnie pulls me forward, following behind her. My smile falters and then falls as I follow behind, defeated. When would I learn I'm not the one who will ever be holding all the cards?

"This is just too delicious. I had come looking for you originally, and what do I find? You with the hint of my warrior surrounding you. You just dealt me an even better hand than I had before, regardless of what you think you know."

What is she talking about? I have a feeling I will find out soon.

# Chapter 14

"OH, GOOD, YOU FOUND her," Sera responds. She is dressed in a white tank top that is stuffed into black billowy pants gold bracelets adorn both of her wrists. She gives a scary smile as she sees Winnie pulling me in behind him.

Beatrice walks into the room, leaving the door open. "You can let her go."

Winnie drops my arm at once but does not go far.

Eyeing the open door, I yearn to run back through it. Forcing my eyes to look around the large room, it is empty other than the other two that were already in the room. Sera stands next to Damon, their bodies close to one another. I remember him from Morningstar.

*What was he doing with her?*

"This is a meeting room that has been cleared for this conversation," Sera states. "I made sure it was empty and not one of the lusher rooms in case things go south." Her eyes shift to Damon.

"Damon, it is always good to see you," Beatrice crows. "Did you have any problems with the cargo or getting it here?"

"No," he states. His face is hard, and his shoulders are rigid. He stands at attention, waiting for his next orders. He wears black on black, and his hair is disheveled as if he just woke up. "Jack was agreeable, said he is where he is supposed to be."

I only met Damon the once. He is the twin brother of Dalia. Natasha and she have some sort of understanding. I guess that doesn't extend to the brother. They are both reapers. If they are around, death will soon follow is my understanding.

Jack comes around behind the reaper. He is grumbling as if he is fighting someone that none of us can see. "Jack," I whisper.

"I have brought you who you asked for." Beatrice guides Jack in front of Sera's feverish eyes. "Now keep your side of the bargain, truth witch."

"Will that be all for my services today?" Damon stands to the side, monitoring everyone.

"Actually, stay awhile. Your service still may be of use yet."

"What is the meaning of this?" Flit demands as he barges into the room.

"All parties are available and accounted for. We may begin." Beatrice says in a loud booming voice as she walks over to the door, closing it. A barrier erects over the interior walls. "The barrier will disperse when an agreement is met."

"An agreement?" Flit looks to Sera. "What is the meaning of this? Who are they?"

Sera gives a simple shrug. "They are not important yet."

"No, I will not listen to this. Make a motion or bring me a plan through the normal channels. I will not be manhandled into a situation like this."

Beatrice walks forward, her heels clicking at each point she makes. "Oh, I think you will. The matter here is more serious now. New information has come to light. This tramp that is your granddaughter…"

"Stricken!" Sera yells. "Truth is not valid. She has not been claimed."

"Fine! She might be your family," Beatrice hesitates, making sure Sera did not hear an untruth. "This trollop has taken one of my snakes and made him all but useless. She has also set free a siren who I had tied to me."

Flint crosses his arms in anger. "The siren. What was his contract?" He rubs his hand across his forehead. "I can't believe I'm even entertaining this. I should be walking out of this room right now."

"He would work and fight for me to earn back his siren soul." Beatrice ignores his rage. "Even you have to keep these obligations when it is brought forward in this manner."

"Which he got back. He has his siren soul." I make sure it is known so she could not twist this to call him back.

"Yes, but he did not get it back from me."

"Where was the soul?" Flit questions.

Beatrice's eyes flick to Sera, then back to Flit. She taps her shoe against the hard floor as she thinks. "I may have made a deal or a trade with it."

"So, the soul in question was not under your care?" He asks.

"Not exactly."

"Then this issue needs to be stricken from this hearing, as he earned his soul back from whoever was in possession of said soul. You should keep better track of things if you do not wish for others to take charge of a tether you left unwatched."

"No." Beatrice moves forward. "The contract says he has to work for me to earn back his soul." Her fists clench as she crowds Flit.

Raising an eyebrow at her, he stands firm, not backing down. "He has been working for you this whole time, correct?"

"Yes."

"And he received his soul, correct?"

"Yes, but not from me it was not earned back from me."

"I would suggest to you that you create a better process when striking your deals then, and be careful in how things are worded. You should have said that you must earn the soul back directly from me, or I must be the one to release your soul back to you for the contract to be completed. Now, if that is all."

"Truth!" Sera bellows out. "Contract complete. Stricken from ordain."

Flit nods as if that settles things.

Beatrice bristles as she turns from him. She flips her long hair before walking off. "Fine on that point, but the snake is a valid reason and I demand the girl be put to death for her insolence."

"Death!" I shriek. Winnie places his large hand on my shoulder, his strength holding me in place. "That's a little harsh, don't you think?"

"Death is a quick solution and the easiest unless you would like to take his place, though I don't think I could use you in the same way he conducted business." She gives a cruel smile.

Watching Flit, he stands there not saying a word. He looks to Sera; my eyes follow his. Sera glowers at both of us.

"Before we get to the punishment of your snake perhaps, we should learn who she truly is." Flit calms the room with his demeanor.

Jack rubs at his hand, murmuring to himself. He lowers his head, not making eye contact with anyone. He scratches at his dreads, tilting his dark brown hair down as he points to something on the floor. Biting his jagged nails, he shakes his head and shies away from Sera.

Sera grips his chin. Forcing him back to her and for him to meet her eyes. Squeezing his eyes shut, he bounces on the ball of his feet. He keeps them closed, not wanting to face Sera's truth or what she wants to pull from him.

"Find your truth somewhere else," Jack states.

"Little prophet, I do not need your eyes to see the truth." Placing both of her hands on his head like she did with me, she closes her eyes to concentrate. "What a chaotic, delicious mess you live in." She grins. "This most assuredly will not be pleasant for you." She bears down on him.

He lets out a high-pitched scream and scrabbles for her hands. "My predictions are not for you," he yells out.

I struggle against Winnie's hold, wanting to go help Jack. His screams are painful to witness as he thrashes against her hold.

"There she is. You hold many of her secrets. What's this about the mountains?" Sera's brow furrows in concentration. Jack's legs give out. She follows him down, pressing into him, not letting him slip from her fingers.

"That's enough," Flit says.

Sera doesn't let up, grounding his head further into the floor. Blood flows from his nose and ears. His hands become weak as his body gives out and goes limp.

"Family, there it is. Just a little bit more," she cackles.

Jack stops screaming. His body struggles to even draw breath the more she pushes on him.

She literally is going to kill him, and no one is going to make a move to stop her. How did this turn  bad so quickly?

"Stop," my voice booms out.

None stop or even glance my way. Winnie doesn't even brace for a fight, just holds me there at his side. I'm not some weakling to be ignored. This stops now! My claws burst out of my fingers as I pull my arms in tight to my side, yanking down and away from his hand. Winnie's hand loosens on my shoulder before he can re-grab me. I take my other open clawed hand and slice up towards his face. He dodges away as they slice through the air.

Rushing to Jack, I throw myself at Sera, tackling her head on, making her release him. She comes away with a scream all her own.

"You want to know the truth. Here is the truth." I grip her hands in my claws, not being careful. My nails slice into her skin like butter as I place them on my head. I sit on her stomach, forcing her to see the rage in my eyes.

She fights for control before I storm into her mind, pushing all my thoughts and feelings at her. "I've seen what you have had to show me. There are too many holes."

"Look harder," I yell at her, pushing down on her, squeezing on her ribs. "How do you like it?" I ground out.

Rage consumes me as I throw all the darkness I feel and how alone I have been through this entire ordeal. Darkness swallows both of us as we get pulled into her truth realm. Memories flick through, skating past. A thick and warm blanket of darkness envelopes both of us. My claws flash out, not wanting to be stifled.

We land in a heap. A large mirror surrounded by stone crashes into me, there are stars scattered around carved into the stone. Catching my eye in the mirror, I see my monstrous form. Knocking me back, I struggle against the blanket that holds me crouching there. I'm in a half form, my badger animal shines through. Dark eyes, sharp teeth, and claws extend from me. Dark black shadows wrap around the rest of my body. My reflection in the mirror reaches out her own claw. I take hers, letting her help me up.

"This is what we could be," a whisper of a voice speaks from the mirror. "We can show her what will be." She looks past me.

Is this what the final fate looks like? Turning my head, I see Sera struggling to get up from the floor. The blanket of darkness twists around her, fighting her at every turn. Keeping her busy.

"She still struggles with her own demons," I say. Gripping her claw still in mine, I yank her forward out of the mirror, out of whatever prison holds her. She breaks free and gives a chitter of an animal noise along with a deep laugh. The darkness that wraps around her spikes into Sera, helping the blanket cover her completely.

My other hand drops to her bare shoulder, holding her back. There is a scar that runs up the side of her neck on the top of her shoulder. My fingers toy with the raised skin. We both look at where my hand lands, not moving from that spot.

"Show her what she needs to see—" Our eyes meet again. "—Please."

"I will show you both, but I can't force her to what she doesn't want to see."

"Then show her a truth she can believe or one she wants to believe."

Future me nods but gives a hard look, not moving from her spot. "You will have a choice to make."

My eyes drift to Sera.

"Not that one," she whispers.

Looking around, I take in this world, but there isn't anything here other than darkness and us. None of this is real.

*What choice is she talking about?*

I just want to make my family whole and get my love life in order. Everything else will work itself out.

"The choice you will need to make is if you will become the villain of your own story or the hero. And if you don't become the villain, who does then? Forcing another into something so you can rise above. Would that make you a hero or villain?" She backs away from me.

My hand drops from her. I turn to keep her in my sights.

"Choices, choices. What will you choose? Make sure to choose before it's too late. Or will you choose to struggle like Sera and deny your consequences? Deny what you must do?" Her eyes slash to Sera as the darkness envelopes her, covering everything except her head. She bends down, brushing her nails through Sera's hair, catching on some hairs slicing through them. "My bad, I forgot you were fragile."

She pulls Sera up with the darkness cocooning around her. Walking over to them, I stand there ready to see what she is here to show us. I'm not sure if this is me or just a part of this realm to show us the truth. Heeding her warnings, I will listen to what she has to say. I will think about what needs to be done later.

We all face forward, waiting for a picture to come forward. Racing over the land, we zip over the grassy plains to the mountains. The air is cool on my face as we get closer to the cold, dark mountains that envelop this world.

I watch the other two, not breaking eye contact with the picture. I brace myself, holding my arms in front of me, waiting for us to crash into the picture and mountains, but it never comes. We are whisked through the hard rock and dirt packed tunnels. Flying down it, we twist and turn in the dark with no rhyme or reason. It feels like it goes on forever, not slowing down. No wonder people became lost in this place. We stop moving as it comes into a large room. There are doors and walkways climbing up the walls and into the rock itself.

There are crowds of regular looking people walking and talking all around us. There are so many of them. "Who are all these people?"

"The voided ones," Sera answers.

"There are so many! I thought there aren't that many, and they come here to perish?" Moving around the folks, I take a step forward. The motion of my body within the motion of us moving makes my head sway. The dark creature steadies me.

"There are more than you think, and they have the ear of the mountains who are not too happy about the turn of events. They thrived here and are doing great."

We pass through people, searching. Dark stringy hair flows down the back of one man who is pointing around him as if he is telling others where to go. No sound emits, so we can't hear what he is saying, but I recognize him right away.

"Ivan," I call out.

*Didn't Beatrice think he was dead?* My heart flutters as a smile creeps up my face, happy to know he is alive.

A sob turns to groans. Sera has tears in her eyes as she searches around him for someone else.

"That is right Sera, he is there." She steps in front of Sera, compels her gaze from the scene. It dissolves, only leaving Ivan's ghostly form there, hanging in the darkness. A husk of a man not being animated by the scene anymore. The creature walks into his body and becomes Ivan.

He stomps forward, his face angry, his fists are clenched at the side of his body. The clothes he is dressed in are dark and hang off his skinny frame. He has changed. "Sera, look at what you have done!" Ivan's booming voice echoes around us. "We had a deal, and you have failed our family."

Bursting out in tears, Sera sobs. "I know, I know. I fell into a truth dream, getting lost for many years. We will make our way there, I promise!"

The dark tendrils tighten on Sera's body as he raises his fist in her face. "Excuses, what a weak witch you turned out to be! I should have never gotten with you."

This doesn't sound like the Ivan I remember. Last, I had seen of them they were very much in love and kind to one another. Is this the future? Me saying these horrible things. Or is this the truth she will listen to and help her move forward?

"I know." She continues to cry the tears flowing down her face as she takes heaving sobs to compensate for the tightness around her chest.

"You will make Flit bring her to me! I will fix your mistake."

"No! I will kill her!" she says frantically. "They can't see one another. If they don't meet, neither one has to choose."

"If you don't, then you leave me no choice. The boy and I will be no more, and you will never have the family you dreamed about so much. I will make the choice for you."

"No," she says weakly, defeated.

"Look at her!" Ivan yells, spittle flying from his mouth. "Look at what you caused. Truth has consequences and for your disgrace in hiding from the truth for so long, you will feel the pain she holds. Claim her, you filth, and bring her to the mountains."

Her mewling cries turn into full out screams as she is forced to gaze upon me. Ivan gets swallowed by the darkness.

Something shoves me from behind, steadying myself against Sera. I whip my head around. Sera still screams out in agony;

a slash appears down my lower arm. My claw shakes in front of my eyes. Blood wells to the surface. Looking at the cuts, searing pain radiates up through it. I hold on to it, holding it close to my body, trying to staunch the flow of blood. Another stab into my shoulder throws me down as my screams echo my mother's. We are both yelling in pain and anguish.

I roll on the floor, holding my arm close to me, trying to stop wherever the next blow would come from. As I roll, I see the darkness unravel from Sera as she struggles to move.

"Stop!" she screams out over the pain that is racking her body.

I breathe in and out in short, hyperventilating breaths. Clenching my teeth, I try to slow it long enough to work past the pain.

Sera swipes at me, throwing me off her. She lunges again. Her fists come down, connecting with my flesh, bruising me.

Curling into a ball, I try to protect myself by covering the important parts from more damage.

"Is this the time to look for your brother or was the last time? Either way, I think we must go now, Lexi," she says in a soft voice.

Uncovering my head, I look up at a blow that never comes. Blood wells up and drops from her hand onto my sliced arm. A dagger lodges in the middle of her hand. The shadows pull back and Flit is standing there beside Sera. His eyes are yellow, his mouth slashes down in disgust.

Back peddling, I crawl backwards away from them, not sure which would try to kill me next. My hands bump into something cold. Turning, I see Jack's body lying there, cold and broken. A racking sob pours out of my chest.

"Wake up, Jack," I shake him, hoping to bring life back into him.

"He is gone," Damon says.

"No, he can't be."

"I'm a reaper. I know when someone passes." He kneels, touching his fingers to Jack's chest, pulling up on an ethereal soul from within. Jack's spirit comes away from his deceased body. Damon holds on to Jack, not letting him go.

"Let him go," I snap.

"If I do, you will not be able to converse with him and he will be gone from this world unless you work with a necromancer. Are you sure you still wish for me to let go of him?" He calmly states.

Shaking my head, I slowly get to my feet. The blood is still gushing from my arm and shoulder, making me unsure on my feet. Struggling to stay upright, I focus on the two wavering people in front of me.

My tongue and mouth feel thick as I force myself upright. "Jack, does it hurt?"

"No, nothing hurts anymore; all is clearer over here."

"Do not lie to the girl. It isn't all sunshine and rainbows, either." Damon growls, tugging at the soul.

A sharp gasp pulls from Jack. He grimaces and shoulders on. "The reaper is correct. It is dank, baron, and degrading on this side."

"The in between isn't meant for spirits for long," Damon says.

"But all the struggles I experienced in my physical form I no longer have, and things make more sense now. Know this isn't your fault. It is a fate that I chose, one that was predetermined. Trust that there was a reason for this. It is the only path where everyone wins."

"I don't know how that could be possible." A hiccup of a sob catches in my throat. "Natasha is going to kill me when she finds out."

"And yet it is. It is okay. I lived out what I was supposed to accomplish. Natasha will understand in time. Pain makes her lash out at the ones she cares for, but she, too, will see one day. And promise me no matter what she does, you will be there for her when she needs it."

Shaking my head, I don't believe him. But it's his dying wish and I will do that much for him. "I promise. I will be there for her, no matter how much she pushes me away."

"Why did you do that?" Flit growls out. "Shadow warriors to me." Shadows pull from under the door and lengthen on the walls as they crawl closer to Flit.

"I couldn't very well have you killing your own granddaughter." Sera holds the knife still in her hand, trying not to move it.

"Kill her? I was trying to separate you two! The damage you did in there was making its way in the real world."

"Alexia, I claim you," her voice shakes as she belts out a scream as if the truth of it tore from her throat.

Flit's face registers shock as his body freezes. He pauses.

"There you have it. This thing is your relation. Now give me what I want. She is on the brink of death as is." Beatrice, who has been quiet until now, walks into view. Winnie follows behind her in full wolf form, a gray silver color and huge compared to his human form.

If she really wants to, she could ride him. My vision tunnels, gripping my shoulder as I try to staunch the flow. The blood loss getting to me.

"Go get medical supplies and bring them back. You tend to Sera, and you tend to Lexi," Flit utters to the shadow warriors.

With a snap of Beatrice's fingers, Winnie turns into a snarling, growling mass facing me. "No tending to her. She is the payment I seek."

The shadows ignore her slinking away; they rush back to Sera's and my side with supplies. The knife comes out easily and they are quick to wrap Sera's hand before more blood can leak out. They pad her hand with heavy gauze. "We will get you to a healer soon." Flit ignores her outburst.

Shaking her head, she cries out as her eyes land upon me. The other shadow gets to work on wrapping my arm and shoulder.

"You have to take us to Ivan, Flit. It is time," Sera whispers.

"Are you sure?"

"I will make you listen to me. Winnie now!" Beatrice screeches.

Winnie lunges at the shadow that is tending to me, grabbing on to it with sharp teeth, tearing it away from the work it is doing. Tugging on me, I fall over easily, holding a hand to my head as I sit there and try to make the room stop moving. He tears at the shadow, shredding it to pieces as dark tendrils hang out of Winnie's mouth.

Beatrice slashes at her arm, blood welling up. Lines of blood flow down. Waving her hand over it, she moves the blood to a point, aiming it at my chest. Morphing it further into something usable and solid, she makes it into a spear; gripping the pole in hand, she whips it to the side, scratching me. She points it back down at my throat.

"Wait," Flit calls out.

She stops the point short, just barely resting it on my throat. The thing is a deep red.

*Who knew blood could be so sharp?*

The gashes continue to flow on each arm and as the blood flows; it pulls into the spear she is holding, increasing its size. The point getting closer as she collects more blood; the sharpness digs into my skin.

"Ties are not the only thing I wield, King of Darkness. I can hold my own and will take what is owed to me."

"Blood control?" Flit says.

"You are not the only one with tricks up their sleeves."

"What do you want?" Flit's fear shines through his voice.

"That is more like it." Beatrice keeps the point at my throat, not giving up the leverage she has. "Your truth witch, knows what I seek. She knows exactly what I want. Though it was what I thought she wanted as well!" Beatrice growls out. "You lied! Not very becoming of one who tells the truth."

Coughing out, Sera moans in pain. "I did not lie."

"That is bull. You wanted her dead."

Tears continue to roll down Sera's face. "Parts of me do, yes." Her head hangs down heavily. Her bandaged hands scarcely hold her up. The bandages turn red with the pressure that she puts on her hands, increasing the blood flow from the wound. Getting to her feet, she holds the hand close to her chest, grabbing the gauze from the shadow to wrap more around it in a tighter formation. Stopping the blood from oozing out. "If she can't have Alexia, then she will settle for you, Flit."

"Get it right, witch. I don't want Flit. This city and everything below it is what I want. I want half of the dark side, land, and power. Meaning he will not oversee this slice of darkness. From now on there will be a light side, a dark side, and a land filled with blood!" She yells out. Her blood sprays out around her, forming a shield.

"What about Blaise?" I ask my voice thready and small, not wanting to move too much for fear of her gouging the spear deeper into my throat. My fingers reach for more gauze, trying to stop the flow so she would not gain more power. The more blood we give her, the more of a weapon she has on us.

"That deal would be for both Lexi and Blaise?" Flit asks. More shadows pour in as he gathers his own power. Shadow warriors pour into the room, circling everyone and causing the room to look dimmer than before. They eat at the light, their forms fighting to swallow all that is bright in the room.

"No, that is for Alexia only. Blaise still has a large debt. I would need more." She gives a cocky smile, looking down at me.

I let the anger in my eyes shine through. The rage in me pauses the spinning room and wipes some of the fuzziness away. Holding tight to it, I let the rage in to my hands as they spring into claws and wrap around the bloody spear, pushing it back at her. "He will never belong to you or anyone else," I snap.

"Is that so? Then my ask for Blaise will be that those two have to finally solidify the mating bond. He will never belong to himself. He will always have a master, whether that be me or you." She throws in my face.

"You will leave his family alone and have no other snake charmer from his village?" I ask.

"Them to be mated? That is all." Flit snarls, talking over me.

"No, that is just a bonus. There will be more needed if I'm not to have a snake charmer to call." She pulls her blood spear back and stands it upright, tapping it against the ground. It rings out as the solidness of it hits the ground.

Standing up, I wrap the rest of the hanging gauze around my arm, holding it tight. I glare at her, knowing this is what she wanted the whole time. To make his life worse, even if I don't want to be tied to him. That he and I would always have to answer to someone. She doesn't know what I already know in my heart.

"I want you to give me a portion of your power and blood, Flit. I also want your added support in the war that I want to wage on the light side."

"Why not just ask for all the land and power?" Flit gives a chuckle. Cocking a hip, he relaxes back.

"Don't kid yourself. One being could not handle the all that you hold as it stands. Pouring that into me would burn out my synapsis and leave me a shadow of a husk. But having a slice of that power over time, it will be called to the one who wields it better. Since I will have your blood, I'm a contender for that power." She gives an evil smile, knowing she holds all the cards.

"Fine." Flit's eyes rove over everyone in the room.

"Deal acquired." Sera squeaks out. "Don't do this," her whole body shakes.

"You are the one that wanted this." I yell out.

"You know nothing of what I want," she hisses towards me. Doubling over in pain, she groans through.

"Why should I trust what you say? Especially after you said that you are on her side of things." I throw back at her.

"You insolent child." Standing up straight, she glares down at me. Walking slowly, toward me. "What are you talking about?"

"I think the little rat overheard our conversation from be-fore," Beatrice comments.

"Our conversation?" Sera asks

"Yea, the one where you said you know the truth. I'm on your side," I spit out.

Beatrice bursts out laughing.

"That isn't what I said," Sera searches her mind, looking for answers. Her eyes land on Flit, then dashes away. Taking a breath, she shakes her head. "I said, you will know if I know the truth and hide from it, because then it hurts me tenfold. I'm not one of your little beasts that you can maneuver onto your side."

"Let's imagine, though, if you did say what Alexia stated. Imagine the places and power we could have!" Beatrice is gleeful at the thought of it.

"Don't do this, Flit," she cries out.

"Sera that's enough. I have no choice." He walks forward, waiting at the edge of Beatrice's blood shield. It lowers, and he reaches a hand forward, shaking her hands.

"An accordance is reached," Sera screams as she races forward, tackling Beatrice to the ground. They roll on the floor screaming and yelling at one another. Punches land on each of them.

"Worthless," Damon says.

Looking back at him, I notice Jack is gone from his side. "Where did Jack go?"

"He moved on to where he should be."

"Oh," is all I say. I wish I would have been able to talk to him more. Jazmin could talk to the dead. Maybe she could get a message to him later.

"Shadows bind!" Flit calls out, throwing his hand out toward the two women fighting. "Sera, the accordance can't be undone. I bind you to the shadows." All the shadows move as one, flowing forward from his hand pouring over them. Sera screams and kicks at them, but they do nothing to the shadows grip. Darkness flows over her, catching onto her clothes, making her a part of them.

"No! You can't do this," she cries out. Her last words come out in a garbled sound as she turns into that of a shadow. Her dark form hunkers down on the floor, sad and lonely.

Flit walks slowly over to her and runs his fingers through the dark silhouette of her hair. "Sleep until I call for you."

Her small dark hand reaches up to catch his, but it slides through it as she lays down on the floor, blending into the ground, her gloom body gone by his command.

"What did you do?" I ask.

"What I had to." He throws back at me, his eyes commanding and yellow. "Now Beatrice, let us discuss in private the land and power that will be given to you. Lexi, don't you have someone to go find?"

"By the way, he should be in his room if you can find it. Though a little tied up, shouldn't be a problem for what you will need him for." She gives a grin. Whistling to get Winnie's attention, she pats her leg as she heads to the door. Winnie trots over to his master, following behind her.

"Damon, will you clean things up here?" Flit asks.

"He isn't something you just clean up after. Jack is a person... Was a person..." I emphasize with force. Letting go of my arm, I rest both of my claws at my sides. "He will be put to rest properly."

Closing his eyes for a moment and inhaling deeply, he lets it back out slowly. "Damon, can you find Jazmin, please? Beatrice, I will meet with you. Just go next door to the next room and I will be right in after I deal with this."

"Very well." She waits at the door. The blood mist circles both her and Winnie as she waits for Damon to walk through, then closes the door, shutting us both in here together.

As soon as the door shuts, Flit's stance is more at ease. His shadows pull in tighter. His face fills with worry and he quickly comes to my aid. He pulls at my clawed hand, checking the dressing that is wrapped around my arm. "Are you all right? We should call for a healer." He sends a shadow to do his bidding even before he ends his thought.

My hands begin to shake, and I lose the anger I have been holding onto. My hands grow smaller as they fall back into their human form. "What did you do to her?" I ask, my voice barely making a sound.

"I made her a shadow that is attached to me. She must obey my commands; I have sent her to sleep for now so that she can rest easy and heal. Her mind has not been right from the start of things. Hopefully, this rest will heal her more so than the first one. She will be okay."

"What if she refuses to wake? Will you just command her to?"

"I will have to remove the shadow curse before trying to wake her. If we want to do things right and for her to not be what you have seen so far, we will have to hurry. Things have never been right for her since the day she lost you and your brother. She was handling things as well as can be expected before that, but after you were taken, there was nothing that could rouse her."

"How did she wake up last time?"

"I asked her that same question. All she said was it was time to," Flit says. His nimble hands pull the gauze free, unwinding it from my arm as he flinches from the wounds that he inflicted.

"Why did you scratch my arm and shoulder? Why did you want to kill me?"

"Did you not hear me before? I wasn't trying to kill you. You were killing Sera. What damage you caused in there was leaking through, and I swore to Ivan that I would take care of her. I could not break my promise to him. Trying to just harm you to get you to let go wasn't working. I would not have dealt a killing blow, but I needed to do some damage to break whatever hold was over the two of you."

A shadow slips under the door coming back. A soft knock taps on the door. "You sent for me?"

Rushing to the door, he opens it and puts his hand up, baring the room from the person at the door. Once Flint sees who it is, he stands aside. "Yes Greg, thank you for coming. Can you heal her wounds?"

"Are you alright?" The man hesitates in the doorway, looking him over. "Do you need healing?"

"No, just the girl."

Greg walks in, he has on dark blue robes and is short. His brown hair is peppered and curly, his blue eyes are warm on mine. The robe of his darkens his gaze.

"Hello."

"Hi," I mumble.

"Greg here will take care of you. He is my personal healer. He is very good at what he does." Flit states his nervous hands, stressing his words.

"May I?" Greg asks, reaching his hands out for my wrist.

I pull my arm up and lay it in his hands gently. The warmth of his fingers cradles my battered limb, and it feels soothing. His fingers glide over the wounds, knitting the skin back together as if I'm clay to be molded. He is gentle and I hardly feel it as he brings the skin back close and removes the bruising that batters my body. The pain and searing throb that comes from my shoulder begins to alleviate and mend. I see the gash knit close through the hole in the shirt. He pulls the shirt threads up away from it before it can seal it away.

"Unfortunately, I cannot mend the shirt as easily," Greg says.

"It doesn't matter," my voice is hollow and dull. My eyes can't tear away from Jack and his lifeless body.

"Jazmin will be here soon. She will make sure he is taken care of properly."

A shocked gasp comes from the doorway. "Of course, I will." Her purple dress is fluffed out. She gathers up her dress and rushes into the room to where I am. "He was a friend of yours?" Giving me her hand, she holds on to it.

"Go be with your snake. We will talk about the future later," Flit pushes.

Ignoring Flit. "Jazmin, will you be able to contact him?"

"Yes, I could do that. But the time to do that is not now. Give him time to adjust to life over there on the other side. If you still want to get a message to him or talk with him, we can try him in a few weeks' time."

Gripping her hand tightly in mine, I hold on to her like a lifeline. My eyes move to hers, tears filling them. "Not right now?"

Shaking her head. "Time moves differently in that realm. Give him some time."

"Okay, but soon, maybe?"

"Yea, let me know when you are ready after the waiting period. Your snake awaits you."

I look down at my blood-soaked cloth. Whispering to her, "I have nothing to wear."

Giving a smile, she gives me a half hug to her, not worrying if blood gets on her beautiful dress or not. A purple silk tie is wrapped in her hair, hiding half of her face. She whispers right back. "I have the perfect thing for such an occasion." Walking to the door, she holds me to her side. "We will get you dressed and ready. Leave your friend to me. I will take care of everything." Her eyes shoot to Flit. "We will have words later."

Pausing in the doorway, she tosses her words over her shoulder. "Damon, you will wait for me to come back here before you start." Her eyes flick to the side as she waits.

"Yes, ma'am," his tone changes.

"Good." She beams a smile as she holds tight, guiding me. "Now let's tempt your snake in ways you never have yet."

# Chapter 15

HOLDING MY BREATH, I let it out in a rush as I barge into the room where Blaise is. "I told you the next time we meet, I would give you what you crave." My voice comes out low and throaty, giving a low growl in warning. The healing left me energized and ready for trouble.

Blaise eyes me from the bed. His tail slashes to the side as he fights to get free of the chains. "You're not real, you're not here, you can't be," he hisses out, fighting the restraints.

The chains do not give but the bed frame bends and creaks with his strength.

Marching over to the side of the bed, I come closer to him into the light so he can see me clearly. Putting my hand on his chest, I push him back down on the bed, holding him there.

He freezes under my touch, staring at my hand and slowly raises his eyes to mine as they melt into human green. "Why aren't you gone?" He moans in anguish. "You should be gone with Domini far away from here."

"Why aren't you with us? Would be a better question."

"She caught wind of the plan. The warrior she can train, another, so she came to get me before I left, forced me in here and let her beasts have their way with me," he says.

Making my touch gentler, I scan his naked form and notice the cuts and bruises litter his snake body. "Bullshit, what happened?" I ask in awe.

"Most of what was done has already healed. I'm her power card. She could allow the siren to leave. She could even let you live if you left. I'm the line she will not cross. I'm in her debt forever."

My lips twitch upwards at that.

"Not forever."

"I will not allow her to take one of my family members instead!" He bellows. "She came and found me when she noticed her siren was missing. Even though I was not going to leave, she still had me punished in case I wanted to change my mind in the future." He wrestles with the chains again. "I now have no freedoms, so here is where I stay."

Brushing my fingers across his lips, I quiet him. "Another deal was struck, one where you no longer belong to her."

Blaise moves his tail, circling it around my waist, pulling me closer to the bed. "What did you do, Minx?"

Going with his tail, I allow him to pull me closer. His tail tightens and makes the dress ride up. His eyes finally register what I'm wearing and notices that it is see through. Pulling me closer, I climb on the bed, the dark sheets contrast against him. His chained hand reaches out to me. He touches the sheer fabric on my stomach. Skimming his fingers against the mesh cloth over my stomach.

"What I had to," I say, pulling away.

His other arm yanks at the chain as he allows me to pull away. He still has me trapped with his tail sitting next to him.

A second tug and the chain snaps, allowing freedom to that arm. Gripping my arm, he unravels his tail from me and pulls me across him. "What did you do, Minx?"

Struggling to sit up, he helps me to straddle his thighs that are molded together into his tail. The dress rides up my bare thighs. My cheeks redden at how close I am to him, my heat directly over his hardening length. I'm already warm and radiating heat for him.

Taking a breath, he hisses out his eyes are wise as he notices I am not wearing any bottoms under the dress. "What are you doing to me, Minx?"

"Don't take that tone with me, snake."

"Don't call me snake or I'll give you one to worry about," he growls. His snake tongue flicks out at me.

Crossing my arms in front of my chest. "As your mate, I can call you whatever I like."

"Is that right?" He gives a smirk as he rolls his hips. He bumps against me, grinding the underside of his penis against my heat. His lower form changes to that of a man. The only part of him that is still snake like is his eyes.

"Are your eyes going to stay that way now?" I cock my head in question.

"Around you, my animal can't seem to stay in check." His fingertips brush against my knee, the chain keeping his hand from moving further.

His hand feels nice against my skin. Grinding, I slide against him, feeling his thick, hard heat next to mine. Giving a moan, my hands roam across his naked stomach and chest, having my way with him without having to stop. His stomach flexes as I ride against him, my hands caress down his hard pecks.

"Minx we can't. Please stop this torture." He closes his eyes, trying to block out what I'm doing to him.

Sliding even further forward, I capture his lips with mine, rubbing me and the sheer dress against him. His one arm comes up to hold me tight, but the chain stops his other arm. Breaking the kiss, I wait till he focuses on me. "Trust me, the torture will stop."

Holding his breath. "I trust you," he wheezes out.

I sit back slightly, teasing my center against his hard cock. Poising it at my hot sheath. I grip his cock in hand and hold it in place as I sink down onto him. We both moan as I sink down on him, riding him.

"Minx!" He strains against the chains.

"Tell me what the next step is, snake." I wiggle down on him, but do not move much more than that. I pull my fingers across my breasts, reveling in the feel, making him watch what he can't touch himself.

"Next step in what?" He rolls into me, trying to move us both.

"In our mating dance, silly." I wriggle.

"In our?" He gives a shake of his head. "But we can't."

I feel him thicken and can't help myself as I move up and down, loving the friction he causes. I wanted more of him, so I let myself go and enjoy the ride. My hips dance as I move on him. Finding a pleasant rhythm, I keep it slow, finding my tempo. We have all the time in the world we can take our time. I rub the see through material against my skin. My sensitive breasts are full and erect; they catch on the cloth turning me on.

"Blaise," I moan to the ceiling.

His arm strains against the chains, no longer able to keep his hands away from me. He punches forward with his right hand and breaks the link on that chain. My hands wrap around his wrist and guide it to my breast as I continue to ride him, not stopping for a moment. He massages me and tweaks the nipple, bringing the fire higher as I try to increase the movement.

Wrapping his other hand around me, he pulls me down, capturing my lips. He holds me there against him, pumping into me at a faster speed.

We both need this. No, crave it. Moans jolt out of me with each thrust.

As he continues to punish me with his cock, his hand moves lower down my back to my ass, spreading my cheeks as he enters me. He rubs his finger down, feeling me and him joining as he massages the spot between us and my ass. His finger dips into my backend, toying with me, bringing me to new pleasing heights.

The extra touch did things for me. I'm drowning in pleasure. Barely able to hang on, I swivel my hips. Moaning into his mouth as we kiss, he slows his speed but increases the pressure that he pushes into me. He matches the tempo of him entering me with what he is doing to my behind. He pushes in when I feel him at his fullest inside of me. Rubbing his finger against me, feeling himself through the wall that separates his fingers from his cock.

Moaning deeply, I tear my mouth away from him sitting up full taking him to the hilt; he presses more of his finger into me as I ride the pleasure that pours through me. Feeling the tingles work their way out. I feel moisture pooling down on him, making everything that much more slippery. He slowly works his finger out of me as he feels my body slow.

I melt into his chest as I rest there, my body catching up with what just happened. My breath and heart try to even out. He is still thick and hard inside me. I feel him there against my mind as the link snaps in place.

"Little Minx, rest for now, but be ready for round two."

"I feel the link once again, but it isn't complete. Tell me how we finish this." The fire is already burning as our tie takes hold. The bliss from the orgasm doesn't last long before I feel like I need more.

Swaying on his cock, I need to feel more of him.

"Fuck, that feels so right," Blaise bursts out. "The re-linking will push us into claiming one another, more so than last time."

I lick and taste the sweat on his chest as I swivel my hips. Stopping to nibble at his nipple, I bite down my teeth, craving the feel of flesh. He bellows out as I sink too hard into his skin. I growl in eagerness. He meets my fervor with his own eagerness.

He gives a quick jerk and the last chain holding his neck breaks free. His hands roam over my sides as I move. He lifts his top half up from the bed, holding me close, but jars my mouth from his chest, making me follow him up.

In this position, he moves us differently, more of a grinding and sliding motion, but the pleasure is still there, along with his pleasant touch. He pulls off the gauzy dress and tosses it off the side. He lowers his head, flicking his tongue over my nipple. Pulling his head closer, I wait till he sucks part of it into his mouth before pushing closer. He nibbles at the nipple in time, with him sliding into me. The pain of his teeth mixes with pleasure, causing my hands to curl in his hair, controlling him in by yanking or pushing on his curls.

"More," I whisper as the fire consumes me.

He slows his movements and raises his head, hugging me close. I tighten around him, hugging him back. My teeth descend as I scrape my teeth along the skin from his neck to his shoulder. I feel the indentation of the scar I left before from my first bite. I open my mouth and bite down in the same spot, though gentler this time.

Pulling him into me in both ways is a little heady and quickly escalates things as my body takes on a mind of its own. I writhe on him as I moan into his shoulder.

He sucks in a breath. "I never want this to stop." He cradles the back of my head against waiting till I am done. Pulling my head back, he bites into the top of my breast, not being able to control himself.

My sharp teeth flash out, striking into his shoulder. I feel my essence go into him and be sucked back out by me. A push and pull as our bodies connect. Once I have taken my last pull, I pull back, flashing my canines. My animal is so close to the surface I feel her there with me, matching his energy. He also let's go and looks me straight in the eyes, his tongue flickers as more of himself loses the fight to passion.

I push down on his chest, taking control of things. "Show me who you are, snake. All of it." I ride him, forcing him to the beat of my drum. "You don't want this to stop? Prove it."

He looks up at me, lust and love in his eyes, with a twinge of fear. My hands skate down his lean form, one hand steadies me as the other skates over my thigh and finds his balls. I cup them and feel them thick and round against my bottom. Caressing them, my fingers dance behind them, press against them as I move on top of him. I feel my wetness seep around him.

"Show me," I whisper multiple times in a chant as I rock him and my pleasure higher.

He grabs my arm away from him as he rolls his hips up into me; the ride becomes bumpy as things morph underneath me. "Hold on."

Pressing down on to him, I press my legs into his hips, keeping me there, trying not to get bucked off while his lower half transforms.

He bumps into me and his smooth scales and body rub against me as he freezes into place.

I still feel him deep inside me. Nothing has changed there, though I don't doubt he can change that. I rest a moment as I take him in. I look back and notice his tail curled around one bedpost as the rest of his tail is on the floor hanging off the bed. Touching behind me, I feel the softness of his underbelly. I keep my eyes on him. His eyelids lower and his tongue flicks out of his closed lips.

"I accept this, I accept you." Moving, I rub against him, purring emits from me as my happiness soars for him. "How do we finish this and become one?"

"You have done most of the work already. You took me into your body all on your own. We exchanged blood. The last step is words to seal it in place."

"Please give me the words. I need this, you need this."

"Repeat after me, okay?" He whispers. His hands hold my hips in place. "Once it locks in place, I'm not sure if I will be able to hold back."

Leaning down, I give a soft kiss. "I can take it. I crave this side of you."

Giving a slight nod, he gives the words needed. "I take you into my mind, heart, and soul to be one with you until this physical world no longer binds us," he whispers out.

"I take you into my mind, heart, and soul to be one with you until this physical world no longer binds us," I repeat. Holding my breath, I wait for something to happen or something to snap fully in place. Nothing happens. Squeezing around him, I feel him still thick and hard there. "Did I do something wrong? What's next?"

He gives a cocky smile. "Next is the fun part. You did nothing wrong, my sweet." His hand comes up and cups my cheek,

brushing his thumb against my soft skin. "You are so beautiful."

My cheeks heat up as I shrink into his hand. I felt precious
and delicate in his arms. A part of me is nervous about being
seen so well by someone else. My fingers run over the hard
muscles of his stomach, my nails lengthen, turning into claws
with all the emotion rolling through me along with the sexual
tension. It is all too much. My badger is here with me, scratching at the surface.

His hand reaches behind my neck and grabs the back of me,
holding me in place.

Freezing in place, I hold still.

"You better hold her in check. Do you understand me? Nod
yes if you understand."

I barely tilt my head up and down before he moves.

"I will stop if you lose control and you don't want me to
stop, do you?"

Shaking my head, I know I have to give him an answer.
The fire ratchets up again; I know he can feel my dampness
intensify between my legs. My animal dances at his commands.

His long, snaky tongue flicks out as his lids lower. "I
can sssssmell you and how turned on you are. You naughty
Minxxxx. I'm going to have you in all the besssst wayssss pos-
ssssible are you ready?"

I rub myself against him in answer, unable to stop myself.

His hand presses on the sides of my neck, increasing the
pressure. I stop what I'm doing.

"Are you ready?"

"Yessss," I bite out. My tongue flickers over my very pointy
teeth.

His strength pulls me away from him as he manhandles me
into a different position. He flips me over onto my knees as

he raises up. He keeps his hand on the back of my neck as he bends me into position on all fours. His tail helps him balance as he slides back into me in one hard stroke. He holds there a moment, taking me in. His tail flicks off the post that is to the side of me and slithers out of sight.

Soon his other hand is massaging my lower back, loosening my muscles there as I lay down further. His other hand releases the tension on the side of my throat as he reaches for something.

"Did you know the tip of my tail is very sensitive?" He brings the tail in question into my eyesight. He brushes it against my shoulder. I turn my face to it and flick out my tongue, giving it a little lick.

His cock twitches deep inside me, as if they are connected. I call my animal back, changing my teeth back to that of a human. I open my lips and suck his tail into my mouth. It flicks with in me as his cock bucks into me. Moaning around his tail, I swirl my tongue around it. Blaise bucks back, pulling almost all the way out before slamming home again.

Doing that takes my breath away as I push back against him at the same time. Sucking on the tip of his tail hard, he does it again. I pull my face away, trying to catch my breath from the thrills that run through my body each time he does.

He takes his tail back and slides it over my spine and ass. "It is so slippery from your mouth. Domini told me how you have been training for both of us." He pulls his cock out, rubbing it against me before slamming home. My hands slide out from under me, and I struggle to get them back under me, wanting to match his fierceness. Heat radiates over me.

He helps his tail into my ass and holds as he slowly pushes more and more into me. I cry out once he stretches me to the brink. He leans over me carefully, letting me adjust. His tail and cock flick in tandem to one another. As his hands rub against me, he finds my nipples and pinches them in time with each flick. Soon I'm moaning and crying for another reason, as I want to move and feel more of him. Leaning back, he pushes into me harder and faster, bringing me to the brink. The carefully timed flicks of his cock and tail send me over the edge.

Screaming out, my voice goes hoarse as he continues to pump into me. Ringing out every last ounce of pleasure. The rhythm becomes choppy as he releases himself into me, bringing another wave of pleasure and comfort flowing into me. Huffing out, I catch my breath; my arms give out as I lower my upper half to the bed. He helps my bottom half stay connected. Removing his tail from me, he wraps it around my legs, helping me stabilize.

The tie snaps in place and I feel him there next to me, mind, body, and soul. My heavy lidded eyes track him as he moves, his tail disappears as he lowers me gently to the bed. He gets up and walks slowly into another; I hear running water and splashes.

My lids fall shut after what we have done, listening to the sounds he makes, my mind wanders in a happy, blissful fog.

Warm liquid and soft hands touch me gently. They are curious and careful. Opening a sliver of an eye, I peek at him as he cleans up what we have done. Making sure I'm taken care of. "You will be sore, but not in pain from anything that happened here. My blood will help to heal you."

"What now?" I ask.

"Now we are mated. The link is whole and solid. It's not going anywhere." He gives it a tug in answer. Physically tugging me back to him so his body molds mine with my back to his front. The warmth pulls me in and makes me feel safe.

Feeling that pluck of our link stirs something lower in me. Giving a little moan, I roll over and throw my leg over his hip. I see he is fully back to human, even his eyes. "Is this how the mating craze is going to continue? Your snake looks sated."

Giving a lopsided smile, a rumble of laughter rolls over me. "He is content with how things played out, yes. Which I do have questions about, but we can come back to them later."

"Later?" I ask

"Yes later. Unlike me, I still see your badger there lurking. She is far from done with me. We are going to play a game."

Running my hand over his chest and nipple, I look up at him with a shy smile. "What kind of game?"

"One where you work on letting all the way go."

"Isn't that what we just did?"

"You tell me." He yanks me closer, wrapping his arms around me, pulling me tight to him as he kisses me passionately. The heat of this man sears me in all the right places and brings me right back to where we started. My body is ready for another round.

Biting my lip, I give a cocky grin.

"More of you will be open to me. Please don't hide what you need or who you are," Blaise says.

"I don't plan to."

"Good, now for this next part, it is up to you what happens. I will give you pleasure as long as you do as I say, and if you don't, there will be a punishment."

"Did you get this from Domini?"

"He may have mentioned some things." He gives a shrug. "We are going to have to take this to a different room though."

"Why?"

"The tools I need are in the other room. Wait here." He rolls over me and leaves the bed, going to another door. He opens it up and darkness is all that can be seen. A light turns on and I can see many kinds of sexual tools and playthings.

Getting up, I'm drawn over to see what this room all holds. It is a small room but big enough for the equipment and a swing device. "Blaise is this?"

"I told you to stay put," his voice comes out gruff. He looks around the room and points to the swing. "Sit," he demands.

Walking over to the swing, I stand before him. He holds the straps and waits for me to sit back. As I do slowly, he adjusts straps and pulls me up to a good height compared to him. He also tethers my feet and hands into the thing so I can hardly move. Straining against them, I test it out.

"Good, that will do." He gives a nod and kneels in front of me, making sure my legs are open and I'm open to him. "Now you know what I have done in the past, so yes, this is something I have done before. Not very often, most come for the animal kink. This is my personal stash, so everything here is clean and has only been handled by me. I get my own room here since I am here often. I have not been with another in here, this is mostly used for training or learning a new technique on my side."

My body relaxes and eases.

He gives a long lick at my core. My legs shudder for more. "By the end of this, I will have claimed you in all ways possible."

"Promise?" My eyes go dark as my animal responds to him.

He flicks his tongue against me before sucking my clit. His hands touch and caress me. "I can do more than that." Pulling over a tray with tools. He brings one up and touches it to my clit until my whole body vibrates with it. He raises it higher and clamps it to my left nipple. It holds on tight and sends a vibration that I have never felt before at my nipple. He brings another and holds it to my clit, the vibrations moving in tandem together from my left nipple to my clit. My body bends as it stimulates me.

He brings it away, making me ease back into the swing before clipping it to my right nipple. He sways me back and forth between his mouth and tongue, teasing me in time with the buzzes.

His mouth moves against my lower lips, kissing me. "I want you to shift a part of you."

"Shift?" I ask. My mind not grasping the concept he is asking of me.

"Yes, let's start with your fingers. Shift them into claws." He gives a long lick to my core and up to tease with my clit as the vibrations are thrumming through my nipples. The swing moves as my body wants to move, causing delicious friction that ebbs and flows. My mind is in turmoil, not being able to concentrate. All I can do is feel what is being done to me.

His mouth stops as he notices my fingers not changing. "Are you naughty? Do you need to be taught a lesson?"

The way his voice is so low and dripping with honey. "Yes, teach me." I yearn for him to bend me until my breaking point.

Adjusting the straps that hold me so that my lower body is in a higher position and my back and neck are at a decline. He walks around and my eyes are at the perfect height to see him. He is still long and partially aroused, but not rock hard.

His thumb rubs against my lips and cheek before he motions me to open. I do so gladly; he rocks forward into my mouth. My arms flail as I struggle, wanting to hang on to him. Pushing my hands fully through the loops, I can rest my hands on his thighs, giving me the solid feel, I need to suck him down properly. I go to work on him, wanting to show him how well I could do what he is needing, even if I could not shift. He lets me control the movements for a moment, but once I get into a rhythm, he holds himself against my face, forcing me to adjust.

He eases back to give me room to breathe. Removing himself, he pulls at two straps that tug my arms in a different position away from him.

"You have been bad; you don't get to control this part."

My eager eyes eat him up as he stands in front of me. "So bad," I agree.

He waits for me to open before he slides between my wet lips. My tongue twirls around his cock, making him harder. He pushes forward all the way, his cock hitting the back of my throat. Sliding in and out multiple times before, he holds himself there at the back of my throat, making me adjust to him. He flicks the nipple clamps, making me moan around his cock. He eases back, taking himself fully away. I use the time to gulp deep breaths into my lungs as my body struggles with the pleasure vibrating through it. Trying to remember how to breathe.

"Still needs something more." Blaise walks over to a shelf and looks at the toys held there. Grabbing something, he holds it to him, hiding it from me. I lay back in the swing, relaxing and waiting for the next wave I am about to endure.

He rubs something large and blunt against my lower lips as it slides into me, making me feel so full. Raising my head, I see his dark eyes light up with mischief. He also rubs a cooling liquid against my butt before sliding another thing that is smaller in. Pulling two other straps down and wrapping a third one from behind and clicking them in place together to hold the toy against me. He holds on to a control and walks back around to where my mouth is waiting for him.

He presses a button, and things start to move inside me at the same time. Things slip and slide, but the straps hold it all in place. Groaning out, I fall back against the swing in pleasure. He takes that opportunity to slip back inside my mouth, going slow as my mouth gobbles him up. Sucking on him, pulling him further into my mouth.

His hand comes down on my clit and slaps it before rubbing the sting away. His arm bumps one of the nipple clamps, pulling it partially off, making it clamp just on the edge. I'm moaning around him as he moves the swing back and forth. He pulls on the other clip, yanking it to match the other one. That sends me roaring. My fingers scrabble in the strap's nails, slice out, but the straps keep them in place suspended in air. Upping the intensity below, it throws me over the edge. I moan around him, letting myself go. He unhooks the clips from my nipples as I bask in the throes of ecstasy. He eases away from me so he isn't suffocating me. Removing his hard cock from my mouth, letting me rest.

Pressing another button, the vibrator below stops, giving me a respite. He lets me just sway in the swing, but unhooks and unwraps me. Removing the vibrator, he pulls me from the chair; he carries me easily in his arms back to the bed. Snuggling me close, he rubs his cheek over my hair.

"We will have to continue practicing your shifting abilities, but I think we have found a better way to make the badger come out willingly without you being scared or angry."

My brain thinks of many things to say to him, but my mouth doesn't formulate the words I want to convey, so instead, I wrap my arms around him and snuggle into his chest further. He makes sure when putting me down on the bed that he is right there with me. My head and upper half of my body dragged over his chest, our legs loop around one another and we stay there in the afterglow of what just happened.

# Chapter 16

AFTER CUDDLING AND REST, my eyes flutter open. They land on Blaise, who is already awake and looking at me. "You talk in your sleep."

I'm shocked at what he says. I didn't know what I expected, but it was certainly not that. "What did I say?"

"Nothing that could be pieced together, really. I heard my name, which woke me up and Flit's name."

"Hmm." I look down at his naked chest that I'm still plastered to. He felt good and comfortable against the chill of the room.

He brings a hand under my chin and raises my face to his, giving me a light kiss. "I think it is time that you clue me in on what happened now. Why were we able to complete the mating bond without repercussions? What did you bargain? Where is Domini exactly?"

"Domini is free and with his people. They came for him and he asked me to come with him, but I could not leave you here knowing that she would harm you."

"You care for me?" He gives an incredulous look.

"Of course, I do. Why else would I be here mated to you?"

He hugs me closer to his side, if that is even possible, and is wearing the biggest grin on his face. "I'm not sure, but you have made me happier than I have ever been."

"He decided it was best to go back with his people, so he didn't start a war and I come back for you. I was going to go to Flit and Jazmin to possibly work out something, but Beatrice was there waiting with her lapdog."

"Is she sending someone after Domini?"

Shaking my head, I sit up in bed, stretching parts of my body sore from what transpired earlier. "No, Flit made sure that their contract was completed he earned his soul back and was free to go. Beatrice should have managed something so important better than bartering it away to be used at that person's discretion."

"That's lucky." He sits up, leaning against the headboard.

Pulling on the chain, I smooth my fingers over the smooth red heart-shaped jewel. "I still have a way to contact him if needed. Hopefully, we will see him again soon; I will miss him in the meantime."

His fingers come up, lightly touching the medallion. "I think I will as well." He looks up shocked that he came to that conclusion.

Giving a huff of a laugh. "He grows on you."

"That he does. What happened next?"

"After talking with Star, who is Domini's sister, I came back the way we went out. Unfortunately, Beatrice was there and caught me. She brought me before Flit to get retribution and demanded my death. Jack, who I knew from Morning Star, was brought here to help Sera determine if we really are related or not. Things hit the fan very quickly and Jack did not make it through." My breath hitches. ". I fought with my mother over it. She had to be made a shadow after it all to calm herself, but before that happened, she had let us know that we must travel to Ivan, my father. He knows where my brother is."

"You have a brother?" Blaise skims his fingers over my side. His fingers dance around my hip, teasing and distracting me.

Nodding, my eyes watch as his fingers move. "Yes, we have to find the rest of my family. For both my mother's sake and mine."

"Why yours?"

Tears fill my eyes, but do not fall. "When you find out that the family you thought was yours isn't and actually treated you terrible all you crave is to find one that might love you and treat you how you should be." The tears finally fall as I hide my face from his view.

Blaise brings me close, rubbing my back, letting me feel what I need to, to get through it.

"But every family member I keep finding isn't what I expect it to be. They are harsh and hiding who they really are, or crazy with power that makes them swing from one way to another."

Patting my head, he brushes my hair away from my face, trying to soothe and comfort me. "You know you can always make your own family."

Blushing and pulling away from him. "I don't think I'm ready for that."

Giving a smile, he shakes his head. "Not what I meant, but good to know where you are at with the children aspect. I mean that you can choose who is your family regardless of if they are your blood or not. You are my mate, so to me you are my family."

"I didn't think of it like that." I scoot back closer to him.

He settles back, hooking his arm around me. "I have a big family. Mine might be all that you need."

"Will we meet them?"

"Eventually, yes. I will send a letter to them explaining things and let them know not to worry, but it sounds like you and I will be dealing with something else until then."

"Oh, I'm not sure if I mentioned it before when we were mating, but your family will be safe. She will no longer bother the snake charmers."

"I remember you saying something like that, but lust took over soon after with what you were wearing." He gives a playful growl, caressing my side. "What kind of deal did you have to make?"

Biting my lip. "I wasn't really a part of the negotiations. I just made sure you were a part of the deal and that your family would be safe."

"What was the deal?" he asks, his dark eyes sparking with anger. His voice is quiet, not yelling, as his anger sits there in check.

"She wanted us mated. She said you would never be free and would always have someone to answer to, whether be me or her." Pulling myself up, I loom over him to meet his eyes. "I also don't think she realized that I was coming back and getting you. Who was I to correct her?"

"What else, my love?" He brushes his hand over my cheek, pulling me down to kiss him.

"Don't you start that." I lick my lips and pull up from him. "Otherwise, you may start something else."

"I never start something I won't finish," he declares. "What else was a part of the deal?"

"The rest was on Flit's side. She wanted power and blood from him along with land. When I came in here, they were going to go over specifics and discuss."

"Which would have been a while ago."

Giving a coy smile. "Was it?"

Rolling me underneath him, he elongates his tongue, licking my lips. "Would you like it to be longer?" He rubs himself against me, already feeling him hard and thick.

"Mmm. Longer." I stretch beneath him, wrapping my legs around his sides.

He slides ever so slowly into me.

We both sigh at how well we fit together.

Laughing out, I squirm under his hold. "Are you sure you want to come with us to the mountains to search for my family? You are a distraction. I'm not sure either of us needs."

"Minx," he chides as he slides out of me, taking this serious. "If a siren couldn't keep me from you, do you think I would let anything else? You chose me and I will be choosing you in every which way I possibly can. Snakes aren't given mates very often. I will treasure this gift that I have received."

"Then we should probably get dressed and find Jazmin or Flit to see how we can prepare for our next steps to find my other half of my family." I frown.

A knock on the door happens at that moment.

We both look at one another frozen there on the bed. "Were you expecting someone?" I ask a little too sweetly.

"If I was, it was not my choice." He plants a kiss on my lips before sliding from the bed. Stopping at the door with his hand poised on the doorknob. He looks back at me, waiting.

"What?" I ask.

"Cover up, my sweet. Domini is all I'm willing to share you with." His tongue flicks out.

"What about you?" I arch an eyebrow in question.

Rolling his eyes. "I will hide behind the door. Fair?"

Giving a chuckle, I roll around in the bed, cocooning myself into the blankets, making sure I'm a properly covered. "Okay."

Opening the door, Blaise stays behind the door halfway as he sticks his head out. Jazmin is there in her purple ballroom gown. Still pretty and sparkly. "Sorry to interrupt you two, but I think it best that the four of us sit down and talk about our next steps. Flit is tired after dealing with Beatrice and me. It is best; we get everything out and in the open now so we can prepare. Also, he will explain what was discussed with Beatrice."

"Where does he want to meet?" Blaise asks.

"Just down the way here. First door on this same side at the end of the hallway here." She points behind her.

"We will be there in a few minutes," I speak up from my rolled burrito cocoon.

"Very well," she murmurs.

Blaise closes the door gently and turns his back to it, leaning against it. Sitting up, I peel the covers back away from me. Looking at the discarded see through dress, my eyes look around the room. There isn't too much in here other than a bed, dresser, and his closet full of toys. That door is closed now.

"I don't have anything to wear."

Sliding by, he opens the door in a rush. "Jazmin," he yells out. She is standing there with some clothes in her hands.

"Already knew you would need something since I'm the one that got her ready in the first place here you go." She pushes the clothes into his hands. "Also, Alexia, marvelous job," she laughs as he tries to cover himself with the clothes.

Pulling the blanket back up, I hide a little smile behind the covers.

He slams the door in her face. We can still hear her laughing as she moves down the hallway. Hiding my face completely, my shoulders shudder up and down as I try to contain my mirth. He throws the clothes in my direction.

"Get ready, bathroom is through there." He motions with his chin as he walks over to the dresser, opening drawers.

After showering and getting dressed, we both are ready to handle what comes next. We walk down to the room that Jazmin mentioned and stand in front of it. Hesitating.

"Do we knock?" I ask.

He gives a shrug, raising his hand he does a quick tap on the wood.

"Come in," Jazmin's voice rings out behind the closed door.

We open it up, and both Jazmin and Flit are there, eating some breakfast at the table.

"Go on, get something to eat and come join us," Flit calls out.

Blaise goes straight to the food, ready to grab something, but I stand there at the door, closing it. My stomach doesn't feel as if it could handle anything, especially food at this moment.

I sit down in the chair at the table, not grabbing anything. Blaise grabs a couple of plates, makes a few trips before finally settling down. He has a whole breakfast buffet in front of him.

He pushes a few plates off to my side that have toast, fruit, eggs, and bacon. Meeting my eyes, he gives a nod before leaning back into his seat, relaxing.

Both Flit and Jazmin continue with their breakfast as we sit there watching them.

"I know you know where the rest of my family resides. I need you to tell me where they are so I can go find them. And don't just say in the mountains, I need to know where exactly."

Flit pauses mid chew for a moment before continuing. He finishes before speaking. His eyes roam the dishes on our side, left untouched. His eyes raise to Blaise, giving him a hard look, before sliding back over to me. "I know where they are in theory, yes. But I can't just tell you where they are located and hope for the best."

"Why not?" The smells from the food were getting to me. My stomach pinches as my mouth waters. I would not have his food before I knew the next steps. The things he offered I didn't need, not from him; I'm strong on my own.

"The reason is three-fold, like all bad things are. I'm hoping Sera will calm down and come back to herself when her family is finally reunited and whole. Second, they are in the mountains which are of the Void's territory. They do not play well with magic users of any kind; they know me and we have done business. There is more business to attend there with this world shrinking as it is, with Beatrice's plans to start a war she will ultimately lose as it stands. We all will if this gets out of hand."

"What are you talking about?" I question as I sit forward. My hand bumps into the silverware on the table as I reach for some water. There are glasses and a pitcher sitting on the side. Pouring it, I do not wait till it is full before downing the water. It sloshes over the side; the cool liquid disperses as it hits the cloth table, automatically getting soaked in. Needing the ice cold liquid, I quench my thirst and hopefully abide my hunger for a little while longer. Once done, I set it to the side, pushing it over to Blaise in case he wants some.

He takes his time but grabs all the glasses around the table and fills them one by one, making sure all were taken care of. He leans back in the chair, relaxing his arms on the rests as he studies the room.

"I must go with you to the mountains if you wish to meet the rest of our family. So I will travel with you, and I'm assuming Blaise will come with," Flit states.

"Yes," is all Blaise says.

"What happened with Beatrice? Yes, I did want to talk to you about the next steps of traveling, but why do you have to go? You said this world is shrinking? What do you know?" My hands itch to ruffle his smooth long sleeve button up black shirt, putting a wrinkle into his plan and shirt.

"We wrote up a contract on what land is hers and the cities that would be contained within their borders. She did also wish for me to take part in the war she wishes to start, but that should take some time."

My hand rests on Blaise's arm, needing the touch for comfort, knowing he would be there for me through it all.

"He told her to put her war on pause while we are traveling, at least till he gets back. He did not let slip the true reason for this trip, though." Jazmin cuts in, pointing a fork at him, explaining things.

Raising a hand, Flit tries to hold off anyone else that may speak. "The Abyss and mountains are taking over the land. They have always moved inward, but at slower speeds, the past decades have begun to increase they are claiming more and more territories. I fear at this speed we will have to leave in less than ten years or so."

"Wait, so the Abyss, that dark slash across the dessert is from the mountains?"

"Only a few of us know that information. But that is correct. A large chasm opened in the middle of it and out of it the darkness erupted." Flit's eyes flinch when talking about the chasm.

My face falls as I flinch away from his words. "If I didn't come here, things would still be okay, or at least no worse. You would have everything that belongs to you and Sera would still be somewhat stable. Jack would still be alive." Sniffling, I hold my sobs back, fighting the tears that threaten to fall.

"Alexia!" Flit gasps out.

Blaise grips my hand in his, rubbing my knuckles. "Both Domini and I would also still be under the control of Beatrice. That would not be for the better."

Shaking my head, I refuse to accept his kind words.

"Sera was never stable. She needs her family back for that, which includes you. There is more than one way to get land and power back." He presses his plate away, not wanting anything more. Taking Jazmin's hand, he holds it to his mouth, pressing a kiss to her palm. "My chaotic darkness, will you stay back to keep Beatrice in line? Try to thwart her plans to pursue this war, at least for the time being."

"Why, of course, my love. It would please me to no end to be the one that thwarts her every attempt to be happy and be the reason she finally falls. Oh, this will be so delicious. I have not been able to have the kind of fun I'm used to."

"I know Sera took all your crazy fun away. She will not hinder you anymore, my dear. But don't go overboard." He admonishes.

My eyes bounce back and forth at the love they clearly have for one another, no matter how unusual it is.

"I will also work on a plan to get your land and power back from her to their rightful place. If that is overboard so, be it," she bites out, accidentally breaking a glass that she held.

He sends out a dark mist covering her hand and the glass that has fallen. He gives her another kiss on her other palm as the mist retreats. The glass morphs into a crystal ball, with dark shadows swirling around, captured within. "For you, in case you need to reach me while we are with the voided ones in the mountains."

She nods and holds the ball close to her, rolling it in her palm.

"So, the world is dying?" I try to get both back on track. Apparently done with my sob story part of it. My eyes slide to Blaise, who is watching me carefully. His hooded eyes seem to relax, but he keeps his focus. He glances at the food, pulling my gaze to it.

"Yes, the mountains have overrun things more so than they have originally. I need to know why it is eating our world and what we can do to stop things. Like I said, it has picked up steam in these last couple of decades."

Reaching for a piece of bacon closest to me, I pop a piece into my mouth, savoring the crisp, brittle bite of it and sigh as the taste blooms in my mouth. Moaning, I sink back as I make the strip disappear, quickly grabbing another.

Flit continues, seeing my mouth full. "We will find out more once we get there. I have a few towns that I would like to stop by that have contacts to better understand it, but once we get there, that will be a different battle in and of itself."

Reaching for a piece of toast, I grab the knife and spread some butter onto it along with getting my fork to spear some fruit on to the tines. "Won't the stops in other towns slow us down? Shouldn't we try to get there as soon as possible?" I say around the food, slowing down enough to formulate my thoughts.

"Again, my reason will be two-fold. With Beatrice taking over we will be heading north and hitting some main towns so that people that I'm close to will put the word out to anyone in the south who needs to move over to our side of things before she can stop people from defecting. Also, there are some items that we will need to collect in order to make it to our destination. We can work on getting you known to your people if you wish it or used to the political side of things as it were."

"That reminds me why does Beatrice think your sons are dead?" I give him a shrewd look.

"Because, for all intents and purposes, they are." He takes a few bites of food, his face a blanket of calm.

Nibbling on the toast, my hunger disappears after a few bites. I sit back with the piece of toast chomping on it.

Blaise sits up fully, moving some plates off to my side in case I want more and others in front of himself. "We can worry about that later, I'm guessing." He says before digging into the food, not afraid of what others thought. If he brought too much to the table, he didn't worry over it.

"Correct, Lexi, if you do not want to be a part of this world. I won't push you into something that you do not want to do and will understand. I only say that in case you want to learn from me or know the ways of our world."

A calmness sets around me. "You do not get to call me that."

Blaise stops mid chew, waiting for my direction.

"What?" Flit gives a careful look; he picks up a cup and brings it to his lips. His eyes meet mine over the rim.

"Lexi. You only started calling me that once Sera had no choice but to claim me. You have not earned that closeness with me yet."

He takes a long, slow drink before he places his cup down carefully.

His cheek twinges as he clenches his teeth together. Breathing out through his nose. "All right, Alexia. I have many secrets and perhaps I will tell you on our journey the one that involves your parents. But you will have to earn my trust like I have to earn yours."

"You said before that this was the only way for things to progress, but I can't trust that. I just want to be careful and know exactly what I am getting into. I have already been through too much."

"Looks like you might be getting part of the political side down. Quintan didn't think you would so quickly." He gives a slight smile.

Shrugging, I'm unsure if what I said is right or not for the situation. But he now knew my boundaries. "Let's just take one problem at a time. First being we need to find Ivan and my brother. Which I didn't know I had till recently. After that we can decide from there. I want to work on my shifting and fighting. I feel like I do not have that down as much as I should yet."

"Between Blaise and I, I think we will be able to help you out there."

"What about Zeek and Natasha? Have they made contact with Shade or Robert yet?"

"Zeek will check back in a couple of days. We should hear an update before we head out. I'm guessing either they are avoiding Thorn or they have their hands full with Shade."

"Shouldn't we go help them first and then travel to the mountains together?"

"Depending on what kind of update we get from them, we will make that decision when we get to it. For now, rest and relax, take in the comforts we have now because while on the road, we might not have such things. We will warp to our first town and from there make our way north to the mountains."

Nodding, I finish up some other fruit, thinking over what I want to accomplish and ready for the next adventure we would be on. This one wouldn't be as scary having some people I trust beside me. Like my mate. I'm still nervous about meeting a brother I had no clue about. Did he look like me? Were we alike? Did he know of me, or is he in the dark about everything like I am? And when we come together, what did that mean for the future of this world? I have decisions I will have to make, and I'm not sure if I want them to come closer or blissfully ignore them until I no longer can anymore. I hide all this turmoil from those around me. They have their own issues to worry about. Mine are insignificant compared to theirs. Until then, I will do as Flit asks, enjoying my new mate and resting. I will face all new things all too soon. Resting my head against Blaise's arm, I close my eyes, my soul content with where I am right now.

# Coming Soon...

## Legend of the Forest (2024)

Mia has a taste for odd things. It has made her an outcast in her own town. There isn't much known about the world outside of it. What stories she can find are far and few between Most are fairytales or only reference the Old Ones. No one has dared to explore the woods and make it back alive.

A Strange Creature is caught in town, leaving everyone to wonder what is next. There are more and more terrors showing up at the edge. Not all are friendly either. Helping this furry dragon get free, she never imagined what she would find when delving into the dark woods.

She meets Haddox, a golden hunk of a man and Grey who is the opposite in every way. Both show her their world. Haddox fills her head and bed with promises and heat, making her feel free like she never has before. With Grey it is very different. They are at one another's throat and can't stand each other.

## A Soul Saga's next book (2024/2025)

Shade's story is about to unfold...

He only recently became human. He also had to betray the person he was meant to protect and take her magic. To save her from herself and protect the world as they know it. His shoulders are heavy with what he has to do. The only one here for him is a tiny flame that goes by Taz. She is a firecracker and the only thing holding him together, since he has no soul.

# From the Author

I hope you have enjoyed the series so far. I would love to hear your thoughts. Please take a moment to leave a review. They are so important to indie authors like me.

- Link Tree – RaquelGabrielle

- Website – www.RaquelGabrielle.com

- Ream Stories (Like Patreon) – https://reamstories.com/raquelgabrielle

- Newsletter (If you would like to keep up to date with my novels and gain access to some free stories) – https://tinyurl.com/4xa4rxkd

*Ream Stories*

*Newsletter*

facebook.com/RaquelGabrielleAuthor/

instagram.com/raquelgabrielle/

tiktok.com/@raquelgabrielleauthor

goodreads.com/user/show/153277018-raquel-gabrielle

bookbub.com/authors/raquel-gabrielle

# Acknowledgements

Thank you so much, reader, for sticking with me and making this dream a reality. We still have a lot more story to get through and even new daring adventures to discover together, so don't go anywhere. The fun is just beginning. You all are amazing and make me so happy.

Thank you so much to the hubby. He helps push me forward at every step and lets me gush and be over excited when I can't say anything yet. This pretty great guy always helps when he can. He is the one that brought romance into my life. Sometimes good things can happen when you're not even looking for it. He puts up with all my ramblings at all times of the day and night; he is an amazing soundboard.

I would also like to thank Kyla, my cover artist. She is always willing to bring my ideas to life. She is amazing and always trying to grow and better her craft. I have seen the time and dedication she brings to the table.

Lastly, I would like to thank my writing group. We are new and just starting, but I already see great things happening with all of us.

# About the Author

Raquel Gabrielle resides in Oklahoma with her husband, dogs and cat. She grew up loving stories so much that she even made up her own tales. Writing has helped her and continues to do so. Writing has always been there for her and something she will always fall back to when things get tough. She loves all things spooky and knows some of the best people come with a bite.

If she isn't writing or telling stories, you can find her hanging out with friends or traveling. She loves to see the world and all its wonders.

She mostly dabbles in Urban Fantasy or Paranormal Romance but has been known to go outside the box from time to time. For more information about her book and writing journey, you can join her
newsletter at www.RaquelGabrielle.com or on her Facebook author page Raquel Gabrielle

Scan for Website          Scan for Facebook Page

# WORSTED

Garielle Lutz

**Worsted**
Garielle Lutz

isbn 978-1-940853-47-5



Cover art by Egon Schiele.

First published in 2021 by SF/LD Books. Deep gratitude to Elizabeth Ellen and SF/LD for permission to reprint this book.



Calamari Archive, Ink
NY, NY

*to Lisel Virkler*

# WORSTED

I REMEMBER THE first wedding I ever went to. The priest sat down next to me at the reception. This was at some fire hall. Champagne was poured, and I offered this priest my tinkling little portion. He enjoyed calling it a fluteful. I had a side view of him and saw all the fine hair fuzzing over his ears. "Mark my words, this'll be a marriage that'll carry," he said. There was boastfulness and leftover ceremony in his voice. He kept talking about the couple— the couple this, the couple that. "Count again," I said.

The distances between people sometimes fill up differently. I knew a man with one of each, a daughter and a son, both now grown, adults. The daughter he could still occasionally get on the phone. The two of them would get together for coffee cake with raisins to pluck out. The daughter would report that someone, a woman again, had taken some sort of interest in her, and the daughter would try to describe the woman graciously but dimmingly enough. The father would accuse her of feeding him postdated information. He would rail. Weeks would pass. He would sometimes drop by her apartment unexpected and demand to use the bathroom. She would always have to make adjustments to it first. Then one day he heard from the son. The mail brought an unsigned postcard with a phone number on it. The only words were: "Do call?" The handwriting looked unsimulated, not at all unreal. The postmark was some untowered town midstate where the man had last heard the son was living. The man let a couple of days pass. He busied himself. He put all new webbing on the chaise longue. He strolled through luggage stores. He marveled at some bananas, played marbles with some grapes. He made the call early of an evening. "Are you working?" he asked his son. No answer. "When did you last work?" he asked. No answer. "What room are you sitting in?" the father asked. Nothing again. "Tell me which room, you goddamn cocksucking motherfucking shit-ass of a goofball," the father said. The son said, "I'm in the glade."

This was a city full of buildings with plenty of entrances easy to miss. The buses at night were lit cruelly from within. Your face got thrown back at you when you looked out your window at the traffic. We were caught in a truth that didn't exactly fit the circumstance. It wasn't a thumping new century anymore. Everyone was resultlessly medicated. Clothing was made to look bigger on people than it actually was. You got used to death tolls getting revised downward come morning after morning.

Very little in the world is lozenge-shaped, but there was something definitely lozengey suspended from the chain of this one's necklace. She was obviously of the region, had the face of a local, was inconsiderately pretty, but not the type to accept compliments without first putting up a fight. Mostly, though, she just sat there and listened to whatever the man had to say. He looked rough and ruined. He chewed his food half-mouthedly. It was the man who was married, I gathered. The woman was there only to hurt the idea of marriage.

I'd tell people their troubles. Back in high school, my only friend, though we were never really all that friendly (I'd never been to his house, let alone been left alone with him in his bedroom, I'd never even taken the trouble to get his name right, I would've been the last person to be inquired about any lifetides still slopping around inside him), took me aside one day in the hallway between algebra and history and told me that his tape recorder was broken and he was scared to death that his father was going to find out. He was dead-afraid of getting beaten to a pulp. A decade or so later (he'd somehow sweet-talked my address out of some softie in the alumni clearinghouse, even though they're under orders not to divulge), he'd written me a long, not unloving letter. In the postscript he let it drop that he hadn't even had a father. His father had moseyed off into eternity right after the birth announcements had gone out. "That's nothing," I wrote back. "For starters, the events related in the order in which they occurred amounted to the woman's saying—shrieking, practically—that they were shy a seat, and then a man toward the back of the bus saying, 'Here's a whole seat,' which the woman's child then promptly filled by half. The bus was on its way somewhere—a world's fair, one could only hope. In time, a few facts came to light concerning this 'child.' As a passenger myself, I was troubled by two facts of bombshell caliber. Number one, this 'child' had a husband and kids. Number two, a city—maybe not the one you're already sick of hearing about, but a presentable city nonetheless, with a central business district and some lonesome sections and an aviary, an armory, a nursing home that had once been the flagship hangar of a regionally recognized airport—grew up around this 'child' the way towns used to assume shape around rivers. Yet in every house, in every apartment block, in the one hotel left in Old Town, in every tool-and-die factory up and down the line, even in the little casino that now had an alderman's office way in the back, the stream from the bathroom-sink faucets kept getting thinner and thinner. Soon enough every son of a bitch within the city limits had no choice other than to start using the bathtub faucet for every little thing that called for water. And not every bathroom has a bathtub, for your information. Some people have to get through life making do with shower stalls alone. But someone like you wouldn't know even the first thing about something like that now, would you?" He wrote back (and had the gall to have it overnighted) that it had always burned his mother up to hear somebody say that some so-and-so or another had just given birth when the truth of the matter is that a birth is always *taken* and that the kid is the one who fucking owes. But it wasn't the first time I'd been worsted like that. I had been a son once myself.

It had been a life of chronic recumbency thus far. I needed to take some decisive, laggard action. I one day walked up Main Street to some municipal museum of all the arts. Not one of them was to have been left out. An underappreciated latter-day abstract expressionist, now in his nineties, was scheduled to give a talk. He turned out to be a fateworn man holding an orchid. He spoke masochistically. During his talk, he led us from painting to painting and from room to room. There were awkward pauses when he had to reacquaint himself with his work. His speech got more and more garbly, then stubbornly exultant. Afterward, in the museum shop, I heard a woman who had just paid forty dollars for the catalogue of the exhibit say toward the man she was with,

"I might as well be nice and go over and have him sign it." She was looking mostly at me when she said it. I was trying to get one rolled-up sleeve aligned with the other.

Even now, at sixty, a mirror is just about the last place I'd ever want to be seen. I've always shaved without looking. I'm not ugly per se, or so I'm told—just lacking in certain of the facial amenities.

I'd often been married, granted. It even looks that way on paper. One wife put it plainly, so I might as well just go right ahead and quote her: "As a fraction of language, *wife* looks and sounds just a little too sure of what it's meant to be meaning. It's got too much of a hold on its meaning for its own good. *Husband* doesn't even sound as if it's fit to refer to a person. It sounds like something extra you have to put on just because you've been told to, even though you feel you're already fully dressed."

This should be just enough about my second wife. She'd always talked a lot about her parents. They'd been sincere but unsucceeding people. She often had us walking over the little coarse-grassed straightaway of their graves. This was in a fenced-off meadow district of the rear woods. She missed getting the birthday money.

"I'll tell you what scares me," she said to me in bed one night. "It's when people say, 'Week in, week out.' Because it makes it sound like it's the same week that keeps getting filled up and drained." I explained that the expression is *day in and day out*. She said, "Baby me anyway."

The way I'd prefer to think about it now is that an acquaintance of mine, a colleague of some kind, even older than I, was trailing after a trailing spouse, somebody else's. I was fifty-seven, fifty-eight, at the time, and I soon found my way onto the trail too. By the end of the first week, we were no longer alone. The trail was already strewn with drained tubes of moisturizer and BB creams, outstretched compression hosiery of violet scent, busted bunion-control screwworks, rectal wipes, mats no longer matty enough to host even a half-decent nap, the crisscrossery of a bra now of sullen character where it landed. Savagely cropped photos of this trailing spouse got passed around grimily from hand to hand. In my mind's eye, she is still a shatterling of unpardonably fugitive beauty stuck in a life not yet marred to the hilt. On the plus side, it was in the ensuing motorcade that I first met Doroth. Poor Doroth! There was only so much you could do when you were so loaded down with youth.

Doroth had a body easily routed around obstacles. Her vocabulary early on was already deep-drawn and awful. She told me her parents had had to be driven away in a long car that seemed to get longer and longer the farther it got driven off. In school, in every grade, the teachers had kept telling her she looked like a Janet, though the classes were already full to bursting with Janets.

She slept in other girls' clothes, found herself situationally enamored of tatterdemalion rich kids, savored that éclat of the unbathed. Early on, she'd let her body debunk itself into something boyishly inconvenient for most of the men she hadn't yet cooled toward enough. But she could never quite buckle down to keeping up the standard spacing between people. Thus her "concerns," as she put it, for me.

My life is always in my way. I went to a movie a couple of weeks ago. I mean, I walked into a theater, an auditorium. I fled before the previews even ended. I thought I was going to black out. I'm now being told I have "benign positional vertigo aggravated by stadium seating, panoramic Viking-invasion extravaganzas, jump cuts, and surround sound." The nurse practitioner assembles her syllables in worthy sweeps. The gelled surf of her hair appeals as well. She's obligingly aloof when I ask where she went to school.

An old friend, a regular, calls around midnight, doped up, rancored, paranoid. His youngest two, daughters, have been placed this time in a specialized detention program that confines them inside teepees for the better part of the day. It's the approved approach. To hear him tell it, his oldest is rarely present for what her life entails, by which he means only that she is never quite actually *in person* and instead operates on a kind of delay, trailing after herself in her own wake, sinking only with reluctance into her accumulated life, then backing out again. There is a husband from whom she is missing, and a job she could go back to and call a career this time. But she's working part-time for a caterer and writing songs about herself. Most of the songs have the same title: "I Do Most of the Business Cards Around Here."

I'd prefer that people stop wasting their opinions on me. For years, I'd go anywhere you had to pay just to get inside.

I liked standing at the sink and watching Doroth wash. She wouldn't wet the arms at all. She'd grit the soap onto the skin, then crack and wax it over the moles and delicate hairs. She'd engross it onto herself until she was caked and coated. Sometimes we took our eyes off each other just to get a better view of all those flights of steps and, beyond the steps, the town itself, with that long, unturning street.

The people I worked with had boiled themselves down to rammish odors I tried my best not to abide. I never did get it straight who was who from one day to the next. There were no promotions or raises, just tiny wrapped snacks dropped onto our desks overnight. The commonwealth in which I lived had spread itself out too wide. I was married to a pettily violent woman who devoted herself to regimens of self-ravishment. Her face started caving in early. Her belongings were carted off with little resistance. One of the movers said, "We don't do miracles here, buddy. We just take things from point A to point B."

Doroth, though, has blade-boned arms, flushes toilets with her bare foot, loses no time in debuting a mood.

We'd hugged just that once.

I felt a stagger or two in her heart.

This might not go over too well, but he came from a coal-mining region that now and then produced lank, doubtful boys who believed in getting a thing pronounced exactly as it was spelled. "Answer" was *an-swer,* with the *w* triumphant. "Iron" came out with a respectful, fair-is-fair *r: i-ron.*

And run he much later did.

From me and my bearings.

But during those weeks, he had bangs and was a slow-moving shadow on the cinder-block wall of our room in the high-rise dorm bordered by cornfields. I had already dismissed him in my diary as somebody untrustworthy and easily steered. But we were tossings from similar families and were soon wearing each other's clothes and letting each other in on things. We meshed a little messily at first. His dick kept keeping itself worlds removed.

The closest city had a sorrily statued traffic circle just barely in the glare. At a lunch counter we each ate a frankfurter served in a sheet of folded bread instead of a roll. Stepping off a department-store escalator, we shook hands with the governor one afternoon but pretended not to know who he was.

I pursued a "concentration" instead of a major. The profs were hirsute dopes I could wow with just topic sentences and SAT words.

I hung and rehung many an unstaying barrette on longish offshoots of my otherwise razor-cut hair. On my face, I practiced with scarcely detectable, traceless powders.

"Don't," he would say. "Or all bets are off."

We suffered corrective bouts of throwing ourselves miscellaneously onto girls. The girls always later told us they had boyfriends smoldering at home. These were boys getting paid under the table for work they did in a warehouse that hulked helpfully in the girls' dreams. The thought of them must have jumbled my heart just a little.

◆

Behind my policy of never entering other people's houses is my fear of the cumulative force of the furniture and the way a low-placed mirror might appear to lop off my head.

There was an imbibing sleep that drank you right in, and there was sleep you had to chase after and bribe. Night was hinged only flimsily to day. A niece who had barely laid a hand on any book in college got herself a job teaching second grade at some lab school or other. In the classroom, she was a sermoning lover of fatigue. The kids loonily welcomed homework and wanted to recite. They stood up when called on, excited by their own politeness. But she lied to them about every subject—kingdoms, phylums, postulates, parts of speech, people of the wasteful world. She was slugged finally by a mother with backing, but did not press charges.

Men of my age: it's not that there are that many more of us. It's just that we get out of the house more often than just about anybody else. We start looking familiar faster.

There's an actress I like. I've studied the articles about her far too many times on my knees. The supermarket where I shop has filthy floors and overadorned baked goods. A couple of nights ago, in the snack-bar alcove, two women about my age, one with a seeing-eye dog, were sitting at one of the tables. They were saying grace before tucking into some fried chicken. I had gone there to buy paper towels. The young woman tending the checkout was happy and exclamatory about everything—the total, the change, the bagging. At home, I threw the sack into the freezer. My freezer is full of everything still individually in plastic bags—paper goods, mostly. I've yet to figure out what's been going on in the apartment beneath mine. At least three people live down there for a few raucous days in a row, then disperse for weeks on end, then return. Right now, their tenancy is active and indecorous. I guess I'll have to go out again. I shouldn't have to need to be here.

When I say "my wife and I," I hope I mean the third of them, the chairpersonage, a trusting soul and later a traitor. I hope to one day be griping in lyrical ways about a marriage that had put us on no map.

We live on different parts of the street now.

I've never been the type to wake up with ambition to spread myself across the day. Things add up, though, in their one-of-a-kind, annihilative way. Then one too many incidents at work, not enough pecans to pick out of a compeer's brownie, lie after lie in an annual performance review that gets printed out and stapled back-to-front by design. I find a job at a music magazine. It's situated in a bystreet townhouse in a low-lying, low-built inland city. The first few days I'm told to read old issues and just let things soak in. I'm given a fitting place to sit. One morning an editor arrives with a bossy, sacrificial haircut and earrings the diameter of fat-lady bracelets. She explains that my job will be to aggrandize press releases into vividly worded personality features. She hands me a publicity sheet and says, "Go to town." I spend the rest of the morning designing artful catchments for otherwise evaporable drops of data about some guitarist not quite a star. The publisher later slides and swivels over to my side, demands my draft, slowly mouths my sentences aloud. He makes it as far as the end of the first paragraph, looks at me, and says, "Who could've put you up to this? This is not a fan magazine." Then he routes my piece to the workstation of a senior assistant editor, who works over most of my paragraph hydrochlorically, then fluoresces the little that's left of it into the house style. The house style requires that after the star of an article has been introduced, the name must never be brought up again. Instead, the star becomes "the five-foot-eleven, 160-pound, Ohio-born, L.A.-reared tofu-eating golden-tressed guitar-slinger and stepfather of two," and suchlike all down the page. I spend much of the afternoon restyling the rest of my piece, tonging out proper nouns, shoving in the requisite cleveresque epithets. The next day, a new dispensation: mandatory alliteration. From thesauruses, crossword-puzzle dictionaries, and penciled word lists that fresco the wall above my work station, I clap together "the freckly, flame-haired fantastico," "the vampish, velvet-voiced voluptuary," et ceterally, then farce the phrasing into the ever-narrowing columns of type the publisher now favored. I make plenty of unauthorized withdrawals from the battered dreadnought of a house dictionary: *gardyloo, gleet.* There's an editorial assistant I don't know much about other than that she always wears a cloche and calls herself Jandy some afternoons and Jandied on others. She's a lukewarm purée of a girl with bedroom eyes and a bathroom mouth. It's her car we take to the taproom after work (she informs me she's an old hand at absinthe), and the bus we take back gets tossed about pretty gently in a storm that's mostly just show. She grills me about my store of the world's knowledge, which turns out to be nowhere nearly as sky-high as she surmised. There's a certain silkenness to the muscles in her upper arms in the sleeveless thing that clings. She says she divides her time between her car and the couchy ladies' lounge at the township casino. She says, "Heebie-jeebied Phoebe Cates is hobnobbing with goblins again!," then keels over with laughter. Within a week, she's left the planet. At the service, I meet the girlfriend. She looks almost upbeat in her first flourishes of mourning. Her wish is that I follow her to a café. "It's just that I never seem to go overboard enough," she says. "I'm just not cut out for appetites." She tries to pay for our coffee with something on her phone, but it doesn't seem to be the right kind. I get fired for breach of policy. (There had been leaks in our pay anyway.) A week later, neither of my remaining names-for-all-the-things-in-this-world books has a name for that deep-set mouth way down in the toilet bowl, into which I've just now tried to reach for the razor that went down so fast with the flush. Things decamp from this life too easily, too early on.

My life reeks of other people, least of all me. As a boy, I'd been daughterish, dawdling—hardly the type to stay put in the lineage. Of my parents' bedroom I remember mostly a bedside table that opened only from the back.

Everybody I know has a secret life, but they no longer seem bothered enough to keep the secrets even decently concealed. Plus I hate it when the voice in my head—the one that makes me hear myself think—gets directed directly at me alone. Sometimes I go right back to work after lunch. Other times, I drive to the mall for some straightforward unease among the crap. I last maybe ten minutes max. Turns out I am unstalwart, and a litterer now too.

One night, later in my rickety fifties, wracked on the toilet again, folded in on myself, chest pressing against thigh, chin nested between bushy knees, I rotated the plastic bottles within arm's reach on the floor until I had arranged a little library of cleaning-product-label life lessons: "Avoid contact with skin"; "Do not mix with other products." I let the bottles and their edicts boss me around until I put myself back to bed.

The sign outside practically every other doughnut shop and coffeehouse that year read, "STRESSED IS DESSERTS SPELLED BACKWARDS." I said, "Why bring it up?" She said, "Because *woman* spelled backwards never even bothers to spell anything. Neither does *man*, unless you count that war. And neither does *kid*, except if you make allowances."

But had I grown up only to incur the spittled wrath of stepnieces, even half nephews barely out of the crib?

This one had her learner's permit in hand. She'd already dubbed me Aunt Uncle. She had only one hand on the steering wheel. It was beneath her to signal her turn.

I once paid full price for a mirror. It was the cheapest one in stock of the comprehensive, head-to-toe bedroom-door style. The idea was to stand up to myself, or at least stand watch. I bought it, brought it home, then never mounted the thing. Tilted it ungivingly against a wall. Let it keep wearing the second, outer frame of cardboard supports it had come in.

She wasn't bashful. She said, "You're no help at all." She said the two of you might as well drive back to the flea market, the one that had to be kept indoors. You figured, okay, for old times' sake for once. A note posted at one booth said, "Back in five." On the counter she found an old laminated sign that in orange letters on a black background said, "ROOMS TO LET." She said, "To let what? Finish your fucking thought."

Doroth wanted to come across as somebody ruggedly unloved. No matter how far she stood out, her body was right away the backdrop all over again. Her fecal swank was often left unflushed. She harped on the disappointment of coming home to her room every afternoon to discover everything always exactly as she had left it.

For a few months in my late thirties, I was altogether secretarial. I knew how to fit in with leached-looking young women in overlit offices with corkboard walls. I was not very talkative or given to reminiscence, reflection, or remorse. There was some justness by now to my every late-in-coming facial crease. During the lunch hour, I'd sit among the crustaceous at McDonald's. They were the very oldest of them all and must have been flushed out of their oubliettes and dovecotes and cocklofts and such for the better part of the day. They bivouacked in booths and cupped their chins in their palms. I watched them stir now and then to buy a soft-serve cone or petition for a cup of ice. Nights, I resolved to be alert at all times, even in my sleep. I really wasn't minding it all that much that I had to be living at home again.

With a police-band radio and a tumbler full of tap water, my father would outspurn any midweek disturbances of mind. I remember his voice breaking for waitresses and peach-fuzzed service-station troublemakers. His rhythms were always a little off: he'd swallow mid-sentence, then gasp, gray eyes watering behind bifocals still lacking the left lens.

And my mother? There was a biographical side to her life, no doubt, though nobody had ever thought to take notes. You were left to assume that certain qualities, tics, and anything plausibly endearable about her would later be attributed to somebody hardly her better.

Resolved: that people who come into routine, daily contact should at least go through the motions of pretending they've never seen each other before and will never cross paths again.

We're owed that much.

How is it that I can't remember having once driven to where there was a town now so suddenly full of sailors? For a time I spoke only to the women accumulating studiously on bench after bench that had been set out in the sand. Enough of them must have been taken in by something or other about me—my intimidating tenderness, maybe, or just the morbid fluency of my touch? You could see the water from the room where we next typically sat, all four or five of us, on a bed that was surprisingly spacious for the price. They must have all thought I owned the place, that it was just a matter of waiting for me to ask them to move in.

Mornings, there was traffic of teenage boys in the street. Their principal trouble was the overpalpable world.

But I still get tired of telling people that I'm not what I'm made out to be, and that I'm not made of money, either.

At work, a fine-toothed janitor in a Harris-tweed sports jacket chewed me out for having thrown a dirty diaper into my wastebasket. I had to explain that the diaper wasn't mine and that I didn't have a kid. I left it up to him to draw conclusions.

Most of the love I've ever felt for people has been inconsiderate and unreturnable.

There's a coupon supplement in the local paper again, and there's an ad for one of those places where you can rent furniture, appliances, dinette sets, entertainment setups. It's only the picture on the front I'm concerned about—the picture of what the place looks like inside. There's much too much of an oversuchness to this picture. I count seventeen people: four customer-service associates (in white shirts, blue ties) and thirteen cleanest-cut customers trying out chairs and mattresses, monkeying with the controls on the TVs, peering into a clothes dryer whose door is open partway, bending forward to fill out forms on a coffee table. These are people on the verge of renting things, and that's their own business. I'm all for letting people do as they please. Thing is, though, there's a clothes basket in front of the dryer—a red plastic number. And it so happens that I own no such thing, even though by this point, I've got a certain amount of my clothes back again. They've been piling up and mattering. So my question is whether the basket in the picture was just a nice touch, making it a display item only, or whether you can go on in and rent just the basket. If it's the latter case, I see myself in the picture. Not literally, but actually. Nobody in the picture looks anything like me, but I can see myself in there, renting the basket in front of the dryer. I see myself stooping over to pick the thing up. The people in the picture are in their lives, whether they're actors or models or just regular people who've had to settle for the day-to-day daredevilry of getting up and getting dressed. They're in their lives and they're in the picture at the same time. But not me. I'm in the picture, but I'm not in my life. I can't manage both.

Birth-order lore held that the oldest would be the last to feel life seeping away. The middle one would see to it that the bills got paid, the tires rotated twice a year. The youngest would be the one to take flight, or finally at least leap.

I cling to the sixth or seventh sense that keeps telling me I might be an only child.

But why go directly after things? Why not settle for whatever's between you and what you want—air still busy with former disturbers of the air? One night I almost wrote a letter to a different woman. I wrote it, I mean, but I didn't mail the thing. She was maybe twenty-two, twenty-three, a student in one of the memoir-writing classes I taught with twinkling impersonality. This was back when I was an adjunct demoted to night duty. She was awfully tall, and she had that kind of punishing beauty you can sometimes make out in the most determinedly lonely of our kind. She'd often smile at me sarcastically during the entire ninety-five minutes of the class. Sometimes she'd sigh excitedly. Other nights, she'd look alert, nod a lot if I was finally making points. Sometimes she'd ask questions to get the class off track. ("I mean, just think about it. Marriage to one person would mean not being married to everyone else on the planet, right? Is that a chance you would want to take?") One evening she brought some voluminous knitting that kept swelling and swelling until she had all but obscured herself behind it. The papers she turned in weren't written very politely. They tended to be rolled into tubes. I'd unscroll the sheets, but they wouldn't stay flat no matter what. On a night of freezing rain she showed up in shorts, with two Band-Aids unloosening on her left shin. Her first appearance in my dreams was a couple of nights after that. In the dream, I had at last found a snack bar and ate a very thorough snack of crackers you were supposed to dibble with a dressing served sloppily on a saucer. The server, a man red in the face, watched me the whole while I ate.

On the phone one night he tells me that for a whole year or so after the truth came out, the most he could get out of his doctor was a placebo-ish starter tranquilizer.

Then my brother-in-law, one of them, the one who'd been made something of: old age, then older age, disputes of an unbusinesslike nature, his having to have always been the snitch, then his stepping off into death just like that!

Farther and farther from where the masses chew their crushed ice, nobody is denying that as a child, a grade-schooler, I stole wheat pennies, old dimes, silver dollars my father collected in the topmost drawer of a bureau. What is being disputed is that I looked anything like the man. My complexion was complicated, turbulent. There were markings on it, rednesses a doctor had to burn off. "Very clever," the doctor said. "You must be very pleased with yourself."

My wife, one of them anyway: her body in those stone-gray, encompassing dresses had no real way of explaining itself. She seemed to move at some remove from her footfalls. You never knew how close she was getting.

She stored most of her clothes not in the shelfy glooms of our closet but in dumpy boxes in the trunk and on the backseat of her car. (She would often outsit the sunlight in that stick-shift sedan that demanded you take the bad with the good.) Her other clothes were stocked beneath the substructional springworks of our bed. This was the marriage in which we finally had a washer and dryer all to ourselves, but my own clothes I drove to a coin laundry down the road. I'd introduce whatever I'd worn—my underwraps, my most companionable pants—into one of the deep commercial drums and let the things confuse themselves with tendencies, valences, still active in the afterpresence of earlier users—anything to get my life elemented more densely. I'd engage whichever dryer had a spent fabric-softener strip left welcomely behind or, better yet, scraps and tinied fractions of dried tissues, sometimes entire pairs of knee-highs or a shrunken, shriveled, stoop-shouldered housecoat. I'd play my load out on top of everything already vital in there. When the drying stopped, I'd peer through the glass at how my things had disposed themselves into unfamiliarizing drifts, open the door, pull somebody's left-behind blouse over whatever else I had on and let a life come down hard on me.

This heavier-set man, hollow-eyed and cherry-nosed, was doing my taxes with admirable dispatch. I had my doubts that he was a real accountant, but I'd been going to him for years. He asked me for a loan of six dollars. I produced a crumpled wad of bills and handed some over. He tucked them into the corners of his desk pad, then resumed his calculations. The mechanical pencil with which he cautiously recorded the figures I'd given him was sleek and looked expensive. He also wielded, with discipline worth having, a big eraser shaped like a Vicks inhaler. His manner was polite and good-natured, and I wished I could have stopped swallowing the tail ends of my sentences when I answered his questions. If I was hearing him right, they were mostly about unrenewable romances that nonetheless left you feeling on top of the world, and venerealizing double binds, affections filched from even a single one of those cold-eyed, high-necked floozies poised importantly behind the cologne counters in the two holdout department stores downtown. I must have answered him truthfully or admiringly enough, having gotten that far through at least that part of my life inventively unmoved.

I have yet to come across an entirely satisfactory explanation for homosexuality, or even a heartfelt argument against that year— it was almost a year—when I was living with a groggily scholarly older man who had long ago failed at both asceticism and lechery. He did not want me to work (he wanted me staying put at home, daintily abed; he wanted me to draw, or at least try drawing, or at least think about how he might one day need to be drawn a little less down in the dumps), and here the poor guy had yet to find out that I had all along been overdoing it with a scathingly blond, preachy, deep-skirted woman who was married and often carried a basketed child with her when she sneaked by to visit—a child on the tinier side, a blightening child whose tininess required the woman to straighten me out (tiresomely!) on every last difference between *tot* and *tyke*. To this day, I restrict how I feel about her—I set limits, and then I cheat. It's darker in a room that has people in it than in one that doesn't.

This flimsy huddle of buildings at whose center I've been meaning to live a lot less irritably—it's not quite a legitimate city yet. There isn't enough spilling of blood in the hotels, and the hoteliers keep eating their sack lunches out back. You can't help seeing that spoiling surplus of deepeningly blue sky from even the lowest of windows. Where I work, the man in charge presides over a day shift of assistants required to wear half-sleeves all year long. He one day hoops an arm around one of the women and with his other hand fiddles civilly with her belt. I'm neither comer nor goner myself, but at the back of life there's got to be something better, or at least at bottom.

Any routine that got me out of the house afforded me a feeling of having outwitted the infinite, but people were always looking at me and saying, "I could say something." Then another voicemail left by that misdialing caller whose voice I'd come more and more to expect: "That was just the documentation stating I *do* have a hernia."

Doroth! Of all the girls with legs and arms detailed so finely with fine-point knifings, I grilled her the most gently. Ideally, she said, every gesture should be ruthfully sexual. Within weeks, our symmetry had come down to this: I came and went as she pleased.

To repeat: There is nothing—not one thing—that says the most about me. But I keep seeing the people looking. At a supermarket I ran into a woman I knew from a previous education. Her hair had been shortened and agitated. This was a woman whose parents had pushed her and pushed her until she could never again be too sure of her footing. She got through life by propping herself up against guideposts and lamp posts, clinging to railings, pilings, mile markers that on some highways came all the way up to her waist. She had nonetheless gotten a whole lot done in her life. She was known for her woe-sprung marriage and for her knack for the vital antagonisms that home life required. That night in the store, she was steadying herself against a shelf. She looked disguisably pregnant. We talked a little about this and that (the big stinks we'd all made when we were right out of college, the swelteriness we kept claiming to feel even when we'd been out in the cold for hours), and there was something almost ambassadorial about her manner. Then I told her I had to go. That night I was a shining example of a person bent on buying something to read later on, a magazine, anything glossy that would lie masteredly flat for me in bed.

Every day the same streets, the same boulevards, but refreshed at least with new traffic, new people, new pedestrians concerning themselves concertedly forward. Then another week pleasingly kaput. I had to go in for my annual eye exam and afterward made a point of picking out frames from the women's section. "Good!" said the clerk, a woman by nature.

In that marriage, we'd had only that one child, a child whose hair had come out straight up and practically ricey. Then one night my wife demanded that in exchange for her pornography, I was to hand over mine. She had made hers presentable, had put it in deliverable form in a yellow plastic crate, but I had to tell her that I had nothing of the sort to show for myself. She found that hard to believe of a man of my ilk, my kidney, etc. I finally let her know that there was a road atlas I looked at privately from time to time because of the colors of the cities, and she said, "Let's have a look." So I got it out from where I'd been keeping it, and I opened it to a page that was taken up by one of those big, boxy Western states. I pointed to the only decent-sized city on the page, an overbright orangey polygon, a hueful metropolitan shape like the shape that shopping malls assume on those maplike directories of stores and restaurants that you have to consult if you're hoping to make it to the restroom just in time. My wife said, "If that's what you want." I never know what to say at times like that. I've never been one to be raring to die.

Maybe it's finally time for the letters of the alphabet to be treated as the tragedies they've become?

Doroth was kept busy enough just being somebody's sister when everybody else had to be out looking for work.

I one day met this sister of hers. She was standing behind a hostess station at a buffet, wearing an usher's sort of blazer underneath a windbreaker. Doroth had thought I should get to know her a little. I ran down a few hours with her agreeably enough. She took me to a place where she said the sandwiches always tasted a little wet. She apparently lived for wish-wash of just that sort. She was brightly unattractive and had ways of carrying herself, of clearing her face, emptying her mouth of not just any old talk but forthright execrations and death threats too. She confided that she had a kid whose adult teeth were coming in way, way too ahead of time. Upstarts, she called them. She wanted them all out. She wanted to know if I knew of a house-calling dentist who would do it if he could be paid off the books.

Once in a while, things should change—if not exactly for the better, then at least for the sake of something else. A wife was in rehab at a new place in a river town, and I drove over there on Family Day. For the most part, the staff kept things moving festively along. This wife and I met with a counselor with a legal pad on her knee. The counselor had some homewrecking music on in the background, with the volume low. She seemed to need to know a lot about me but conducted herself without much curiosity. A few days later, I was ordering supper in a diner—my life was finished—and it was one of those Pennsylvania Dutch places, called, I believe, the Distelfink, where you get your money's worth, where they make sure you get your fill. Even after you feel you've finished ordering as much as you can possibly handle, the waitress comes back and says, "You're entitled to another vegetable." I watched the busboy clearing neighboring tables. I told him he might as well take my place mat too while he was at it. The place mat was entitled *Brain Teasers*, and at the center of it was a cartoon drawing of a smiling, large-jawed, wax-mustached, chef's-hatted chef scratching his chin, and arrayed around him was an aggrievement of puzzles, mazes, scrambled-word games, illustrated riddles. None of these were of much interest to me. The busboy was a towheaded, rangy kid in a white short-sleeved shirt. An ID bracelet with huge links was sliding up and down his arm as he took the place mat away and added it to accruing crud in a plastic bin. Things looked simple enough the way he did them. But the trouble I've always had with getting rid of anything—with taking out trash in general—has nothing to do with the location of the Dumpster itself (at the edge of the parking lot of the apartment house) or with the requirement to bag the trash securely in thirty-gallon bags (the lease has much to say—two obese paragraphs—on this score). My trouble is with the open-endedness of the disposal process itself—the untransactedness of the transaction. Because unless I'm completely missing the boat here, all that happens is this: you bag the trash and carry it out to the Dumpster, and once a week it gets hauled, along with everyone else's bags, to a dump or a recycling plant, and that's it. At no point do I get a sense of there being anyone, any one actual person, on the receiving end who acknowledges the arrival of any one particular piece of trash in any one particular bag— anybody, in short, who actually bothers to take it out and look at what it might be and register the fact that somebody has had to get rid of something. This is where my concern arises. This is where the trouble starts. Because with certain things you throw out, you don't necessarily want them to just disappear. You want them out of your way, for certain. But what you really want to do is to put them in the way of somebody else. Because you can't be too sure that anything is out of your hands for good until you have proof, even a guarantee, that it has found its way into somebody else's hands, the hands of somebody who cannot help knowing what he has on his hands, because it's right there. The hands are the important part, *gloves or not.* Without the hands, nothing has even begun. Because there has to be somebody else who knows what was yours at one point. That's all I'm saying. What was yours has to get inserted into somebody else's life, at least for however long it takes for it to get itself looked at. Because it has to sink in. There has to be a person for whom it sinks in. If it doesn't sink in, you might as well still have the thing itself. In fact, I'll come right out and say that, as far as I'm concerned, if it doesn't sink in, you do still have it. Nothing will have changed hands. Nothing will have changed, period.

Life sometimes throws a little something my way, but this can't quite be humanhood as intended or as usually understood.

*Keep your mind's eye to yourself!* I've had to be told once too often.

With mostly browns, umbers, russets, I filled in the outlines of several feelings that might have had to do with her, and I entered the results in a coloring contest at the mall. Didn't even bother to lie about my age this time.

Besides, I'd been young once. I'd been entertaining the offer of a job that would involve my doing a lot of work, of an as yet deftly unspecified nature, for somebody in another state. I'd have to pack up and move, naturally. An apartment was going to be part of the deal. The promised apartment would be on the second story of a four-story building that the offerer of the job claimed to have been in the family for generations. The way it was explained to me, though, there wasn't any door to keep anyone working in the offices on the first floor from walking up the stairs and right into the apartment. The offerer of the job said that she herself would have no interest in whatever else might be going on up there, but she was in no position to speak for any of the others, though these people, she guaranteed, were too insolently negligent about everything concerning their work to even think of doing the honors of climbing up some steps. I told her I'd need more time to think things over.

My first day on this other new job, though, I make the rounds of the cubicles, get everybody's name right (there are tagboard tags spelling things out), make apologies for even the most well-meaning of mispronunciations. Everyone says things like "The tape is erased!"; "No offense taken!"; "Let's talk soon!" Later on (the first week's pay is withheld), there's a constructive potshot taken at my "sexual welfare" and one long, anonymous, terroristical letter, printed out in great-sized Gothic, that reaches me a day or two later in an envelope of exorbitant dimensions. The concern of the letter writer is what it supposedly looks like I'm doing when all I'm doing is just fishing deeper and deeper in my pants pocket for my keys.

She'd stop speaking to me for weeks, then promote me back into her emotional protocols. I discovered that through the mail she'd ordered gadgets, appliances, devices for marriages not quite going right. She must have been getting some use out of the things on her own. I find a little galaxy of them in the closet. They're in one big box high enough that even on a stepstool they aren't that easy to claim.

They're made of just about anything you could name. Silicone. Neoprene. Glass. Stainless steel.

I give them a try. Her smell is still smelly on most of them.

I enter myself from behind. I consummate things just for the justice of it.

I lowered my standards, and then commenced that period of periodic nice gestures on my part. I interviewed my parents that time we were all on the waiting list at the same motel.

There was a time deep in my forties when the people who handed me my change in the stores would hand me bills that were mostly torn. They must have sized me up as a person who accepts without protest. They dealt the bills forward from the bottom of their register drawers. I would take the things home and had to find somewhere to hide them. I often settled for the mouths of the castaway cordovan loafers I kept on the floor in shoddily cobbled mockery of my life.

Something came over me a couple of nights ago. It was that funny feeling again—the conviction that comes from having had too much dumb luck in the very year set aside for backing out of life. I walked downstairs (though this time not taking my time) and got into my car. I drove to a home-improvement store and bought a nice piece of lumber—a big shrink-wrapped slab of plywood. I brought it back to the building and hefted it through the lobby and up the stairs (there's an elevator, but I never use it) and into my apartment and set it down atop some plastic crates stacked two high. Okay, there, I've got a table now, okay?—that's as much as what I must have been telling myself. I sat down on the floor beneath the table. The minute the evening rates went into effect, he called. He said he had a hamburger story to tell and a gro-cery-store story. I had a hamburger story, too, but he told me to make it quick because he wanted to go to bed. My hamburger story required some background, because it was actually two stories—one about that day, and one about the day before, both involving the same burger asylum and the same counterdamsel who, both times, was on break and sitting at a booth, but who came into the picture, by her own doing, on both occasions. The man wanted me to describe her, but I was in no mood to go into bodily specifics or deification. This displeased him. His girlfriend had gone away for ten days "to think some more," he said. He said she'd been calling him overcontained, emotionally finite, untrustable, lumpily aloof, too picky about the things he'd taken to keeping under his pillow. He wanted to know what I was wearing, and I lied. He must have known I was lying, because he said, "That's why you'll always be living alone," then hung up. It had all been on his bill anyway. He always spoke in an overenunciatory, speech-teacherly way that could be hard to take when he was in the wrong. I turned off the ringer. I got up off the floor and arranged a few things—the batch-let of hospital-patient bracelets I couldn't stop collecting; snippets of necklaces that had long since run their course—atop my new table. At some point I walked to the kitchen and started boiling water in the big pot I'd bought a month or so back. This was the first time I'd tried to use it. The boiling water was going to be for egg noodles, evidently. I couldn't go through with it. The next night, it started on my bill and after a few minutes switched over to his. He insisted we limit things to hamburger stories from this point forward. His new stories involved novel ways to make him-self look uneasy when going to places like that, as if he were forced by circumstances to eat there now. I told him I already missed talking about other things. He told me to shut up. I defied him and resorted to endearments. He hung up. He was never big on getting together (he kept saying we lived so far apart), but we had met up one summer at a suitable lake that had a boardwalk (few lakes around here do) and at one point we shared a large coneful of French fries I'd been the one to pay for. I believe I was the one holding the cone. In those days he still smoked. He had a cigarette in one hand. He very deliberately but very casually jabbed the burning end of it into my palm. He said, "I can't eat and smoke at the same time. Don't keep expecting me to." He always had it pretty good. He'd worked in Human Resources for years. All he had to do was teach new hires the easy way they could tell the difference between the professionals, the paraprofessionals, and the people on staff without ever once being a pest. There was a simple trick to it, he'd assure them. He'd have them looking at drawings of all three walks of life, and from the drawings he went on to portraits in oil, altarpieces, carvings, tapestries, watercolors, acrylics, double-exposure photographs, overhead-projector transparencies, slides, videocassettes, eight-millimeter film reels of cherishably garish coloration, charcoal sketches, gouaches, otherwise unclassifiable works on paper, one-offs and one-of-a-kinds (he insisted there was a difference). He'd tell every new hire she was a quick study, butter her up, then send her out into the corridor to fall flat on her face.

Whenever we had to walk together toward the car (we were on our own again, just for the day), my mother only ever had that one thing to say: "We're on our way to see the little boy who *did* ask to be born."

Then the days when I would feel, by turns, humored or depreciated by the attentions of the woman living in the apartment overhead. She seemed to be taking her every cue from me. She went along with pretty much everything I did. I would rush around my rooms, deranging the place. I'd hear her doing the same. I would overexert myself in approximations of exercise, mock aerobics. She would, too. Or I'd skip meals, lie motionless for hours. Not a sound from upstairs. Once, I went as far as sneaking out of the apartment with an overnight bag, gentling the door shut, taking a bus to a motel. For two days, I watched cable TV behind drawn drapes, walked to fast-food places, bought newspapers just for the obits, the police blotters, the bingo updates. I imagined the woman immobilized, directionless. The night I went back, her footsteps tracked mine from doorway to living-room floor, where I must have finally lain down for certain.

Looked at in a different way, it's all well and good to fault yourself for thinking that you have another life when you're not quite asleep, when sleep is hovering just above you—and that that one's the life in which you're most at the beck and call of who you more likely are.

And me?

I'm just like everybody else.

Only never at the same time.

My parents had held on to the same telephone number from long before my birth until well past the triumph of their having both gone deaf. Then came their flauntingly expressive deaths, one after the other, in a matter of weeks. Then at some point, everyone's area code had to be changed in that corner of the state. I finally had to have the entire number nulled and voided. But it's a rending sequence of digits I still fall back on out of habit when I pick up the phone to call somebody, to call somebody out.

Looking back, I guess I was my mother divided by my father, and not the other way around, if I have to be a quotient of any two ill-lived people.

I hadn't had much of an upbringing after the incidents.

Depending on whom you made it a point to talk to, my second wife was either good about keeping marital hours, showing up for housewarmings, and working at sexual odd jobs, or else put in her time as a friend of my sister's when my sister was better off without me and my always having to be a couple of years older. My sister was misdivorced and always making up her mind again about the man. He'd furnished her with a baby to look at, somebody to see as just another life spinning off in ordeals beyond her own.

This second wife of mine was always good at giving advice on how to make anything look lost. She could carry a worry over into even the way she walked, but there was only so much deadweight sympathy you could keep feeling for people. Your emotions would always feel stolen from anybody else anyway.

I go into her bathroom for a change of scene. The sink is kaput. Not even any pipes beneath the bowl. The wastewater simply splatters into a plastic garbage pail underneath. I empty the pail into the tub, then rinse out the pail, rinse out the tub.

After the wedding, she acted as if nothing had even happened. Some people just have that gift. I later figured it all out because it is exactly what I would have done myself. In fact, it's how I continue to make a point of doing things. For instance, I later described something—some granules, or grains, of sleep somebody had swiped from the pages of a frail-spined library book and then finger-swept into an envelope. This person (whom to this day I picture as a womanish youth whose growth spurts had brought nothing but scandal first and disappointments later) then sealed the envelope and on the front of it wrote (and then thrashily underlined) the title of the book, the name of the author, the copyright date, and the call number. This person took the envelope home (I let myself picture just one room in the place: I permitted myself just enough vision of close-cropped carpeting over which had been thrown an oval rug, with an outer band of maroon, to put people in mind of a racetrack) and most likely intended to return to the library and run through the same procedure with many other books in hopes of founding a lasting library of such meekly cornucopian envelopes at home. But this person was nobody even remotely in the same boat I was in and most likely never even went back.

I bring this all up because I wanted to have a look at this description some years later in a residential hotel where I was overseeing the after-dinner outlandishments of circumstantial homosexuality with little regard for how narrow and bare of window the room actually was. I let it be read to me, rather, by somebody many downblown years my junior. She read it over and over in every accent she could muster. But the envelope was barely in the description at all. It hadn't survived. Just about the only thing left in the wording was something about how little a woman golden-lockedly like herself had been loved from limb to limb and how the man always managed to get enough money together to go everyone else one better. I remember having to kill a fate-scorning amount of time on the toilet afterward, doing my damnedest to try getting everything out but probably just blushing down there. Certain other events, ensuances, would have to stand out if this were to be the story that finally served everybody right.

We were, as usual, down on somebody's floor at some point. People had to step through the **V**'s our outstretched legs had made. Besides, tell the truth: as soon as something gets itself described, who needs it? Tear it the hell down.

Any kind word and she'd be right away bound for the bathroom to check on the bleeding.

I've still got the notes she wrote to me in the raw, leaning alphabet she could so easily fake.

Doroth filled me in on a lot. She was conversant in all the kinks and countertop pharmaceutica of that half-circle of dream-blinded kith and kin. She sometimes talked in a commotional, bullet-pointful way when she should have already been getting sleepy:

- All those years I'd been living with the conviction that if somebody leaves you, it's understood that you're to follow!

- I actually already have a kid! It's out there somewhere in a family, holding the whole family together!

- Those sidewalk caricaturists with the easels and sketchpads? Suppose you sat somebody really ugly down in the chair. Then what? What would they draw?

- We were just two women in the scramble of our early twenties, barely breaking a sweat. My fellow feeling kept coming out funny!

- Please don't make me have to do the thing with my voice, the thing that makes me sound like what I am!

- An empty face should know enough to collect things on itself. Any old blemish will do!

- Denise was different. Our intent was to touch off just enough of the end of the world to get us through this little bit of brittleness between us. We'd each been a little sick of the other of late!

Her sister came back provisionally OK'ed from a physical, talking about "the life behind the life."

Sometimes we stayed at my place, first on account of her and then, after she must have fallen afoul of herself anew, on account of how the rooms were spaced out and yet stayed contentingly connected. She kept walking from one to the next. I figured she was describing the rooms to herself, lugging the description around, pitting it against what was actually on the floor, on the walls.

But I can't bear the thought of having to keep lugging around how the street outside looked to *me,* which would be in competition with what it must have actually looked like, the car door still open, her sister howling, even though the light had already been long enough green.

It was later suggested that I show up for a workshop on how to punch up my obituary-in-progress. Mine was said to still be spotty in parts. "Don't leave it up to the bereaved!" the guy in charge, the facilitator, told us. "Get it all down now!" He was a shakily exhortative depressoid trying to look sporty. (He was out on loan from some mortuary consortium.) His big thing was a technique he claimed would make it easier than ever to take the "bitch" out of "obituary." "This ain't no résumé we're talking about, future deceased peoples," he said, then put an outline up on the board but erased it before I could finish copying most of it down on my palm.

He passed out some paper and had us each get going.

While we wrote, he walked around the room, stopping behind every desk to read over our shoulders and offer suggestions.

"Nice, very nice!" I heard him tell one woman.

"I try," she said.

I put some things down that I figured would sound like reasonable enough predeath doings, deathworthy pursuits and the like. When he got around to my desk, he read what I'd written, then shook his head.

"Those are *hobbies,* butch," he said. "You're positive anybody even knew you had them?"

Then: "Let me ask you this. Exactly how alone do you live? What's it like on the floor in your bathroom? What's the most pillows you've ever owned at one time?"

I mentioned a book I'd taken up with, a company-keeping library discard that was not on the only subject dear to me but now and then brushed up against it vagrantly. I could not exactly follow the gist (the meanings, the sense, had long since passed back into the lineations, into the peaks and underproppings of the letters themselves), but I found I could press a fingernail deep into a page, make a private indentation next to any line I considered worthy of return. The book thus filled with ruts, depressions, all my own. They would smooth themselves out, though, before I ever reached for the book again, so I could never find my way back to those pages.

I could have said more—I wanted to broach the prospect that one or two women could still be talked into coming to my door to come forward—but he cut me short, hurried across the aisle to a woman counting on her fingers. "This one I was married to, this one died of you'd-never-guess-what, this one was living with his mother in a mobile home he would one day set fire to, this one had had way, way too slow a head start, this one actually had me believing his office was in one building even though the work itself was in another . . ."

"It can't be about *them!*" the facilitator shouted. "It's got to be about you! It's got to give off a whiff or two of a full, unstunted, ripe-rot life."

"Let me think," she said.

He came back to me.

I'd **X**'ed out everything I'd written and tried to start on a new tack. I wasn't getting anywhere.

"Look," he said. "Picture yourself blue in the face. What will people miss last of all? Tell you what, tell me about just one person. There must have been some woman friend who could put up with just about anything."

I mentioned a rank-minded woman who'd kept all her textbooks from college. They were all still covered with kraft paper, still glutted with folded worksheets and quizzes. But I'd liked being kept company while trying to put myself to sleep, to put sleep over on myself.

"We're talking way too many ages ago, pal. Look, have you fucked in this century yet? Or been enfucked? Have you presumed upon a man of your own sex ever or even just lately?"

Silence.

"Okay, be mum. But listen: mourners these days like a little something to do. People like to stay active these days, even in chapel. They need to be kept busy. We can pass out little cards. The cards can read something like 'The deceased requests such-and-such,' something along those lines. What's your pleasure, buddy? A little hand play? Little tugs of the arm? A styptic kiss? What would you want from them? If somebody shows, I mean."

No answer.

"Listen, you look like you've got a bit of money. You'll be up there on a bier, man."

No response.

"I hear it can be real nice up there. You can really lord it over on people."

He moved on to another desk, to somebody else still rockily, busybodily alive.

When the session was breaking up, he came over to me again. "Look, bud, I hope I've at least given you a little something to look forward to," he said. "It'll be the best of both worlds."

Doroth on the floor of my car, coming to:

- Where at last is a body in which things get done differently?
- I wish I could just walk into a room and not feel like I'm belittling it!

- Things keep coming out of me first-personally when I want to be seeing everything from some other side!
- Long as I don't have to level with people, I'll be fine!

I finally find a file folder that might as well be bearing the title "With Whom She Had a Son." Inside: a photocopy of a driver's license, expired. The face in the photo: features gone ghostly from toner going low. Eyes (green) and height (5'11"), but you can't always go by those. (Bodies are fickle.) Age: behind mine, naturally, though by only a nice slice of a decade. Last name: lacklustrously Eastern European. First name: like something you'd want to run past the patent office, not give to a kid who'd soon enough have to live through all the timidities life would require.

A killing unfinality to the rest of the stuff. Mostly just blurred ATM receipts, some blunderedly brain-spun poetry on notebook paper, very unlike her but with no effort spared.

I felt her pulse once. It felt like an opera was going on in there.

I wouldn't know any other way to put it: The boy toiled at his play. Much of youth had already eluded him. He had balls and dolls—he'd been given a little of everything.

He woke up one day and no longer could walk.

He had to make it to the bathroom. That was the most he would try. He had to get there. He had to go.

He took a step, a niggling one, with one of his feet, the left one. The other foot reneged on it, cancelled it out. He tried again. This was no advance. He was not getting anywhere.

He was being thrown off himself.

He kept landing on the floor.

The boy had only the vaguest of bodies strung beneath those heavily sewn bottoms.

People will naturally want to have misread that adverb as "heavenly." No grudge will be held.

A doctor had to be brought in. The doctor spoke of "an evasiveness of the bone." Things of this sort were not unheard of, he said. He said the bones would stop equivocating soon enough.

The mother and the man notionally the father put the boy to bed for a few days with one of the puzzle books then popular. It had been bought for the many pages that asked, "Which line is longer?" These were floorers.

A day or two would come and go. The bedsheets were soaked. The boy longed for a bite to eat—a marshmallow maybe, maybe just a corner of his mother's marmaladen toast.

He fell each time he ventured out of bed.

Another doctor was sent for. He said, "Hear me out. It is not a disease presenting itself to us here. It is neither injury nor handicap. But something in or from the world has been communicating itself to your son."

The mother said, "Communicated what? From who?"

The doctor said: "I am not the right person to be directing the treatment of this boy."

Everyone by now gathered (the mother, the man long regarded as the father, a couple of girls regardable as sisters, a wailing aunt or two, two or three stoic uncles cast in the same mold and with the coming evenings of feast-making no doubt frontal in their minds, neighbors wearing whatever black they still hadn't gotten around to giving remissly away) watched the doctor's nostrils narrowing themselves further and further as he talked. It was as if the doctor's nose were closing itself off from the rest of the world. The voice of this doctor kept thinning out. Everyone must have been thinking exactly the same thing: "This man wants to suffocate himself! He's going to keel over right in front of us! Go ahead! Let him do it! It'll serve him right!"

The third doctor brought in did not speak in figures of speech. He had an orderly mind, and the order he had in mind was this: wheelchair (six months), then a brace (give or take a year or two), then crutches (six months to start), then watch and wait, then wait and see. Everybody thought this doctor practical and worth parting with their dollars for.

The years had their unfavoring way with the boy. One of the boy's feet was now a size and a half larger than the other. A man was known who was known as a sneak. He claimed he had once sold shoes in a neighboring town. He bragged that he could switch the halves of two pairs to form one pair that might just fit. He was sure he could get away with it. He still had all sorts of keys. This man had been gone to school with.

The boy grew up to be mistaken for a clerk in the stores in which he walked haltingly from front to back and from open to close in that unmatching pair. The left shoe fell short of true leather. There were so many eyelets, row after row after row, that it had been cutthroatedly hard to find the right kind of long-streaming lace. What else was there to do in a town that puny but pretend to be hard at work in every store he kept limping through? People would ask where articles of this, that, or the other might be found. Handkerchiefs. Lint rollers. Dress shields guaranteed to absorb even the most negligible and dewy of underarm sweat. A child's first sham planetarium. He would have to tell the people, "You wouldn't want anything like that. Take my word for it. It's junk. You'll have it broken in no time." They would want it anyway. He would lamely lead them toward the counters, the bins, the clearance cases. They didn't care how long it would take. He would say, "See how shoddy it looks? You couldn't even ask for anything more shoddy. It's even a lot shoddier than it comes across. Pick it up again. Really look it over. Something like that wouldn't last. I wouldn't even think of taking your money. Take your business next door."

He would be next door in a quarter of an hour.

Am I even partly in the wrong for spitting it all out this late over so many gloatingly blameless people now so gutsily dead?

*Mind me.*

Mind me a little till the end of time.


I signed over my bank account, gave her my credit cards, asked her to change all my passwords behind my back. She told me I'd have to wait for her monthly drain of my finances to become a pleasure entirely mine. By now she was opening all mail addressed to either one of us. She became an adept at signing my name. The furniture she picked out was petite enough to fit only her. (I remain a futile six-foot-three.) She started paying me a monthly pittance with which I bought her thoughtful but modest gifts, things that could never compete with what the others kept having delivered. The woman she was seeing was excitedly unhappy but otherwise awash with life. This one didn't care for my outer nature, my ethnic demeanor, the way my penmanship kept coming out so oddly canted in testimonies of worked-for woe.

Everything ever after was to the tune of some other tune or another—never the one stuck in your head.

# TRANSFER OF TITLE

FROM EARLY ON, I'd had to be taught to never be heard from again, but at some point in my forties I began noticing these three who rode buses all day long, just as I did, and their ridership looked even more devotional, more engrossing, than mine. The towns the buses passed through must have begun bunching up in their minds as a single, solitary place that any lore had long ago run off from, a place to turn their backs on, until the driver ordered them off. I always thought the driver meant me, too, but he always made a point of saying, "Not you, lady," and then I would say that it was my stop anyway, and he would try to trap me in some small talk. By the time I'd work myself free from him, the girls were always already gone. Was it so terribly wrong, though, for me to wonder where they went?

They looked to be in their twenties, and they looked to be uncheerable, and a different sort of person would probably not have been so quick to dismiss them, the way I sometimes did, as women whose sorrows must have already been scaled back to an eliminative balefulness expressed mostly through their diet: I pictured prissy water crackers left to go stale before sun-up on an otherwise bare table in an apartment bare of any giveaway pawings from a bed.

And those buses: they were forever bruising their way beyond some verge or another, and the terrain out there was mostly blunt, relieved here or there only by an offscape of warehouses or a lake about to be drained. Our state was one that showed up almost perfectly rectilinear on the map, but the borders were in fact hackly, jagged. Departers often felt torn up inside once they got out.

Except for the occasional older person, the only other ones ever on these buses were men in whose faces I could make out the unluminary trance of workers done for the day with their work. I'd listen to them talk. But these girls, these miserably tressed cusses who always sat as close together as three people can get on a bus: there was a falsery to their faces that you couldn't quite take the full measure of without resorting to a stare. "If they're even women," you couldn't help sometimes doubting, because you were through enough with most things too. It was expected of you to have a weakness for people even weaker than yourself. A going explanation, should one be needed, was that nights were a hardener of whatever had most gone loose in a day, and my days, to be cruel, were trash. Things always felt a little too early to already be too late. I was in my stunted forties, as I say, and I went about perspirantly in snugging unfinery of an unvarying hyacinth violet. These were dresses that cropped me into someone a little thinner, I hoped, and somebody a little less fed up.

I now and then wondered if they were sisters, these girls. They had no features in common, but people in those days spoke of "blended" families. Then again, these girls just looked tossed together, unstirred to any uniform consistency.

Then one day they had seated themselves as far apart from each other as they could manage. The driver's usual howl for them to get off gave me a start, and as they worked their way to the front, I got up too. I got close enough to one of them that my fingers trended trickily toward hers. She caught mine first. We stepped off, and she led us away from the other two, saving face, I guess, by talking speedily about a houseplant of hers practically at death's door. Then, that quick, she said, "We could never be friends," and I didn't think to ask whether she meant her and me or her and those other two.

We were in some town, close to what seemed to be the center of it. (A butcher's stall, a little hostelry with a slanting sign.) She led me down the street and into a building, an apartment house, and up two flights of stairs, and down a corridor, past a line of doors, and she then tried a knob, found it unlocked, and went in. I followed.

"He's probably not due back for a while yet," she said. She was quick to shut the door, throw the latch, the bolt.

The apartment was just that one room, windowed on only one wall, and the window got the better of the town. There was a couch, and we were already sitting at opposite ends of it.

She felt it only fair to say something up front about her brother, though he was only a stepbrother and was still in school, scarcely untucked from childhood, purposeless in his growing. Then she got up on the subject of herself. When she was a kid, the doctors had been thinking along lazy-eye-syndrome lines and patched up her good leg so she no longer could put any weight on it. She crawled back and forth to school, dragging her good leg. She'd always been built differently, and for a long time it was still too early to live and learn. Her parents hadn't believed in parting the curtains or, behind the curtains, raising the blinds. Her one real, unstepped brother was just somebody she rarely crossed paths with anymore except when he was showering people with gifts. Until lately, she'd been banging around in mathematics, then dropped out, found a bunkmate's narcotica in a tube sock, had no luck with any of the capsules and tablets, moved out, bought work shoes to wear to work, lost one job after another, went back to school but the education wasn't telling her anything and she was merely attracting attention, the professoriat sweated onto her clothes, her parents were off again taking their ease in distempers of maturescence—it got to where she couldn't even go to a grocery store and pick up three or four things for a simple little dinner without the checkout clerk looking at everything she'd laid down on the belt and jumping to conclusions, construing it all as somehow recapping her life. Her last job had lasted exactly three and a half hours at someplace restaurantial where the owner, or the shift-manager, whoever he was, kept staring at her until she felt as if her features had gone runny and were about to bleed off. And as for the two girls she rode the buses with (I could see her wanting to reach a conclusion), she had long since been of the opinion that you can't keep a double life from getting itself halved and then halved again.

This all sounded to me like territory gone over long ago.

"What about lately?" I must have said, because she right away said, "Trying not to put out an eye." She pointed to lots of solitary nails driven into the walls at what looked to me to be exactly her eye level. (I gathered that there must have once been lots of things to hang.) She said she'd tried twisting the nails out with her fingers, prying them loose with pliers. When that hadn't worked, she'd resorted to impaling pieces of paper onto the nails, or hanging clothes hangers on them, as grave reminders to watch out, but somebody kept tearing down the paper and putting clothes on the hangers and later putting the clothes away in the closet.

"The guy whose place this is?" I said.

"He'd never do anything like that."

"Who else comes in here?"

"Things get kind of communal at times."

"Those two girls?"

"Let me show you the closet."

But she made no move to get up.

She talked about the man. She made him sound creased and faraway because of his height. In the description, late-day hair was appreciating on his cheeks and chin and on the curve above his mouth. He otherwise came across as a man who always got himself overdressed on the days it was up to him to drive, which, I gathered, didn't come around often enough.

"If he comes, we'll have to leave," she said. "He usually knocks first, though."

She reached for a little wooden case under the sofa and brought it out, opened it, set it on my lap. It was full of freehand, haywire jewelry—bracelets and other devisings of obviously her own lurid and private manufacture. I'd be expected to try some of these on? I saw that I'd already folded my hands, and I kept them folded.

By now, I guess I'd had her sized up as a lean-minded and narrow-hearted lover of malarkey, but I made a pledge to myself that I'd give things another quarter-hour.

"Shall we exchange names?" she said.

I said I'd been named Laney, after a vivid and sometimes awfully sweaty aunt, but right away that made me wonder, for once, who or what I might have really been underneath that name or, worse, without it. Now that I thought about it, it did sometimes seem as if nothing but the name alone had been propping me up all along.

The girl said she'd lately taken to calling herself Patrice but wasn't averse to responding to Carly.

"Now that we know each other," she said, and reached for my hand in a companionate way. We sat quietly holding on to each other for a bit. It wasn't so ridiculous. "Come closer, Laney, my Laney," she said. "You're not tired of me, are you? You don't think I'm too tied to my belongings?"

Then the man himself knocked, and in he walked in all of his heights. He took one look at me and turned to her and, talking too fast for me to follow, gave her what I took to be a summing-up dressing-down of a peppily violent kind.

She shoved some of the jewelry onto an arm and said, "I guess I'll be going out with him for a little while. For just a little bit, okay? Please make yourself at home. Stay as long as you like. Here, let me give you some money? All I've got is fives."

The man did not even glance in my direction on their way out. The girl first gave me a quiet little kiss. It was a kiss not of the plenishing kind, but the kind that draws something cloudy and possibly important out of you and leaves you feeling dry and unvital.

After they left, I sat for a while on the sofa and must have fallen asleep. I got up a few times in the middle of the night and turned on a light to see if I was alone. A sheet had been draped over me, but there was no sign of either of them. I went back to a sound sleep.

I spent much of the next morning in her closet, horning myself into her wardrobe, nudging myself into her every getup (she had some very nice things, if they were hers), then let myself out. I waited for the bus.

At the time of which I now write, I lived in an apartment, and days when I wasn't riding the buses, I was driving a car, but only locally, to a drive-thru, one of those handy microphone-and-speaker setups, because that way you never had to look people in the face when you let on what it was you really wanted.

The building where I lived was a block long, with friezes, trefoils, even cupolas—the builder hadn't missed a trick. It had a lobby with three couches arranged to form a **U** of sorts. Nobody ever sat there unless they were waiting for a cab, and there were only five cabs still on the move in this town. The day the building manager was scheduled to escort the appraisers through every unit, my idea was to pretend not to be at home. I spent six straight days—starting from the day the notices were taped to our doors— throwing everything that was on the floor into boxes and crates, then piling the boxes and crates high against the walls, vacuuming the cleared centers of the rooms. When appraisal day came, I hid, unimaginatively, in the bedroom closet, behind trash bags stuffed with sweater dresses. I'd expected to hear no fewer than five or six sets of footsteps but could make out only two. To my surprise, the closet door was never flung open. Nobody said, "How old did you say she is by now?" All a voice said was "Looks like somebody's all set to move."

I had lived in that building for an awfully tawdry decade. My sleep, when it came, was mostly monotonous. Come morning, I'd often hear a lady outside in the hall saying, "I must've run into her on the stairs ten times today already. It's not even nine o'clock. What's her rush?" The landlord kept raising the rent and promising to knock out a wall or two to give us a better chance at the view. I often went out for walks. The town's observatorium wasn't popular anymore. There weren't enough people around for me to play favorites. I felt useless in the sceneries outside— shopping centers off to the side, or parks where somebody or other did in fact now and then park, then sit with windows rolled up, awaiting attentions. I'd make my way back to the apartment house, loom behind other tenants at the line of mailboxes right after the mailman had left. The older ones were always the first to abstract their bent little mailbox keys from robe pockets and change purses, but they'd say, "No, you go ahead. You look like you're on your way to work. We've got all day." There would be nothing in my box, of course, and I would have to be seen fluttering my hands to make the lack of letters, circulars, parcels, seem a relieving inconsequence. No matter how loosely or foolishly I was dressed, I would have to charge out the front door again afterward, pulling nobody visible behind. That was primarily why I came to walk so much and why people on the sidewalks came to say, "Yes, I know you—I mean I recognize you, I've seen you everywhere, we all have—do you deliver messages?" Then the world would have to quickly reduce itself all over again into streets, alleys, gutters, candy-bar receipts in the gutters. The town still had a morning paper and a late-afternoon paper, but by nightfall you were on your own.

My life should hark back and forth to the time, not even all that much later, when I suddenly had a husband, a raw-headed, speculating fellow, somebody straight from a fair-game but profitless infidelity to some other sexually petty brunette (to cite one of too many already), somebody good at pointing people away from himself, someone who nevertheless could never pass up a hitchhiker, somebody who wanted me to wear themed hosiery and fix him sandwiches of parsleyed bologna, someone whose mind you could sometimes actually hear clearing itself up, but it wasn't long until I was given to understand that there was the man you loved, and there was the man you married, and then the man who took off with your married man.

After the divorce (the last time I had much of anything to say to him was on one of those old phones, my words draining away through the sieve of the talk-cup), I took note of what people were doing now with their lives, liking what it would have been like to be out of the picture entirely, and I tried doing a little of that. It was always a labor of wrongs from the start, though—even those months when I lived with a younger woman who was unemployed all the while I knew her but dressed night and day in a uniform that was pleaty and acorn-colored. She claimed she could get along with anybody but haggled over any affection I asked for. She had a couple of little kids who, come morning, would ask, "May we wake up now?" These two, these girls who sipped lemoned water from bowls and lived mostly on cold cuts, were polishedly despondent already, their hearts already scrambled. They were unsure of their places on the furniture. Their smiles were always turning a corner. They would each manage to get me alone, then say, "You're just trying to get me to say something bad about her." Our evenings got dragged out with public spirit on local talk radio. The few times we had company, the visitors (confusional cousinry of hers, usually, whose lives could have used some doing) would point to things in the living room—any old barefaced clock, or a whatnot to which hairpins had somehow gotten themselves stuck, even a library book gladdened up with Mylar—and expect there to be a story about each, as if each had all along been sheltering some threatened history. Afterward, full of homebody behaviors anew, the woman would look at me with a sparkle I found defiant. We would coach each other forward into bed, where she always thought she ought to owe herself something first.

Life kept heaving itself away at me, and I'd have to throw myself aside as well.

There were later others I've also got to get covered up in recall:

The second man I married (we'd batter away at our appetites, then try to dampen any afterclaps), and then I'd gone off with that woman I'd always found looped around one man or another except at the Laundromat, where she kept to herself.

Then the one with the cavities in what little she still felt for people, and the one who figured out the way to get all the dishes to stand up straight in the sink, and the one who spent all day needing people leading themselves clockwise around her at work, the one who had always been taught that the words *woman* and *female* were originally intended to have meant something different—life had yet to menace any of them just right.

I lived with just one other one afterward. She was a woman on whom loneliness must have missed its mark. She had bambooish arms and worked in a cashier's cage. "People will be people," she once claimed, then quickly corrected herself. There was a refrigerator that sumphed and exhaled, and the color had long ago gone out of the walls. Most of all there was a book she kept reading. Even a single sentence on a subject that concerned her not in the least could make her feel berated to the point that she had to be stopped from punishing it back.

A couple of sisters of hers were still alive close by, but their viewpoints seemed squandered on us. Truth to tell, I was practically sixty by now myself, still seeking a final outlet for my youth. Yet when you touch someone—if you're going to take things that far—where all must the hand really go?

A few people are to be known here only as her unfit children, sisterly boys grown now and gone, fending off the hours in untowering towns of their own.

I later knew one of them only well enough to say, "May I lie to you?"

I told him part of everything—your part in it, anyway.

# A LOW-HANGING TOWEL

THE MAN'S LAUNDRY had been piling up in baskets again. He was out of clean things to put on.

The man heeded all this from the standpoint of his furniture, which set limits on where he could be, on which positions he could take in life.

The ones who beat him to the laundry room this time didn't have the look of tenants. It was two women. One had a loose-fitting, indistinct body that she wore as if she could fling it off at a moment's notice and reveal herself to be just about anyone else. The other was all skin and bone inaccurately clothed.

There were just three washers, three dryers. The man saw that the women had all of them going. He had brought a basket of veteran underwear. He gave the women a look, and they returned it right away, just to get things squared.

He carried the basket back to his apartment and decided it might as well be time for a bath. The apartment had an outsize tub with disobedient faucets. He had sworn off showers months ago and started on the baths: he tried store-bought bath salts and foams, tablets, fizzing sweeteners, syrups. Then he stopped being so particular about what he brought in with him. Things no longer had to bubble or dissolve. Newspapers came apart soggily and blackened the porcelain. Some days it was picture frames or anything else he had pried off the walls on his way in, though he drew the line at whatever was unjustly sharp. Other days it was just cake mixes, leftovers. He liked it when the water got thick and chowdery.

When he stepped out, he never bothered with a towel. Whatever might have clung to him in the tub stayed stuck there. Sometimes the air in the room dried enough of him for whatever it was to peel itself off.

You'd get no argument from him about the importance of reorganizing and concealing the few sounds that came from his apartment. These days, there was little more than sneezes, intestinal ructions, thunders from the rectum, coughs, throat-clearings, unexpectedly loud yawns, snores of his own that awoke him from naps. He had long ago discovered which fan— the rattly box one on the floor, the oscillating windowsill one, the hooded ventilation fan above the stove—could offset or undo any disturbances of the body when the thrush and slutch of the TV tuned to a vacant channel or the sink's running water would not be enough to do the trick.

Sometimes the toilet seat got stuck to his rear end when he got up after further of his chores there. Then the seat would free itself and clunk down onto the porcelain. Would the neighbors have known he'd had to go again?

He sometimes made headway from room to room on his haunches.

He had a little radio, and on the mornings it snowed, he listened over and over to the lists of school closings until he knew them by heart: Kellerville area, Longstead area, Mount Holly area, all the outlying athenaeums, all the Our Lady of's. Sometimes there was only a two-hour delay, and he wondered what it must be like, to have the boon of two extra hours like that.

Some days he was free to dote on all the sweets and excellences of his body, the reach of his esophageal acids, the sting of his bile, the shackliness of his carriage when he started off toward another room with a new resolve to set some money aside.

The town itself lacked much longitude, it was a sponge-colored locale, the parsnip-shaped dome of the courthouse was the one and only landmark, and there were blind spots among the population. He had not kept up with how the people managed to make their behavior stick from day to day.

It was not a town he would have chosen himself, but when he was growing up, a sister of his had reached for something, touched it in a way they had all been taught never to let anything be touched, and then she died. The family thereafter had to move shrewdly and afar. He had been told he would be no less himself where there were mostly trees. The thing was to get himself soaked up by surroundings. When he was old enough to get himself enclosed in a marriage, the woman he chose had snooping fingers and fingernails left undazzled. She kept thinking that teetotaling had something to do with math, pursued backyard agriculture with unsuitable tools, banged up against his mother once too often at the stove, seemed to be snoring herself hoarse the one night the two of them were going to try something new. They were already too old to have ever had friends. She had once had a couple of nieces to take shopping for community-college clothes, but then they graduated and found husbands and lost track of themselves and all of the bodily wonderments.

For the longest while, he had a record of perfect attendance at the table when meals were readied on time.

His wife grew solid, unbudgeable. She weirdened barely further in her chair. Then one day she expected him to try on some sort of abridgment of a pair of pants—not shorts, exactly. He could already picture the townspersons taking one another politely aside to say, "That shouldn't be."

The members of the committee that granted divorce in that town had it in for each other and could almost never get anything done. The town charter required that all six live together and share one big bed that was just a decorated platform that required going up a couple of flights of steps. They were always in each other's way but were required to say, "No, no, you're good."

The man had studied their group photograph in the paper. The paper came out only every other week. In the photo, one of the members looked barely out of her teens. Her breasts were just rude blurts. Also in that edition was an opinion piece about the new generation. They were said to be having trouble with coming out of one hour and getting going in the next without first forgetting to have brought something along as an offering or encumbrance.

You could spend a whole day reading this paper. The man clipped an article about a "bedroom community" going up just down the road. Things could be taking a turn, he thought.

Days came and went, but the nights had magnitudes all their own.

The man set about ignoring his wife until she thought better of things. Then she bought herself a car. It was an unsporty, slabby hatchback the manager claimed would behave like an angel in alleys and on highways alike. She right away moved out. She perished not even a month later on her way to get some follow-up thyroidal blood work done on a whim. Roughhoused relations of hers came out of the woodwork and pinned all the blame on him. The exception was a young woman in purplish-blue gym trunks, fraying, who stayed after the others drove off. She claimed to recompense her child for any daily interest shown in astronomy. Would he care to make a donation? She showed him a star chart the child had made. He couldn't make anything out in it. He looked and kept looking for anything poking out of a night sky rawly drawn.

It was hard to miss the volumes of feeling rising and falling within her—the flushes and blanches again and again.

"Did you know about her?" she finally said.

It turned out she was another of the nieces of his dead wife's. In lieu of a medal, he gave her some lackluster silver dollars, saw her off, sat down with the paper again. The classified section was by far the largest, but it was mostly one notice of name-change after another. A Joel was now a Jo Elle, a Leni now a Lenny, and so on down the alphabet, which cooperated.

In weeks to come, any people the man thought to call could be heard reaching right away for anything close by to eat: a suddenly unforgotten blockful of peppery cake, a sandwich incompletely dressed. People needed to have a reason to have their mouths open other than on the man's account alone.

Then a letter arrived from the niece-person. It came without a return address. In it, she explained that the child wasn't hers. It was a kid she'd sometimes babysat, but that had been years ago. Could she be forgiven? Might it be possible for her to return the silver dollars?

He went about his business, in no mood to argue with himself.

Another letter came a couple of days later. The envelope was weighted with coins, more than he could remember having given her. She claimed to be almost forty, claimed to have lost a baby somewhere along the way, and had a lot to explain about why the upper deck of her teeth was in better alignment than the lower. Would he have any interest? Could he see her as a politely unhappy, cleaned-up, sunny-faced drunk he could maybe shrug some of his life off on sometime later in the week?

Again, no return address. No way to write back.

The postmark named a dump of a place a few locales beyond. There were reasonably distracting things on TV, if you gave them a chance, one show devoted entirely a countinghouse about to come down, and he one day stopped at a bakery he had always made it a point of shutting his eyes to. The things they sold as croissants lost their curves once you got them home. At home they looked like pieces of sheet cake.

The third letter, a week to the day later, was all of six pages about some man she had let live with her for a little over a month. The two of them had each wanted the other to be the mightier of the two, to be just the one to see better days, then report back. Then one night, something came over her. She told him, "Don't stop being a valentine on my account, if you think that's what you are." She set him up with a brother she said she'd neglected to mention. The brother lived in a better part of town. Her man went off to live with the brother in a rented place that had a lone turret in which her man sometimes hid himself for no reason and to no effect, because it must have felt good to keep getting roughed up so regularly for once. She sometimes came over so the three of them could sit and all hold hands, with her in the middle. "See?" she'd say. But this brother of hers had a number of court dates and soon had to report to jail every third weekend. She would see him off each time. It was all well and good to have remembered his kisses, because they had been austere to a fault, and arousingly acidulent, but hindsight after so many years was no good through eyes ruined so excitedly on men of that laxening kind. Her brother would come home Sunday nights and scold her man for not having done enough around the house, for not having cooked something sufficiently exquisite. Her brother's thing must have always been awfully red and sore after just those two nights away. Her brother gave her man the preliminary okay to go back to her, but she had already found somebody else and was enchanting this new one in that brute, rote way of hers. But he turned out to be a valentine too. Every one of them did.

So what did he, the recipient of these missives, at long last think? The one good look he'd gotten of her after his wife's funeral—was it enough? He was patient. He waited for another letter. None came. There was a bus that ran every other hour to the postmarked township. He one day took the bus, got off, walked around. There was little to see or do—houses barely presentable and windowed ungivingly, a few large apartment buildings whose stairwells he scaled, then climbed down, then scaled again as if in exercise (nobody was around). He presented himself at a restaurant. The waitress wasn't her, and from what he could make out, the cook most likely wasn't either. He ordered what the menu termed a "two-ply beefburger sandwich," but on the plate set before him was a gravied consequence of veal. "You're not still working on that?" the waitress returned to say. "You've got no further labors ahead?" He walked around a department store that was mostly just one huge room, with ramshackle scaffolding overhead. Nobody there was her. The department store had a candy counter. He bought a minority of loosened chocolate to contend with while waiting for the bus. The chocolate tasted dry, off.

The bus driver took his fare and laughed in his face. "Nobody finds her," the bus driver said. The chuckle sounded practiced and apropos.

"All right," the man thought. "I am sloppy and old." Sundown was on schedule. On some days you felt the loss of human nature within yourself more than on others. From the bus stop he walked back to his apartment. There was only the one exercise he knew how to do. He had once tried to explain it. "That might not technically be considered an exercise," he'd been told, but he did them on a mat by the unimproving hundred. That night he made a tally. Sixteen hundred at one go!

He started loitering his nights away in the shallows of the slipcovers. He had a dream in which he was berated for having brought home the wrong kind of bread for that corner of the world. The berating voice was hard for him to place. His unsickenable mother with the beginnings, finally, of a cold? His late wife?

In another dream, he was once again at the counter of the only fast-food place left in town. (In waking hours, he had long since begun making a second home for himself there.) In the dream, the counterperson assembling his order propped the packet of fries against the wrapped sandwich. That way, none of the fries would have to touch the paper place mat on the tray. Things could be eaten cleanly.

In a follow-up dream, the counterperson, now a lowvoiced woman with a dampening role in life, explained that it wasn't technically called a place mat—the name for it was *tray liner*.

That dream had a sequel, too. The counterpersons this time were mostly men, grown and curtailed and uncaringly attentive. His "for here" food was handed to him with madcap displeasure in a paper bag stapled shut. He woke up braving his own affections with a hand squeezing his upper leg.

The months came and kept coming. He didn't know anybody anymore. Those he didn't know he read about in the paper as they went about overturning their marriages or dying out of spite.

The man turned up his nose at all locally available venereal fare. Then one month he let himself be put through some duping, computerly long-distance amours with women from the big, smirching cities of the North. One of them had jerked herself free from some dulling family saga, though she still kept tabs on a brother. There was a rubicund delicacy to her adult acne. It looked embossed on her professionally. She wore shorts in all weathers as a way of settling some score or another. The other woman was finessive about her milky good looks. She liked to get the conversational ball rolling by whispering, "Funny how things happen." She cinched all of her eye-opener dresses with the same flimsy cloth belt. Her breasts looked packed onto her. Neither of these women knew about the other. For a while, he felt a muddle of something uncustomary in his groin and gut. He took buses to visit these two in their hampering, loose-carpeted apartments. He held their hands in a clowning way that came as no surprise. Their pasts lacked any chronology he could master. A tasting-menu meal here, a riverward stroll there among other suppositious couples tugged toward each other in one emotional fracas or another over somebody else—he figured that this much would be highlight enough. Enough of these trips, though, and these two turned out to be plain-hearted and barely germane to him anyway. And were they really rescuers?, he wondered. They might as well move even further hindward to their own kind.

Then on a day already frail and failing, a woman approached him on the sidewalk. She had a man's billfold out. She nodded toward a car in which a younger woman sat in darlingly timid, sleeveless unease, looking as if any earlier life of hers had been sheared away. What might engorge?, the woman wanted to know. The billfold had been shaken open to reveal the greenery of hundreds upon hundreds. He kept walking.

After long absence, he was finally welcomed back at the school where he had long ago taught vo-tech communications at half price on nights and weekends. It was a community college aggrandized with dorms. Each building had its own smokestack. The young removed themselves from local households and learned to love the clop-clop of books as they were dropped, one after another, onto the tiled floor.

It was to be understood that he was no good at instruction but at least was better than any of the applicants who had made it in for interviews. It was to be understood that he would be considered staff, not faculty. Over the phone, a voice he did not recognize said: "You're sure to understand that we can't pay you a salary or by the hour, but we'll see that you get some money at the end of the month, though it'll vary. Whether you want to take anything from students is up to you. We'll be looking the other way. We figure you've got some inheritance, but still. If these terms are agreeable, say as much after I turn on the machine. Hold on just a sec. Okay, now."

He said yes.

At the end of the first month he was handed an envelope sagging with coins, but inside he also found a batching of dollar bills, and a couple of fives, and a suspiciously crisp fifty he figured he dare not use. Sheets of fast-food coupons had been folded with consummate unconcern.

One afternoon a prickly kid who had stopped coming to class came to his office with a hundred-dollar bill and said, "My pop says to give you this."

He reached for it.

Another afternoon a girl in unworldly getup came by, mostly to vent her youth. But she had a paper bag in hand. "Here," she said, before leaving. "Sometimes my mom bakes."

He took the bag home, unopened. Curiosity got the better of him by week's end. These were cookies of an unmitigated rustic spice, stale but divertingly chewy all the same. Within the hour, his bowels unlocked.

The classroom lacked a door he could shut. He put the kids through keyword-recognition drills, taught them how to see to it that a paragraph got a topic squared away. One day, in the standing water of their early thirties, the students would look back and remember that his lectures had meant, if not the world to them, then at least a thankfully forgotten part of the world. He liked how they felt so tenderly about themselves even now. Some of them had been taught all along to "get something out of" whatever they read, so they came at books in a spirit of ransackery, entered them pryingly. Others were mostly free-mouthed girls who rarely sat up. They wore floor-scraping, drabbled skirts that kept even their shoes a secret. The one with the dumpy arms was morbidly lively while she slept through class. The workbook required for the course was mostly blank space. Quizzes were taken on little sheets torn from a rainbowed scribble pad and were over before you knew it, but for the exams he passed out rag-content paper of regular size, and there was time for each student to commit to the page an odor of her own and get it fussed into the fibers of each sheet as the base of the palm got dragged along behind the cramping fingers that conducted the pen. When the papers were turned in, he could count on finding a warpage to many of them, as if water had somehow come into the picture and then been mysteriously drawn off.

His office was a by-room, a sideroom, and his desk was more like a dresser. The top drawer held soaps and slop cloths. Sometimes there would be a knock at the door. "I'm guessing these must be yours for Saturday?" a voice would say. A popular secretary would then hand over a carrying case full of the eyebrow pencils, the slant-tipped and arched-claw tweezers, the acutely styled vials of nail polish, the cemeterily vaselike bottles of nail-polish annihilator. These he would set aside for possible resale during tutorials.

It was mostly students who dropped by, students in curricular dishevelment. He would manage to get a book into their hands, get them to sit busily with the book, to give it some play, play their hands over it, achieve a mastery at least of its dimensions and heft.

One kid had learned to run his eyes over a page until he found a word he liked and might want to take home. Another could take up a pencil and draw a line down through the spaces between words and make a maze of the page.

Once in a while he would get a student on the lookout for herself in anyone she met. There were never enough of these. They usually wore balefully detailed shoes and barely sipped the soda they were always lugging around. They often had a flutter in one knee, the pitter of a pulse nearly visible in a wrist. One of her kind once wanted advice. This one had a blond floss on her arms. She talked about her "sitch" and her "cirk." Her cirk was her circumstance—her trouble with keeping up with the encouragings of the other girl's parents whenever she was allowed over, and then with never knowing for sure how much of a holdall the other girl's heart actually was. Her sitch was her situation, the limelight she was in with the two males always after her. She took out a catalogical notebook and showed me the sketches. There was a plussage of stark hair on their faces that was never quite a beard.

She was bold enough to show him one after another zone of her upper arm where their hands had kept landing.

She brushed her fingers along the shoulder of his sweater.

"Tell me something I can take to the grave," she said.

He had sat through this sort of puckery before. He would've known this shade of lip gloss anywhere. (Storm-washed ash-gray it almost always was.)

What was he to have told her anyway? That a lie was just the truth with the facts staggered just a bit differently in it?

He was pushing the furniture around in his office one day, trying out different perspectives and sightlines, when he discovered, behind where the tall bookcase had stood, a hole that had been drilled into the wall. It gave out onto the office next door. He got down on the floor and could see clear into the other office. There weren't any lights on, just light from a window. He couldn't make out any human presence. He got up, went to his dresser, pulled out the businesslike, middle drawer. A pencil looked inessential in there (the point seemed weak), so he took it out and returned to the floor, fillipped the pencil through the hole. He could see where it landed on the carpet over there. He pictured the cleaning lady eventually stooping for it gamely, blood-boilingly, like every damn time before. He pushed the bookcase back into place. He had a class to get to. He was late by seconds at most. He broke the ice for the first five minutes or so, then asked a girl something simple about the reading assignment. She answered pianissimo.

That evening, though, it was just like him to have forgotten that all these years he had all along had that other sister, the one who kept seeing floaters in front of everything she saw. He called her and was told he was more than welcome to come live in the little stone-floored outbuilding at the edge of her property however he saw fit. She described the grassy extremes of alleyway he would probably enjoy noticing from the room-length span of window. She said people hadn't stopped tramping up and down that alley night and day as big as they pleased with no regard for its being private property. They treated it as just another place to dump just about anything they no longer had any use for—tube tops, those U-shaped neck pillows more and more used on abortion runs, club chairs, bolts and bolts of sea-blue gauze, a barrel-shaped table lamp with something almost overweening about the triple stitching on the lower rim of the shade, intrauterine contraptions, the kinds of thick-fleeced socks that in those days customarily doubled as mittens, pouched-out backpacks barely worth the bother of going through anymore—but never the one thing she could have actually used, cardboard boxes, the crisp and spruce and clean-edged kinds of cartons she collected by the roomful upstairs, though the things they could have come in handy for were now never going to happen. She had always had specks all over her face, but now she had something even more posh that was wrong with her.

He hung up, packed.

It was mostly patio furniture and yard pieces when he moved into the place out back. The little there was of upholstered stuff—that sofa, for one thing—was steeped in the sharp smells of somebody else, certainly not that spoilsport sickling of a sister. This was the smell of somebody who had circulated her furors farther and wider. He pictured her as somebody generally on the mark when she shot language back at people. She had probably been taking up criticisms of her pronunciations one by one for years. If by this point in your life you hadn't been put wise to the fact that the *i* in *short-lived* was to be as long, and as long-sought, as all get-out, you might as well have been dead all this while yourself.

For the hindmost of his days, there was just that one low-hanging towel—the lower left side of it for the face, the lower right for the hands.

# PRESSED POWDER

SHE HAD ADVANCED disposedly toward me in so many passageways at the community college that at some point I must have stopped waving her off. Like me, she had a futile disposition, or so she claimed, and she felt astray in herself, and had gone back to school, like me, to study office machines, office furniture, retail shelving. We were in some of the same classes. She was a participator. I liked the way her flesh fit her. She usually wore the same thing—a buttony shift-dress of cucumbrous green. You could tell she conducted her life with a certain venerealian pomp. You'd take her for the type who could show several true natures, someone who would ditch herself in others for a month here, a holiday there—someone who collected herself as she went along.

She caught up with me one day on the way to class, hung one of her arms over my shoulder, and said, "So what else is there in this world of yours?"

There was a test that day. Only one of the profs ever gave essay exams, and this guy was the one. She was good at being evaluated, though all I'd ever managed was to arrange what had been taught into a fresh, glaring ignorance. But this time I found myself writing down everything I could remember about suit forms and droplights, risers and waterfall racks, island displays, complexion bulbs, demonstration cubes. I suddenly had a smug run of the subject.

At the campus coffee shack, she liked to talk about her two brothers, so we went there after the exam, and she talked. One of the brothers was a "boulevardier" benched these days in vestibules, lobbies, waiting rooms. He was against people using the word *I* when there was nothing behind it, nothing to back it up. The other was a pipefitter who ailed alcoholically and was known mostly for his panoramic absenteeism from work. Pricks were the easiest thing for him to get his hands on.

"Am I keeping you from anything?" she grew fond of saying. "Have you got anything anywhere?"

It's all well and good for me to overlook how hidden I was even from myself in those days. This business of changing my address every other month, of making certain I was unheard of differently—I was, to be honest, a little tired of always feeling as if there were still hours and hours until whatever time it already was.

So, yes: I started sending her little tributes, honorings, keepsakes cheeky and affordable, through the mail, in care of the college.

I treated myself to feeling something for her. I toiled away little by little at how little I still felt.

You could always count on people wanting a bite to eat, but she must have still been in an "I'm different" stage, dramatically needing nothing. I sometimes drove us to a hamburger sanctum down the interstate. Like all women of such time and place, she kept running to the restroom, though she called it a bathroom and always came back to the table with her hair looking wet. She always spiced up her returns with a confession. Did I know she had a kid? The kid was too small to be much of anything yet, though, so there wasn't much more for her to tell me, other than that the kid had its grandfather's tattered hair. I pictured a lightly saddenable, girlier version of her.

In class one day, the Photocopying Sciences prof was looking right at me when he said the part about "no roving eyes," then handed out the midterms. I was sitting next to her for a change, but only to throw her off a little. I hadn't studied. I didn't even read the questions. I doubt I even turned a page. I just signed my name on the answer sheet and distributed my #2-lead ovals in what I hoped would spell out something suitably, aptly terminal and crowning. But how much can you say with just A, B, C, D, and E? A BAD CAB BADE ABE and A CAD BEDDED DEAD DAD and BAD DEED were the most I could come up with. I repeated these a few times down the sheet, then reblackened all of it before turning everything in. The prof said, "Thank you," and I went outside to wait.

She had taken her time, and when she came out, she took my arm and led me to her car—a first. "I'm taking you home," she said. She drove us toward her part of town, pointing out features of buildings along the way, factories that now housed apartments for people to further themselves maritally or not. She pulled up in front of a notary public's office. "I've got the upstairs," she said.

Up there, in her place, was a man, a robed and orthopedically shod, concerned-looking person, in maybe his bottommost thirties, who looked a little like an unfiltered version of her. He said, "I called Mom—no, wait, she might've called me," but there wasn't any kid I could see.

The two of them offered me breakoffs of bulky candy they said came in crates all the way from the old country, showed me unkempt kindnesses of every sort, beat around every sort of bush, then walked me through what they miserably and lengthily professed was the notion of the truly biological spouse. It was like a team-taught lecture.

Then they wanted to know if I'd stay for a movie on TV. I did, but only out of courtesy, I'm still guessing, and afterward I could see that there was no place left on them to put what they felt onto each other, so they put it all on me.

# YOU TOO

"YOU TWO" WAS how we were known, to the extent that we were known. As in: "How many nights will you two be staying?"

Will people sit through a list of the state parks themselves? Can the names of the campgrounds count just this once as common knowledge?

I remember maybe five or six.

Boulder Run. Hickory Hollow. Beech Falls. Stony Lake.

French Crossing. Holly Creek.

Cedar Trails.

Hope Furnace.

In the mornings, when I was told to wash my face in the basin set up for my benefit outside the tent, what I did was dip my index fingers into the cold water and then rub them gently against the corners of my eyes. That was as much as I did. I touched my face as if it belonged to somebody else.

Afterward, I had it in me to sit on a folding chair that I set out at the side of the road that the other campers took to get to the lake. I put a ruckus on my face that I thought would faze whoever walked past.

He went into me every night as far as he could go. Everything within had to get packed tighter and tighter together to make room for what he had to do. I tried to picture the bloodied lining of my life inside, the stringy stickiness of it. I worried about what might fall out. I worried about how I would ever get all of it wadded back in. How would I even know where things were supposed to go?

I know I got skinnier.

It was sinking in that I was not out of school the way other people were out of bread or kerosene.

Here is how to this day I still picture a person who is beside himself:

Sooner or later the other side of you comes into view.

You see it out of the corner of your eye.

How close does it come?

Does it bump right into you?

Does it take your part?

# I'M NOT FAMILY

MY SISTER MARRIED a man who had once dropped some ice, tiny brilliancies of it, into the shallows of a drink she was holding out for somebody else. (That person was awfully big about it and backed off.) I didn't show up for the wedding. This husband was the manager of the service department at a car dealership. After a car had been put up on the lift, he would step out of his office, enter the waiting area, approach the owner of the car, and tell him, "I'm not saying it can't be driven, it's not something you have to drop everything right this very minute to get rid of, but it's not getting any younger, the engine is throwing itself open to all manner of trouble, just about everything's shot, you might want to hold on to it for parts, but, look, you're not going to make me lose sleep worrying about you racketing around town in it (are you?), we've got plenty new models out there on the lot," and then the owner of the car would either cut him off and demand to talk to the mechanic face to face or else be on the verge of tears and just ask meekly for the keys. I'd already become a regular in that waiting room—it was more like a lounge, to tell you the truth, and was a good place to rest your eyes, with free coffee you could help yourself to and a fraternity of vending machines—and for hours some afternoons, I would not so much keep to my chair as grip the arms of it and rutch my rear end up from the well of the seat and clear myself of it almost entirely, exercisingly. Whenever I'd get up to go, my sister's husband would come out from his office and say, "What's your rush?" If I was insistent about leaving, he'd say, "Well, then, why not do something about yourself on the way home?"

I might have been thirty-four, thirty-five. There was never the right amount of me left over after a night of sleep.

It was typical of a day like that to be seamed with mealtimes, but I might have just been hungry anyway. This time, I ducked first into a corner store, a ma-and-daughter. The girl at the register had coffee-mottled teeth.

I loved the fuss of the bubbles in the bottle of Coke I'd started to shake, then the chordal shower of a kid playing electric guitar outside. A lot of his inner life had been set out to be registered. I like it when people look so *unneeded.* I went to the place where the waitresses always competed with each other not to have to wait on me. Each was a uniquely slaughtered dream of somebody just a little bit better. The one who took my order that day was new to me—just a scheme of bones.

I had the candied chicken with some stuffing far enough off to the side.

Two men were talking at a neighboring table. The hair on the first one's arms looked like feelers, practically.

The other one was saying that when both partners cheat, there's a kind of cross-ventilation going on that can sometimes do a marriage some good.

"Your wife," the first one said. He weighted the words just so, until it seemed that nothing could hold up much longer under that kind of pronouncing. I could almost make out the beat of the grievance that made him tick. He was a man of overcopious eyebrows over the simplest of eyes, watering just a little just now.

Whenever talk turned to marriage, as it often did, you had to wonder which end of an overreaching penis might be the one that could point toward anything worth keeping.

My sister's first marriage had been to a man whose dreams never once left town. Like all husbands, he kept getting bigger and bigger. He'd said as much about me.

I ate, to be sure, as if the fork were just a sorrowmate of the knife.

I asked for my check, paid the girl at the counter. The chicken-pox scars on her forehead formed a tidy little triangle she'd swiped over with concealer.

Outside, the world might have been many different things to different people, but one thing it wasn't was a place where there's something you don't see every day. There was a doctor whose office you could just walk right in. He was against appointments, paperwork, patient histories. I didn't even have to wait. He was a bearded-over general practitioner who cut me off in mid-complaint, said, "Blood sugar," and jittered out a prescription on a piece of paper that I carried out to the street, where somebody said, "Quick, give me that, I gotta write something down." He snatched it. He had a pen out and was already using his palm as a desktop. He wrote, "15, 04, 12, 23, 09," then said, "Play these tonight, and you'll have someone to thank tomorrow."

Have I as much as said that this town, the low-pitched clapboardy entirety of it (pop. 13,386; elev. 1,017 ft.), could likely be chopped down in a matter of hours?

There was a line at the pharmacy. Men, mattering women—I fell right in. Something kept coming up, true, but I was thinking not about the thing but around it, putting a hollow where it really was, putting it at the center of something I could keep backing away from. What had my mother said? I'd been young. She'd one day told me never to let anyone stick anything up my fanny. Or she might have said heinie. But it put an early wrong idea in me—that I had plenty of storage space inside. It was another ailing way of having to see what lay ahead.

When it was my turn, the pharmacy clerk was graceful about wanting my name, my date of birth, my benefits statistica. Everything came out of me as the sob story it was.

I chewed the first of the ellipsoidal pills on my way out. I've always preferred a full mouth.

Plus, I'd grown up thinking that all I had to do was put on a pair of glasses to get my eyes hidden well enough.

Then back to the house. The room looked as if somebody had spent an hour, maybe a good hour and a half, on the bed all the time I'd been out, and then, with signs of a great struggle, made sure to leave everything exactly as it had been found.

My sister: all she lacked was whatever it took to keep me from insisting on the significance of the mattress's being raised, platformed, *staged* above the floor.

When you stir up a marriage, though, what rises first to the top?

Me in my sister's husband's bed again? Even if it was only a hand of mine she'd laid on one of her husband's when it was holding its own on that thing of his that barely even quivered?

I wish this were all there was to it. I moved to another end of the earth. I'd call my sister on Sunday nights to rub it in that there were still hours and hours of daylight left at my end of the line. I later lost touch with her altogether.

This was a town with a sheeny river, and towers unfit for a sky practically periwinkle by midmorning, and a woman about my age whose teeth had already lost their looks.

One thing I'd always felt safe to say to anyone on a street of just that sort was "I wouldn't if I were you" or "You must've been at it longer than me," but this woman just wanted to take me home to her daughters.

I tagged along. She struck me as a capably dangerous woman of pains by turns blunted and honed. There turned out to be just two girls at home.

These two were debasing, telltale, mutinous multiplications of their mother, but they will have to count, for now, as just one, the more slivery-armed and ensnaring of the two, the one already risen well out of her teens—a namesaken, unsunned thing in shorty pajamas.

She unclamped one of the snappish binder clips from her hair, and the mouth set going in the face was doing nothing more than asking her mother what might be expected for supper if her sister wouldn't be coming back for the night.

The mother said, "The two of you'll have to have the balance of that stew."

Then the mother, my host, left me with this daughter, disappeared into what I guessed was her bedroom, came out of it with some awfully twinned, awfully thickset luggage, showed me where the kitchen was, kissed her daughter on the brow, said, "Can't a mother do things for her girl?," then left. I heard a car starting.

The rubber bands braceleted on the girl's wrist were glazed-looking things, gone rotten and inelastic. She snapped them off one by one.

If it helps, she said, "You going to live here, or commute?"

I said I was staying at the hotel.

"Live here," she said. "Save yourself the back-and-forth."

She walked me to the hotel, and I checked out. There wasn't all that much to carry. Most of my clothes were stacked in a rucksack. She played a hand into the pocket of my parka, came away with a dilapidated cigarette, brought it up to her lips, tossed it. We stopped at a restaurant for the soup-and-salad special. I like it when people come right out and say, "Does this bread look all right to you?," but she buttered hers without even seeming to think about it. The salads were awfully mussed, even haggard, but the soup had ample assets of carrot and pork. Nothing tasted the way she thought it ought to taste, though. I said, "Because of all that lipstick?" She said, "I can't believe they're letting us eat here! My mother knows the owner."

Back at the house, I settled in, adapted. Stones had been arranged in the bowl of the toilet, so you had to find somewhere else to go. The girl ate out of paper bags and relieved herself in wastebaskets. There was hardly a day that her mother was gone that her arms didn't go out from her sides toward whatever was taking up the world. Some kid—some Jeffo or a Jasp, I now forget— sometimes came over to play games with her on a weakening TV. Together, the two of them would carry things to new places. The boys eventually knew enough to get up and leave. The girl would be looming soon again against me.

The two of us mostly just sat out in the kitchen. I had to be afraid she'd drift too far away from herself anytime another breeze arrived.

It was obvious she was living in a body already getting a jump on how it would look a decade later, and yet you right away wanted to ask what she was already doing so far from her past—you could see that she knew what it took to keep herself looking looked-after. Any father she remembered was a man whose fingers were creviced with paper cuts, somebody who read books, booklets, circulars, the paper, not for any news but to put things, anything, in place of what he already hardly knew anyway. And such a strange lacunary outspelling of his name on the signature line of the checks he'd stopped sending her on the sly and which she'd never cashed anyway because the tellers had such loppy arms and looked so gratingly indistinctive!

She claimed to have trouble with putting on blouses—telling the difference between the inside of them and the outside, then knowing what went through what, which buttons were the ones that would ultimately count. The one she was wearing was more of a shift, over bottoms that were drawstringed and a little loose. (Everything the green of surgical scrubs.)

Her dresses, jumpers, hung from the ceiling on hooks intended for hanging plants.

She wore her hair as if it were a notable stronghold no matter what.

Outside of being a girl, she claimed to be taking shop classes, and said it was always better to keep getting held back in school, because that way you got to know your teachers over the long haul. But the way she talked, she could cover any subject, concealing it completely. Other times, she kept her vocabulary curbed.

I asked her why she wasn't in school that day.

I've never minded big, fat lies, but hers came out in what I still recall as only a sachet of modest and plausible untruth.

The house was fastened nicely enough to the neighborhood.

But I wasn't too sure of my room. (It had pillows and plenty of bedding but no bed to host them.) In my booksick days, I'd once read one of the better single-volume encyclopedias that treated the subject of roomage, of roomery through the ages. (It had been given as an unwrapped gift.) The book went into everything—even why it always came to be that once a building got razed, the rooms were in fact never part of the debris; they kept to their space, entirely intact, no matter what else might go up later on the site, and this explained why people in the new buildings often said, "Gosh, I never thought I'd be able to spread out like this in here!" or "Don't these windows even open?"

For the first few weeks, the mother popped in for an hour or two every couple of days. Everything she wore looked pricily asymmetrical. She might have had just about anything broiling inside her. She'd spend a little time with the daughter. I'd look for any signs of interpersonality between the two of them. They were each sick of this hemisphere, true, and they each had hair the color of butcher paper, and breasts that looked underprompted by those bras, and each, I imagined, had a heartache not yet put to enough ungoodening use. They didn't so much finish each other's sentences as keep putting an end to them.

The mother would ask me barely anything other than "Finding things okay?" or "Need the name of a good all-around guy?"

Then the mother would get up to leave. Her daughter would kiss her pretty menially.

Truth to tell, watching the two of them saying their comfortless good-byes like that, I often found myself reaching for beer pretzels out of a dented tin and feeling not all that much of a departure from what I'd always usually felt—i.e., there are loosements in the world that needn't concern us every minute of a day. But would my eyes one day be veterans of the way the girl's arms trailed off into the rest of her when it's usually the other way around on people?

I sometimes got up and made my way to the girl's room, making it look as if I had found her by chance. Her room was heaped, huttish, unventilated. Once or twice, she would be on the floor, signing greeting cards spread around her in a semicircle. There must have been dozens. The front panels of the ones I could see always read, "From the two of us," "From both of us," "From all of us," "From ours to yours," etc.

"I mind being witnessed," she said.

She had been brought up behind drapes, mind you. The way she talked about her life, the way occasions had swung toward her and then away, made the world outside sound even farther off than it probably was. It was in a wet, capsulizing voice that she spoke only of something that had been worked loose from the underside of a trickishly valved band instrument she had been made to play in school. It had to be lathed and then machined even further until it fit her. I wish I could have taken what she said and made it go elseward.

Those first weeks or so, though, went by surprisingly fast. From the living-room window, the girl and I would watch people getting into cars or coming unbelovedly out of the locale, then ducking back in. We gave each other lulling household names. I liked how words crispened in her mouth and were followed by ambitious, draining swallows that might as well have taken everything she said right back down again. Talking like that, she sometimes couldn't help getting things caked with more description than they could bear—e.g., that business about her stepbrother, with scarcely a "stitch" of hair on his head, who was spoiling in some "system" in a lakeless limited inland urbanation that had gone up "hollowly," a city now boasting an opulently domed train station, okay, but the train was run for amusement only and would never be any good for definite departure. A second set of adult teeth had sprung through his gums, knocking out every one of the first, but he never cut her in on any of his injuries. All of this should have had cause to be untrue but more and more struck me as stinkingly indisputable.

Every day, after a late, uncontenting lunch, she would pack herself into the cramping bathtub to souse, with the drain, the catch, open only just a hair, the water going slowly about its desertions. She'd want me out in the hallway to have things explained to, and sometimes to explain. (Beds roam only pokily, but go they do, what with those casters they're set up on nowadays; at work, her father had been reassigned from "projects" to "tasks," though it wasn't a demotion, the supervisor had assured him in her lilts, but then one day he fell down on the job, or it gave way underneath, was pulled out from under him, and they'd had to hire a woman to make plainer and plainer to irate callers that he was still too very far away from his desk to ever call back by day's end; besides, what's a wallet to man anyway, other than something to give some rumped warmth and adhesiveness to things you'll later have to pull apart?; and you could whimper all you wanted about a boyfriend who finally turned his dick on himself or about a wife who spoke too deeply within a marriage for even you to hear, but anything else was little more than mere behavior.)

Listen long enough to other people and all you'll hear is the story you've only just now stopped telling yourself.

On shopping days, she took her jumpy place among the outnumbering in the one jumble shop that would let her in. The one time I went along, she paid with rolled pennies, a single bill held together with sallowed tape. It was a store where the people who were buying weren't called "customers" or "guests" or "clients"—I forget what they were said to be instead. What she was buying was mostly just longer and longer spans of the sprawling carmine licorice she could never get her fill of. She said, "They should carry the kind of tablet that has stuff already written on it, thoughts and whatnot, to spare people." Along all the walls, the greeting cards were arranged by category: "Relationships by Blood"; "Recipients of Dismemberment-Insurance Payouts"; "Must I Have a Reason?"; "Imminent Deaths of Secret Admirers"; "Playing Along as Long as It Takes"; "Moving *Again?*"; "Life Is Death's Stopgap, Darling"; "Turning a Blind Eye to You Just This Once More"; "Every Hour Seems to Have Ramparts Around It Now, My Dearest One. I Can No Longer Fight My Way Out."

She now and then left the house on her own to sit at a diner and drink time-killer sodas. She paged through the free apartment-listing weeklies, the monthlies for seniors which got printed in giganticized type. But she wasn't much of a reader. A book was just page after page of redistributions of the language. ("You run across so many of the same words from chapter to chapter!") On the homeward stroll was a church with a marquee that on Wednesdays vouchsafed something lighthearted ("'susej' is 'jesus' spelt backwards by somebody too dumb to spell 'sausage.' Just kidding! Join us for a sausage supper this Saturday! $9.55 adults; $4.50 children under 9. 5:00-???") but on Thursdays went back to scraps of scripture. The minister often sat on the steps and more than once tried to take her under his wing. He tried it with comically broidered kerchiefs, wafers beset with chocolate, mock massages. He'd once put a Bible into her hands, but all she could do was picture her hands atop all the hands that had already held it.

There was a tiny throb in her thigh muscle whenever she brought up any affections still rotting for her father.

Food was brittle and scrimpy unless I took her place at the stove. She wanted my fingers first on everything that was hers. (Sandwiches cut on the bias, broccoli chopped to chafe the gullet on the way down, blonded brownies rigged unconvivially with nuts still shelled.)

That plenum of pores on her cheeks, the lengths of lamp chain strung around her wrist, the dry-boned severity of her knees, the way the spiraling umber-brown hair on her shins didn't look so much as if it were issuing from within but as if it were suspended, even levitated, half an inch above the skin, the tang of how she must have smelled here and there as the day wore itself out on her: I had to remind myself that her body was never quick to sensationalize itself, she held to the household commandments ("6: You can never be too bonny for a best friend, but you daresn't have more than one"), she didn't drive ("They'd always be running my plate"), and she'd now and then think to ask, "What else can you tell me of everything?" Either that or she'd want to know what I'd be like as an enemy.

Some days, she had a kind of self-chaperoning air about her. Nothing she felt for me was ever more than "emotiony."

Other days, she'd say: "I feel I can tell you anything. Can I?"

"Even if I loved you, I'd be lonesome," she'd say.

She'd say, "My mouth is your mouth?"

To feel the day having tacked minute by minute toward this!

We'd swap misgivings, finish more schnapps.

One day she seemed to be doting on one thing, but her mind was already on something else. She told me that she had a considerably older sister who year after year kept giving birth to the same child. The newborns always came out with their fingers clubbed together, and they made their way into life with neither publicity nor flamboyance. The staff at the hospital was getting fed up with this mother and her "miracles." The doctors had their own little toaster oven in the lounge, and the nurses respected the fact that it would one day never be theirs. The only orderly who was a woman was kept around mostly because she shed light. The light came off her not in a fixed, steady beam but in sloppy gushes she had no real control over. It spattered all over the place. Off the lobby was a display case housing jars of nursily preserved gherkins of stool, all said to be the posterity of the founding surgeon. The administrators didn't want word to get out that the place was on the verge of becoming a museum. At closing time, the doctors went home to spouses to go over the day, overspread it, get it coated over. The nurses were delicately wrathful midlifers who arm-wrestled each other in darkening apartments.

"Tell me about this niece," I said.

"Nieces," she said. "I can tell them all apart."

Then: "Makes no matter to me. Long as I'm not the one mothering or the one getting mothered."

One day, the girl said, "I should probably go back to school tomorrow. They've probably been wondering. It's probably time. I definitely should go."

The next day came and went. She hadn't stirred from the chair where she'd slept.

"The world's not exactly lacking for me," she said.

The daybed held throws instead of sheets. There would always be that skeptical tilt to her lips, that obscured maturity in eyes unwarming.

One night she wanted to know something about me. I coughed out an account of myself. I tried to make a case for having once wanted a full and tiring life. I described a bounteous enough marriage to a wife summarily venerated, a wife who sipped at life through last straws—a cumbersome, beseeching roughneck with a typewriter going day and night. I counted on the shatter of all that letterage striking the page to cover up whatever noise I might have barely kept making with anybody else in what had to pass for the utility room in that cottagey lodging where we were easy enough to buy for but had no flair for having already done just enough with adulthood.

The girl said, "I've got a wristwatch that blips on the hour. Let me go get it."

She brought it back, set it out on a hassock. We waited for the start of a new hour and harked.

She said, "The polite thing is to find whatever's really yours, then keep your eyes way the hell away from it?"

In due time, though, there was one day a knock at the door. "I don't answer when this happens," the girl said. She was quick to disappear.

I opened the door. A woman was standing outside in a navy blazer. Pinned to it was a badge from the school district. On the paperwork she showed me, the penmanship was round-shouldered and wearying. This was a large-grown woman looking plenty of girlhoods old. Her cheeks had been scuffed with blush, and she was keeping her voice low. I had to help her off with her coat. I swore I could smell other personnel on her. I might as well have been preparing for this all of my life. I might as well have been all along brought up to this height for nothing else but.

She said, "It would help an awful lot if I could just see her bed."

I said, "I don't believe she ever makes it."

She said, "Doesn't matter."

I led her into the girl's room.

I'd never seen a bed suffer such toilsome scrutiny. She bent over it, got down on her knees, sank her chin into a corner of the mattress, inhaled clinically. Her eyes were shut, their lids not aflutter.

She tugged at a sheet. "These are bleached?"

I said, "I think they go to a dry cleaner."

She sank her chin practicedly into a pillow. Her eyes closed for further finical inhalations.

"Think she would notice if any of these went missing?" she said. "I think I'll just go ahead and help myself."

She got up, tucked a pillow under her arm. She was writing things down, and I stared at the bed, into it, at how the sheets looked as if they'd been caught mid-ripple from one end to the other. It looked as if whitecaps were forming here and there toward the corners.

The visitor backed away even further from the bed. She said, "You know what I think? This is strictly between you and me, but I think the joke is on the kids in some really close family, a really tight-knit one. Because what can they do but get even closer and then grow up and have to marry outside of it anyway?"

Then: "I don't mean to be throwing cold water on anything you've got going here, the bed is certainly all right, it's okay, but there's usually a talent—there's usually a parent or a live-in aunt saying, 'I don't know where she gets it from.' But with this one, I just don't see anything coming to the fore. I'm just not seeing you or anyone else getting much more out of her. Maybe she's just a brat. Lots of them are. Life'll be shredding her up soon enough anyway."

Then: "Oh, I need to ask—does this one ever wear glasses?"

I rummaged around in the drawer of the night table. I found the glasses, handed them to her. The plastic of the sidepieces had gone a little pale and cloudy from the potent oils of the girl's hair.

I watched the visitor go after the inner surface of the nose pad and with her finger sweep away a little indecently oleic deposit, almost a paste, that had collected during who knows how many sweatings over a greeting-card message panel or another menu for ordering in.

"See, this is what I mean," she said. "This is nothing but smush. It's not even steeped in anything. There's no point in even having this sent out to the lab. I hate to always be leveling with people, but if I was you, I'd do something soon. Can't you just shoo her out? Have the locks changed—that'd be one route to take."

I saw her to the door.

The girl nimbled out from her hiding post. "I've disappointed?" she said. Before I could even answer, she started in about how, come morning, if the sleep had been just so, she could sieve the utterest of things out of what was left of her dreams, even the ones that were just arabesques or affronts. It was almost never anything bigger than a trinket (souvenirs, she called them), something still lapidating and taking on color as it met the air. But when I asked for samples, she said her sleep had been off the mark lately. I had to coax her and coax her to produce any proof. She went to her room, came back a quarter-hour later with a shoulder bag I hadn't seen before, and brought out from it (1) the torn half of an index card treated with some sort of buttery matter; (2) a footlong share of electrical cord, one end of it looking as if it had been misled through a pencil sharpener; and (3) a concentration of shaved hair sportily preserved in a corner torn from an envelope.

All of it looked just whimsied up for me on the sudden.

These new tears on her looked whimsied, too.

I'm to also have regarded it as a failing that the one thing she gave me in parting (it took me practically no time to pack) was a squeak toy in the shape of a rolled-up newspaper. The squeak has long since gone out of the thing, but I still sit on it sometimes in these leaf-laden outskirts where the woman with whom I'm now married prefaces every sentence with either "Please know" or "I'm to tell you" or both—e.g., "Please know that I'll never not keep putting food on the table"; "I'm to tell you that I won't breathe a word"; "Please know I'm to tell you that every moment won't always be expected to be just a redress of the moment before." We sleep at diagonals to each other, and her good looks have come out even better on this kid we now have. This kid is clear-skinned and moon-eyed, beating me already at peekaboo and night frights.

This kid will grow up to leave a heritage of assery on high chairs, campstools, love seats, rollaway beds.

This kid will soon enough lose its place on its blunt stub of a body.

The eventual chip of its shoulder will mature into a hunch, a stoopening hump, that'll draw every last hurting eye to it.

I'll be the one you'll keep counting on to stick around even longer to see that every part of life going on behind my back can cover only this much ground.

# THE WATER TABLE

THESE WERE MURDERABLY tall, dry-skinned girls with yam-colored hair. I was no different.

The beds we were led to had been run ragged. The sheets were rotten.

Everything tore.

We had to wait until we were sure that the new girls were totally asleep. I turned to my sister.

"What are we trying to pull?" I said.

We raised ourselves from the mattress, dressed, left the house. My sister found a job waiting on tables. I left her conducting shallow plates of doughballs to women she could not lock in the face.

I kept walking. In either direction there were dove-eyed women looking uprooted and pale. I went to work in one of the larger houses. The rubblework outside was decorated with wreaths, adornments, that lady travelers could not miss. The place could not have been mistaken for anyplace else. It was on Old Airport Road. The travelers would stand luggageless on the porch and wait to be discovered, not wanting to be the ones to make a move.

There was a flight of steps I always had to lead them up. I would gallant them along a hallway and around spilled hoards of coat buttons. The first thing that always came into my head and out of my mouth was that I was their sister. This put gaps and resentments in how the travelers felt about me from the start.

In the room, the narrow light from the pinlamps would silver our bare arms and legs. I would be asked, "Did you hear that?" or "Did you smell that?"

I would say, "Hear what? Smell what?"

"Good," I would be told.

I taught myself to stop cooperating with my body, to stop pretending to be its accomplice, to dumbfound it toward whatever was always dank underneath every one of these rough-toothed women in slitty flannels and wraparounds. Afterward, there was always an orderly roteness and redundance to the declarations, the promises and proposals. But I soon had money. I walked with vigorous finality down the staircase. I walked in moonlight toward the center of town. Come morning, I consoled myself with the notion that whatever light delivered to our eyes to see is not necessarily being neglected elsewhere. I went to live along a much wider road. The apartment belonged to a sleep-weighted, unchattering woman. Neighbors above and below said I was an oil-bearing likeness of daughters the woman had once paraded through the halls. I had to be taught that the long corridors of the spine did not necessarily lead out into the world.

"It's the other way around," I got used to hearing. "We're sisters first, then the other."

But everything we did looked both nervy and demeaning, like some showy feat of the disabled.

What made us sisters was that we let things be held against us, or up to us, to see what colors we had that would match or compete.

Counting myself again as a girl, there were three of us some days. Right or wrong, there was always something going up on our block.

It was later demanded that we make music of our own. It was expected to be both choirlike and catty. None of the others caught on that they were being sung about to their face. The wording of the words was to be kept secluded. I sang without ever knowing when taking a breath would do me any better.

I was stuck watching them double up, twin themselves around whomever they could reach.

I later came to a rest in a building set far back from the street. There was a stack of unbothered-with mail. The address had been crossed out and revised in hookish postmistressly backhand. There was a treeless lot out front that I was taught to say would one day get built upon. "A house will go up on the lot" is the way I was taught to put it. The house, once risen, would not exactly cancel out where we were living but at least would make it harder to be seen from the street.

Inside, the mother and her friend, a woman herself, discussed everything freely. When I could not keep my mind on their talk, I made a game of sitting in places from which the girl, my sister, had already departed, lowering myself onto whatever had kept her off the floor—hassocks and stepstools and such, but mostly shelflike projections, juttings from walls.

After that, we could barely keep our heights and weights separate and apart.

Those days, I was barely carrying my body on me, hardly wearing it at all.

I relied on handholds, footstops.

One night, our stomachs had been settled with sandwiches and some milk, and in the bathroom mirror, with light only from the hallway, I had what I thought was a lunar face, its latest lasting acne crispening under some packed-on greenish corrective sluck. The wall behind me was all warpings and corrugation.

I will have caused no ruins I later knew of.

Then school started all over again. The teacher would point to papers I turned in full of punctures where the pencil-point had assailed the page.

"Don't go handing me any more Braille," the teacher would say.

Most days there was a new word to be used in whatever we turned in. The things I wrote were not so much statements as just stickily coiling trumples of cussery.

I talked back one day when I didn't know the answer. "It doesn't matter where it comes from as long as it gets here!" I screamed.

In time, a pageful of misexplanation in one of the books had me speaking of the world as a wide, noisy flourishing of rot, bosh, slibbersauce.

I did not so much learn as encumber what I'd been taught with what I already knew.

There was a pane of stickers on the teacher's desk from which she some days lazily abstracted the one-word appraisals ("NICE!"; "BETTER!"; "WOW!") that she slapped onto the upper margin of our worksheets, next to where our names had been bared in huddles of roundabout penmanship.

We were one day expected to play look-alikes and, on another, duets.

Some of our papers had to be hand-stitched together into booklets that the teacher took forever to grade. Mine came back weeks later with ruddy question marks all over every page. What she wrote at the end of it was "No way, shape, or form are there people anywhere who live like that. How would you know any of this? You're not even worth your cost in shadow."

To the smartest girl in the class, every subject was nothing but anatomy.

We were the last of what we already were.

When we were lucky enough, as I once was, to one day sneak out of school and out into one of the shallower fields, you might have figured out how it was done, how the water was made to come up over them, how it got coaxed straight up from below, out of the earth, and not, as you would have thought, horizontally, from some off-run of a lesser river, or pumped from some far-off lake, and you would have seen how their legs had gone out from under them, the hundreds of them, the thousands and thousands, and at first you would have turned up your nose at them, at all of that running of blood, and turned your back to their wider shoulders; but if you had waded out close enough to any one of the drownlings to finger where it was different, where it was sometimes stiff and graspable, you could not have helped finding the new coolness of your hand agreeable, and would have been in no great hurry to come back around your own body, as I keep doing, to discover how you were suddenly forever no longer wasting your breath, on me, alone.

# UNNATIVELY

I LASTED A LITTLE longer than a semester at that rattlebox of a state college downstate. It was only long enough to pull to myself a boyfriend and all that pubic civility of his. From the dining-hall windows we would look out at the cemental realms of the physical plant. We'd turn up our noses at the girls always provoking new schisms among our classmates. His father paid a visit one evening. He talked as if he was never entirely sure of his right to use the words. They came out of his mouth with critical parts missing or ground down. He'd come to move his son into a one-room apartment. This new place was a little out of true with the campus but turned out to have room enough for me. Once, for a weekend, I was left alone in charge of a dog, a raggy, sleepy-souled thing missing his collar. I forget his name, but even when I knew it, I didn't go along with it, wouldn't say it (it didn't fit), but instead, when the poor thing was drowsed on the mat in the bathroom, I would loudly take the name and suffix it outlandishly (often with *steins, olowoskis, inskis*) or flip the consonants around. The dog always clodded his impeccably afflicted way toward the chair where I was sitting, then clodded back to where he could go back to sleep. I finally stripped his name down to just the howl of its vowels. The dog did not come. I had to move back with my parents after things that soon enough happened with the boyfriend, things the slumlord had written up in mishaps of townie legalese. This was when my parents still lived in that zagging line of underheated rooms above a four-car garage. I got in the habit of standing in the front yard and picking fights with the neighbors until my father came out to ask if I was starting to get hungry. The three of us mingled only at meals. I slept in the bed where my mother ordinarily would have slept. I had always been good at keeping my life separate from my body, but now I had to be extra careful about how far I let my sleep get away from me. I had to keep mine separate. Evenings, she spent a lot of time with the newspaper—"going over it," she called it. This involved not so much reading it as trying to find a better way to pat it down, get it folded novelly, test its page-span, maybe even urge it into flight. Sometimes she carried the paper into the living room and sat with her back to my father. She would move her hand across the newsprint and not let anything stop her. After she laid the paper aside, I sometimes took up with it myself. I was at the age when you read only enough of a story until you're convinced that you're safe, you're not in it, it doesn't concern you at all. When I found work in an office, I thought I was doing my co-workers a favor by ignoring them. I thought I was creating an above-and-beyond, heart-robbing impression that I was not about to get in their way, as if to whisper, "Look, I know I'm not as good as any of you." Then every couple of weeks, I would work my way around the room and ask them one by one if they were mad at me. "Heavens no!," they would say, or "Don't be silly!" So I'd smile and say hello and accord them each a "Good morning" for a couple of days after that, then go right back to ignoring them. It was a piecemeal blond I got married to first. Up until that point, she had been just a figurine in her parents' life—someone whose mail they could easily go through. We each entered the marriage expecting the other to handle most of the matrimonial folksiness and whatsuch. No matter what I would say, she would say, "I see."

She didn't believe in answering the door. Of the second wife I remember mostly that we were one day out in front of her unit (she had been living in a housing project, and I'd been approved to move in), and she was trying to fix something wrong with her car, was awfully busy under the hood, working up a sweat, and I was in the passenger seat, paging through another book of quotes. A fat kid, a neighbor, was directing her. He some days seemed to have the whole neighborhood orchestrated. In the line of work I now was in, I had to see to it that people got most of the stars taken out of their eyes. The coming divorce would be just temporary, I had to keep telling myself. Those days, too, my days would continue straight into my dreams, as if there needn't be a difference. It was getting to the point where everybody at work was expected to have a story to tell about having almost choked to death. In my case, I was big on hard candy—drops, lozenges, pastilles— and I sometimes worried about losing track of whatever I'd just got revolving around in my mouth, then swallowing the thing wholesale and going unacceptably blue. The worry was whether I'd have it in me to make it out to the hallway and tap on doors. Another worry would concern how I would be dressed, whether I'd have anything on at all. Days it was better for me to want nothing to do with myself, I made sure I found a place to stand in a line. There was a convenience store where you could always count on one that was good and long. I'd stand behind people who struck me as painstakingly spoken for, argued about, laid into. The good had obviously been already seen in them, and they were left with little else to show. I would be buying two newspapers— the local and one from wide away. There was a college, a small one, a branch of some bulging university, within walking distance of the complex where I now lived. I enrolled in a course during the day and the identical course in the evening with the identical instructor. (I figured I'd need a refresher.) In the evening course, everything was different from how it came out during the day. In the day class, the instructor went on and on about the inhabitants, the elevations, the roadsteads and water-bearers and leastways of certain places he claimed to have lived for a while unnatively. He showed film footage of all he had seen. Students came and went, ate perkily or slept, sometimes shouted, "Focus!" At night, the instructor spoke straight to a different purpose. He always had a different load on his mind. The man didn't give us a minute's peace. I had to stop by his office one time to pick up a handout. I'd never seen so many window ledges and so much metal shelving in a room as small as that and painted so maroonly. He opened up about his ex-wife, who still had his vacuum cleaner. He wanted it back. It had no sentimental value, he claimed, but it was exactly the right size for the place where he now lived and for the sorts of impurities on his floors. He offered to write me a far-darting letter of recommendation right then and there and to put in it that I was a "young man of goldened homeliness." I will remember this later-strangulated man for his gangling sentences on the overhead projector, his shadowing, fibrillous arm on the screen, his hair-haloed hand, the way he'd every now and then stop mid-lecture to roll up the legs of his trousers and then powder the backs of his knees. I later traveled in what little was left of his pack.

# RULES FOR TENANTS

1. TENANTS ARE EXPECTED to have grown up with a live-in aunt who concealed all of her pregnancies by circulating among the rooms in a curtainlike organization of hangings and overhangings—wraps and swags and cleverly projective aprons that kept her body, and the thrivings within, at a decorous, uninspectable remove. Over the years, the house thus became brilliant with her children, a hardmouthed and unhidden assembly of brats fighting over imagined borders between bedsteads. *No pets on premises.*

2. Any tendency among tenants to throw their presence upon others living in the complex is to be curbed at all times.

3. Any references to another complex said to be overtowering ours but occupying the same address are not be countenanced.

4. Sidewalks on the property are to be made to show the effects of great, presentable crowds. Each tenant is expected to grind the sole of one shoe onto the concrete until such time as the desired effects have been satisfactorily achieved.

5. You are to have served well enough, at one point or another, as a high-school guidance counselor who asked students questions about things you damn well knew were none of your business— what they would buy if they were in charge of grocery shopping for the entire family, to what degree they would mind their mind's playing a trick on them every now and then, what the first thing

in their head was at the instant they woke up, what their shins smelled like by the end of an especially miserable, overladen day. The questions were on a form you'd designed and had printed with your own money. There were sixty questions in all, and most of them called for a multi-sentence response. Nothing involved checking things off a list or filling in blanks. The kids were always cooperative and often apologetically thorough, because this kept them out of class. At the end of the last page was a seven-square-inch bordered space above which was printed, "Anything else you would like known about yourself?," and that alone could keep them busy for a good fifteen minutes. You would be sitting at your desk—your littered, splintery ruin of a headquarters—and thinking about how you would take the forms home with you and add them to the others you kept stored in the box your toaster had come in. The only time you ever read the things was after another botched night out with your spouse. There had only ever been just the two of you in that marriage.

6. [from *Articles of Tenantal Comportment*, rev. centenary ed., with permission]. "Any tenant deteriorating pretty noticeably in personhood in the usual, dead-of-afternoon manner shall be reported to Management"; "Hate is expected to be expressed intimately but at a remove"; "Tenant agrees to inform Management of which closet to hasten toward if tenant is at peril of imminent death—particularly if said closet has been used to store sexual treasures."

7. The bus that makes a loop of the parking lot twice daily is to be the only one of the fleet that will have been painted to look like a trolley car. It is to be called a Dart.

8. Waiting for the mailman's truck also means waiting for the mailman's truck to leave. Each tenant shall be allowed ten (10) minutes afterward for other tenants to claim their mail and read it silently but publicly in the lobby, on the bench brought out daily for that purpose across from the bank of mailboxes. Each tenant is not to have brought his/her door to a complete shut on the way down; said tenant is to stop just short of engaging the lock and thus save all others from an extra sound on the way down and an answering sound on the way back.

9. Any tenant venturing into the downtown district shall return with a description along these lines: "At the heart of the district are two or three blocks possessed of the simplified, primary-color diversity of cities one often sees in children's picture books— books contrived to steep a new generation in the notion that almost any urban block holds in brilliant, shadowless embrace a marqueed movie house, a limestone bank, an arcade-fronted midget department store (a water tower on its roof), an awninged greengrocer's, a round-the-clock dental operatory set just a little bit back from the line of other storefronts, a haberdashery that now sells mostly women's ready-to-wear, a hardware store with a recessed entranceway, a long-shuttered burlesque house, and a restaurant with nothing even the least bit recondite on the menu's list of daily specials. A little of this is eclipsed by a vividly passing bus whose passengers look leagued together in smiling regard of the other side of the street." After such a recital, variations are permissible; e.g., "It was in this block that I first glimpsed the woman. I fell in line behind her at the bank (I had wrapped some primal dimes), considered the elegance of her fingers as she

browsed some counters in the department store (wallets, scarves, gloves reaching almost to the elbow), advanced to one row behind and one seat to the right of hers in the movie theater (it was a costume drama plotted to a certainty), established occupancy in a booth where I could face hers in the restaurant (I put through an order for the identical select toast and unbubbled cola): we thus sat there for hours, never touching the squares of toast after they had been set before us, never unwrapping the straws for our drinks. After sunset, the woman remained vibrant enough from headlights trafficking across her face. The waitress eventually removed our plates and glasses of outlasted soda. We were later led out of the restaurant by a man presumed to be the owner. The hardware store was still open. I followed the woman as she went in to inquire about whatever novelties of implemency would be required for her to remove a picture hung high on a wall. Its removal, she said, would need to be definitive this time. She asked to use the restroom before the clerk rang up the sale. The men's room had no men in it. At the bus stop afterward (the sign was a disk mounted on a pole with a darkened base), the woman pretended to be just another poor thing. I was having none of it."

10. Any tenants with cars must park the cars out of the range of all other tenants' windows so that others will feel a need to walk out of the building to settle to their satisfaction whether particular owners of particular cars are at home or not, though it is to be understood that the presence of a car on the lot cannot be construed as final proof that the tenant has not gone out, for tenants are sometimes led away by other people with transportation of their own.

11. There shall be no further course of human events between 11:00 p.m. and 7:00 a.m. on weekdays and between midnight and 8:00 a.m. on weekends.

12a. Each tenant's portfolio shall include a certificate attesting to meritorious completion of the workshop (held fortnightly) instructing tenants on how to wash their hands without subjecting others to the noise of a running faucet. As a courtesy, instructions are summarized here: i.e., apply to the palms almost however much is left of the soda in a can, rub a cakelet of soap between the palms, pour almost the last of the soda onto the palms, then brush the palms on a receptive span of the carpet. The backs of the hands will never have need to be washed. Soda is available at vending machines on each floor.

12b [as applies]. Don't act as if the two of you hadn't gone to high school together and weren't renting that slattern of a duplex on O—Street. One night the man of you (his posture having lost the simplicity people had always claimed to admire) tried to remember some of the others he might have graduated with. He looked up their names in the phone book. Then one night he called one of them. A voice (likely female) answered, with TV noise brimming behind it. He hung up. (The contents of a heart are not so easily sorted.) A night or two later, neighbors were out on the porch. He opened the door and looked out at them through the screen. "We seen," one of them said. He could see the rocks in everybody's hands.

13a. *Visitation policy.* Two (2) women at a time, if on record as unswerving sisters of copious soul, may be admitted to any unit whose lessee is a lustless, watery-eyed male—provided that conversation flourishes within five (5) minutes of admittance. No men are to be admitted to a woman tenant's apartment under any circumstances. Children are to be regarded, at best, as prompts to remember that we all unsettle and ebb.

13b. You'd been distracting yourself onto enough people for long enough (correct?), so go ahead and admit it: you could see things through the body on her. You could see straight through to the carpeting underneath and what for months must have been tossed onto it: scarcely used cap erasers resembling turrets, to be sure, and those tearings from a big toenail, and, that being said, what you took to be stickied, fuzzed-over chewable vitamins, unwrapped fractions of unenlivening candy—take a moment, in short, to admit to remembering when you had started to grow up and girls started having that smell and you didn't.

14. (A) If you are a man who intends to go on living as a man, the following will be expected to have been your past: You were, for some years, an adept at abrupt, sidelong marriages that meant no one any harm. The divorces felt to you at first like little more than personal soilures but afterward had some sort of encircling effect. (B) If you are a woman of a mind to go on being a woman, the following is to be your lot: You are to have been married industriously at least once earlier and hurt in ways that never finally sufficed. Any women you bring into your unit must be unequalledly shaven, heart-shoving, and overcreated. To put it horribly, sleep will still exalt you. You will have long ago begun addressing any oiliness of skin by smearing dish detergent onto your nose and then letting it dry there. You are to shop only for

sundries, if at all. Cutoff dates are to be revised and/or renewed as needed. You are not to have enjoyed or been enjoyed. You remain representative of a kingdom apart. You shall nonetheless continue to outface the outfacing parts of others.

15. Tenants shall lease their units with the understanding that (a) they will never be in a position to know what the entire, ever-accumulating noise of their tenancy will sound like to other tenants, and (b) shutting a cupboard door ever so gingerly is a learnable skill (tenants shall see Management for instruction). A corollary to this understanding is an acceptance of the fact that however much they might experimentally turn on every face-saving appliance; activate all entertainment apparati; run bathtub waters both hot and cold; rummage around for that old tape recorder, rewind the cassette to the point where they were caught yowling in their sleep, and dial it up to maximal volume; even call a friend to ask that friend to be a friend for once and call in exactly one (1) minute and let the phone ring and ring; and then, and only then, fling open the door and step outside of their unit and stand there listeningly, or walk the halls in some dumb show of ennobling caring for others for once—even then, in sum, they will never come even close to hearing what everybody else has to put up with every morning, noon, and night. Tenants are to live with this understanding the way they will by now have roved out to the parking lot for a smoke and been told somebody else's troubles that are to become their own troubles now too.

16. Each tenant agrees to have the leased unit fitted out, at his/her own expense and within the first two (2) weeks of occupancy, with

a hellhole commodious enough for the tenant and two (2) guests.

17. The following policies are to take effect immediately upon annual renewal of the lease: (A) The newsstand in the lobby will no longer stock out-of-town toilet goods. (B) The tenant shall hereafter be referred to consistently, unavailingly, as "you." (C) Tenants are expected to drop everything at a moment's notice to remember a long-gowned grandelder's having once said, "Put something on those feet," because it was the feet alone—the terribility of those bunioned big toes, the upcourse of veins and hatch of black hair on the instep—that others, downlookers themselves, took stirring notice of each time you stepped out onto the harsh carpeting of the crossway on your route to the garbage chute or that westernmost pay phone, the one just beyond the laundry stall. (D) Whenever the cashier hands you your change (you are to have found yourself, as usual, in a sporting-goods store but are once again buying something that might be bought cheaper at the dollar mart on the corner or at the dry cleaner's off the lobby), the hand of yours that claims the coins is never once in a million years to be the same hand that puts them in the pockets of your pants or housecoat. (E) From here on out, *I* is the initial of a person, not a personal pronoun by which you are permitted any further, ensuing references to yourself. There is to be a tickle, a kind of irritation, deep in whatever ready understanding you might now manage of how you are said to have once been friends with anyone, let alone this person whose initial now is *I* and who has a shovy way in his sleep, who seems to be shoving things aside in his dreams. You are to be barely the bearer of yourself, but, hold on, we're not dictators here, you'll still get your wished-for nervousness when

the time comes and you're asked what you're doing out so early. (F) Even if Management goes so far as to concede that you actually were that girl, the one who had less and less luck getting things off her chest but who compiled a simple list of everything blood had turned out to be no thicker than, what of it? This is mostly about the other one. This other girl backed her way into the room, sat down behind the drums. She picked up the sticks, slowly brought one of them down and let it tap the head of the snare drum ever so lightly along the rim. The snares began to rattle a little. With her other hand she quickly muffled the things. (Politesse?) Then she let the other stick fall. She looked at us (repeat: never once at you). Then she brought both sticks down together, bounced them near the rim, worked them slowly toward the center of the drum, faster, louder, building up to a firm, reverent roll. She stomped onto the pedal of the bass drum and smacked a stick against the edge of the ride cymbal. Then, resting her hands, she sat quietly and looked at us again. None of us did anything. (You stood there as if there had been three of you out there with her? You were the oldest, with a flashlight under your arm? You were the one who said, "You're our aunt? You're sure that's all you are?") So she started up again, a lot louder and faster this time, arms crisscrossing as the sticks struck the tom-toms and the cymbals, her feet pounding on the high-hat and bass-drum pedals. She kept at it, sweating by now, her mouth and forehead creased, the muscles in her arms tightening as she shaped the thuds and chops and cracks and bashes into something we wanted to trust because it was obviously hurting her so dearly and so worthily much. *You* were the one looking as if you'd gone through life being told, "Gee, you smell like soap" or "It's not working, if you know what I mean." But don't come crying to Management if it turns out that the one thing required in death is that the blood not stay long enough where it belongs. (G) You will have had to look out the window until you saw the car pull up and then have to lock up the apartment and walk the three flights of stairs down to the lobby and get into the car with the woman for the same reason that, decades ago, in elementary school, from the third grade to the fifth, you once a month had to leave school twenty minutes early to go to the "clinic," and your mother would be waiting outside the classroom door, and it was months until a teacher finally stepped out with the two of you and said, "What kind of a clinic are we talking about here?," and your mother must have had the answer prepared for years—rehearsing it must have been one of the things that kept her going while you were at school—because it went on and on, the words getting bigger and longer, then shorter and fouler. But the woman waiting in the car this day decades later was not your mother. You knew this woman from work. She'd done something for you once, completely unmeaningly—unclogged a copier, probably. This woman, you'd heard, later bought a house. (The walls were all colors of clay.) She lived there perfectly fine for a while. Then it began to pain her that the house had been lived in before, that she had not gotten to it sooner. Then this final time you'd see her. You were both topping out of your forties by now. People more and more felt entitled to each other's privacy. It helped that the two of you had all along kept painting over your true colors again and again, until you could no longer make them out.

## ERNIE BUSHMILLER
## ALREADY A DECADE DEAD

OUR DAYS WERE numbered but not flavored nearly enough. This is not even an hour ago. I walk down the street to a pay phone. I dial the operator and ask her to put through a call to my own number. I need extra steps put between any two things I do.

I wait.

He answers on the fourth ring.

"You," he says.

"I couldn't help it," I say. "Say something."

"I threw out all your plants. Records are next."

"Seriously," I say.

"More than that."

Weeks later, I run into her, the one I threw him over for, in a drugstore on Newport Street. She's picking up photos she's had developed.

"Don't count on Texas," she says. "I think I'm losing interest."

Outside, on the sidewalk, she flips through the snapshots.

"This is a picture of *me*," she says. "This is a picture of *me* and all three of my dogs. This is a picture of *me* and my mother in front of her house."

"Walk me home," she says.

I run into her at the Patio a couple of days later. "Loan me a quarter for coffee," she says.

I reach into my pocket for a quarter, hand it to her, and say, "You won't get a cup of coffee for a quarter."

"I only want the milk."

"When you get to be my age," Norah's telling me the other night, "you're going to go out and buy one of those books that tell you how to identify birds. That's all you'll have to look forward to. And trees—you'll want to know the name of every tree when you're walking down a street." She's a good seven or eight worse-off years older than I, and high-handedly smart, undriven, and she keeps going unclaimed. Her sundress smells perfectly worthily of her. Coke from a can tastes awfully dirty sometimes.

On the drive back from the capital, we were expected to talk about people. We could think of nobody but Norah and Phil, and then only because of how openly nature was running its course through both of them.

I talked about the night she'd turned to me at some toss-up of a party and said, "Why don't we just walk around the block?" As soon as we got out to the pavement, she said, "My mother couldn't wait for the day I hit puberty so she could teach me the proper way to do it to myself." She said her mother called it "charming oneself."

"She's been freezing spiders," said this passerby of a lover, this woman with me in the car, Leslie's car, with neither of her hands any longer on my lap.

These were deedless, deplenishing days of my twenties. I was getting better at shying away from myself.

The next evening I'd been walking around town for another half hour or so, then stopped at another pay phone. Again, no answer. I felt a tap on my shoulder. The person I'd been calling happened to be walking past the pay phone at that very instant. "Go to a movie," she told me. Not "Go to a movie?" or "Let's go to a movie!" She was merely telling me where to head next, without her. Then three insultingly warm and sunny days in a row. More of the snow is missing. Four wrong numbers this afternoon alone, and the only thing unusual about my nightmare last night wasn't its plot (I'd been accused of rummaging through her things again, I was protesting my innocence, I wasn't being believed) but the way it fizzled out: there was buzzing and humming, then the sputtering of sparks—as if there were some foul-up in the transmission of the dream, or faulty reception on my part.

After Norah, it wasn't that I wasn't particular about people. It was just that I couldn't see the point in eating out with them in better places. You couldn't concentrate on their unmanaged futilities and on your food at the same time if the food was any good. How I wish this were pettiness instead of just plain good sense.

I met the plank-chested one through the personals. She claims she lifts weights. She claims that at work they had her painting fire hydrants. We'd been out to eat only once, but it took hours. (You could tell that the waiter—a petulant lollipop of a kid, aspiringly bearded—was intent on sensing something.) I'd been meaning to use a ladenly blank stare to mark an end to that part of my life, but she called me a day or two later, and we talked about how it was expected that you would think back on things, on people you could have hurt differently.

She wanted to borrow money. She was particular about how she wanted it and what she wanted it for and why she wanted it coming only from me.

Later, broke, I'm eating the last of the storm fare, taking M&Ms in constellations of five and seven.

There are no lady accountants listed in the phone book, and the men are mostly in practice on streets I've never heard of. They've got some of the streets technically counting as avenues now.

This dress I'm in—too tight!—ties in the back, is sleeveless. I feel hollowed by it, though.

The hair on my shins looks practically chromed.

You get heckled when you walk the sidewalks of this town. That's why I take my walks in stores.

One of the dreamier things about the cafeteria at this Kmart is the whipped-potatoes machine. The countergirl turns it on, it hums and whirs, and then it discharges a pittance into a dinky plastic mold.

The girl gets everything lopped onto a plate she then hands me with what I'm afraid I take as effrontery.

But Laundromats enthrall me so little, I've been doing all my wash at home—in sinks, buckets, dishpans. Socks, a vagrant plenty of them, mostly biscuit-colored by now, are drying on the radiator to my left. On the radiator to my right: four lopsided T-shirts of a fickle, indiscriminant pink.

I don't want to think of myself as a slob. I want to think of a slob as someone who doesn't put things back where they belong. In my apartment, things were never anywhere in particular to begin with. Everything is simply where it lands.

Childhood? I was always being beaten up, always. In third grade, it was singing time, and we each had to share a songbook with somebody else, and I was paired off with some Dolores Gerson who hogged the book—I couldn't see enough of the words to even pretend that I was singing them. In college, in a dorm at Flagship State, I'd have the index finger and thumb of my left hand ringing the one part of my boyfriend I could have done without. I'd be looking out the window at the snow stocked squarely at the edges of the parking lot below. I'd be trying to decide whether I'd had too little needless sleep or entirely too much. "I'll get the notes" is what I usually said.

Wait—I've got this all wrong. It wasn't Topics in Cultural Geography I had at ten; it was one of the lowermost biologies. I'd pack myself and my curricularized baggage into a seat close to the back of the amphitheater. A few rows under an overhang never got as overheated as everywhere else. Girls bent over their notebooks as if taking dictation, enthusiastically uncomprehending.

I slip through stores and admire some drearily beautied vendeuse piling striped woolen sweaters onto a counter. The short sleeves of her white blouse are rolled up to reveal muscles a trifle too humdrum.

In the car, driving from mall to mall, I listen to polkas, C&W, faraway talk.

I'm barely a broth of whoever I was even an hour ago.

I try feeling my way back to the body-shaped clearing on the floor where I'd been so hustlingly asleep even just minutes ago. I end up having to stretch out in a new region. There's the crackle of newspapers underfoot, the sloshing of soda in rolling, overturned bottles, as I get myself settled among uncased cassettes, bags of chips, devastated tape dispensers. Ideally, nothing should do for a pillow.

At the Laundromat, the young man with shrunken cheeks and a bowl haircut, busy with a loose-leaf notebook that's easily a ream thick, each page looking covered with blackouts from a heavy marker: he's tearing out some pages and flicking them into a trash basket, stuffing others under his shirt.

But which summer was my saddest? The one between seventh grade and eighth? One morning, I dared to watch an old Abbott and Costello show. I expected my mother any moment to rush back in from her clotheslines and start shouting, "Get out of the house! Go outside! Or are you afraid somebody might see you?" I watched Lou Costello buy a "slice" of vanilla ice cream from a vendor in a park, and I wanted to run out to the kitchen for the half-gallon of Weis Carnival-brand van-choc-straw (the cheapest, waxiest kind anyone then could buy) still forsaken in the freezer. I wanted to knife it into slices. I wanted to get everything life-lorn about this life slit out of its wits.

There's only the one bar I go to. You have to take about ten steps down just to reach the first of three doors. The stool I usually choose is right where one of the sides forming the U-shaped bar begins to curve toward the other. This way, I can see just about everyone else in the house, as well as the awfully prominent clock. You look at someone, and you likely find her looking right back at you, and then her eyes jet off.

It's a man who comes over to claim the stool next to mine. He has one of those names that sound as if a part of it got chopped off. *Geoff.*

I've soon got him saying, "Oh, gosh, you're sweating already."

Not even eleven o'clock yet. I get to know the one I go home with, a slop of a girl keen on men except only this once, just long enough to figure out that when people tell her, "Better you than me," she always takes it the wrong, aggrandizing way.

One after another they come, beery postcards from the cream-colored East, the pile amounting by now to a chronicle of sorts, with intimations of motor-court bacchanalia and breezy dashboard exultations: another friendship about to end.

Tomorrow is Sunday. That's always the worst. No, not true— Monday and Tuesday are also the worst. The worst of them all tend to come in packs of seven.

Plus, I was not in love with him, I never felt hinged to him in any way definite, he didn't pick up after himself, he didn't take after anybody, though he had a sister I knew from the union hall. They still had a pay phone there. Her scalp kept pushing out precocious grays aplenty. She was eating an orange after the vote got taken. The orange seemed to keep being a disappointment to her.

This other one's story, the story of this sister of his, was only that you get your childhood honed into a tactful loneliness, you get your gamine bearings from an imposingly thin-spun but touchable friend a little older, and then you grow up and end up doing all the dirt that was always distinctly yours to do. You figure out what other people are using now for money, and you try using some of that. (Thirty's about the age, but some get to it sooner.) Hence the sum of additions added on to a house already too big for people you've already left unendeared within.

I was sick of living in the surrounding areas but always kept moving farther out from the core. One night to the next, I'm never pointed in quite the same direction for sleep. When I wake in the middle of the night (I do it seven, eight times), I wave my arms in front of my face to make sure I'm not up against anything sharp (swing-arm lamps, elbowed lamps, jut out all over the place, clamped onto boxes, crates) before I make major moves. The first thing I look for is the window (dim light from the parking lot is always coming in through the blinds), and then I treat myself anew to the very features of the room. I'm soon up for good anyway. I'm reading a book flaunting far more than enough biographical befallings of somebody not even the subject of the book. I'm a sucker for reading about anyone longing for a baby to lose interest in, to get her nowhere.

I feel as if I've gaited my life to the slow crawl of somebody else's days. I pivot onto a side street of florists, costermongers, shoe-repair shops. I'm passed by a purposeful young woman, celestially secretarial.

At Burger King, I was behind a fuddlesome old man. I overtook him once I got inside and fell in line behind an unworldly teenage girl with a kid. When it was my turn, I ordered a hamburger, small fry, medium Diet Coke "for here." After the countergirl rang up the sale, placed the things on the tray, then pushed the tray toward me, she asked for the old man's order. What he said should break my heart: "I'll have the same as whatever you just gave that lady."

I do a lot of demolitionary daydreaming. So many things go unwailed. The night after some holiday almost nobody gets the day off for, I'd been sitting across from my best friend of the time, at a booth in a diner even farther midtown. He'd already finished his fries and was helping himself, uninvited, to the last of the potato chips rimming my plate. He had his foot propped up on the cushion of my side of the booth, blocking me in. This alone gave me surprisingly immeasurable satisfaction of a sort. But I thought about saying, "I have to get up to use the ladies' room," because I expected him to say, "No, you're not." I bring this up only because I later fell asleep to scrambled smells, as of ashes that had been pissed on, then subjected, in due course, to dish soap pretty citrussy. Morning, I reach into the fridge for juice in a box—an exploit. I retrieve my voice. Another occasion for the world to sort itself quickly into rivers, the skyline, purse strings, people, the foods people more and more bragged about doing without. I find him asleep in the bathtub, looking laboriously human and untreasurable, in every way offending.

The human body—must there even be such a place?

Someone was pounding away at my door (it was midafternoon; whatever else I thought I was doing, I must have been sound asleep on the floor), and I listened to this person keep it up. Then this person stopped pounding and started turning the doorknob back and forth. Then this person gave up. I could hear footsteps receding out into the hallway. Nobody had shouted, "I know you're in there, so open up, or I'll have to break down this door," so it couldn't have been anyone of importance. I went back to sleep.

The telephone is too personal an instrument, too private a device, practically a self-help appliance when you get right down to it. Three days ago, I pinned my hopes on a haircut. I'm always saying there's no quicker way to get a lighter head.

The stylist looked longstandingly herself. I forget how little old she actually was, but she'd said.

Nothing's any different now, and my hair's no shorter by even a quarter of an inch.

My upper lip trembles as I pluck.

Another unstately solitude I've gotten myself involved in. E-mail's too unearthly for me still.

I always make it a point to buy a paper. I walk into Burger King with it. Saturday's the one day I open it to the sports. Saturdays a page is given over to letters to the sports editor. The letters are reliably, comfortingly, brief and bellicose. Tonight I've been pouring Drano down the bathroom sink. The thing's been clogged for a month. All that time, I'd been thinking, "Okay, fine, you're not the only sink under this roof." So I let well enough alone. I was willing to go along. Then a few nights ago, the faucet started leaking, and the bowl started filling up. I used an old dish to scoop water out of the sink every half hour or so and pour it into the tub, but that meant not leaving the apartment. I'll have to do something. I'll have to buy something. I'll have to add something to my life.

But this one had at least a good two and a half decades on me, had been living too long overlooked. She'd gone back to college to finish what she called her "spinster's degree." All she ever had on her mind was how they kept coming up with newer and newer things to come down with, how there were breakthroughs in ways you could now take to your bed. She figured that sleep apnea must have been a labor of love to discover.

I don't know why I stopped by. She's still got a pinched mouth and a look of being put out, put upon, as if her body weren't home base after all.

She's as drily hygienic as ever. We once again go about defiling something or other about life (*her* life, she cries) on that divan.

The only thing she wants to talk about afterward is how she ought to have a daughter or two by now.

She talks about kids as if they were a refreshment no one had ever offered her, something sweet-spun that would have really hit the spot.

We make plans.

To myself I vow to do more work on my absence.

It's going to need a lot more sweep.

I'll dilate it this time until it'll fill intersidereal spheres.


I've always liked taking aptitude tests. I'd love to have aptitudes. It's only Brach's chocolate stars I eat when it's astral chocolate I require. On the live version of "The Girl from Ipanema" on the Astrud Gilberto CD I bought secondhand in the city yesterday, there's a single, startling, seductive swash of feedback—pure grace—after the second line of the first verse. The quality of my own mistakes might be said to be improving? They show more initiative?

Nothing much glinting in the days we were given, either, but this one's bracingly unappreciative, and she's got good looks gone a little gummy. The money from her husband helps. Nightly visits to a restaurant are required. She skirmishes with the waitresses over market-rate seafood she'll eat only if coaxed. Lengths of silver keep getting twisted intemperately around her wrist. The husband before this was somebody paramount in lewd local art. To spare us another lull, I talk about how I've taught myself to recognize people from the back. I talk about how handy it comes in on sidewalks when you'll otherwise end up overtaking someone you don't want bringing up your rear.

She interrupts.

She loves me on a sliding scale. Her body keeps cutting into middle age. Lucky for her, her every move is mine.

But her bags were packed.


My life has yet to ray out in any real direction. In one dream, my thumb comes apart. But today I am uncomplicated and readily fathomable, ready for work. The job is not even just seasonal anymore—it's only the three weeks before finals they say they'll pay me for. I stalk errant commas and stray apostrophes in preposterously awful rough drafts. I excise malignant paragraphs. I hose down feculent sentences. I oil creaky syllogisms, pull platitudes up by their roots. The papers are always due tomorrow. The one I've been sleeping with parochially? It's all there in the planes of the face, in the geometry of the smile: she'll one day hit the ceiling once too often. Part of it is that she's in sales.

Plus I could've eaten sliced chicken with garlic sauce right here in town, and so much the cheaper, but I drove the whole raw way into the city. The people eating in that place—everybody looked like an official—seemed to be enjoying full-blown metropolitan sorrows instead of county-seat miseries and setbacks. Then I tramped the fifty or so blocks back to my car and drove to a large, darkish indoor flea market with mildewed air and roof-leak buckets everywhere. Tonight I'll watch TV only if I've got enough things to block the lower half of the screen.

Snowed all day, but not all roads were closed. Drove to the plowed safehold of Burger King and ordered in a deep-sunken voice and read a long article in the paper about how teenage girls conceal their pregnancies from their families and even from themselves. The babies turn up later in Dumpsters. I heard one countermaiden ask another: "Will we have people?" She must have been reading the same article.

You can die in your sleep, but you can't live there very long. My days of late had all been irkingly Sundayish again, but it was on a calendar Sunday that I met her. Some people you sleep with just to recoup something of yourself. This one is a hardy twenty-three, with blunt, boyish knees, and lives in some underfoliaged suburb, works for a freebie weekly in some guy's sunken living room: she's dubbed it the "editorial basin." She says every sex always turns out to be the opposite of hers. She feels implicated in every suicide she reads about in the paper. Once or twice, she's tried lapping warm, days-old water from a cereal bowl she'd left out on the floor. Her history is otherwise suspiciously gistless. But she wants the nutshell version of me—the company-keeping, the comeuppances.

I tell her I'm no match for my life. It would be better off inside somebody else.

But are we kissing or just eating each other away?

Then something went wrong with my toilet, and for three or four days, I drove to Kmart every time I had to go. But I was good about it: I always bought something.

Other nights I count on things to get turned around in my sleep. Another night, still snowy out, I was admiring some Brittany spaniels at a pet shop. I heard a woman saying, "He was killed in his outfit overseas, but the bird wouldn't shut up about him. I had to have it taken back."

But when did I start having such a hard time talking on the phone? Days the thing rang, I'd let it ring itself sick.

I'd be ready to look up to whoever it might have turned out to be.

Too often I'm on the verge of worship.

Thunder, rain, the ticking of the wind-up clock atop a photo album I've yet to empty out: everybody but me so debilitatingly beloved.

From the entranceway to the bathroom is a trail of blankets, rumplings of the Sunday newspaper, cast-off camisoles now a little too tight, TV-dinner trays, vacuum-cleaner attachments, grocery bags all weekend still unpacked. "Twenty-eight isn't 'late in life,'" she's telling me from the toilet.

I feel free to explore life more mediocrely.

Phone just rang. Weekly call from my brother. "You do know tomorrow's the Fourth of July?"

Good question!

Still down in the car is the box fan I bought at the Kmart two fouled townships over. I hate to be seen carrying big boxes into the building and up to my apartment. I don't like looking like somebody *acquiring*.

They should have put a rider on my birth certificate to the effect of "Promptly refrigerate any unused portions."

Yvette was another of the ones a little too often unwanted, and I had to feel bad for her, because in the city she'd now moved to, people looked too much like people in the city she'd just fled. Not in the overall mass, she explained, but in the individual, up-close nose and elbows, in the bolder and bolder organization of their hair. It was a misfortune to come face to face with people who stopped just short of being a ringer for your mother, or the supervisor you'd reported to, or your favorite screwball waitress at the pasta place, even some girl you'd dumped because of something ungovernable in her budget. Worse, what good did it do you to cut them dead when they had no notions of who you even were? You might as well have smiled at them even more outstrangeningly. So in due course she moved back to the first city, but people who should have now looked familiar and welcoming were instead looking incompletely distinguishable, stupidly diffuse in everybody else.

"Level with me," she said. She'd been staring first at my fingers, then at the motion in my knees. "Were we together? Or you're here to tell me we've never been apart?"

Early on, people were already saying I was one of the ones who listen. The bus I took to the city today passed a church named Covenant What So Ever and spelled as such. In a store I bought a little bag of Dipper Skippers, imitation M&Ms. These leave a pleasing chemicality on the tongue.

Plenty of events I would now gladly overturn if I were button-eyed and forgiving like Francine.

I loved her even though her name was like a lid that had been placed over her life and never did quite fit.

Earlier, though: another of those especially drawn-out and morose episodes of the sort in which you try to get out of the way of somebody coming toward you, and then he changes his path, then you do, too, and then you're practically on top of each other.

People are married as far as the eye can see. (I speak in general.)

You could be looking at him—you could be standing right next to him—before you realized you were looking at a person.

I'm fond of overpriced turnpike food. My best blanket goes way back to high-school days.

I'd been hoping to discover that with some doing I could be made to derive from anyone other than my parents and any of theirs. Beyond that, there were due dates, red-letter days, three-day weekends, though nobody ever bothers to come right out and tell you that everything else is going to be either a disappointment or just more sodomy down the road.

I was shredding the last of my parents' bank statements, receipts for final things they'd bought for me and my drenched sunburst of a brother. How could it be the weekend already? It hadn't even been much of a month. Not everyone had set out that year tc become just another sitting duck. There must have been other ambitions. Why must a body keep being a burlesque of the person within? Corrine hadn't been so female herself. She'd stand for quarter-hours at a time beside embankments of people waiting anywhere in line. She'd barge alongside the first large family idling outside a restaurant. She was good for tips on how to get anything to look even harder to find. Her wreckful attempts at loving me were a gentleness felt too late.

But Maura? She lived for any resets in the gladiatorial suavities of office politics. She'd let morning light blemish her afresh. She'd learned to defer to drink, to drugs halved and handed over by enqueering friends still up and already awaiting the new day's welcome deflations of itself. I'd have her clipping coupons for any hell to be had of it. In the middle of the night, she'd have me listening to all the shit sizzling out of her. Nobody else is up for humoring her now.

My Double Whopper for dinner was assembled by a thin and very serious woman, an erect and conscientious subject of the broiler.

I eat at that place so often, I should know everybody's name by now. At least they don't know mine.

Once again I'm told she asks after me every now and then. I'm told she's usually moodily polite when she asks.

Her life crops out between people, but she can get awfully selective.

Later, I couldn't fall back to sleep. A man was talking gravely in the apartment next to mine. I tried to imagine enough of a voice in pleading answer to his own.

Mollie called me in the middle of the night. She said she was pregnant. She said she would need an abortion. The next week, she called me in the middle of the night and told me she'd just been raped "so to speak." Last night, she called to tell me about a "petite" shotgun she'd found in her bedroom closet. Did I know anything about how a thing like that might have ended up in there? Some love is too difficult to keep getting itself tendered. The new apartment is just okay. I'm tired of being the only one around at the very instant people decide to change their lives.

One morning during the worst of another arctic spell, I had no way to get to work other than to call X. (Couldn't even get a cab.) I hadn't spoken to her in months. The wind-chill factor was about thirty below, but X arrived with undried hair. She drove with characteristic disregard for the traffic, feeling no duty. I never once looked over into her face. She said that a few days earlier one of her brothers had to have one of his feet taken off. It was the brother I'd once bought shoes from at the mall. I'd tried them on, then begun to unlace. "Wait, I do that," he said, the way people always talk when I'm just about ready to get something started.

# CHEAP NIGHT

I WAS EVENTUALLY sent off to a number of different people, a second round of specialists, about everything else that was said to have still not been set right. One was a man with an office on a sliver of a street in what was left of the business district. He had me sit in an anteroom with him while he filled out the first of the forms without ever looking over at me. Then I followed him into the better room, where there was a desk. On a sheet of a tablet that had been printed to look like a prescription pad, he wrote down the name of a woman who he said cut hair in ways that helped people along.

The appointment was for seven that evening.

This was a tall, damp-looking woman in a smock. She asked no questions. She set my head backward into a narrow sink for a hurried, turbulent shampoo. Once her fingers got moving across my scalp, she barged a portion of her limited side-flesh informally against my shoulder bone. The result was maybe some useless, cradlesong warmth—nothing more, I am sorry to report. The next thing she did was seesaw a towel back and forth across my skull, then tug me toward the barber chair and wrap me in a sheet. It was a routine haircut after that, I guess, until she pressed her palm against my cheek. She kept the hand there, detained it professionally, as it were, until the skin heated up. Whether it was departing heat of mine or a transfer of hers I could not at the time decide, but here I had the handicap of a wall before me that was solid mirror, and in going wide of my own reflection, I could not help unpiecing the woman's face into, first, a powdered-over replica of the large-pored, forthcoming nose of the specialist who had referred me there, and a chin of his own depthlessness (though here again given cosmeticized redefinition), and his wide-set, shittily brown eyes.

I muttered something about nepotism, kickbacks, etc., tore myself free of the sheet, stormed out.

At a pay phone, I called my only friend, a very good acquaintance of mine, someone I hardly knew enough to think of except at times like this. He said he had right that very instant finished ruining an hour in an adult-book store with an invalid video machine and a man suffering love-cramps of his own.

This friend said he wasn't up for getting together.

On my way home, what the hell, I stopped off at my stepsister's. I found her in the living room, her arms spired above her head in a shortcut rendition of an exercise some woman was enacting on the silenced TV.

My stepsister was in trunks, baggy socks, an undershirt. She struck me as no more than an enlargement of her scowly daughter on the sofa.

I compiled myself onto one of the baggier side chairs. From this privileged elevation I watched my stepsister, now down on the hardwood floor, bucking around on her stomach, raising her rear to a resultful summit—not a push-up exactly.

It was the daughter's idea that the three of us should go out for a bite to eat. "Unless you'd not rather," she said to her mother. Her mother said she'd tag along. We drove in the daughter's car to a below-stairs eating place she knew. Running the length of the wall facing the street was a band of windows that took detailed notice of the lower legs of passersby—skirts of coats, slow-going feet of people coping.

The daughter called our attention to a blemish on her left cheek, a little pink difference. She kept her fingers on it, twiddling at it, kneading away at her cheek, until the disturbance itself seemed to vanish into the environing complexion. Then she took her hand away, and the blemish reappeared with a renewed sickliness.

"But catch me up about you," she said.

I guess I was a kind of handy, convenient mystery to her, and every fact I gave her had an efficient way of instantly separating itself from any larger certitude. I have never liked feeling a point of view being trained on me too sharply.

My stepsister motioned toward the arrowy sign that pointed to the restrooms, then got up, taking her handbag and jacket. The daughter mentioned having seen an old teacher of hers faking a vacation in a chaise longue one neighborhood over. She spoke of little shares of chocolate she had once arranged and rearranged until they were practically mush and had to be licked off her fingers by more than just one lonesome mouth but her boyfriend was nowhere to be found. She'd had to recruit a girl she knew from the public pool who kept perfecting more and more ways of looking marooned. And this daughter said she could no longer feel any connection to lengthier and lengthier spans of her life. They no longer seemed hers to have lived through. She claimed she did not so much crawl out of her bed in the morning as originate anew from it.

I felt threats already piling up behind everything she said.

"Blow into my life," she said.

My stepsister returned to our table, settled in.

I was looking out of my face at the two of them. I could feel the holes I was looking out at them through. Everything looked rimmed and rounded around. My body must have been sitting behind me or just to the side. The two of me did not quite coincide.

"You have this responsibility," she said.

# CHALAZION

HE SAID, " WE'RE in that van."

He waved toward a small truck idling on the shoulder of the two-lane. The truck was one of the regular white ones, with the red and blue stripes. He walked far ahead of me. Tree branches were thrown all over the road.

He opened the door of the van and led me into the back. I got a quick look at the driver, a man in a sweat suit, before the curtain was parted and we went behind it. He pointed to an armchair upholstered in lima-green vinyl.

"You can have the chair," he said.

I sat down. He sat at my feet, facing me.

"The fellow driving, he don't hear," he said. "He won't know what we're talking about."

"Will we?"

It should not forever have to bear repeating that there are people whose line of work is to make sure that mail gets lost in the mail, and then there were people like me, even at that age.

◆

What "well done" meant to the waitress and the cook didn't jibe with what it meant to the girl's father, which is why the slab of prime rib traveled back and forth between the booth and the kitchen.

The girl had already finished her sandwich. There hadn't been much to it. She looked out the window of the restaurant at the afternoon. It was a rain-blurred gloss on all previous afternoons.

To the best of her knowledge, the girl would never catch up with other girls her own age or even younger. She was merely very clever. Her life was laid out for her in tiny furies.

Her father was absolutely right in his conviction that you have to level with people, that you can't just keep leading them on. His one flaw, he well knew, was that he never got any credit.

Therefore, what? Drive to a discount fashion outlet where they watched you like a hawk? What else would be open?

The father looked across the booth at his daughter. "Well, what's on the agenda?" he said.

The girl opened her mouth.

Shreds, strewings, chippings of an alphabet fell out.

◆

A person at work is under the impression I come from a medium-sized city on the other side of the state. After any holiday, this worker says, "Did you get a chance to go home to . . . ," and then the worker says the full name of it, not the nick one the locals are said to favor. I of course always say no, but I'm not past the point of buying and studying maps of the place. I've learned the names of streets and neighborhoods, of buildings that take up entire blocks. These aren't inroads, though.

◆

The mother says to the son's doctor, "Just so he gets his hair where he'll need it."

The doctor says, "He might be holding it in on purpose."

◆

The day had come. Or at least the sun had come out. On the parking lot I ran into a woman I knew from a former marriage of her husband's. Her features looked a little different. The lower half of her face barely made it up to the upper half anymore. I must have said something courteous enough to her. She must have said something enough in return.

In other words, I asked her, I never should have been parented by or have married or even befriended or been a party to the births of or pursued any of the enmity of the people I had in fact had?

I waited.

I looked at her mouth. It looked definite on her.

"I want an answer," I said. I waited some more.

Neither of us could get one thing to stand for another.

◆

We spent most of an afternoon sifting through the dirt until a neighbor girl finally reached into the pocket of her shorts and fished the thing out. It was a stainless-steel coil with a rubbery carapace over it.

We wanted to be taken for babysat kids. We wanted to bury it in the yard.

Nobody knew what the right tools would have been.

◆

The professor had written his poem but was having trouble finding just the right epigraph until he turned up something in a treasury of zingers from antiquity. But then the damn thing would not stay put at the head of the poem. It kept flapping its way into the left-hand margin. Then it was anagrammatizing itself into unflattering statements about the off-duty life-whiles of the professor.

It started going too far.

The man felt there was no shame in seeking professional help. Wires were set to be run from the serifs of the letters of the words in the epigraph and through the sockets of the hairs in the professor's beard. The risks had to be explained up front. The most serious risk the patient ran was just a soupçon of electrocution (or might it have been electrolysis?), in which case a supplementary wire would then need to be run through the professor's crotch, an even more iffy operation and no longer an outpatient job.

The professor gave the go-ahead in pages and pages—reams— of permission.

Neither procedure was pronounced a success. The professor lost his beard and much of his crotch. The loss cost him his job. The poem was published without the epigraph. The title and all the words in the poem had to be changed. The gist, too, had to go. The changes were made without permission. The poem is now said to be about something else—somebody still patiently lying in wait, all set to be fingered and finagled. It is not for attribution.

◆

People, *persons*, kept getting overheard running off in pairs.

One of these said, "A grown man does not have 'friends.'"

The other said, "Whatever you want to call them then."

♦

All of this should have happened the way one day people would be forever claiming it never once even did. There must have been all three of us this time out. One of the other two had a way of hiding things in her nostrils, in her ear canals: midgetries of tin or rubber, table scraps, the tiniest offcuts of plywood. She could still get her body to depict just about anyone other than herself. May I later be said to have broken something of hers? May it this time be a toy she must have been hoarding for years? Because she had exiled it to a narrow idealizing box beneath her bed. I had not intended to do much harm to the thing. I was only trying to turn it to use. That night I pressed her for its whereabouts. "Something might have happened," I kept saying and saying. I was trying to sound my gravest. I followed her to her room. There was always one more thing I'd know before I knew it.

♦

This might have been in Pittsburgh. Just this once, I did not raise a big stink. In the driveway was a car I could already drive, an automatic. I got in. I drove only as far as the first big building. Inside, I was directed right past HR. A woman in the ladies' room took a load off my mind by telling me I looked exactly how you'd expect a visual learner to look.

"You're all set!" she said.

I later saw my first associate out in the hallway—a woman hurtling toward me in cahoots. I could feel all it—the training, my life—finally of use.

She let on that she was just a go-between.

"Watch," she said.

A man in a suit walked by, a client, bearing a wide, full-weight flagrant envelope. She snapped it out of his hands. When he kept on walking, she handed it off to me.

"What now?" I said. "Look inside."

It was a photo of the neighbor lady.

She had tender sentiments up hers.

◆

It does you no good to be abutting any of the others, but there we sat on porch chairs until our hungers came back.

For groceries, we bought the starkest to be had, brought them home and harrowed them even further with nothing more than the key to the car. It took all three of us to be free to stay or go.

◆

She's had this apartment on her own a long enough time now. She calls it her "affordance." Her feet usually land on my lap as I poke through her husband's mail, both the foolish stuff he gets and the stuff he still sends her.

He keeps saying he's still her husband in every last one of the latter. Set any object at all in front of this guy, and he'll have already seen it through all of its sidelines, things it has yet to be egged on to do.

Her eyes hold everything in.

♦

The mother has managed to rig up a makeshift curtain between the front seat and the back. It's a folded-over yellowing bedsheet secured by clothespins to the roof and to the backs of her seat and the father's too. Then the swack of the father's palm against the mother's bare arm and her cheek as he tells her what all he's found out. The kids trying not to listen to everything the father's saying that's sounding more and more as if it's furnaced. In the backseat, the whispery sibling invents a game. "Close your eyes and open your mouth," the kid crools. "I'm going to put things in, and you've got to guess."

Chewed-off shaft of pencil.

Pinkie.

Corner of tissue.

Toe of sock, but with the toe inside the sock bent back.

AAA battery.

House key.

Something somehow somewhat not.

♦

You can't keep putting a stop to geography. I worked as one third of a team. The fourth of us had quit. There was a small office in which we did the work and a larger, outer one where the woman went when she had to take a call often ten times worse.

♦

At least once every couple of weeks I would have to bring in somebody new, which meant more time outdoors going from person to person and saying, "I'm just getting started, I'm just starting out, you know what it's like, I'm not asking much, have a heart, at least come in and have a look."

Once they made up their minds, I'd let them bring X amount of luggage.

"I'm not your friend," I'd tell whoever it was. "No pets, no visitors. Aside from that, you've got the run of the place."

One or the other of them might get started by deciding to scour the tub. I'd hear every time the can of scouring powder got set down again on the rim.

More and more it was just that women preferred to be done right by themselves, and men were afraid of themselves half the time. Some of the men often lost the very thing I was supposed to be wearing.

But then I've had others who could get up, get dressed, eat a breakfast, watch a talk show, just like that. I mean, A, B, C, D, E— you name it, they'd always know what was next. And then others who'd spend a whole day getting themselves to the brink of being theatrical for people later on.

Just for once I'd like to know just what it was those two thought they were eating.

Not that I would touch it.

I was brought up to let a day go into detail on its own.

♦

There was a father with four daughters who were each a letdown
to him, even in the ice-cream flavors they chose when they each
got a turn.

He looked unfitly astride humanity even in his sleep.

It was the other aunt who dreamed of moving in.

♦

It's true that the fried chicken they served was not beyond compare.
The way they cut it and shaped it so you couldn't tell whether you
were getting a breast or a thigh or a wing—that was novel, though.
In no time I knew what all the cooks and counterpersons looked
like. The issue of dependency became an issue.

Please understand that I did not make conversation with
any of these people or even pretend that I recognized them from
previous visits. I did not assign them names or even nicknames in
my head. For their sake, I pretended that each visit was my first:
I squinted at the menu board and took my time deciding what
to order. I am confident that I made absolutely no impression on
them, that I had not been filed away as the guy who came in every
night and ordered the three-piece special, double mashed, skip
the roll. I stopped by only during the hours I knew they would be
busy, and I ordered take-out only, though the tables looked nice.
So nice, in fact, that I let them be a lesson to me, a lesson about
how much better my betters actually were.

Which naturally means I had a father who lived at a picnic
table in the living room at home—from which it follows that I had
a father with horizontal wrinkles on his forehead that always made
me think of slices of bread stacked on a plate—which explains why

the only bread I allowed myself in those few moments when the thought of bread alone wasn't enough to make me retch was the darkest of toast.

For instance, this is how my father lived at his table: he lived there in a yellow shirt. When I came home from work on Friday nights, he would say, "Well, do you have your week in?"

I'd barely be in the door, and already I'd have to think of the week, the whole trail of facts and toiletries, as something that, in his eyes, had to be wedged, or shoved, into something else.

More often than not, I would be carrying a bagful of fried chicken. More often than not, I would be somebody going back on history not a bit.

◆

The woman's husband was sick. The poor man had been sick for weeks. She kept having to go to the store for things the husband in his sickness kept on needing.

She was there at the store so often, and for such longer and longer times, that other customers, not finding what they were after, started to ask her if she worked there.

She was soon sick to death of having to answer.

She went to the minister for guidance.

The minister was in his fifties. He met parishioners by appointment in his signature condition of shirtlessness, a vein wigglesome in each upper arm.

The woman seated herself, not uncomfortably, at his feet. The feet were shod in chukka boots with deep-cut, pristine tread.

She unburdened herself of what kept happening to her at the store.

The minister told her he had once been met with similar tribulation. His wife had once been very sick. He was often in the store three, four times a day. Customers would ask if he worked there. They wanted help in finding things on the long-stretching, high-rearing shelves.

These were tactless people trying to get their hands on uncreased bags of nut-sweet bread grain, smartly tapered jars of bleached beef-apple hash, thin-cut bars of citron-and-molasses-grass chocolateship, foil-wrapped and duty-free.

He soon tired of inquiries.

Who did these people think they were?

Man of God or not, he was fed up.

He went home to write a book once and for all, so he said, though it turned out to be not much more than a booklet. He'd been afraid to show it to anybody or even bring it up with anyone until now.

"Wait here," he told the woman. "I keep it in a distant room. I've certainly got my walk cut out for me!"

He got up and left.

She could remember the wife he had mentioned. She could picture her, memorially enough, as a spoiled, light-thoughted chippy from the low plains, buried to the nines in a low-cut shroud.

She tried other ways to keep herself busy there on the floor while she waited for the minister to come back. She tried to think about the woman he now was with. She'd been in her company no more than maybe once or twice. This new woman of his gave herself airs of someone far more critically impaired. She remembered hearing this woman boasting of having a daybed and another bed just for nights. Such a cunt, and now with a minister yet!

She thought she could make out from afar the labored rataplan of a manual typewriter set up, no doubt, on a raised plane of sheet metal. The bell of the thing she was certain she heard and then kept on hearing.

An hour must have passed. The minister returned with a little aggregate of papers, at most two or three sheets of brutal typing, triply stapled but not quite in true.

"I'll tell you what," he said, standing over her. He was sweating messingly above her. He tore out the central sheet of the papers. It was typed on only one side. "You take this chapter home. You won't need the whole book."

She thanked him and walked home with the page to her husband. She looked in on him, a sleep-stinkened man busily ablaze with all his afflictions. On the floor to the side of the sickbed was the pallet where she slept, with a striped beach towel for a blanket. This was no time to lie down.

She went into the other room to study the sheet of paper. It held a chapter all to itself. The title was "What to Say." She read it reveringly.

It began, "What to say will depend on your mood." The chapter included lots of examples with a cautionary note that said they were just that—examples. The book went on to say, "Not every individual who is setting out to shop for a spouse at death's door can be expected to pass through the same moods as another, much as the bodies of the spouses themselves hanker differently after disease."

She read the chapter and did her studious best to memorize the things to be said if people were to ever again put to her the question "Do you work here?"

Block quotations are unsightly, an abomination, but we are left here with no other choice. What follows is but an excerpt:

> Should your mood be one of annoyance, then say, "Oh, but do I seem to be wearing a name tag, or a smock, or a vest, or any other article of attire identifying me as an employee of this store? You say I am apparently not thus garbed? Then fuck you." Should your mood be one of affability, though this doesn't sound like you even one little bit, then say, "Funny, but I was just about to ask you the same thing!" Should your mood be one of hostility, then say, "You look exactly like the type of peon I'd expect to find working in a shithole like this and no doubt begging for even more hours." Should your mood for once in your life be one of modesty, then say, "No, I filled out many an application and never made the cut, never got called in for an interview, but, heck, I might as well keep trying." Should your mood be one of atrabiliousness, then say, "Why, yes, I do, but we no longer wait on your kind." Should your mood be one of the coldnesses that come from one interruption too many, then say, "Yes, I am the store detective, and we've had our eye on you for some time now. Would you be so kind as to follow me so that the strip search by committee might commence?"

The woman studied and studied, memorized and memorized, then went off to her pallet for the night.

In the morning, she returned to the store.

People talked back.

# THE COURTESY OF A REPLY

SEVEN OF THEM in attendance, of the twenty-two who should have been present. (I hadn't yet worked out the distinction between *attendance* as a function of the body and *presence* as spectatorship, receptivity.) The males who had settled for the course as an elective fitting their time slot were mostly gone by the end of the first week or the beginning of the second. The classroom had no clock, but students not wearing watches discovered how to reckon time manually, sounding the quarter-hours with accurate spanks of the knee, marking off the minutes with ticky clicks of ballpoints. Individual minutes were fractioned down even further by measurely eyeblinks that exceeded what muscles or habit required. I could count on students to bring the smells of the weather along with them into the room. These kids were young but youthless. Some of them were doers. At their seats, these would count pocket money, attend to overdue housecleaning of their wallets and handbags, write bill-paying checks, wrap gifts, perform chairbound calisthenics. Others dined. Still others brought babies or strays. I enjoyed the mutter from the heat ducts. The students favored overlarge, overgreat wand-like pens. There were accidents in their spelling: "treatise," often as not, came out as "treaty." When I passed out handouts, a lot of these kids would not move. They wouldn't reposition their outbent legs or backpacks. The required reading for the course was a paperback with a cream-colored cover that attracted the reader's blemishing fingerhold and afterward blackly hosted whatever soots and grimings the hand had brought along. The book came shrink-wrapped and disintegrated, came unglued, with each turn of the leaves. I heard many complaints about this book. A cloud of some sort, a massive woolpack, was said to occupy the entire works. Other students claimed that even though the words were set out only seven or eight to a column on the double-columned pages, the reader got chased straight into the margins. One girl complained that the words either sank deep beneath the level of the page and blurred away or else shot up and jutted right out at you. Another maintained that the pages, if tilted toward the light just so, could be seen to have glazings and frothings, or else a ghost aurora. I countered that the title page looked like a welcome mat and that I'd taken many a lap of the chapters myself. Plus, in this edition you got both a "Preface to the Student" and a "Preface to the Instructor," and there was a chummy intimacy to the former and, to the latter, a satisfying approximation of having gotten into somebody else's mail. Most days, I had the students read out loud. I liked to listen to their voices run down. One day I called on a front-row woman whose self-conscious soprano began to fail after half a page. It was as if the entire voice structure inside her were coming apart. A silence started to cumulate around her. I had to take over midsentence, and after class the woman trailed me to my office. I had to show her to a chair that had wheels underneath it. As soon as she sat down, I could make out every disturbance in the foreground-background relations in her face. Like others in her generation, she called me a troublemaker, an agitator, a provoker, and a busybody, and there were of course no framed photos of anybody on my desk, nothing on the wall I could point to or even glance in the direction of, so the woman had her big, fulfilling tantrums and withdrew. I had another class in five minutes, but I fell to work, entering grades into the thick looseleaf registrum.

Once the door to the classroom gets shut from inside, knowledge tends to widen and dilate a little. I at least had the run of the subject matter, though I sometimes put different, cooling words to it.

The syllabus—the scheme of assignments, the slate of due dates, the dress codes ("Don't wear anything you'd sell in a pinch") and other policies of bodily conduct—had been filched from something I'd once read way in the back of a law library. This syllabus was a great-sized affair but was available in abridged, booklet form as well.

It's true that in class I talked a lot about shoplifting, because that was something I still kept a hand in myself. I'd bring to class some articles from my "levitations," as I called them. Rolls of store-brand shelf paper, those overscaled safety pins for kilts.

The ideal test was one that a student could pass without having studied but instead by having spent some time in the company, in the proximity, of the "material." The answers were not so much written out as pounded onto the page.

The few males left tended to have beards. I can understand a face wanting to cover itself up. Each sulky set of students had a distinct, rain-or-shine personality, but nothing else was ever axiomatic enough about them. People of that generation were swift-spoken, scented like sun-showers. They welcomed themselves to cots in the nurse's office.

They liked to copy and recopy their notes and keep their fingernails bitten bare.

After class, things would be left behind at chairs I couldn't remember anyone having sat at. I would carry everything to the lost-and-found chest at one of the outstations of the security department. It would more often than not be a left-behind notebook full of re-agitations of some facts from a lecture, tight curls of words, the first line of a fresh page indented no matter what, the pink pinstripe of the margin breezily unheeded. "At the end of the semester, come and get it," the security officer would say. "It could all be yours."

In my office, I'd piss into a soda bottle, a sixteen-ouncer, plastic. It was better than being seen patronizing the restroom every twenty, thirty minutes. I was someone who always had to go.

The phone would ring and ring. If I answered, I'd be told there was "another concern."

I loved telephone numbers in and of themselves, though. I loved the medial, intervenient hyphen keeping those two groupings of digits from getting too close.

I began referring to my classes as seatings: there was a ten-o'clock seating, another at eleven, others at one, two, and four.

The departmental secretary was chirkingly polite. She was quite the quiz. She always knew how fast everybody's marriage was crumbling into dust. There were slumps between everyone's legs in those days.

If it wasn't a clean life, though, it was a life in which there was much that could have still been kept pretty clean, if one had been of a mind.

The house where I lived—it had *been* a house. It was now more like a dorm. I lived there with other men in unguessable hierarchy, one to a room. The rooms were hut-like and entire unto themselves. I think some of the men might have been getting paid to live there. All night long, I'd hear their stirrings and by-turnings, their every thunge and flomp. (To this day, I'm told, people reorganize themselves at all hours.) The one I sometimes talked to referred to his midget TV as "the vision." It was not exactly what I would call talk, though. He brought words together, or brought them almost within reach of one another, but that was usually as far as he got. He sometimes got a word sunk in a running murmur he then kept up. I mistimed my own swallows. His face was the type whose features looked smeared on, as if they hadn't been allowed to settle just yet. I was interested, I suppose, in reconstituting my own loneliness in those days too. There was much to remodel. I never got very far in my sleep. I'd fallen into the habit of waking up exactly on the hour or half-hour, even though the digital clock—the little band of digits I'd read off a display on the fax machine—was off by five, six minutes.

I'd kept the fax machine because there were still two or three people to whom I now and then thought to ask, "What are you getting out of this?" or "Who else do you expect to get to go along?," then have to decide whether it was worth the bother to wait for a reply.

My life still drew ants.

# WRITTEN AT WORK

A STORY OF this sort can't wait to get itself over with. No matter how hard I try to drag the thing out, it keeps stopping short. It's very much to the point and apropos of anything else people were saying about me in those days that had deluge after deluge of truth in it.

To wit, I once had an officemate with dandruff in his eyebrows—steep ridges of it crusting visibly through the fringe of blackest hairs. He taught several renditions of beginners' math. This was at a for-profit business school in one of the outbuildings of a mall now obsolescing pretty awful. Toward the end of our first week together, this officemate confided to me that before lights-out every night he had to lather the eyebrows with a tar-extract shampoo, the strongest and the most likely to sting of the ones still allowable by law. He explained that he would pinch the shampoo deep into the flesh beneath the hairs, leave it set there until just before breakfast, then rinse with some preparation said to be a blend of soothing waters all the world over. (Back then—I was in my inelastic, middle twenties, scarcely eligible for inner life—zealotries of any uncourtly sort could win me over in an instant.) Mornings, from my desk, I would watch him swipe a finger gently, exploratively, through the eyebrows to see if any flakelets would start drifting down onto the lenses of his spectacles. If any did, he would drop whatever else he might have been doing—drafting a memo of understanding, most likely—and rub his eyebrows raw. After a few minutes, he would take off his glasses and swipe a finger across each lens until he had a greasy mass of grayish scales piled against the nose pad. Then it was time to decide whether to deposit the scales into a lenient envelope he stored in the file drawer of his desk or smear them onto the mouth of the plastic bag lining the wastebasket. He kept some water in a Styrofoam cup on his desk. He would dip his fingers into it after he was finished with his brows. The other thing about this man was that he suffered from a not uncommonplace allergy a good three or four months of the year. His nose would run and run, and he would try to stop it with a handkerchiefed finger up a nostril, but there was no point in returning the handkerchief to his back pocket afterward, because he was only going to need it again moments later, when his nose started leaking again. In no time, a lone handkerchief would be drippled, drenched, good for nothing. This explained why, during allergy season, his desktop fixtures—the tape dispenser, the stapler, the calendar pad, the cardless rotary file for addresses and telephone numbers, the telephone itself, also rotary (it dazes me to this day that the man apparently had no mathematical trappings at all)—got blanketed, ghosted over, with handkerchiefs soaked through and through. Sometimes he would have as many as a half dozen of the things going all at once, in rotation, counterclockwise.

I was there the afternoon the marshal of the math department and the hierarch came by together. The hierarch gave me a couple of pats of approval on my shoulder, then withdrew. The marshal threw some file folders onto the floor. They fell open to batches of exams my officemate had graded with check-marky underexertion. My officemate had not yet cleared off the lenses of his glasses after lunch—they were already pretty snowy again— and he had a handkerchief, the first of the new hour, spread napkinwise on his lap. The marshal told him he would be placed on probation for another two pay periods. He was also told to put more thought into what he said over the phone, both to students and to any howling elders of theirs no longer made of money. This I thought was a point worth making. I'd never heard him get very elaborative on the phone. I'd never heard him say anything other than "The question you have put to me is beyond the scope of my life, my work, and my life's work."

The reprimand went on for a while. I picked up a magazine I had already read partway and read it a little further. I always got stuck on an article in there about a woman neither thriving in the occupative guise of a bagger at a supermarket nor feeling her way to any other shrewd callings in life. I was a woman myself, many times over—shushed and plain-eyed and within reach of another dead end of my personality. My heart was running out of hoaxes to put over on itself.

At the retrenchment party for some furloughed co-workers, a man whose job had been spared in this round told me that at the last outfit he'd worked for, he got stuck with field-interviewing people newly pauperized, and some woman answered his questions while peeing pleasantly into a tureen on the floor. He kept his mouth open for me just a little, exposing startlingly straight teeth the yellow of canned corn. A few others approached me, mostly to say, "I'm not about to coax you," though every now and then it would be "Or would you rather I be frank?" After I left, I didn't feel up to going anywhere close to homeward just yet, so I made the first of my customary stops. A senior administrator—the one that was housemotherly temperamental and apparently nobody's fool—was pushing a cart out of a supermarket just as I was making my way across the parking lot toward the store. We ignored each other triumphantly.

Once, in my earlier twenties, I was visiting my parents for leftovers, and they decided we should make the drive to a mall about an hour and a half from where they lived. This was a mall none of us had ever tried out before, an already moot place with boarded-over skylights. We were working our way through a large-appliance department when a middle-aged saleslady with a drugstore complexion threw a halting arm out toward me and said, "So *here* you are! Where have you been keeping yourself? You been in hiding again? You get tired of me, or what?" My parents later said, "What was that all about?" There had long been other things about me, too.

My title, my position by that point, was Auxiliary Junior Administrative Adjunct. They had me teaching only one half of a course every semester in addition to practicing lower-order mathematical devotions at my desk. In the classroom, I was unopinionated, unquibbling, open to anything anybody might want to say about anything adjacent to the topic or even at crooked removes from it.

There was a dreary-eyed chit here on an internship a while back. A promontory of reference books stacked at the front of the desk kept her mostly out of sight. Crayolan hair, inflictions of wire glued to her teeth, a bulk of chainworks troubled around her neck, sleeves that belled outward as they reached practically all the way to fingertips sleekened alternately a smoke-grimed blue and the brownish orange of terra-cotta—there was nobody to accuse us of what the two of us were doing, even if we were barely doing it. My eyes tend to water a little when I know I won't be caught.

People with a quiet way of entering rooms see more than their fair share. I grew up the third of three girls. We'd had our lives cut out for us. What was cut out for us didn't have much in the way of give.

I once killed a month in turmoils of marriage to a man out of my caste, a man who never once stopped bragging of better lives he could resume as soon as we called it quits. Hair of the blackest grade had authority over his arms, his legs, his chest, and there was the respiratorily reckless way he slept, the jubilating way he paid out of pocket for pharmaceuticals that left his moods unimproved. There had been a lot of guesswork in how we expected love to arise finally between us.

The truth was that I was always prissy about my toothaches and was a diabetic in the making. I had no outside interests, but getting away from that apartment of ours—of *his*—as many times a day as possible was my only true calling.

I'm typing this in the new office I'm being treated to temporarily. It's just until the leaks in my ceiling get fixed. Minutes ago, I wandered down the corridor to the ladies' room. A man was knocking on the door of the men's room, and a voice within cried, "Yes?" These are one-toilet units, and there's an inconsistency in their design. To lock the ladies' room down here, you have to turn a little dial one way, but in the ladies' room upstairs, the one I frequented during months and months of collywobbles, you have to turn the dial the other way. I get confused, so almost every time

I walk into the one down here, I immediately have to step outside and re-enter, this time playing with the lock, just to make sure. I don't want to be barged in on. I have twice walked in on show-offs who didn't bother to lock, and it's unsporting to see people, people you don't prize, in the semi-fetal crouch of a mist-wreathen workplace crap. Both times, though, they apologized to *me*, and I rushed off, all nerves, to do something careerwise, anything Xeroxably arcane.

I sometimes reward myself with an extra hour or two for lunch. One day I wound up at a budget steakhouse, in line behind a couple of thirtyish men wearing identical rings. One of them was balding and manicured to a fare-thee-well. I might as well just go ahead and call him Paul. Paul had a medium build and dirty-blond hair. Paul's husband—I'll call him Sal—was slouched and paunchy. A size-and-inseam label was still tacked to the waistband of his pants. They both ordered some sort of grandiose duplex cheeseburger and the salad bar. They worked their way along the cafeteria-style counter toward the cash register, and Paul fingered a stack of coffee cups, examining one cup after another without ever committing to one of them. He asked the girl behind the register if he could speak to the manager. The manager, a man in his late twenties, appeared lickety-split but with little magic to his arrival. Paul said to him, "Where does one find things like these?" The manager said, "Oh, anything like that we get from Waldplatz." Paul said, "Do you suppose I could buy some? I'd take at least six." The register girl said, "Why not just buy two and just keep washing them?" I think all of us, except the girl, must have colored a little. It was as if we could look all the way through her, back to when she'd been babysat. But we could picture the babysitters only partway, only about as far up as just above the knees. Anything farther up on those girls must have long ago been crossed out or cut off. Their breasts, their arms and faces, were as much as zilch to us. Their voices might as well have been smoke. But why is it that there's never enough to people? Why must my own life remain to be seen?

I never knew what to think, or what it must be like to keep smacking thoughts around in your head all day long. My only remembered dream from last night involved a heated argument with a co-worker about the differences between the ordering of sections in the local paper and in *USA Today*.

Pets aren't allowed in the building where I now live, but in the stairwell I keep running into a woman who has a dog of a junior sort, a mousy and unvocal thing with trouble maintaining its shape.

The parking lot is all ice. I traversed it with a box of light bulbs an hour ago. I put a new blade in my razor—typically a pick-me-up.

I turn on the radio. The forecast calls for "isolated snow."

I make pasta. Then the unexpected good fortune of turning up a Long John Silver's plastic fork to eat it with.

I never got good at spreading things thin. I needed everything thick and threatening. That Sunday at the mall, I would make sure to drop by my parents' bench every twenty minutes or so. On one visit, my mother tugged at my tank dress and said, "Feel how heavy my handbag is." It was packed with fast-food napkins and straws and individually wrapped white-plastic spoons and forks and coupon caddies, but it wasn't heavy at all, and I told her so. During the next visit, my father said, "I want to ask you a question, and I don't want a sassy answer or any more fibs: You're saying you're sure your microwave still works?"

It's not that there aren't one or two people who will still open their doors to me if I keep up the pounding. This one, rummaged-looking in a raisin-black robe, admits me after the third round. She says she went fishing earlier with her ex-husband and caught an enormous catfish that refused to surrender its life. It continued to flop about even after she dragged the thing home. Her housemate, her ex's brother, whacked its head repeatedly with a ballpeen hammer until the thing stopped moving. But when she began cleaning it, hacking away at it, discovering in its stomach crawfish and minnows and a sackful of eggs, she at last came upon a tiny heart still beating with pestering regularity. She punctured it with a pin. Blood spurted all over the table. Tonight we eat clammy pasta and later kiss more pettily than ever while the housemate does the dishes.

In a book of narrow, mattery columns, too many to a page, it was explained how to ask your parents for your birth certificate when the time finally comes.

I must have needed mine for some concern or another at work. My parents right away told me they knew of no such thing. They spoke practically in unison.

If I drove into the city, I usually parked sixty, seventy blocks away from wherever I thought I ought to be going. Walking was the only point to being at liberty in a place as big as that. There was an eatery there called Pizza Care. Last night, I met the woman who lives above me, over me, however it has to be put. She came down to complain about the noise.

"Noise?" I said. I stood in the doorway looking at her. She looked half vanished.

"You know what I'm talking about."

"No. I don't."

"Things being gone through. Things being chewed over. Lips smacking. Arms being crossed. Pulling yourself together till all hours. Always standing on your own two feet. Always putting yourself first."

I'll probably wait another week to have my car towed.

Driving home from work, I got stuck in single-lane traffic behind a vintage station wagon with the gate down. Lounging in the back, facing me, were a tressy boy, maybe twenty, and a close-cropped girl maybe a year or two older. Both were triumphs of molding and sheen. The boy started staring at me. It was a loaded, unnegotiable stare. He moved his lips, just barely, and then the girl was staring at me, too. Then we were stopped at a stoplight. I visited my own stare upon them—a stare that cored, you best believe. The light turned green, and the boy pivoted around to say something to the driver. He never pivoted back. The girl was still facing me, squinty, looking drained.

Back at my apartment, I write another song on my guitar. I write two sets of lyrics, one for Jenni (bilious) and one for Senta (moonstruck anew). The melody is sixties-ish, watered-down pseudo-Beatlesque. The refrain in the Senta version is "Can't we just ditch this business of shifting for ourselves?' It's this version I record on cassette. The vocals are mumbly but reverent, rectifying. There is nothing between Senta and me by this point but piping-hot buddyhood of a type. She lives on Doritos and sundae cones. I let her smoke in here. For an ashtray, she uses a lemon-squeezer dish I bought at an odd-lots place. She tells me that as a kid, nothing scared her more than being told, "Get ready for bed!" She'd think, "What does that even mean? Exactly what is it I'm supposed to be preparing myself for? What all's going to be happening to me there?" She's twenty-five, twenty-six, with little left ungiven of herself. I'm all set for passing anything up.

From my late teens until my mid-twenties, I had a Christmas Eve routine. I would walk to the sorriest discount department store in town and not leave until they closed. (The sorriest of these was a place where you had to pay to use the toilet, though the store had its own barbershop.) Customers, mostly men, would be hectically grabbing anything boxed festively enough, and I'd wander the aisles, looking at whatever could be bought and taken home in an effort to placate or to pointedly disappoint.

I had to get my driver's license renewed. I kept putting it off. I bought time by buying a temporary from a jocularly skeptical notary, but the thing had a typo. Today I felt I could no longer postpone my visit to the Photo License Center, because in a dream last night, I was trying to tell a woman behind a counter that the spelling of the name of my street was off by more than one letter. In the dream, the woman said, "But I want to hear all about it! I hope you'll feel you can tell me everything! Please don't hold anything back on my account! But first I have to quick go do something in the back!" Then she backed away from the counter and vanished. I'd rather not think of her as a stand-in for my mother. My parents tended to spill beans, the really big, emotional, gas-firing ones, only when we were seated around each other at already crowded food courts. ("Now, Annie Ann, we want you to know that we've got a cemetery plot just for you. And your father is triply unwell. I'll wait till we get to the other mall to tell you a little something clinically newsy about myself.") Today, at the Photo License Center, I withheld an assortment of my troubles from a woman in a wheelchair who tried her best to take my picture. "Your eyes have to be open," she said after the first shot. After the second: "Now they're open, but I can't see them. There's too much glare." Then: "Nope. Tip your glasses up just a tiny bit. No, no, not like that." This went on. I left with another temporary.

At home, the tone of the building has changed yet again. The tenants beneath me must have become different people. They've substituted new noises for the old, familiar ones. I'm just assuming it's still the same people down there, just somehow better refreshed in their woe.

My phone rang the other night. I picked it up, but the thing continued to ring. I kept saying hello, and the phone just kept on ringing.

The rental house across the street—a ramshackle, shingled affair, long and narrow and low to the ground—had been dark and quiet for a few months after a downcast family had to have their furniture trucked away, but it's got new tenants: students at the beauty academy downtown. They must be in their early twenties, these slight young men with toasted-brown hair who wear uniforms that look like a cross between a fast-food worker's costume and something almost astronautal. One of them, girlish, sits on the front stoop a lot, sometimes with a book, maybe a textbook. He's conveniently there most evenings when I pull into my parking space after work. But tonight he was walking up Main Street just as I was walking down it, on my way back from an hour or two at Emily's again. (She's usually good at falling asleep loveworn in my arms, but tonight her hair, normally upswept, was an awning she kept lowering and lowering until it covered her eyes and most of her nose, and she didn't have a kind word for me or my devotional distaste for people she hated even more.) He looked me up and down, this unmiserable cosmetologist-to-be. My apartment has lots of windows—eight of them, in fact—but not a single one faces that house that he not only lives in but no doubt overruns. I stoop to making up excuses to myself to stay outdoors (inspecting my car, say, for freshly indefinite vandalisms) in order to keep an eye on him. Life keeps throwing a little something my way, though it's never anything handledly human I could use.

One night at a department store, an employee, a woman in a commodious sort of middle age, says to me, almost sweetly, "You're in here an awful lot. You're a price-spy, right?"

It was only a week ago I found myself standing before a bank of telephone directories at the public library downtown. I was in an exploratory mood and tried to run down a few names. I found a childhood classmate on a bonnily named drive in a suburb of a city not too far away, but it was probably somebody else laden with the same middle initial. In elementary school—either first or second grade—I'd sat across the aisle from her, and we'd pass notes back and forth on coarse gray tablet paper: "You are a car," "You are a house," "You are a street," "You are where my dad parks on the street." During recess, she'd walk over to where I'd be leaning against a fence. She'd look at me, erupt into giggles, then run toward the trees. Is it to her, then, that I most owe my having decided tonight to empty out my living room and get everything stacked up in the other room until it looks just as ungathered and suspect there? The grunts and whoops in the apartment below might be the fruits of nothing more personal than football on TV. Dinner will be some frozen stuff that'll stay frozen down in the car until I feel up to going out to fetch it.

From an upper level of the municipal parking deck where I sometimes hide, I one day saw a group of four or five people in their twenties, possibly a tad retarded, walking along a road that leads to a mall, each clutching a jumbo bag of popcorn.

Linni? The closest I ever got to myself was when I watched her take me into her eyes. Later, from my vantage on the bed, her ass had a visage of its own, practically. Almost every day I run into the man she's involved with. At a quick-serve Chinese place, I'm served a bowl of rice with a hair in it, and I tell myself, "Good, I've got some company." People add up like that.

You'd want to think, the next one said, that there had to be a seductive and irrefutable progression from living room to kitchen to bedroom. She asked if I'd be up for picturing her life as continent after continent of graph paper not even written on a little. Such are the sweatful exactions of somebody trying somebody else's damnedest to be somebody else still.

Then one morning my car wouldn't start. A grave-faced little boy (from the building, I supposed) approached my car and tapped at my window. I rolled it down pretty irritably, I confess. The boy pointed into a wastebasket he was carrying. In it was a puzzling miscellany of grisly auto parts collected who knows how. I rolled up my window and sat there until he left. The engine eventually aroused itself somehow. I made it in to work. The workday was boldly dulling. The cash registers at the snack bar were on the fritz, so orders had to be written down, totals reckoned with a calculator. I got through the afternoon by thinking about a girl I'd tried to get to know in college. She had always managed to stand with her back to the world, so how come I kept remembering her in a blue windbreaker zipped up without pity to her neck? How come I could still make out the unmockable outpoking of her breasts? I came home to a note posted on one of the front doors of the apartment house: "INSPECTORS PLEASE GO TO THE FOURTH FLOOR." I still live in alarmist carnivorous disorder on the third. Dinner, though, was another smorgasbord of mashed potatoes and candy on the floor. Afterward, before my bath, I pressed my ear against a wall and could make out the sounds of at least friendship on the other side. Something eventually got itself expressed catarrhally. I'm certain I heard positions on cushions being shifted decisively. I moved to the wall at the other end of my apartment. I heard a woman's voice say, "We'll do the laundry once we get to the motel." I assumed it was evictedness I was hearing in her tonations. My sleep later that night wouldn't stop making fun of me.

I don't expect straight answers from anyone, or questions put to me without insinuative curvilinearities.

I get asked to give a talk to a class of grade-school kids. The topic is "being smart when it's time to choose a vocation." I get things stretched out to seven minutes short on specifics. From the questions put to me afterward, I gather that the kids thought I was trying to talk about where to go on vacation. The teacher later asks them to write thank-yous on mulberry-purple construction paper. The notes arrive in a beribboned sheaf. They all turn out to be variations on the theme of the first one I unfold: "You look aloned."

Then a workday so full of incivility at every turn that midway through my final meeting, I came close to walking out of the room, but I kept thinking, *Walk where?* Afterward, I set out on another desultory tour of the local shopping plazas, and, over the course of two and a half hours, I stood at the snack bars of discount department stores and put away a grilled-chicken sandwich, two hamburgers, a large soft pretzel, two orders of French fries, a handsomely pouched threesome of chocolate-chip cookies, several Diet Cokes and Diet Pepsis, and an odalisque of a hot dog, sickly pink and asprawl on its untidied bed of bun. All of this was paid for with the eighteen tatty dollar bills handed off to me by a nomadic buyer of textbook desk copies who'd caught me halfway through some hyperventilations during my mandatory office hour midweek. (She'd looked around, motioned playfully, or at least tried to, and said, "Maybe police this place up a bit?") Then I drove to the video-rental place but left empty-handed. Then I shoved my way through a couple of supermarkets. I bought a ten-ounce bag of Nestle Toll House morsels. I stuck it into my glove compartment. I drove to a mall and looked at the puppies in a pet store. I kept my eye on a dachshund adoze in a pail. Then I drove home, but I couldn't stay put. I got into my car again and drove to Walmart and bought some fruitless soap. There was a young woman, maybe twenty-six, twenty-seven, sitting dejectedly on a bench near the checkouts. I looked at her, and she might have looked at me. I drove home and looked in a cupboard to see if I still had the butts of any of the cigarettes she had smoked in my apartment three or four years ago (but, no, they weren't there; I must have tossed them out after further rounds of being let down by her), because, several nights a week, she had shown up, out of the blue, to tell me, in installments, the story of her life, which was mostly about how a succession of men had applied themselves to her in not unwelcomed bad faith, and I'd wound up writing her three songs (recording a rhythm-guitar track first, then overdubbing a lead-guitar track, and then, above those, a vocal track, my voice mortal, untuneful, inexcusably intemperate), a cassette of which I dispatched to her in an overstamped padded mailer. She was, she claimed, a seer (though the things she foresaw, she added, were better left uninterfered with) and a budget-minded compulsive shopper: she already felt free enough to ask if she could stash some things at my apartment (a Mr. Coffee machine, a dustpan and brush, some cleaning buckets, a business traveler's hair-removal kit, a couple of featherweight pastel dumbbells, a set of plastic wine glasses shaped exactly like tumblers just to keep people fooled) because she was still living with her scantling of a father and didn't want him to find out she was planning on moving in so soon with her girlfriend, a cosmetologist of local renown and with a face (in the snapshots I asked to see) looking eternalized and perishable all at once. "But I'll always love you, too, honeybunch, and I'll call you every day," she right away better have damn well said. The girlfriend ditched her within a week or two. She wound up next with a surgeon—a veterinarian, it turned out. By that point, she was intent on becoming somebody fond of leaving people undeservedly behind. We always sat on the floor at opposite ends of my bedroom. We never once touched, even by accident by the door. Her new place was on the third story of a dormered rental. She claimed somebody kept sneaking up to the attic at night to spy on her. (She had a periscope or two of her own, though one was just the kiddie kind.) She called me at work one day and told me to meet her at the Denny's closest to her. I was first to arrive. I waited an hour. She showed up ruiningly buoyant but smelling like a brewery again. She explained that an art-history professor eight states away was ready to leave her husband and her kids for her. They were going to have their own lake. She told me she'd found a job at a factory where she operated dangerous machinery that she alone would one day tame. Her hair had been newly reduced to a crew cut. She was already tattoo-sleeved by then, and a little bossy about picking up the check. I now run into her maybe once or twice a year. The second-last time was at a Wendy's. Her hair was growing out again. We pretended not to see each other.

Yesterday the maintenance man stopped by to inspect the air-conditioning unit. He walked straight toward the thing, taking care not to look at anything else or at me in my tissuey shorts, braless, my breasts already goblins gone soft.

I later find a bag of rolls, a half dozen of them, kaisers, nice and green by now, behind the little chest of drawers next to the bathroom sink. I remember buying them, just not carrying them that far.

Some people are geniuses at moving from one thing to the next. They keep this up all day long. They know how to get ahead, even if it's only spending an entire morning ironing things they'll never dare wear in front of people even more inglorious in their pinings and their drives.

There's little point in my going any wider of the facts. I think it was four days ago that somebody smashed a glass tumbler in the parking spot I always claim here at the complex. (The shatterings are still there, unswept.) Two days later, I called in sick—my first time in years. I got myself dressed: pencil skirt, scoop-neck top, half-sleeved cardigan. I spent most of the day lying on the carpet, as if convicted already. Midafternoon, I got up and drove to an enlarged supermarket several towns south. At the deli counter I chose the greasiest of the chickens in rotisseried rotation. I carried it into my apartment. The bottom of the bag split. The chicken spilled out onto the carpet. I had no other food to my name. I told myself, "I'll eat only the parts that didn't touch the rug." I still had some vinyl exam gloves left over. I slipped on a pair of those. I ate as self-endearingly as I could manage. I later turned up a lump sum of cheapest clumped chocolate I'd forgotten about. I took some interest in it. This was back in the days when the phone company still had you paying by the minute. That month, my bill topped off at about three hundred and fifty dollars. Even now, I talk but do not engross.

Everything people said or did in those days was bedeviled with a vague and unsettling valedictory air. I might as well get something out of my system about my sisters. They were born a year apart but passed themselves off as twins trying feebly to differentiate themselves from each other. (One never learned how to drive but could always tell you the day's price of gas down to the fraction of a cent; the other was almost never not sewing and preferred love that was a little grueling.) They'd each had their shot at loveliness of a sort, that upsoaring of beauty every woman with some youth left in her enjoys for at least a season or two, but they never seemed to know what their hearts might be up to, and in time they let life bunch up on them, and both ended up marrying pretty much the same man, a plumber in one case, an electrician in the other, and they stuck it out with personal touches that must have gotten the job done. I saw them during the holidays every other year or so. They wrote me off as a cheat, a backbiter, a vilifier, and a slut.

My heart had always liked to horse around. There was a fondling at the bank I'd switched to for the free toaster oven, the checking with interest. We were of similar stooped height, similar wobbling views of ourselves as adults forever new to adulthood. I could recount the weeks of leisurely unrest we squandered with chemicals that bleached all imagery out of our dreams, or, on the contrary, I could be furious that I should have once owned such telltale Melmac plates the two of us ate from in such underlit fetid undress, but, on balance, she introduced me to her sister, a woman odorless everywhere on her, a bookworm who read combatively, putting up a fight against everything the words said, even if all they were saying was how it will have once seemed that everybody was living more than one life at a time and that every busy hand, sealing an envelope or washing a dish, had become a semaphore, flashing the signals to welcome you into a secret, difficult love.

I make it a point not to keep up with people. I make it a point to look as if I'm living in some other streaming course of things completely.

Then Ingrid, though: she'd been married and again and again tried to explain the marriage (there was some sex she was technically still owed but intended to forgo, there had been some showboating infidelities of her own, etc.), but I was used to hearing pretty much the same thing from practically everyone—that too much had happened not too long ago without enough benefit of surroundings, of duration and enduringness, but as soon as they ever got enough cash together, they were going to round all the people up and have it happen all over again, then back off even quicker this time.

"What about you?" she says. (This Ingrid has manners.)

I tell her that life might have had enough of me already. I tell her that the place I live is mostly transients now. Weekends, there's a tractor-trailer cab parked in the lot, and early on Monday mornings, it's out there idling for hours, waking everybody else up.

"You go out at all?" she says.

I mention a midafternoon sprint into CVS for two packets of M&Ms. "You're throwing money at me!" the plus-sized counterwoman had screamed, because a couple of quarters flew toward her as I fished a fiver out of the pockets of my slacks.

"All anything should call for is an easy-enough signature," she makes sure she says plainly.

The only person still talking to me at work confessed that life wasn't fodder enough for her anymore. She looked good in blue, though, with that typically sticky frosting of makeup. She had somehow expected the office to be more of an erotic environment than it was turning out to be. There were accruals of something possibly cruel in her eyes. She'd grown up in a family unusually shorthanded when it came time to scatter any affection around. Her father had had a godsend hernia to nurse, her mother sent all her prayers overseas, and there was a sister she never got in good with. Her roommates in college had left her alone, and her first love had been a woman in the last storm surges of her early thirties. This woman—an Elona, I later found out—could be scaldingly self-contained one minute, then the next minute have trouble getting herself back up to life size. Elona had no use for what her body wanted her to do. Elona would have been satisfied with any end in sight. Everything was Elona this, Elona that for a while, and I was soon making it a point not to keep up, though I wasn't tiring of the details themselves. The last my new friend had heard, Elona had tripped into a marriage with a man whose past was said to never once show through on him. Again, I never minded listening to my friend, if I may keep getting away with calling her that, go on and on about herself. I've usually preferred people with little to spare in their nature. She was soon sharing photos of her furniture, of her parents' beflowered gravestead, of her sister, now wracked in a chance marriage, looking impassionedly nonchalant behind a register at a fabric store, a prune-purple bruise on the one forearm showing. We started observing each other's birthdays. We cheered each other on through the hours until we could wring a day free from its drivel of minutes and see each other off (her commute home involved two tricky transfers; I typically now walked, in merriments I had no right to feel just yet). Some nights she called me near tears but never ready to cross any threshold. I was always struck by the breadth of everything she never suspected about me. She would sometimes put the phone down without hanging up. I could sometimes hear her taking her time on the toilet. (Those days, I was quick to take anything as an overture.) Some mornings she brought me things she'd baked—cookies with abstruse names ("shuckerwinkles," "ladyskins," "doodlehusks," "pappy peels," "redcaps") that were often as not hard on my teeth. Other days, she would dive for cover in her folders, her portfolios, then ignore me altogether. The winter that year was beyond tropical. The dress code had to be relaxed, and then relaxed again and again, until the house modiste was calling for hemlines that went all the way up to the waist. You could gape through practically anyone to everything and everybody even farther beyond. When spring came, there wasn't all that much left that hadn't already been spritzed to the breaking point. Then the drought set in. By summer we were, all of us, coarsened, raw-hearted, assassinative. Fall returned us all to tact and timidity. Through it all, all through the year, I sometimes lost sight of my friend for weeks at a time. (She alone was given dispensation to do some of her work from home.) Then her calls stopped. I got used to going unscrutinized again through week after week. People walked loathingly past me on their way to other people. She gave her two weeks' notice. (I remembered her having once mentioned a background in something or other that entitled her to be a leading light in off hours and on weekends.) It turned out to be a good thing that people were starting to get me mixed up with somebody else. (One morning alone, I was taken for a Lisa, a Cindy, an Andrea.) It was a good thing because it got me thinking that I might possibly have the makings in me of some other person completely. One hand may wash the other, I mean, and both hands may wash the face, but the shoe is always on the other foot.

# acknowledgments

The author expresses deepest gratitude to Derek White, to Elizabeth Ellen, and to Anna DeForest, Lauren Leja, Alban Fischer, Keith Jones, Christopher Kennedy, and David Nutt.

The author expresses much gratitude also to the Foundation for Contemporary Arts.